Happy Mother's Day, Carol!

With warm
and many blessings.

Sheen K. Parsons

20!

The First *Rose* of *Summer*

Eileen K Parsons

WestBow
PRESS
A DIVISION OF THOMAS NELSON

WestBow Press books may be ordered through booksellers or by contacting:

WestBow Press
A Division of Thomas Nelson
1663 Liberty Drive
Bloomington, IN 47403
www.westbowpress.com
1-(866) 928-1240

ISBN: 978-1-4497-3298-1 (sc)
ISBN: 978-1-4497-3299-8 (hc)
ISBN: 978-1-4497-3297-4 (e)

Library of Congress Control Number: 2011961479

Printed in the United States of America

WestBow Press rev. date: 12/5/2011

THIS BOOK IS DEDICATED TO

MY LATE GRANDFATHER, ARTHUR VANRY, who believed I could
accomplish anything and always encouraged me to follow my dreams.

ACKNOWLEDGEMENTS

Trying to decide who to thank and how to thank them has proven to be difficult. So many people have assisted me and encouraged me over the past year and a half that I'd have to write an entire chapter to thank them all individually. Thanks to everyone who has been a part of this.

My wonderful husband, Eric – I am so very thankful to the Lord for blessing me with you as my life's companion. Your support and understanding during this project (and every other part of our life together!) has meant more to me than I could ever express. I love you so very much.

My son, Daniel – thank you for the many days you came home from school and said, "Mom, you write. I'll get the door and answer the phone!" I love you, my son, and I'm so proud of the young man you've become.

My parents – Jacoba (Jake) and Rick Spearance – Mom, for the hours of praying with me, reading, proofing and encouraging me to keep going, and Dad for being the great dad you are. I love you both.

My mother-in-law – Sharon – without your help, it would have many years down the road before my dream would have been realized. Thank you also for raising up a wonderful son to be my husband! I love you lots!

My grandmother – Mae VanRy – for your encouragement and words of wisdom. You are a great lady, a woman I love and cherish, not only as my grandmother, but also as my friend.

My cousin, Jeff VanRy and his wife, Melinda – for the weeks and hours you spent pouring over the manuscript, giving me the "brutal honesty" I asked for. Without your sharp eyes and editing know-how, a lot of mistakes would have remained, and every English teacher in the civilized world would be chasing me with a red pen! Thanks and God bless you both!

My cousin, Angela Gleason – for the afternoon you spent using your photographic ability to produce my author portrait. You truly are talented, and I appreciate the hours you spent finding the perfect pose. It was lots of fun!

Pastor Chris Cooper – for opening the first door in my life to real writing. The years I spent writing the article for the church bulletin and the newsletter helped me in so many ways. God bless you!

So many friends – too many to list – for the almost daily emails, Facebook messages, and Tweets of encouragement to keep going, trust the Lord, and never give up!

And most of all – **My Lord and Savior, Jesus Christ.** My life is proof of His wonderful mercy and grace, the depth of His love and forgiveness. I pray that the words that follow give Him all of the glory, honor and praise!

ONE

THE SUN WAS SETTING OVER the bay. The evening chill moving in with dusk came as a reminder that summer wasn't quite here. It also meant that it was time to lock up and go home. The lobster trap had been Steve's only pressing project of the day. Pete, one of the local fishermen, had stopped in an hour earlier to reclaim it for the next day's fishing trip.

"What do I owe ya?" Pete had asked.

"Wasn't more than a half hour's work. No charge. If a treasure chest makes its way into the trap instead of a lobster, save me a few gold coins. Otherwise, a prayer at sunrise before you go out is all I really need, Pete," Steve replied.

"Thanks, Steve, and God bless!" Pete left with a smile.

Most of the local fishermen were longtime friends. On the good trips, when the fish seemed to just flop up onto the deck and shrimp crawled willingly into the nets, Steve could go home with lobster, crab and more fish than he and Marian could eat in a week, thanks to the "gifts" from his friends. It wasn't uncommon, however, for the crews to go out for days at a time and come home with empty nets and traps. He didn't feel right about making a huge profit off minor repairs to their gear.

Steve Matthews had been awarded contracts with the local police department as well as Maine's Department of Environmental Protection to maintain the vessels they used to patrol the bay and neighboring waterways. Many customers were the wealthy who lived in luxurious Florida homes during the winter months, then rented 3,000 square foot cottages or time share condos in Rockport for the summer. He felt no guilt in charging premium rates to take care of their yachts, sailboats and cruisers. He had even been "commissioned" by a retired senator to rebuild a cabin cruiser that looked like it had been around since the ark. Half the hull was rotten and the entire deck had to be replaced. It would have been cheaper to buy a new one. Steve had expressed this opinion to the senator, but the senator disagreed. "No, no," the senator had replied with his too-white, toothy smile. "This old girl has sentimental value!" Steve would definitely be able to pay his bills this season. His friends were often less fortunate. No need to bleed them dry.

Steve ran his hand over the repaired side of the hull one more time, checking the caulk for bubbles and gaps before putting the tools away and sweeping the wood chips from the floor. He stopped and stared out the window at the sun's continuing descent. The tide waters could be heard lapping at the piers. Seagulls crooned overhead.

His thoughts travelled to the unfinished project in the next bay, a sailboat that had been started during his older son Paul's senior year of high school. It had been the only thing that kept them together on the weekends Paul had come home while still in college – weekends that had become less and less frequent. Since starting his career, Paul only came home for the bigger holidays, his new life and misguided choices keeping him away.

"God, please be with him. Bring him back to You. You know what he needs. My heart breaks, Lord. Do what it takes to make him see the truth. Make him see how much he needs You back in his life."

After setting the broom in the corner and turning off the lights, he looked around the shop one more time before arming the alarm and going out the door. He locked up and looked over the marina. The sky was a postcard perfect purple, orange and red. "Sailor's delight," he said quietly to himself. Such calm, everything so peaceful. The only sounds were the waves coming in from the bay and a motor in the distance.

Taking a deep breath, he turned to walk home, praying all the way that his inner-turmoil for his son would pass. He had a deep sense that a storm was brewing in his son's life – and only the hand of God Himself would be able to bring Paul through.

TWO

BROOKE LOOKED AROUND THE ONE-ROOM flat. Everything from the whitewashed brick walls to the green and white checked tile floors reminded her of the locked-down, high security psychiatric wards of the movies set in the 50's and 60's. She could almost see the restraints and shock treatment jumper cables materializing in a corner. Brooke chuckled at the image. Her father had always told her that she had an almost dangerous imagination. Perhaps he was right!

The kitchen was the only updated corner of the loft, with modern stainless steel appliances and built-in microwave oven. The full wrap-around counter made it seem like a separate room. The cabinets were polished oak with brass pulls instead of knobs. One cabinet had window-pane style glass doors.

The only truly separate room was the bathroom, its claw-footed tub visible from the kitchen. The bathroom's only light, a frosted globe that hung above the pedestal sink, cast a dim glow onto the chipped mirror of the old metal medicine cabinet, adding to the loft's institutional appearance.

The windows were all square, hand-crank, awning style, with the exception of double French doors on the front of the apartment. "That will have to be the living room," Brooke said with a smile, walking over to examine the antiquated doors. She pulled the doors open, the panes of glass rattling in protest. A warm breeze pushed into the room, carrying with it the traffic and street noise. Black, wrought-iron bars scrolling from the base to halfway up the window frame were all that separated Brooke from the eleven story drop to the street below.

Brooke scanned the loft a final time, her eyes pausing at the kitchen and finally coming to rest on the doors. Their rustic appearance and the view into the City decided for her. She couldn't wait to move her few possessions in.

"Dad, please say something." The silence from the other end upset Brooke more than if her father had yelled his protest. "Dad, please."

"Brooke, tell me you haven't paid anything yet. Tell me you haven't signed a lease." Her father made no attempt to hide the frustration in his voice.

"I can't tell you that, Dad. I paid the deposit, first and last month's rent and signed a 6-month lease. I move in Friday."

More silence.

"Dad, I'm twenty-four years old. It's time..."

"Time for what, Brooke?" her father interrupted, his voice barely audible. "Time to get mugged, raped, killed! Why couldn't you stay at Ruth's? Didn't she tell you that the room was yours as long as you wanted? I thought you liked it there? I thought Ruth treated you like a daughter? You were safe there. You had other young women around you there. Why now?"

"Dad, I'm the only one left from my class. I graduated two years ago! Only one other girl is a student at NYU and she's eighteen years old! The other girls aren't much older, and I have nothing in common with them. I have a good job. I'm on my way to living my dream. I'm closer to Papa. I like being in the City. I'm even closer to my church. Dad, I'm ready to start my life." Brooke closed her eyes against the tears. Her father had always supported her goals. But his over-protectiveness often made her crazy. "How old do I have to be before I can grow up, Dad? I am a woman now. Someday you are going to have to accept that."

"You're my baby, Brooke – my only baby. I grew up in New York, remember? I know what that city does to people. I know how dangerous it is – the crime, the depravity. I left for a reason, Brooke. I just don't want to see you hurt. You're all I have. I love you."

"I know, Dad. I love you, too. But Syracuse has its share of problems, too. When was the last time you went for a walk alone after dark? And I'm not living in the slums. It isn't high society, but I'm not going to be shot when I walk out my front door. It's a secure building. There's a doorman and a security guard. There's even a parking garage for tenants and visitors only. If you don't have a sticker on your windshield, you have to be announced to the person you're visiting. I'll be fine, Dad. Besides, how many angels have you prayed for God to send my way?"

"More than I can count! But don't for a minute think I won't be praying for more when you move into this new place of yours!" Brooke could hear the smile in his voice.

"God has never failed me, Dad. His hand is ever on me. You taught me that, remember?"

"I remember, Honey." His voice cracked as he spoke the words. "I want to come out Friday and help you move in. May I?"

"Of course, Daddy. I'd love to have you here. Could you stop for Papa on the way? He wants to be here too."

"So, the two of you are in this together, huh? I should have known he'd be in on this somehow!" He tried to mask his laughter as he spoke the words. "That'll give me time to give him a few words before I get to your new place!"

———

Brooke picked up the key before 8:00 Monday morning, bucket, sponges and cleaning supplies in tow. She had even brought her clothes, toiletries and makeup so she didn't have to go back to Ruth's before having to get to the theater that night. She had been able to switch her hours with Rachel so she could have the weekend off to get moved in. The landlord had agreed to let her move in before the end of the month in exchange for cleaning the apartment. She hadn't realized how filthy it was when she'd looked at it Saturday morning. The mold around the bathroom sink clung like a stubborn enemy refusing to leave. "How could anyone have lived like this?" she'd wondered as she attacked the mold with another spray of bleach. She left the bleach to do its work and went to the kitchen to see if the oven cleaner had done its job.

Brooke had her head and shoulders in the oven, chiseling away at the burned on drippings when the buzzer sounded. "Great. Just when this was getting fun!" she said, pulling off the gloves and wiping her hands on a paper towel. "Yes?" Brooke asked as she pressed the button on the speaker. *"This is going to take some getting used to,"* she thought as she awaited a reply.

"It's Miss Ruth Howell, Miss Barsanti," the doorman said through the speaker.

"Oh! Please, send her up!" Brooke could hardly wait for Ruth to see her apartment. She wished she had coffee or tea to share with her first visitor, but all Brooke had brought in the way of food was a cup of Starbucks and a danish. She could see Ruth was thinking ahead as always when she stepped out of the elevator with a box of take-out, coffee and doughnuts.

"I assume you neglected to think of lunch, as usual, my dear," Ruth said as she put the packages on the counter and hugged Brooke. It was after 1:00 and Brooke hadn't even noticed her hunger until she caught the scent of sesame chicken wafting from the Chinese container. Brooke shrugged her shoulders and smiled at Ruth. "If you had seen the grime in the place when I got here this morning, you would understand my lack of interest in food. I think the landlord added another layer of dirt just for me!" They laughed and stood at the counter eating their lunch.

Ruth had been like a mother to Brooke since she'd moved to New York. Brooke had rented a room in Ruth's house since the week before starting classes at NYU and continued to live there after starting her job with Broadway Theatrical Costumers. Most of Ruth's girls moved out within a year or two of starting school. Those who remained through college moved out as soon as they'd graduated. There was only one other girl who had stayed beyond graduation and her situation was similar to Brooke's. She, too, had lost her mother at a young age. The love that Ruth easily poured out filled the void left by such a loss.

"Martin called this morning," Ruth said as she finished her rice. Brooke put her empty containers in the wastebasket and went to the sink to wash her hands. "What did Daddy want?" she asked, turning slowly to see Ruth's face.

"Sweetheart, he just wants to know you're okay. You are his entire world. Don't worry. I reassured him that you'd chosen a safe, perfect place to live. I told him how close you are to church, the theaters you work in, and to your grandfather. I told him you could almost see Belvedere Castle in Central Park from your window. He laughed at that. He seemed relieved to hear that I approve of your choice. He expressed his concern, but I think he's coming around."

"You can't really see Belvedere Castle from here, you know," Brooke laughed. "I am closer to it though, aren't I? So, I guess it's almost true. He and Papa are coming Friday to help me move in. I've been so nervous about his reaction when he gets here. I don't feel so nervous now. Thanks, Ruth."

Ruth hugged Brooke tightly. "Come on, Sweetie. Let's see how much cleaning we can get done before the stage calls!"

By the time Ruth left and Brooke was locking the door to leave for work, the bathroom was spotless and the kitchen would pass a health code inspection. It wouldn't take long to get the rest of the loft cleaned up and ready for moving day.

Ruth helped Brooke every day that week to clean the windows, wash the light fixtures, scrub and polish the floors, and hang curtains on the windows. She had even helped Brooke replace the cabinet in the bathroom. The landlord had given permission to install it with the understanding that the old would be put back in place when the time came for her to move out. She had found a lovely, ornate cabinet at the flea market that gave the bathroom a Victorian look. She bought a small toolbox with screwdrivers, a hammer and wrenches so that she could make easy repairs on her own. She wanted to avoid bothering the maintenance staff as much as possible. By the time Brooke had to leave for work Thursday night, the apartment was ready to move into.

"I have one more thing to do," Ruth said, taking a small bundle from her bag. She walked to the living room, pulled the step stool over and went to work above the doors. Within minutes, beautiful lace panels had been hung, giving a simple elegance to the corner. "I've hung them so that you can push them back and still open your doors."

"Ruth, they're so lovely!" Brooke fingered the lace, marveling at the intricate rose and ivy design that ran through it. "They look old, Ruth. Where did you find these?"

Ruth stood beside her. Taking the lace into her hands, she studied the material for a moment before responding. "They were my grandmother's. They once hung in her bedroom. I want you to have them, Brooke. I don't have a daughter of my own. I never will. You mean more to me than I could ever tell you. They're yours." Brooke hugged Ruth, tears running down her face. "Don't you start that now, Sweetie. You don't want to look like a mess for work!" Ruth kissed Brooke on the forehead. Smiling, she turned and left the apartment.

THREE

IT WAS ONE OF THE best Italian coffee bars in New York. *La Regina Dei Caffe*, "The Queen of Coffee," was owned by an Italian family who believed in keeping everything as traditional as possible. Gianna, the granddaughter of the couple who opened the café in the late 40's, maintained the traditions set by her family. There were no to-go cups. If you wanted a cappuccino to-go, you'd better have brought your own cup. You couldn't get a breakfast sandwich with ham or bacon – those were dinner items. The choices were simple and sweet.

Despite the resistance to Americanization, it was one of the more popular cafés in New York. Most mornings, dozens of patrons stood around the bar sipping espresso, munching on biscotti, or dabbing jam on toast. There was a deep reverence for the little bar that held true to its heritage. The regulars had great respect for the robust woman behind the counter who did her own baking every morning and served her customers with pride.

Paul Matthews didn't have an Italian bone in his body. He was New England born and bred. His family could be traced back as far back as the Boston Tea Party. He had travelled Europe when he was a senior in high school, a reward to the school's high achievers, and fell in love with the cuisine while in Italy. *La Regina* was one of his favorite coffee stops in the morning. The coffee was a rich dark roast, smooth and bold – perfect for getting the blood flowing the morning after a late night.

Gianna smiled at Paul as she handed his travel cup back over the counter. He ordered biscotti and paid the young woman at the register. She smiled flirtatiously at Paul and glanced up at him from under her dark lashes. Paul had never seen her before and was amused by her behavior.

"Maria!" The girl quickly averted her gaze as Gianna scolded her with a fierce Italian tirade.

Paul chuckled and turned to leave. The small café was definitely over its "maximum occupancy". People were struggling to go out the door and more were waiting outside to get in. Paul waited by the counter and watched the flow of people coming and going. An old man holding a pastry box stood by the door and gestured for a woman to go first. She smiled a "thank you" and barely made it through the door when a young man pushed his way past and knocked the old man into the wall, the pastry box falling to the floor.

"Sir!" Paul set his coffee cup and bag on the counter, and rushed to help the man up. "Are you alright?"

"Fine. Just bruised with embarrassment." The man winced as Paul took him by the arm to lead him to a stool.

"I'm not so sure about that." Paul lifted the edge of the man's torn shirt sleeve. Blood was seeping through the fabric. Paul examined the scrape that extended from his shoulder to just below his elbow. "This may need to be looked at. Can you move everything okay?"

The man flexed his elbow and rotated his shoulder. "Good as an old fellow like me can expect. It feels like a bruise, nothing more."

Gianna was muttering in Italian as she pushed her way through the crowd with a dripping towel in her hand. She stopped in front of the old man and shook her head before dabbing his arm with the towel.

"Gianna! *Sto bene*! I'm fine. Stop fussing."

"Fine, you say! Then stop bleeding on my wall, Nicholas!" She picked up the scrunched pastry box, brushed it off, and slapped it on the counter in front of Nick. She nodded once, turned on her heel, and marched back behind the counter.

"Such a gentle, understanding soul, she is!" He shook his head. He turned to Paul and extended a hand. "Nick Barsanti. Thanks for the assistance."

"Paul Matthews." Paul smiled at the man as he released his hand. "Do you have far to go? Let me help you."

Nick nodded his appreciation. Picking up the pastry box, he allowed his new friend to lead him out of the café. "I'm old enough to be the woman's father and still she insists on mothering me. I've known her since she was in diapers. Though don't ever let her know I told you that! She'd probably put rat poison in my espresso! Here we are." Nick stopped in front of an old building. "This is my stop."

Paul looked at the building. The trim around the windows was chipping. The window seals were broken, allowing the moisture to seep

9

in and coat the tight space between the panes. In the window was a faded "For Rent" sign. Vertical blinds blocked the view of the interior.

"I live in the apartment upstairs." Nick gestured to a narrow door to the right of the main entrance. "Shop's been vacant for some time now. I'm particular about my tenants. My children tell me I'm too particular. Thanks again for your help, young man. If you hadn't been there, Gianna would have spent the rest of the morning trying to doctor me. That isn't the way I want to begin my day!"

"Can I help you up to your apartment?"

Paul's arm was quickly brushed away.

"I'm not so feeble that I can't make it up my own stairs." Nick nodded to Paul before unlocking the door and making his way up the stairs.

Paul waited until he was certain Nick was safely to the top. He took out a business card and wrote his home number on the back. "Call me if you think you need a doctor. Hope you're okay." He tucked the card into the door's window pane. Glancing at his watch, he grabbed his briefcase and hurried toward the subway. He should make it just in time for his first appointment. It wasn't until he was seated and the train was moving that he realized he'd left his coffee cup and biscotti back at the café.

"Great! Nice start to the day!" He shook his head and tried to ignore the rumbling in his stomach

FOUR

THE SUN SHINED BRIGHT AND warm Friday morning. It was the middle of May and already the temperature was in the seventies. Brooke had stuffed as much as she could into her trunk and driven her car from Ruth's to the parking garage after work the night before, to avoid the morning rush hour. The parking attendant had merely shrugged and given her the "Tenant" window sticker she needed for her car and then followed her with his eyes as she walked out into the City noise to hail a cab.

Her father had hired a moving truck to bring her bedroom furniture, and Grandpa and Grandma Merriweather were sending their old kitchen table and chairs. He promised to have the movers stop by Ruth's to pick up the odds and ends she still had there. She didn't have much else. Papa Barsanti had given strict instructions not to buy anything as he had a surprise for her. She hadn't dared to buy even a toaster for fear that he would scold her for not listening.

Brooke entered through the parking garage and unloaded her car. She stopped at the security counter in the lobby to give a list of names of the people who would be coming and going from her apartment that day and received information from the doorman about the use of the freight elevator before she made her way to the main elevator.

"Brooke!"

She turned quickly and stopped the elevator door with her foot when she heard the familiar voice.

"Pastor Brian! What a surprise!" She smiled, struggling to not drop everything as she hugged him and then his wife, Lauren, as they stepped into the elevator. "I didn't expect to see you."

Brian was a large man, well over six feet tall with broad shoulders and an even broader belly. His skin reminded Brooke of dark chocolate. He had a bright smile and gentle manner. Lauren was petite and shapely, a foot shorter than her husband. She had a quiet dignity about her. Brooke had been drawn to her from the moment they'd met.

Brian had been the church pastor for seven years, only a year longer than Brooke had been in New York. Despite their youth – they were in their early thirties – they had proven to be invaluable to the congregation and had quickly won the respect and support of even the most skeptical parishioners. The flock had doubled in size since they'd come. They had even developed new programs that helped the communities surrounding the church. Brooke had felt at home the minute she'd walked into the building. It was more than a place to worship and hear the Word spoken on Sunday mornings. It was truly a family.

"Can't have you moving in without a little apartment-warming blessing. Besides, Lauren baked more cinnamon rolls this morning than any normal man can eat. We figured your moving crew could help me eat them."

"Don't you believe the man! He would've eaten every one of these if I hadn't kept his hands away from them! You don't think that belly grew without his help, do you?"

Pastor Brian smiled at his wife. "Her fault. She's the best cook in New York!"

Brooke laughed as they reached her floor. She unlocked the door and showed them into the empty apartment. "This is it," she said while dropping her bundle on the floor by the door.

Brooke gave them a quick tour of the loft. Pastor Brian and Brooke spent a few extra moments commenting on the view from the French doors as Lauren admired the cabinets in the kitchen.

"We can't stay very long. We're doing hospital visitations this morning. We'd like to pray for you, though, and your new home," Lauren said, turning back to Brooke.

"I'd like that, thank you." Brooke accepted Pastor Brian's and Lauren's hands in a circle of prayer.

"Lord, bless our sister," Brian prayed. "Help her as she begins this new journey in life. Her eyes and her heart have remained on You, Lord, through the trials of college and the beginning of her career. She's had a constant loving hand to guide her during these times, Lord, through our Sister Ruth. Brooke has allowed herself to be accountable to Ruth, to live by the Godly rules that Ruth requires her young women to follow while living in her home. Brooke will be without that motherly accountability now. She will have to rely on the guidance of Your Holy Spirit and live in the Truth that she carries within her. Help her, Lord, to stay on the path you have set before her, to keep her eyes fastened to You, never turning away from what she knows to be good and right. Bless her, protect her, send your angels to cover her and let her, Lord, shine her light bright and true in everything she sets out to do. In your mighty name we pray, Amen."

"Amen," Brooke and Lauren agreed as the prayer was closed.

Pastor Brian and Lauren gave Brooke another hug and made their way to the door. "If you find you need some help tomorrow, let us know. We could be here first thing in the morning. I could probably even get a couple of them crazy kids from the youth group to help if needed," Pastor offered as he left.

"Thanks, but Daddy and Papa will be here soon. Ruth is also planning to come over. You know Ruth. She'll have this place fixed up before I know it!" Brooke laughed.

Brooke closed the door and gathered the things she'd left on the floor. She put most of the load in the corner where she planned to arrange her bedroom. The bags with paper plates, cups, and napkins she put in the kitchen area so that they would be available for the day. She noticed a package on the counter next to the cinnamon rolls. She opened the attached card and read *"To help you start the life God has planned for you. With our love and many blessings, Pastor Brian and Lauren."* Brooke carefully opened the box to find a set of dessert plates with a wreath-like fruit design around the edge. In the center of each plate was written in gold lettering: *"In all things, give thanks."*

"Thank you, Lord, for my wonderful friends." Brooke smiled as she unpacked what she could while waiting for her family to arrive.

———

Ruth arrived, shopping bags and Papa in tow. "Found him loitering around the entrance. I was afraid if I didn't bring him up with me, the doorman would have him hauled away for vagrancy."

Brooke noticed the battered pastry box and the way he favored his arm. "Papa, what happened to you?"

She took the box from him and looked at the red scrape running down his arm. "You look like you had a fight! Are you okay?"

"I'm fine. Don't you start fussing now! I was run into by a rude man at *La Regina* this morning and was pushed into the wall. It's nothing." Nicholas flexed his elbow and fingers. "See. Nothing's broken. I didn't fall. Just a scratch. And, thanks to a young man – who was very handsome by the way," he added smiling at Brooke, "I was not completely molested by Gianna. Had he not been there, I would probably be hooked up to life support right now. That girl just doesn't know when enough is enough!"

"A handsome, young man, huh? Don't get any ideas, Papa!" Brooke laughed at her grandfather. "Where's Dad? I thought he was coming with you?"

"Oh, he called early this morning and told me to come without him. He had some issue with a customer - a sticking drawer in an armoire he recently delivered, or something like that. He and the movers will be here directly. Now, open the gifts I bought you and let's get this moving-in party started!"

"Party, you say? I hope you remember that in a few hours, after the work has begun," Ruth said as she handed the packages to Brooke. "I know you, Nick. By lunchtime, you'll have found a comfortable place to nap and will be quick to remind us of your advancing years!"

"Well, what other advantages are there to having one foot in the grave? I can do what I want, when I want, and nobody can do a thing about it! Now, let my granddaughter open her housewarming gifts!"

Brooke decided Papa had cleaned out the kitchen departments at every store in the City. She wouldn't have to buy a single appliance. He had purchased everything from toaster and can opener to food processor and coffee pot. The coffee pot was a multi-function pot that made coffee, espresso, and cappuccino. She didn't want to try and guess what he'd paid for it!

"Let's get that pot cleaned up and ready. I brought coffee to go with the cookies I picked up from Gianna. Let's make sure it works okay!"

Brooke smiled as Ruth got the coffee started. It had just finished brewing when her father arrived. "Just in time!" he exclaimed as Brooke opened the door. "I could smell that wonderful aroma in the elevator!"

Following close behind her father were the movers, two men who were built like tanks, their muscular chest and arms stretching their shirt fabric to the limit. They entered the apartment with what Brooke knew immediately to be a couch, despite the brown paper wrapping. "Daddy! What have you done?"

"I had nothing to do with this. You'd better look at your grandfather if you want to blame someone."

"Wasn't anything," Nick said when Brooke started to protest. "It's been in storage for years. I had it cleaned is all."

The movers put the couch in its designated place and removed the paper wrapping. Brooke recognized the couch from pictures of her father's family. It was upholstered in beautiful, dark green damask, its arms, legs and back trimmed in wood. It had been her grandmother's. "Papa!"

"I put the parlor furniture in storage after we sold the house in the Village," her grandfather explained. "Your grandmother had become ill and living above the shop, closer to the doctors made more sense. We had tried to squeeze it into the apartment, but it wouldn't fit with everything else we had. I'm surprised it survived all of those years locked away like that. I know Sophia would have wanted you, the first grandchild, to have it."

The day held many such surprises. The movers were quick and efficient, removing the brown wrapping from the furniture and putting it where Brooke wanted it. In addition to her bedroom furniture and the dining set her grandparents had sent, her father had a small wardrobe. "Ruth mentioned that there weren't many closets. Thought it would be a good way to get it out of my shop!" had been her father's reply when she asked about it. He had also brought boxes of what Brooke assumed to be what she had left in her room. Before long, the loft was filled with furniture and boxes in need of unpacking. Where in the world would she put it all?

Pastor Brian reappeared at lunchtime with sandwiches and extra help. He had finished his visitations early and wanted to lend a hand.

"Shaun didn't have any classes this afternoon and volunteered his time," Brian explained.

Shaun and Brooke had attended some of the same art classes at NYU. He taught art at one of the local middle schools. The common interest in art and their shared faith helped them to quickly become friends.

"I appreciate all of the help I can get. Papa is busy making everyone believe he's too old and feeble to do any real work and Daddy is busy trying to make everyone believe he isn't. Without some more muscle in here, I'm afraid he'll give himself a heart attack." Brooke's father just shook his head in denial and went back to putting drawers into her dresser.

After a short lunch break, they went to work getting the apartment in shape. By dinner time, all of the furniture was in place. Many of the boxes had been unpacked. The contents were scattered around tables and counter tops, waiting to be put into their new homes. The only real challenge had been Brooke's drawing table and supplies. The one space large enough with an outlet nearby was the area that appeared to be intended for table and chairs. Her drawing table, easel and supply carts fit perfectly. Beside them, she had set up her sewing machine and sewing table. The dining table and chairs were arranged in the center of the room.

"Well, maybe an area rug will make it look like it belongs there," Ruth had offered when they considered the set up.

"I guess I'll have to think of it as an artistic arrangement," Brooke commented. "I don't see any other way to set it up. I'll get used to it."

Pastor Brian and Shaun left, offering more help the next day if needed. Ruth volunteered to take Papa home.

"What time do you have to be at the theatre?" Papa asked as he stood to leave.

"Heron let me switch my hours with Rachel this weekend. She didn't mind as long as someone was there. Rachel was happy to switch. That makes last weekend her final for this show. We were given the contract for costuming *Shakespeare in the Park* this year. That means I'll have to work all week from 9:00 to 1:00 doing sketches and then be back at the theatre to finish up our current show from 6:00 to midnight and then work the final shows next Friday."

"Heron?" her father asked. "Is that really her name or is it some stage thing?"

"It's her real name. Her mother is a dancer from Jamaica and her father a professor from South Africa. She's a talented woman. She has been a team leader with the company for several years now and she's only thirty," Brooke explained.

"Name fits, too," her grandfather added. "She *looks* like a heron. Her legs are about as big around as pencils and her nose sticks up in the air like a beak!"

"Papa, be nice. I think she's a beautiful woman. She is arrogant, I won't disagree with that. I think things have always come easily for her and she believes she's above everyone. God will show her the truth someday. She's an atheist. I guess her mother is Buddhist and her father is an agnostic, but she has totally rejected the notion of God."

"You're right. One day she will be shown the truth. Whether or not she's willing to accept it is another thing," Ruth said as she left the apartment.

Brooke said her "thank-yous" and "good-byes". Her father planned to spend the night with Nick, but wanted to have dinner with Brooke. "I'll be along shortly, Dad," he told him as they left. "I have to be back in Syracuse tomorrow afternoon, but would like to spend the morning with you. I just want to treat my daughter to her first pizza in her new place."

"Sounds good, Son," Nick said. "See you in a few hours."

Brooke closed the door behind her family and surveyed the loft to see what more she could get done while waiting for her father to return with their dinner. There wasn't much left to do. Brooke had purchased some dishes and flatware, pots and pans, and basic kitchen items that she'd kept hidden until she was certain her grandfather hadn't gone crazy in that department as well. Ruth had loaded all of the dishes into the dishwasher, dried them and put them into the cabinets. She had even handwashed the dessert plates Brian and Lauren had given and arranged them in the cabinet with the glass doors.

Everything was a reminder to her of the love of her family and dear friends. Her bedroom area was somewhat private now, thanks to her father setting the wardrobe up to serve as a wall. Ruth had purchased two, old fashioned privacy screens that helped to add another "wall" to her bedroom. One of them had solid wood panels with roses carved into them. The other was a more traditional one with fabric in the center of each panel. Ruth had replaced the original fabric with a rose-patterned tapestry.

"It's taking shape. It looks more like a home," Brooke said, looking around the room. The throw pillows she'd made for the living room had a rose design similar to the fabric in the privacy screen. The curtains and table covers further softened the appearance of the loft.

Brooke went to work putting her clothes into the wardrobe. Her father had completely refinished it and replaced the old shelves with cedar. *"He thinks of everything,"* she thought as she folded her sweaters and placed them carefully on the top shelf. His attention to detail was one of the reasons his business did so well. People knew he took pride in his work. Everything he did was to perfection and if anything didn't meet the customer's expectations, he would do his best to make it right.

Every part of his life reflected that desire to give his all – including his life as a father. He had done his best to make sure Brooke knew that she was loved. He had accepted early that he could never replace her mother, but did what he could to keep her alive for his daughter with photos and stories.

His faith was strong. Christ was the foundation of his life. Even when he'd lost his wife and newborn daughter, he never turned back but had shown an acceptance that it was God's will. Brooke knew he had mourned and asked the why questions, but he'd never turned away. That example had stayed with her. It ignited a fire that grew within her daily, an assurance that no matter what happened, she could trust the Lord to walk with her every step of the way.

FIVE

PAUL DIDN'T GET HOME FRIDAY night until almost 7:00. It had been a long day. He had been called into the director's office within minutes of returning from lunch. His meeting that morning had been successful, resulting in another client and another portfolio to manage that was in the millions. He needed only to make a few minor changes to the contract and it would be his.

The call into the director's office had caused him concern. What if the company had changed their mind about the contract? Should he have cancelled his lunch appointment and completed the contract immediately? His worries were quickly allayed, however, upon entering the office and seeing the CEO sitting in one of the leather chairs, smiling as he rose to shake Paul's hand.

"Our miracle worker!" Marshall Appleton squeezed Paul's hand and motioned for him to have a seat. "Gregory called me this morning after your meeting and informed me that you and you alone would be required to handle the management of his finances and investments. Can't turn this one over to someone else. You made quite an impression, young man!"

Paul expressed his thanks. "The Appleton, Murphy, & Young name got me in the door. The rest was simple persuasion."

"Nonsense. We've tried three different times to get Gregory Fillman to allow us to manage the whole package. You are the only one who's been able to get him to make the commitment." Pratt Young shook his head in amazement at Paul's ability to sway the toughest business executive to move their accounts.

Pratt had been the Director of International Business for 12 years and had never met anyone like Paul. "That kid can move the most massive mountains," he had remarked to Marshall before calling Paul into his office.

"We want you to join us tonight to celebrate your success! We're having a little gathering at the Waldorf. Some folks we want you to meet will be there. Plan to be there around 8:00. That should give you time to go home and change – nothing formal, just business. Again, great work!"

Paul had found himself on the other side of Pratt's door before he knew what had hit him. "Guess it's a good thing I didn't already have plans," he had said to himself as he made his way back to his office. An invitation from Marshall Appleton wasn't an invitation. It was an edict. Paul decided it wasn't a bad thing. To be put in the same room with these men was a great opportunity. Twenty-six years old and already on his way to the top!

He had spent the rest of the afternoon making changes to the Fillman contract and calling prospective clients. In between the meetings and phone calls, he had to keep up with the management responsibilities. It took more than landing the clients. Keeping them was often the greater challenge in this business.

The exhaustion hit him the minute he walked through the door to his condo. He wanted nothing more than to change his clothes and relax. He didn't have that luxury, unfortunately.

The cleaning lady had been there – he could smell the pine cleaner from the front door. *"I hope she didn't use furniture polish on the piano again,"* he thought, dropping his keys and briefcase on the sideboard and pushing the button on his answering machine – six messages. *"Susan probably left five of them,"* he thought as he picked up his pen and notepad to write down anything important. "When will that woman get it through her head it's over and has been for months."

Three had been from Susan. He deleted them at the first sound of her voice. Two had been from his father – the usual "missing you, loving you, praying for you, Son" messages that his father liked to leave. His father's second one had an urgent sound, but still said nothing really important. "Have felt a strong urge to pray for you today. Hope everything is okay. Call soon and let us know you're okay. Love ya, Son"

"Yeah, yeah, okay," Paul said as he deleted the messages from his father. "Pray on, Dad. Maybe that's what got me the contract today." Paul shook his head at his parents' continued religious push. He wasn't a kid anymore. He believed in God. He still went to church on Easter. He had outgrown all of that weekly Sunday School stuff years ago. Times had changed. He didn't expect his parents to change, but resented their constant push to mold him into what they thought he should be. They would be a lot happier if they'd just accept the fact that he was not them.

His other message was from Nick Barsanti. "Thanks again for your assistance this morning. I also appreciate that you left your business card and home phone number. I'm doing fine – no permanent damage. If you find yourself in my neighborhood, stop by. I'd enjoy talking to you again." Nick finished by leaving his phone number in case Paul wished to reach him.

"What possessed me to leave him my card?" Paul asked himself as he wrote the old man's number on the notepad. "Now he'll probably call me constantly." Paul put the pen and pad down by the phone and went to get ready for the Waldorf. "Nothing formal" meant no tux. That didn't mean casual. He still needed a jacket and tie.

He pulled out his grey silk pinstripe, a clean shirt and tie. He showered quickly, shaved and was ready to leave by 7:30. He decided he should drive rather than take a cab. The purpose of the evening was to impress prospective clients. His Mercedes would have a greater effect than a cab. Besides, he loved that car. He seldom drove. He lived on the subway and in cabs during the week. Driving in this city made little sense during the workday rush hour. "Rush hour" wasn't exactly appropriate. There was little rush and lots of "sit and wait." The weekend was about the only time he had the chance to show off his car. Tonight would certainly allow him that pleasure.

He wasn't out of the parking garage long when he started to question the decision to drive. Traffic was at a near stand-still. "I could have walked faster than this," he said to himself as he inched forward. The pace finally picked up. He pulled up to the hotel with time to spare.

Paul had been through the doors of the Waldorf-Astoria only twice before. The first time was for his second interview with Appleton, Murphy & Young. The second time was for a breakfast meeting with a long-time international client that was threatening to take their account to a competitor. Both times he had been a nervous wreck and was still struck by the grandeur. Now, he was able to walk through the lobby with a sense of purpose, belonging. He felt like he was finally finding his place in the world.

———————

The evening was the perfect end to the week. Paul shook hands with current and prospective clients, as well as two senators and a former governor. Pratt Young left his side only twice – once to go to the men's room and another at the beckoning of Marshall Appleton.

Pratt returned from his short conference with Marshall and steered Paul to a small group on the other side of the room. "Marcus," Pratt approached the man at the center of the group. "I would like you to meet Paul Matthews. Paul, this is Mr. Marcus Reed."

Paul shook the man's hand. "Pleased to meet you, Sir." There was something unsettling about him. He appeared to be in his mid-fifties. He was average height, slender, nothing extraordinary. Paul still felt uncomfortable with the man.

Mr. Reed smiled as he shook Paul's hand. "Pratt has told me a little about you. I believe he mentioned that you interned in Germany during college?"

Paul shot a look at Pratt. Pratt gave a small nod, shook Mr. Reed's hand and excused himself from the conversation. "Yes. Part of my studies allowed for international interning. I spent four months in Frankfurt."

"Quite an exciting city. I've been there several times myself. My daughter enjoyed the museum the year she accompanied me. Tell me, did you enjoy your time in Europe?" Mr. Reed motioned for Paul to sit at a near-by table.

Paul spent the rest of the evening discussing his time in Germany, the challenges of international Finance, as well as the similarities to business in the United States. Marcus Reed showed a deep interest in Paul's experience. By the end of the night, he felt more at ease with the man. Paul even found himself discussing his family, his modest beginning, and his goals.

It was midnight before Pratt resumed his place beside Paul. "Pratt, thank you for an enjoyable evening. I don't often have the opportunity to just talk to someone without having the feeling I'm being set up for some corporate pitch. It was a refreshing change," Marcus said as he shook both Paul and Pratt's hands. He moved around the room saying his good-byes and left. Paul noted that most of the group that had originally been gathered around Marcus left with him.

"Was I supposed to come away from that little conversation with a new client?" Paul asked Pratt after Marcus had left.

"Not yet. Tonight our intention was for everyone to get better acquainted. You know, become friends. I think you succeeded."

"I've never heard of the man before, Pratt. I don't even know what kind of business he's in. Whatever it is generates enough wealth to put the man in Armani. I also can't believe a simple business man would need a bodyguard." Paul looked at Pratt, waiting for an answer.

Pratt laughed. "You don't miss much, do you? What makes you think one of his friends was a bodyguard?"

"I've never seen a Bluetooth like what the guy had stuck in his ear. And, unless the guy's had a colostomy, the little bulge on his left side was a gun. He spent the entire evening standing stiff and as alert as a guard at Buckingham Palace. He never smiled. All he drank was water. And, no, I don't miss much. So, who is he?"

"Just a friend, Paul. No, he isn't a client and he may not ever be. But, he is a friend of Marshall Appleton – a good friend. We thought it was time you met him. You're moving up in this company, Paul, and it's important for you to meet the people who are important to us. Come on. Relax, have a drink. We've got the suite for another hour. It's been a great week!" Pratt squeezed Paul's shoulder, pushed a drink into his hand, and turned the conversation to politics.

An hour later, Paul crawled into a cab. He was completely exhausted – and intoxicated. Though he hated leaving his car, there was no way he could drive home. The doorman of his building laughed as he made his way through the lobby to the elevator.

The ride up made him feel queasy. Paul had never been a drinker. His parents had spoken against it while he was growing up. He had tried alcohol once during his rebellious teenage stage and didn't enjoy the effect it had on him. It didn't make sense to impair himself. He preferred to be in control. He leaned his head against the side of the elevator wishing he had stuck with the juice and soda he'd started the evening with.

"Just don't be sick. Don't be sick," he said to himself over and over as he dragged himself out of the elevator and to his door. He closed the door, dropped his keys on the sideboard and stumbled to his room. He was asleep before his head hit the pillow.

———————

Paul felt the gentle rocking of the boat. Waves gently lapped at the sides. He felt like he could sleep all day. He awoke to the ringing of a buoy in the harbor.

Paul sat up in bed. It took a moment for him to realize the boat had been a dream. The rain pounded the windows with a steady rhythm. The buoy rang again – it was the doorbell. Paul jumped out of bed and grabbed his robe as he made his way to the door.

"A package for you, Mr. Matthews," the doorman said.

"Thank you." Paul closed the door and looked at the envelope – Waldorf stationary.

"Wonderful. What did I do last night that I can't remember?"

Inside the envelope, Paul found the valet key for his Mercedes and a note from Marcus Reed. *"Hope you arrived home alright last night, Mr. Matthews. I thought you may need your car, so I had my driver bring it to you. Please let me know if anything is unsatisfactory."*

Paul groaned at the poor impression he must have made on the man. Pratt would not be happy. More importantly, how upset was Marshall Appleton going to be?

Paul called the hotel and left a message of thanks to Mr. Reed. He turned on the coffee pot and took an extra-long shower. By the time he toweled off, he felt halfway human again. He retrieved his newspaper, had a light breakfast and drank his coffee before deciding to spend the morning in the office.

Few people came in on Saturday. It was the perfect time to tie up loose ends and get a jump on the next week. There were no interruptions, no expectations, no set schedule. He was in his office and had already started on some changes to Monday afternoon's proposal when Pratt entered his office. He leaned against Paul's door frame and crossed his arms.

Pratt chuckled as Paul looked up.

"Okay, Pratt. Give me both barrels. I know I must have humiliated the company some way last night. Mr. Reed had my car delivered to my building this morning, along with a note. He left long before I did. How did he know I had been an idiot and had to take a cab home?"

"He was in the lobby when you left." Pratt pulled a chair closer to Paul's desk and sat down. "He called Marshall this morning for your address. He was impressed with your *'better judgment,'* as he called it. What are you doing in here this morning? I figured you'd be home sleeping it off."

"Surprisingly, I don't feel bad this morning. The elevator ride to my condo was terrifying last night, but, other than feeling a little tired, I'm not bad today. Remind me next time, though, that I may not be so lucky. I think I'll stick to cranberry juice and club soda! I thought about a few changes this morning that I wanted to make to the Morris proposal for Monday afternoon. I didn't have any plans this weekend anyway. How about you? What are you doing here on a Saturday? I usually have the place to myself."

"Marjorie and the girls went to Boston to visit her mother. I was supposed to go along, but Marcus Reed requires a lot of entertaining when he's in the country. At least, that's what I told Marjorie. I hate going to her mother's. The woman has hated me since the day I met her. The feeling's mutual." Pratt rose from his chair and slapped the top of Paul's desk. "Come on. Let's get out of here. You need your weekends. Can't have you burning yourself out. Let me take you to lunch."

"Sounds good. Let me just finish up and I'll be right out." Paul saved his changes to the proposal and logged off his computer. 11:00 on a Saturday morning. Nothing to do – nowhere to go. Might as well take Pratt up on his offer.

He turned off his light, grabbed his jacket and joined Pratt, who was deep in conversation on his cell phone all the way down to the lobby. Pratt ended his call just as they stepped out into the chilly air.

"Typical New York weather. Yesterday it was seventy and today it feels like snow again. At least the rain has stopped," Pratt said, pulling his jacket on. He waved down a cab and turned toward Paul. "Like French? There's a great French place over on West 68ᵗʰ. Cheap, but great!"

Paul climbed into the cab with Pratt. Pratt gave the driver the address and immediately his phone rang. "Marjorie. She'll call or text about a hundred times while she's gone. Drives me nuts."

Paul wondered how anyone could be so unhappy in a marriage. His parents never seemed to have problems. Even when finances were tight, or when Paul went through his rebellious stage in high school, his parents were always the picture-perfect couple. He'd never heard them fight. They still held hands and talked about everything from the critical to the mundane. Maybe that's why he hadn't met the right woman yet. He wanted someone he could share a life with the way his parents had. His father attributed it to their faith and the bond they had through Christ. His father always put a religious twist on everything. Paul believed it was more their ability to understand each other.

Paul was watching the foot traffic out the window when Pratt nudged him. "Marjorie wants to talk to you." Paul looked at Pratt quizzically. "She was just wondering what I was up to."

Paul took the phone. "Hi Marjorie, we ran into each other at the office. You know Pratt, always the workaholic!" Marjorie spent a few moments grilling Paul on Pratt's activities since she'd left. Paul told her about the important business meeting the night before and the need to have a working lunch now to discuss some upcoming appointments. "I promise I'll keep him out of trouble," Paul said before handing the phone back. Pratt finished his conversation and tucked his phone back into his pocket.

"Woman doesn't trust me." He shook his head. "You're one lucky guy right now. Free as a bird. Enjoy your freedom while you have it. Don't get yourself into marriage and family too early. I love her and the girls, but there are days…" He looked over to Paul and shrugged his shoulders. "Sometimes I'd really like a little change of scenery."

The cab stopped in front of the restaurant. Paul stepped out, and Pratt paid the driver. They were soon greeted by Marshall Appleton and Marcus Reed. "Hope you don't mind, Paul. I called Marshall when you agreed to join me for lunch. It's a good day for a few friends to get together."

Pratt smiled at Marshall and shook hands with Marcus. Paul followed the men into the restaurant. He felt awkward. Last night he felt like he belonged with these men. Now he felt small, unimportant. He loathed the feeling and determined to change it – whatever was required.

SIX

NOTHING COULD WAKE BROOKE LIKE the smell of coffee brewing. The aroma swirled around her head, drawing her from her sleep. *"I'll have to thank Papa again for the coffee pot with its timer,"* she thought, as she made her way to the kitchen. Every morning when the coffee-smell woke her, she could think of her Papa.

Brooke took her coffee cup to the living room window and looked out at the rain drumming on the panes and the street below. The chill that penetrated the glass promised a cold, dreary day. She didn't have much to do. There was little left to unpack and find homes for. She did have to go to the market and fill her empty pantry. She also wanted to see Papa. Despite having seen him the day before, they hadn't had much time to just talk and she missed him.

As the rain pounded harder on the glass, she thought about her father, driving back to Syracuse. He was very careful, but the drive was long and he hadn't left her apartment until after midnight. She knew he'd be up early to have breakfast with her grandfather and be on the road before most people were out of bed. She would have to call later to make sure he'd made it home okay.

Brooke sat on the couch with her coffee and pulled her legs up under her. She took a sip and savored the peace she felt. "Thank You, Lord, for blessing me," she said quietly as she listened to the rain. She considered the many blessings in her life. There weren't many young women who could say they had a strong relationship with their family. Most were so busy "finding themselves" that they forgot to cherish the people who should be most important to them. There weren't many who had the relationship with Christ that she had. She realized she had far to go, but she also recognized that without Christ in her life, it would be empty.

Brooke finished her coffee and finished unpacking. It didn't take long to put her things away and make note of some things she thought must still be in Syracuse. Why her dad hadn't packed her box of pictures and albums but had sent her ballet slippers was beyond her understanding. She hadn't worn the ballet slippers in years, but the box of pictures she looked through whenever she was home. She also realized her mother's jewelry box was not with her things from Ruth's. She would have to call Ruth and have her look for it in the closet of her old room.

She made a list for the market and took a shower. If she could be done with her morning errands in time, maybe she could take Papa to lunch. It would be nice to sit with him for a while and enjoy his company. She would never tire of his stories and sense of humor. She could think of no better way to spend the rainy afternoon.

The morning didn't run quite as smoothly as Brooke had hoped. The post office had a line out the door. She'd had to wait nearly an hour to take care of a change of address. The market wasn't much better. *"Grocery shopping must bring out the worst in people,"* Brooke thought when two women started to shout at each other in the produce aisle. She couldn't imagine oranges were worth fighting over, but people got upset over the silliest things. There were only three checkouts open and one was express. It was past noon by the time she was finished with her errands and her cab pulled up in front of her building. The cab driver didn't offer to help with her grocery bags. He took them from the trunk and dropped them on the sidewalk in the puddles and rain. Thankfully the doorman, David, came to her rescue with a large metal shopping basket. He loaded her bags for her and rolled them into the lobby.

"Thanks, David. I was afraid I was going to have soggy bread and squished tomatoes!" Brooke laughed, shaking the rain from her sleeves and wiping the drops from her face.

"We have a couple of these hidden here in the lobby. Let us know when you're going out and we'll have one waiting for you. When you're finished unloading, just bring it back down so that it's here for someone else."

After unloading her groceries and returning the basket to the lobby, Brooke took the subway to Papa's. By the time she reached his building, the rain had stopped. A colder wind was blowing in, threatening to bring more winter weather to the City. Brooke enjoyed the changing seasons, but she was ready for spring.

Brooke tapped on her grandfather's door. "Papa? It's me. Are you busy?"

"No. I'm in the kitchen. Come in."

Brooke went in and hugged her grandfather. "You haven't started to fix lunch yet, have you? I would like to take you out."

"Haven't eaten yet. Your dad and I had a late breakfast. You kept him out too late last night, you know? He didn't get here until after midnight! We stayed up talking until after 2:00 this morning and he wanted to be on the road early. He didn't make it. It was after 11:00 before he got out of here!"

Brooke laughed. "Don't blame me! He's supposed to be an adult! We had a lot to talk about. He seems to be handling my moving into my own place better. We talked pretty easily last night. I was afraid yesterday was going to be a disaster after the conversation we'd had earlier in the week. He'd sounded like I was going to have to live under Ruth's supervision the rest of my life."

"Not the rest of your life," Nick said. "Just until you meet the right man and get married. Then you were supposed to move out of Ruth's and have a life of your own. He still thinks you and Shaun belong together."

"Shaun and I are close friends, Papa. We have lunch together now and then, and we've even gone out a few times, but he's like a brother. Besides, he seems to have his eye on Rachel. He's been asking me a lot of questions about her lately."

Brooke put away the dishes he had been drying and steered him out of the kitchen. "Where do you want to eat lunch? I'm starving, so whatever you want. Just grab your jacket. I think winter is making a comeback."

"Oh, you know me. Anything. How about that little deli in the park? The one by the zoo. They have great sandwiches." Nick put his jacket on and started down the stairs.

"Papa. Why don't you use the elevator? I'm so worried that one of these days you're going to fall down these stairs."

"I haven't used that elevator since Sophia was wheeled out of here on that gurney! I'll consider it when I get too old to climb the stairs. Seventy isn't too old to climb the stairs!" Nick gave his granddaughter a look that settled the issue, at least for the moment. Brooke was like her father and would likely bring it up again in the future. He was glad she cared but he never liked to be fussed over.

"So. Shaun's got his eye on Rachel. How'd that happen?" Nick looked at Brooke with a little twinkle in his eye.

Brooke laughed. "I know what you're doing, Papa. No, I'm not jealous. Shaun is a dear friend. And, well, Rachel is a very beautiful woman. I don't blame him. He met her one afternoon when she and I were having lunch. He was head over heals before I could even introduce them. I still haven't figured out how to set them up. He hasn't seen her since but mentions her often."

"She is a beautiful woman," Nick agreed with his granddaughter. "You, however, are much more beautiful. I don't understand why he has never pursued you."

"I think you're just a little biased. Anyway, he had a girlfriend in college. I was a *friend* in college. I was the one he talked to about the everyday stuff. When he and his girlfriend had problems, I was the one he came to for advice. When they broke up, it was my shoulder he cried on. I think it's hard to get past that "we're just friends – you're like a sister or brother to me" thinking when that's how you've seen each other for so long. He's definitely the kind of guy I'd like to fall in love with, but, well, I don't know." Brooke shrugged her shoulders and looked up at her grandfather. "I guess I'm not in any big hurry. I'm happy just designing for the stage and working with some great people. I like being able to volunteer at church and do what I like to do. I like being able to hop on the subway whenever I want to visit my grandfather without checking with someone else. I'm not sure I'm ready to give that up. I like my independence."

"I understand that. I just don't want to see you alone. Remember, God gave Eve to Adam to keep him from being lonely. Life is much better with someone to love and share it with." Nick squeezed Brooke's hand. *"She truly is a beautiful young woman"*, he thought as he looked down at her. He just wanted her safe and happy.

"What about the people He calls to serve Him who never marry? They live their lives completely for God, living a life of sacrifice. What about those people, Papa? What if I'm one of those people?"

Nick didn't speak. He looked down at Brooke, his brow scrunched in thought.

"Papa? Did I upset you?"

"No, you didn't. You don't believe that's God's call for you, do you? I can't see you alone the rest of your life. I know you are the one who has to decide, but I can't imagine that being His desire for you."

"I can't either. I just want to keep my focus. Everyone is always pushing people my age to find the right person, fall in love, get married, have children, and by the way, make sure you have a career so you have a purpose in life and don't lose your individuality. I'm not going to run out looking for a husband just because it's the natural next step at this stage in my life. Right now, God is my Companion. If I keep Christ my focus, I can be more certain that the choices I make are in line with His will for me. I have to keep things in perspective." Brooke shook her head. She wasn't sure he understood.

Her grandfather was from a different time – a time when people were expected to marry and have a family as soon as they were old enough to make the decision. He also didn't have a relationship with Christ when he was at that stage in life. He was a religious man, raised Catholic, and respected the rituals and teachings of the church. But, he hadn't *known* Christ. He merely knew *about* Him until he was well into life. Brooke was a child when he gave his life to Christ.

Brooke looped her arm through his and rested her head against his shoulder as they walked quietly through Central Park to the deli. She loved this precious man. She never wanted to disappoint him and she knew he worried about her. Out of his seven grandchildren, she was the only who ever spent time with him. They had a special relationship. She treasured every one of these moments.

They were seated and waiting for their lunch before Nick said anything more. He took a sip of water and grinned at Brooke. "You are a sweet girl. I know what your problem is. You spend entirely too much time with an old man! You need to get out more!"

Brooke smiled at him. How he loved to tease her! She'd worry if he didn't.

They spent the rest of their lunch talking about Brooke's upcoming busy schedule. Memorial Day weekend was the end of relative quiet and the beginning of utter chaos in her life.

"I'm going to Syracuse to see Dad Memorial Day weekend. Why don't you come along?" Brooke popped the last bite of her wrap in her mouth and wiped her lips with her napkin. "I plan to take the train, but we can drive if you'd be more comfortable."

"Vince and Rhea are planning a cookout. I was planning to go out to see them. I haven't seen my newest grandbaby since shortly after he was born. He'll be grown before I know it. They've been so busy, with the business and the kids."

Vince was only three years younger than Brooke's father. He had twin sons, from a previous marriage, who were only two years younger than Brooke. One lived in the City, only a few blocks from Papa. The other lived in Vermont. Neither had visited Nick since their father had remarried. Vince's remarriage had caused tension in the family, as his new wife was only two years older than his boys. Rhea had a baby girl seven months after they were married. Their son had been born only 18 months later; he was nearing his first birthday.

Brooke knew Papa was making excuses for them. They weren't in another state for goodness' sake! They were only on Long Island, much closer than Syracuse and her father saw Papa more often than her uncle did. She couldn't remember the last she'd heard of a visit from her aunt. Maria was the youngest of Papa's children. She lived in New Jersey with her husband and 2 teenaged children. She too was close by and couldn't be bothered to spend time with Papa. Brooke knew it had to hurt him to be ignored by his own children.

Brooke paid the bill and let Papa leave the tip, as was their tradition. It saved an argument over who wanted to pay the bill. He would never let her pay it all, so she gave up trying to convince him otherwise.

"Say hi to Uncle Vince and Aunt Rhea for me. I haven't seen them since the party the week after the baby was born."

The walk back to his apartment was much quieter. He looked tired.

"You okay, Papa?"

"Fine," he said, nodding. "Just up too late. If you keep your father out too late next time he comes, he'll just have to sleep at your place! Do you have plans tonight? A date, perhaps?"

"Getting back on that topic, are we? I do have plans, but not a date. I'm meeting Ruth for dinner. It's funny how I miss her. It's only been a couple of days since I moved out, but I miss her almost as much as I missed Daddy when I first moved here for college."

"She's been good to you. She's a sweet lady. Give her my love."

"I will, Papa. I love you, and I'll call you soon."

Brooke looked at her watched and rushed down the stairs. She and Ruth were to meet at the restaurant at 6:00 and it was after 4:00. She hurried down the walk to the subway, quickly becoming a part of the flow of racing people.

———————

Paul left the restaurant after apologizing for not being able to join them for drinks that afternoon. He wanted to be alone, to take a walk and clear his head. In a matter of a week, he'd gone from being a hard-working, trusted employee to being "friends" with his bosses. He'd always gotten along well at the office, and had joined them a few times for parties and gatherings, but never like he had that weekend. His head was spinning from all of the excitement.

"Mr. Matthews," Marcus Reed caught up with Paul as he pulled on his jacket and started for the subway. "Please, join me tonight for dinner. I have reservations at the Bull and Bear in the Waldorf for 7:30 and would enjoy your company. Meet me in the lobby and we'll go in together."

Paul shook Mr. Reed's hand and promised to be there. That same feeling of unease washed over him as he squeezed Paul's hand and smiled like he had already known Paul wouldn't say no.

Paul continued to the subway. He stood despite the seats available. He didn't want to sit. He wanted to walk, run, anything to help him clear his mind of the clutter that was piling up. He tried to close his mind to the noises around him – the baseball debate between fans of opposing teams, a child's whining and his mother's scolding, a couple arguing. The chatter whirred in his brain like stones in a blender. He had to get away from it.

Paul got off at the next station and trudged up the steps into the City's cold air. He found himself on the same block as *La Regina*. He went into the shop and breathed in the inviting aroma.

"Back for your coffee cup?"

Paul looked over at Gianna who was smiling at him from behind the counter. "It's still here?" Paul asked with a smile.

"Of course! Washed and ready for a refill. You look like you need it." Gianna filled his cup and handed it over to him. "Maria, package some cookies for our friend."

Maria nodded and caught herself before she looked at Paul. Paul decided she didn't want another verbal lashing like the one Gianna had given her the day before. Maria handed Paul the box of cookies and turned to another patron.

Gianna waved the money away when Paul tried to pay her. "You helped a very dear friend of our family yesterday. And, you left without your breakfast. I don't want your money today."

Paul smiled at Gianna. "How is Mr. Barsanti? He was a little banged up yesterday."

"Fine. He was here this morning, stubborn and difficult as usual! That's always a good sign."

"Thanks, Gianna."

Paul had an inexplicable desire as he left the café to check on the old man. He walked the short distance to Nick's building and stopped suddenly. The woman hurrying away from the door leading to the old man's apartment was incredibly beautiful. She passed him quickly, looking at her watch and picking up her pace as she rushed toward the subway entrance. Her dark hair and full lips burned into his mind as she disappeared from sight. Paul was thinking about more than the welfare of his new friend as he pushed the buzzer to Nick's apartment.

SEVEN

CLOUDS BANISHED THE SUN AND poured cold rain down on the City throughout the day Sunday. The view from above the City was a collage of colorful umbrella crowns scurrying down the sidewalks toward shelter from the cold. Bus tires splashed water onto the sidewalks, drenching the shoes of any pedestrian too close to the curb. Rainwater gushed into the storm drains and plunged into the depths below the streets.

The downpour battered the church windows with an echoing force that drowned the voices of the worshippers. "Gives new meaning to the phrase 'shout to the Lord,' doesn't it?" Pastor Brian joked as he stepped up to the podium. Laughter filled the sanctuary. "The title of my sermon today is 'The Floodgates of Heaven.'"

Umbrellas flapped open and were quickly turned inside out by the brutal wind gusts, allowing the bone-chilling rain to soak the parishioners as they exited the church after the service. The torrents that had been flowing into the storm drains were now rolling over the curbs and onto the sidewalks, the steady flood of water too great for the drains to contain.

Sometime before dawn Monday, winter briefly returned to New York. A few early risers witnessed the falling snow that replaced the rain. Patches of ice on the sidewalks threatened to pull the feet out from under any unsuspecting intruder and throw them quickly to the ground. The traffic on the City streets looked like bumper cars at the State Fair.

By the time Brooke stepped through the door and into the morning air, however, the sun had pushed through the clouds. The patches of ice had melted into small puddles and the traffic was once again moving along at a normal Monday morning crawl. She breathed deeply the brisk air and walked to the subway.

Brooke spent the week in fast-forward. Her days were spent doing sketches for the "Shakespeare in the Park" costumes and submitting them to Heron for approval. Her nights were spent at the production currently at the theatre, a part of the team that stayed backstage to make any repairs that may be needed to the costumes.

The close of the show Friday night was a welcome end to the exhausting schedule. The cast & crew party that followed lasted until after midnight and by the time Brooke was seated in a cab and on her way home, her eyelids would no longer remain open.

"Are you ill?"

Brooke's eye shot open at the sound of the cab driver's voice. "I'm sorry, no. Just tired."

"I will talk to you. Maybe that will help."

Brooke smiled as the cabbie talked about his wife and infant son the rest of the way to her apartment, even pointing to the picture taped to the dashboard as he talked. He was certainly proud of the precious child and smiling wife in the photograph.

He waited for her to enter her building before pulling away. Brooke appreciated the rare act of kindness. Most wouldn't have cared about her safety in the cab and certainly not at her building.

"I could use a day of rest," Brooke thought, locking her door and looking around her apartment. "I haven't had much time to just enjoy my new home. Tomorrow won't be any quieter."

To close her hectic week, Ruth planned an "apartment warming party" for Saturday afternoon. "Don't worry about anything. I'll bring all of the food and make all of the arrangements. You just notify your building security and be ready for a full house," Ruth said when they'd shared dinner the previous weekend.

"Thank You, Lord, next week is a short week," she prayed while getting ready for bed. Sleep found her quickly and by the time the Saturday morning sunlight danced through her window and pressed a warm kiss on her cheek, she felt rested and full of anticipation for the party.

Party was an understatement. What Ruth had planned was more like a festival crammed into a small space. Brooke hadn't even realized she had so many friends.

Papa arrived just before Ruth and helped set up.

Pastor Brian and Lauren had offered Ruth their help and brought enough food for an army. Every inch of counter space was covered with food. Ruth borrowed a folding table from the church and covered it with a lovely tablecloth that couldn't be seen through the trays. No one would go home hungry.

Brian's hearty laughter filled the apartment and infected everyone else in the room. It was impossible not to have a good time when he was there.

Her team from work was there, with the exception of Heron who never replied to Ruth's invitation. Brooke's employer, Meryl, stopped in long enough to congratulate her on her new home and then had to run off to a meeting.

It seemed like half of the church congregation was there celebrating with her and laughing along with Pastor Brian. "Hey, since we're all here, how about a sermon?" Pastor Brian suggested at one point.

"Okay Brian, I think you've had enough sugar for one night," Lauren said in response, eliciting applause and laughter from the entire room.

Brooke hardly heard the knock at the door through all of the noise. Shaun hugged Brooke when he entered the apartment, his eyes immediately darting around.

"Looking for someone, Shaun?" Brooke tried to act like she didn't know who it could be. "Pastor Brian and Lauren are in the living room."

"Oh, um, thanks." His face lit up when he noticed Rachel. He did a poor job of acting indifferent to her presence.

"Rachel, you remember Shaun, don't you?"

Rachel smiled, her gaze never leaving Shaun.

"Easier than I thought it would be," Brooke thought when Shaun and Rachel fell easily into conversation. They were by each other's side the rest of the afternoon and into the evening. They left together, Shaun saying that he wanted to make sure Rachel got to her car alright, Rachel smiling brightly.

Most of the guests were gone by nightfall. Ruth stayed to help Brooke clean up, and Pastor Brian and Lauren volunteered to make sure Nick got home okay.

"I'm perfectly capable of getting to my own home, thank you very much! I'm not an invalid!" Nick shook his head in disgust. "Why do people think that when a man gets old, he needs to be treated like a child! Let me be!"

Brooke just shrugged her shoulders apologetically at Brian and his wife. They hugged Brooke and left without Nick. Ruth found his hat and jacket and helped him on with his jacket.

"Papa, they were only trying to be helpful. You know I worry about something happening to you and I don't think you're an invalid. It's just that you never know what can happen in this City," Brooke offered as an explanation.

"I know. I worry about you, too, when you're out roaming on your own. But I don't insist on sending a babysitter to make sure you get home okay. Just stop trying to do it to me, okay?" Nick kissed his granddaughter. He muttered under his breath in Italian as he left the apartment.

"I wish I'd learned my family's language so I could understand what he was going on about," she said to Ruth after he'd left. "On second thought," she laughed, "maybe I'm better off not knowing!"

Ruth shook her head and laughed along with Brooke. "He just wants to keep his independence. You can't blame him for that."

"No, I guess not. I suppose my fussing over Papa isn't much different than the way Dad fussed when he found out I was moving in here. I should try to be more understanding."

Ruth left shortly after Nick. Brooke resisted the urge to call him to make sure he'd gotten home alright. Brooke tried not to worry, but she had a hard time settling down. The ringing of the phone made her jump.

"Hello?"

"Hello, Dear. Just wanted you to know that Nick is home safe and sound," Ruth reassured Brooke from the other end. "I stopped by before driving home."

"How did you manage that?" Brooke asked in surprise. "I'll bet he was furious."

"No. He forgot his scarf. Somehow it managed to get tangled up in my coat when I was getting his off the coat rack. Not sure how that happened," Ruth replied slyly.

"You are rather devious, Ruth!"

"I know. But, you have to admit, it worked! He didn't suspect a thing!"

––––––––

Paul's week was busier than usual. He succeeded in signing contracts with two of the three clients he'd pursued early in the week. One was a smaller account, but had a big name. The larger account would net the company millions.

Tuesday afternoon he made what seemed a risky suggestion to purchase a particular stock on behalf of three mid-level international clients.

"I don't know, Paul." Pratt's pacing and constant adjusting of his tie made it obvious he didn't agree with the idea. "That's a huge risk, especially with clients who stand to lose a lot. If we're wrong, they could be facing serious financial distress."

Paul spent over an hour explaining the changes that had taken place in the market over the weeks prior and his reason for believing it would be a sound plan. "The stocks will be worth twice as much in less than a month. The clients can either keep them as assets in their portfolio or sell them off and make a huge profit."

Marshall stared over the table at Paul, his fingers steepled under his chin. He bounced his chair seemingly in rhythm to his thoughts. He ignored Pratt's frantic look.

"Do it!" Marshall finally said. "Call Val and Marty. You can't do anything with their purchases without talking to them first. We have full discretion on the Oldman account. Just do it. Make sure you tell Val and Marty I approve."

By Friday, Paul was the talk of the company. The stocks didn't double in two weeks as he'd predicted. They'd tripled by the closing bell Friday. Pratt and Marshall insisted on champagne in Pratt's office before they were to meet with Marcus Reed for a private party. Paul's star was rising. He smiled as glasses were raised in his honor. *"By thirty,"* he thought. *"I'll be a millionaire and my dreams of wealth and position will be within my reach."*

EIGHT

BROOKE WENT TO WORK MONDAY anticipating the short week and the coming long weekend. Meryl surprised the staff with a four-day weekend in honor of Memorial Day and to give them time to rest before the start of the busy season. Brooke planned to spend the long weekend in Syracuse with her father. She didn't get home as often as she'd like and looked forward to the time with her dad.

Having a short week, however, didn't mean there was less to be done. There were still costumes to complete and fittings to be done. Heron wanted the entire team at the Delcorte Theatre early the following morning, ready to make any alterations.

Brooke spent the day in the sewing room cutting patterns and stitching costumes. Sewing boxes with extra buttons, matching thread, and garnishments were assembled for each costume and loaded onto carts for delivery to the theatre.

Rachel came into the prep room where Brooke was readying the clothing racks and cartons for the delivery team.

"Well! How long did it take Shaun to walk you to your car Saturday?" Brooke asked when she noticed Rachel.

Rachel smiled shyly. "Only a half hour or so."

Brooke laughed. "I had a feeling it might take a while. What do you think?"

"We had lunch after church yesterday and we're having dinner tonight. We'll see, but he really is a sweet man, isn't he?" Rachel squeezed Brooke's shoulder and went back into the main studio.

Brooke felt a brief pang of jealousy. She dismissed the feeling and considered how perfect Rachel and Shaun were together. She was happy for them. Why she had waited so long to help them get together, she didn't know.

Tuesday greeted the team with a promising sunrise and warm spring temperatures. Heron gave her nod of approval for Brooke's work from the day before and moved on to the other racks of costumes. Heron quickly found fault with some of Rachel's work, and had her near tears before the final cartons had been opened.

"Shake it off, Rachel," Brooke whispered. "Just let it go. You know how she gets."

"Why does she always seem to come after me! Every costume I did came from an approved sketch. I did what she told me I could do!" Wiping her eyes, Rachel looked over at Heron. "I think she just doesn't like me."

"She doesn't like your *faith*. She's given me a hard time, too. Remember last spring, the fit she threw when she saw my Bible in my bag? She ordered me to never bring it to a job again. If Meryl hadn't stepped in, I wouldn't be able to have it even on my breaks. She knows our faith, Rachel. That's what she's attacking - not you."

"Doesn't make me feel much better, but thanks for reminding me. I just wish she'd look at our work and leave the rest alone. Mara reads those trash novels and nothing's said to her about it. Julie's costumes were the ones we spent most of our time repairing during that last show, but I've never heard Heron yell at her. You're the best designer we have, besides Heron and Meryl. Yet, she's always giving you a hard time. I just don't get it. When we do a good job, she looks good to Meryl and everyone else in the business." Rachel shook her head and went back to her costume rack. She had a lot of work to do in a short time.

Brooke wished she could help her, but the last time she tried to help out, she was accused of neglecting her own work. *"Better leave it alone,"* she thought, rolling her clothes cart to the women's dressing room.

It always amazed Brooke that it was the extras who strutted around like the biggest stars in the world of theatre, not the real celebrities. Two Hollywood names were taking part in the festival, and they were both down to earth and easy going about everything. They were being costumed by Heron and two other long-time team leaders. Brooke and Rachel were the part of the team who costumed the extras.

Brooke's first fitting was easy. The actor was a very quiet man, turned when asked and never spoke to Brooke unless she asked him a question.

She was finished with him in less than an hour. Her next assignment, Leslie, wasn't as quick.

"I hate this fabric! Whatever possessed you to use this?" she snapped at Brooke before the first pin had been put in place.

Brooke smile at her patiently. "We were instructed to use this by the theater company."

"Well, don't think I'm not going to complain about it! This is terrible!"

Brooke had her step onto the stool to pin the hem of her skirt. "Don't tell me you plan to leave the waist like this! It must be tighter and the neck line must plunge! Don't you know anything about the works of Shakespeare? Where did you go to school?"

Brooke took a deep breath. "I didn't want to make it too tight. I'm concerned about the seams remaining intact if you have to make any abrupt movements."

"What are you implying? That I am not slim enough? How dare you?" The woman looked ready to claw Brooke's eyes out.

"I'm implying nothing of the sort. This material is delicate and pulls easily. But, I will make it smaller if you'd like."

She pinned the waist and bodice tighter. She could tell Leslie was sucking her stomach in. She couldn't understand why. Leslie was very slender and certainly didn't need to make herself look any smaller.

"I can't breathe! You made this entirely too tight! Loosen this up!" Leslie snapped, glaring at Brooke.

It took two hours to finish pinning the costume. By the time she finished, Brooke was ready for a break. *"What makes these people so arrogant?"* she thought, taking her bag and a bottle of water outside for a few minutes of fresh air. She sat in the grass and read a few verses from Psalms. If anything could calm her, it was King David.

After a few minutes of rest and quiet prayer, Brooke put her Bible back into her bag and returned to the dressing room. She went to work on her next costume, unaware that her difficult morning was about to get worse.

The rest of the fittings went well. There weren't many adjustments to make, and she'd have no trouble getting them back to the theatre the next morning. Brooke was labeling the costumes on her clothes rack when Heron stormed over.

"Leslie told me what you did to her during her fitting! What did you think you were doing? How dare you insult the cast of a show?"

"Heron, I didn't insult her. Please, let me tell you what happened." Brooke tried to explain, but she could tell Heron wasn't listening.

"In addition," Heron shouted. "I have told you that waving your religious stuff around at people is completely inappropriate. Yet, you take it upon yourself to have your own little church service while working! I should fire you for this!"

"Church service? I read a few verses from my Bible during my break. Meryl told me I could as long as I was on break. I didn't do anything wrong!" Brooke was shaking all over.

"Well, that's not what Leslie reported to me and after the way you treated her..." Heron clenched her jaw and didn't go on. She glared at Brooke. "You will remain in the studio until further notice. Leave now! Finish the work you've already started; then wait for me to tell you what to do. You should be grateful you still have a job!"

Heron marched off, leaving Brooke shocked and overwhelmed. She knew that nothing she'd say to Heron would help. She packed her patterns and sewing box and took a cab back to the studio.

It was quiet. She was more or less alone. A few interns were cleaning up and sorting through material and notions. She prayed quietly and hummed a few songs from worship on Sunday, but her thoughts kept returning to Heron and the way she'd been treated.

"Lord, I don't understand. I know I'm not supposed to question You, and I know others have been treated far worse than I for their faith, but this is America, not some primitive culture! I just want to do what's right and be treated fairly," Brooke prayed quietly. She finished her alterations and loaded the costumes onto the racks for delivery back to the theatre.

Brooke was clearing her work table when Meryl came in. He glanced around, looked at Brooke and frowned. "I thought you were at Delcorte with the rest of the team. What are you doing here?"

Brooke couldn't meet his eyes. She didn't want any more trouble. "Heron sent me back to make alterations. She wants me to stay here until she decides what else she wants me to do."

Meryl wasn't a fool. He knew something had happened and Brooke wasn't the type to complain about anyone. He also knew Heron's temper and attitude.

"Go home Brooke. You look like you've had a rough day. Take some time to relax."

"Thanks, Meryl."

Brooke went out into the afternoon sun. She walked for awhile, hoping to clear her mind. The frustration and discouragement continued to grow. *"I need Papa,"* she thought. If anyone could cheer her up and shed the proper light on the situation, it was Papa. She stopped at La Regina for biscotti and walked the few blocks to his building.

She knocked lightly and opened the door. "Papa?"

He didn't answer.

Brooke put her purse and pastry box on the entry side table. She followed the smell of coffee brewing to the kitchen, but didn't find him there. She checked his bedroom and the spare room - no sign of her grandfather.

She stood in the living room trying to decide what to do. If the coffee hadn't been brewing, she would have thought he'd gone out. She was considering calling the police when she heard the elevator.

"Papa! You scared the living daylights out of me! What were you doing? And why are you taking the elevator? Are you okay?" Brooke nearly cried with relief when he stepped out of the elevator. She moved to hug him and stopped quickly. She had never before seen the man with him.

He had dark brown hair and was a little taller than her grandfather. He was dressed in what was without a doubt an expensive suit. The blue silk tie he wore was loosened slightly. His piercing blue eyes glimmered in surprise. His expression changed to one of recognition.

He stepped out of the elevator and extended his hand to Brooke. "Paul Matthews. Pleased to meet you." His voice was deep.

"Yes, sorry. Brooke Barsanti. Nice to meet you, too," Brooke stammered in embarrassment.

Paul released her hand reluctantly. She was more beautiful than he'd remembered from the day he'd seen her leaving Nick's apartment. Her eyes were such a golden brown he had trouble taking his gaze from them.

Brooke looked over to her grandfather. "Is everything okay, Papa?"

"Paul is the young man who rescued me from Gianna at La Regina the day I was pushed. He merely stopped by to see if I was healing well."

"Thank you, sir, for helping my grandfather," Brooke said, glancing again at Paul then quickly looking back at Papa.

Paul chuckled at her, amused by her shyness. She hadn't appeared to be a bashful woman. She had carried herself with dignity and confidence when she'd passed him several days before. Now, she seemed the most timid creature he'd met.

Papa looked at Brook and shook his head. "You're the one who wanted me to start using the elevator, aren't you? Now you're upset that I am! You make little sense, child!"

"I also remember you saying that you wouldn't use it until you couldn't climb the stairs anymore!"

Nick smiled at Brooke. "I was just giving my friend a tour of the shop. It was easier to take the elevator down and go through that way. Come to the kitchen, both of you. The coffee is ready."

Paul and Brooke followed Nick into the kitchen and sat to the table. Nick served the coffee and sat down with his guests. "So, what's wrong Brooke? Don't say 'nothing.' You've had a look since you got here. And it's still two hours before your workday ends. What happened?"

"Oh, just one of those days. Meryl sent me home early." Brooke took a sip of coffee and looked over at Paul. "Mr. Matthews, what kind of work do you do?"

"Finance management, investments, that sort of thing. Mostly international. My newest client is from Cairo. I really enjoy the work." Paul smiled at Brooke. "Please, call me Paul. When you call me Mr. Matthews, all I can think of is my father!"

Brooke laughed. "Okay, Paul it is!"

Paul and Brooke spent the next hour getting to know each other better, under the watchful and satisfied eye of Nick. He was pleased with the way they were getting along. He didn't like Brooke being alone and was quite impressed with what he'd already seen of the young man.

"Well, I must be on my way," Paul said, rising from his chair. "I have a dinner appointment with a man who will not be left waiting! I enjoyed meeting you, Brooke. Would it be inappropriate for me to ask you to dinner sometime soon?"

Brooke smiled and gave Paul her phone number before he left the apartment.

"You look quite smug, Papa! How long have you been planning this?"

"Not planning so much as praying it would happen. He saw you leaving here the day we went to lunch and asked me about you. He mentioned your beauty and I had to agree. He is a very nice young man. Don't you think?"

Brooke hugged him. "Come on, Papa. Let me help you cook dinner." They worked together to fix a simple supper. Brooke set the table and sliced some bread.

Papa prayed over the meal and told her about Paul's visit. "He thinks he might have someone interested in buying the building."

"Are you going to sell it?" Brooke couldn't imagine anyone else owning the shop, despite its being empty for years.

"I don't know. If the right people and offer came along, I might consider it. I'd have to find another place to live, though, too. I'm sure a buyer would want to do something with the apartment. I would have to think about it. I'd want to know what the plan was for it before I'd agree to anything." Nick took a piece of bread from the basket. "So, when are you going to tell me what happened today that brought you to my door so early in the day?"

Brooke filled him in on the day she'd had, beginning with the way Heron treated Rachel and ending with Meryl finding her in the studio. "I'm not sure what to do, Papa. Heron is one of the best in the business and has been with Meryl since she finished school. If he had to, I know he'd fire me to keep Heron happy."

"You don't know that. He seems to be a fair man. He still owns the company. I wouldn't start looking for another job just yet."

By the time Brooke left, she felt better. Her grandfather always knew what needed to be said and how to say it, even when he didn't agree with her interpretation of things. He seemed to know how to put things into perspective. She made up her mind to go to the studio in the morning and do her job without thinking about Heron's threat.

Brooke spent most of Wednesday morning cleaning up the prep room. There wasn't much for her to do and it was making her crazy sitting around and waiting for Heron to call her with a task. By lunchtime, the room was cleaned up and organized.

Brooke was at her worktable getting her purse when Meryl and Heron came into the room. They stopped in the doorway, still deep in conversation. Heron looked unhappy and Meryl looked stern.

Meryl turned from Heron and left the room. She stared at Brooke for several moments before going to her own office. Brooke sighed and left for lunch. She was sure Heron would be waiting for her when she returned.

––––––––––––

It was a note from Meryl that read "Meeting in my office" that greeted her when she returned. Brooke took her sketch pad and a notebook and went to Meryl's office. She tried to prepare herself for what was sure to come.

Meryl's door was open when Brooke arrived. He and Heron were sitting at his conference table, discussing the previous season. Meryl looked up and motioned for her Brooke to enter. "Come right in and have a seat! We were just getting started. I have exciting news! We have the 'Madame Butterfly' show!"

Brooke was confused. She'd never been included in Meryl's meetings with the team leaders.

"I know there's still a great deal of work to be completed on the 'Shakespeare in the Park' costumes, but we have to get to work on this right away. I don't want to give this to another team – this is definitely a show for you, Heron, and your designers. So, Brooke, I have a plan that will keep you busy doing two things at once. Are you up to it?"

"Yes, sir," Brooke answered, hoping that she hadn't agreed to more than she could handle.

"You don't even know what it is yet!" Heron snapped at Brooke. "Shouldn't you first find out what's being asked of you before you put your head on the block?"

Meryl looked at Heron. "I believe she already knows how I work, Heron. You've taught her well and I have every confidence she will do fine." Turning back to Brooke, he explained "I need someone to finish the Shakespeare alterations this week and also start the sketches for the 'Madame Butterfly' submittal. I will pull a few of the others back in from Delcorte to help, but you are one of the quickest workers. I know with you at it, the costumes will be back out within a few days. If we can wrap up Shakespeare this week, we can dive into the new show when we return next Tuesday. I've already decided to send Ruby's team out to take care of any repairs needed during the festival. It's just maintenance now. What I'd like to know is, who would be best to bring back to rush through the alterations and completions? Who do we trust to do it right so that Ruby won't have serious damage control? I don't want a repeat of the last show. Who did the costumes that required all of the repairs?"

Heron answered quickly, "Rachel. Her work is substandard."

Brooke spoke without thinking. "Heron, those weren't Rachel's. They were Julie's. Rachel spent most of her time fixing Julie's mistakes. Rachel would do a great job on the alterations."

"I know you two are friends, Brooke, but you don't have to defend her!" Heron glared at Brooke.

Meryl cleared his throat. "Alright. Heron, you know who can and can't handle this. Make the call. Just make sure whoever is left on this doesn't let us down. Brooke, I know Heron has put you in the studio for a reason and I will honor her decision for the rest of Shakespeare. Your work will be done from here. Once we get to work on 'Madame Butterfly,' however, you will have to go out with the rest of the team. So don't get comfortable here in the studio." He looked at Heron to make sure she understood what he was saying.

"Okay ladies. Let's get to work. We have a lot to do in two days!"

The next two days were non-stop. Everyone worked late Wednesday and Thursday nights. The costumes were quickly finished for 'Shakespeare in the Park', labeled and put back on the racks for the delivery team. 'Madame Butterfly' was mentioned briefly, more as a reminder of the upcoming week than anything else. Brooke left Thursday night feeling better about the way the week had gone.

She was excited about the following week. It was the first time Meryl had included her in any of the decision making. It was also the first time she was given access to the information about a coming show. Usually she was told with everyone else on the team which extras and roles they were designing. She felt that Meryl was somehow trying to send her the message that, despite Heron's mistreatment, she was valued by the company. It meant a great deal to her. Now she could go home to Syracuse and truly enjoy the weekend with her father.

NINE

PAUL SAT IN HIS CAR with his fingers wrapped around the steering wheel. He stared out the windshield at nothing for several minutes before taking a deep breath and getting out. His home looked the same. Nothing ever changed here. Sometimes he was relieved by that. Other times, it irritated him that no one in this town ever seemed to step out into the real world and grasp all it had to offer. Irritation was what gripped him when he closed the car door.

How he'd let Pratt talk him into to going home for the long weekend, he didn't know. "The computers in the office are scheduled for upgrade and maintenance for the entire day tomorrow," Pratt informed him Wednesday afternoon. "The office will be closed, the computers unavailable, until Tuesday morning. Get out of town! Enjoy some fresh air; do some boating, or whatever it is you do when you go home. Just take a break!"

Paul had tried to work on his laptop Thursday morning but received the warning on his computer that the network was unavailable. Annoyed, Paul packed his suitcase, left a note for the cleaning lady and was on his way out of the City by 7:30.

He'd spent the next seven hours driving up the coast, mostly through small towns and villages, trying to muster up some enthusiasm about seeing his family. It hadn't worked. He stood there in his parents' driveway wondering why he'd listened to Pratt. He could have stayed in New York and enjoyed the long weekend with friends rather than sitting through another of his father's endless religious spiels.

"Too late now," he thought. He looked up at the house and shook his head. "I'm not ready for this." He walked down the driveway and headed toward town.

Paul could hear the piano from the sidewalk. The music floated out and met him, a sweet welcoming sound. He smiled and went up the path to the house.

Knocking while turning the knob, he called in "Grandmother?" The music stopped and he heard quiet conversation before the music started again.

Jillian Matthews didn't look anywhere near the age of seventy-five. Her gray hair was still long and thick, pulled back away from her face, but allowed to flow down her back. She could easily have been mistaken for Paul's mother rather than grandmother. She stood tall and had a grace that never diminished.

"Paul! Steve and Marian didn't tell me you were coming! What a surprise!" She hugged him then turned her cheek to accept a kiss.

"They didn't know I was coming. It's a surprise to them, too. In fact, unless they've seen my car in their driveway, they still don't know that I'm here."

"Come in. I will send my pupil on her way and we'll have tea." Jillian instructed her student on her next lesson, sent her out the door and went to the kitchen to put water in the kettle.

"Still have the same piano," Paul commented, more to himself than to his grandmother.

"She's a dear friend," Jillian smiled, coming back into the living room. "Come. You look like you need to relax a little. What's on your mind?"

Paul sat down to the piano and ran his hands over the polished wood. How many hours had he spent at this instrument, learning everything he could from his grandmother? "I have a baby grand in my condo now. I love being able to sit down and just play whenever I want to. It's relaxing."

"Good. That means you haven't stopped practicing. Play a piece. I'll bring the tea in when it's ready."

Paul started to play. At first, it was nothing in particular – just a stream of random notes. Those notes soon flowed into Chopin's Ballade no. 2.

Jillian returned to the living room carrying a tray with her silver tea service and a plate of petite fours. She stood in the doorway and watched him play. His eyes were closed; his fingers danced gracefully over the keys.

"You must be in a fuss. You've always picked that piece when you've had a bad day." She set the tray on the table. "Come. Sit with me. I want to know what has you in such a state. Is it a woman?"

"You never did worry about diplomacy, did you Grandmother?" Paul smiled at her. He sat in one of the wingchairs and took a sip of his tea. "I have met a woman, but we haven't gone out yet." He spent a few minutes telling her about Brooke and her grandfather.

"Well, if her grandfather approves of you, that's a good start. What else has been going on?"

Paul filled her in on his recent successes at work and his unexplainable apprehensions about Marcus Reed. "I just don't know what to think of him. In fact, I don't really know anything about him. I know if he were ever to become a client, it would be with the international side of the company, but I don't even know where he's from. I can't figure out his accent. Pratt and Marshall have been really vague about the guy. The problem is, he's a close friend to Marshall, and Pratt seems to worship the guy. I've spent hours with him over the past few weeks and still don't have a clue. Am I being paranoid?"

Jillian put her cup back on its saucer and sat back in her chair, her hands folded in her lap. She said nothing for several minutes. She searched Paul's face. "Have you ever known your employer to do anything illegal or immoral?"

"No, well, not illegal. Nothing immoral in business. I wouldn't be the least bit surprised if Pratt was having an affair on his wife, but that's personal."

"Follow your instincts, Paul. But it may be that everything is happening so quickly for you that you just haven't been able to adjust to it yet. I'd keep my guard up, but don't let it get you into such a condition. You'll know soon enough."

Paul visited with his grandmother for the next hour. His time with her helped him relax. When he left, he felt better about seeing his parents. He decided to go to the marina before going back to the house.

He walked the short distance, past his parents' home and down to the bay. The sea air was clean and fresh. He couldn't resist breathing deeply the wonderful scent and smiling at the childhood memories that came flooding into his mind. Within minutes, he'd reached the marina.

The only change Paul could see to his father's shop was the security system. *"I'm impressed. I thought guardian angels were all that Dad would ever rely on,"* Paul thought sarcastically as he entered the shop.

Paul looked around the room, noting the cruiser on the lift. It was an impressive vessel. He ran his hands over the wood, observing the repairs that had been made. It looked like a lot of work had been done to the hull. Paul heard a drill in the smaller workshop. He took a deep breath and went to find his father.

"Dad," Paul called out as he pushed open the door to the work room.

"Paul! It's you! Wow! This is great!" A big man put the drill down, removed his safety glasses and marched over to Paul. He hugged Paul and grinned at him.

"Hi Herbie. Dad still working you to death?" Herbie was 40 years old and had worked for Paul's father for 20 years. He had a mental disability that gave him the personality of a 12 year old. His father had hired him as part of a school-based work program that trained the learning-disabled in a skill. He was always happy and worked harder than anyone who'd ever been employed by his father. Steve had decided to keep him on and he'd worked for the marina ever since.

"Oh yeah, don't you know it! I got promoted, sorta! I get to put hinges and stuff on the cabinet doors now instead of just sweeping up and cleaning stuff and sorting stuff all the time. It's really cool cuz I get to use the drill and 'lectric screw driver and everything! It's real neat!" Herbie beamed with pride as he filled Paul in his "promotion." "You gonna work with us again?" Herbie asked innocently. "It would be real cool if you could! We had us a lot of fun, didn't we, Paul?"

"We did, didn't we, Herbie? No, I still have my job in New York. I'm just here for a visit. Where's Dad?"

"He's down at that stupid pier that keeps getting broken. The man that parks his boat at it rammed it two times this week! Don't you just know he gots to be drunk or somethin'? Nobody with a lick of sense would do that two times in a week!" Herbie shook his head at the thought.

Paul smiled at the man. "I think I'll go down and talk to him. Stay out of trouble, Herbie! Maybe I'll see you again before I go back to New York."

"Okay Paul! Bye. Don't you get into trouble neither!"

Paul left the room and looked out the window toward the main part of the marina. He could see his father looking over the damaged pier. Paul turned away and went into the inner bay of his father's shop. He looked over the unfinished sailboat, running his hands over the wood as he considered the many hours he and his father had spent on it. His strange dream briefly crossed his mind, the sounds of the waves lapping the hull, the sun beating down on his face.

"Hello, Son."

Paul turned from the boat to see his father standing in the doorway. "Dad."

"Didn't know you were coming home this weekend. It's a nice surprise."

"It was a last-minute decision. The office is closed for the holiday and well, I decided to drive up and surprise you and Mom." Paul looked back at the sailboat. "I'm surprised you've never finished this."

Steve moved to stand next to his son. "You shouldn't be. It's *our* project, Paul. Someday we'll finish it together."

Paul shook his head. "Dad, I don't know when I'll ever be able to come home long enough. Why don't you and Jason finish it? He's right here and seems to have more time than I do."

"It isn't your brother's sailboat, Son. It's yours. Let's not get into this again. You already know how I feel about it. Let's go home. Your mother is eager to see you. She called about an hour ago. She saw your car in the driveway. Where have you been all of this time?"

"Grandmother's house." Paul shrugged. "I just wanted to see her for a few minutes and it turned into an hour. It was nice to visit with her."

Steve nodded his understanding as they made their way out of the bay. Steve's mother had always seen Paul as her favorite. Paul had often escaped to her house when he was having a bad day or if things didn't go his way at home. More than one disagreement had occurred between Steve and his mother concerning Paul's upbringing.

Steve sent Herbic home, wishing him a nice holiday weekend, and set the alarm. "Never thought I'd see one of these here, Dad," Paul commented as Steve entered the code.

"Two businesses were broken into in a week's time. I decided it was time to move into the 21st century and put one in. I didn't realize it would save money on my insurance. It's also given me peace of mind."

"Sure nothing's bothering you? You've been on my mind a lot lately. You look exhausted," Steve asked as they walked the short distance to the house.

"No. Nothing's wrong. I've just been so busy. I have a few new accounts. I made a huge, somewhat risky decision a couple of weeks ago that was quite successful. It really impressed my supervisors. I've been spending a great deal of time with some powerful people these past weeks. I'm happier than I've been my entire life. I've been putting in some long hours, though. I know that's why I'm so tired." Paul smiled over at his father. "Coming home this weekend should help me with that."

Steve simply nodded. They stepped through the door and into the kitchen of the family home. "Look who I found, Honey," Steve said, kissing his wife softly.

"Paul." Marian smiled and hugged her son. "I saw you pull in and wondered where you'd gone. Is everything okay?"

"I'm fine! Why does everyone keep asking me that? Since the minute I stepped into this town, everyone has been asking about my welfare – Grandmother, Dad and now you! I'm fine! Can't a guy just come home for a visit without having something wrong? Good God!"

Paul noted the hurt on his mother's face. "I'm sorry, Mom. I didn't mean to fly off. Really, I'm fine. I'm just tired and I guess a little temperamental. I've been working a lot of hours and just need some rest. That's part of the reason I'm home. And I wanted to see my family."

Marian smiled weakly at Paul. "Well, bring your bags in and get settled. Dinner won't be anything special, but maybe Jason and Lydia could bring Sarah over this evening. You haven't seen your niece in months."

"I'd like that, Mom. Thanks"

Paul retrieved his bags from the car and carried them up the stairs to his old room. His mother was already busy putting clean linens on his bed. "I can do that, Mom."

"Nonsense. You unpack and let me take care of my son for a few minutes."

Paul went about unpacking and putting his things in drawers. He never liked living out of a bag. He put his toiletries in the attached bathroom and helped his mother finish making the bed.

"I really am sorry, Mom. I didn't mean to yell at you."

"I know. It sounds like you have a busy life and just need to relax. Don't worry about it. It never happened." Marian hugged her son and prayed a silent prayer. Her mother's heart could feel the struggle going on inside her son. It was there, whether he recognized it or not.

They walked together down the stairs to the living room. They were talking about Sarah, Paul's niece, when they entered the room. "You should see her, Paul. She's the cutest little girl – the biggest brown eyes and dark curls. She looks like a little angel!"

"She does," Steve agreed with his wife. "I think there's a little devil lurking behind those long eyelashes, though," he said, laughing.

"She's only a year old, Steve! How in the world can you think that?" Marian said indignantly to her husband.

"She's got you wrapped around her little finger!"

Marian shook her head and laughed. "I guess I can't deny that now can I? She has a pretty good hold on you, too – and you can't deny it either!"

Steve chuckled and nodded in agreement. "Hard not to be in her little grip. She's such a sweet little thing!"

Paul laughed at the conversation between his parents. "I can't wait to see her again."

"I should see what I can throw together for dinner," Marian said, excusing herself from the conversation.

"Wait, Mom. Let me take you two out to dinner," Paul said. "I haven't had the chance in such a long time. Where would you like to go?"

Marian and Steve looked at each other. "Well," Steve said. "I think that would be fine. Should I call your brother and have them meet us, or just have them over here later?"

Marian shook her head before Paul could answer. "I don't think they'd want to wrestle with Sarah all during dinner. I'll call and have them come over later."

Steve and Marian insisted on a little diner near the marina for dinner. Steve wanted Paul to see the locals who asked about him regularly. "A lot of people miss you, Son," had been Steve's response when Paul asked about someplace quiet.

Despite the regular interruptions by people wanting to say hello to Paul, dinner turned out to be pleasant and relaxing. Even after their meals were finished, Steve and Marian talked steadily, one picking up where the other left off, about Jason and Lydia and the delight Sarah had been to their lives. When they ran out of family talk, they turned to business at the marina.

"I saw the cruiser on the lift," Paul commented when Steve mentioned his contracts for the season. "Where'd she come from?"

"Do you remember that senator who resigned last year, that Senator Maxwell?"

"The one with the bad comb-over and teeth too big for his mouth? If I remember correctly, wasn't there some sexual harassment accusation against him?" Paul asked before taking a sip of water.

"That's the one," Steve nodded. "He still claims he's innocent and withdrew from the race and resigned to "save the face of the party" as he put it. He brought me photos of the cruiser, got a quote and insisted that no price was too high. Between his boat and the two local agency contracts, we won't have to worry about paying our bills this year. That's a great feeling."

"I know exactly what you mean, Dad. With the accounts I've pulled in just this spring, and the impression I seem to be making on Marcus Reed, I won't have to worry either."

"Who's Marcus Reed?" Marian asked. "I don't think I've ever heard you mention him before."

"He's a close friend of Marshall Appleton. He isn't a client, but Marshall thinks highly of him. I don't really know much about him, yet. It's only been a couple of weeks since Marshall and Pratt introduced us. We've had several working lunches and dinners. I don't know if they're hoping to get him to sign on as a client, or if he has some pull overseas, but he's someone of great importance to the company."

Marian glanced up at the clock on the diner wall. "We should go home. Jason and Lydia will be there soon."

Paul went to the register to pay the bill as his parents stopped to chat with some of the families scattered around the restaurant. Paul went back to the table, dropped a tip and walked over to where his parents were deep in conversation.

"Hello, Paul." Reverend Shaffer stood and extended his hand.

"Reverend," Paul replied, shaking the outstretched hand.

"Steve and Marian tell me you're home for the weekend. Hope to see you Sunday. It's been a while," the reverend smiled at Paul.

"I don't know. I haven't decided yet whether I'm leaving Sunday or Monday. I guess we'll have to see."

"Well, I hope you can make it." He turned to Steve and Marian. "See you Sunday and hope you enjoy your weekend."

Steve shook his hand and spoke his thanks before leaving with Marian and Paul. The drive home was quiet.

Jason and Lydia were already in the Matthews' living room when Paul and his parents arrived home. Lydia smiled and hugged Paul. Sarah was curled up on a blanket on the floor. Asleep with her fingers in her mouth, she was the picture of pure contentment.

Jason hugged his brother, slapping him on the back. "Paul. Glad you made it home! How's life treating you?"

Paul filled Jason in on his recent business successes. He emphasized his financial increase and the rise in his position with the company.

"Haven't heard you mention a woman yet. Still no one to keep you in line, huh?" Jason reached over and squeezed Lydia's hand.

"No, not really. I have met a beautiful woman, but we haven't gone out yet. We've spent some time talking at her grandfather's place, but that's it." Paul spent a few moments sharing his encounter with Brooke.

"A church girl, I hope," Marian said quietly, smiling at her son.

"I don't really know, Mom. I haven't had the chance to find out her religious or political standings," Paul replied, his tone harsh.

"Don't get defensive, Son," Steve said. "Your mother and I just want you to be happy and find a Godly woman to share your life with. That's all."

"That's all? Why can't she just be a nice, intelligent, gorgeous woman? Why does she have to be straight out of the Bible? I told you a long time ago that I've outgrown the religious stuff. Why can't you just leave it alone? You wonder why I seldom come home!" Paul stood up and stormed into the kitchen.

Steve's jaw was set, his hands clenched as he followed his son. He moved close to Paul, his anger evident. "You know how we feel! You know and have known your entire life that God is and always will be number one in this house and in our lives! Don't come waltzing in here, throwing your wealth and power in our faces and spit on our faith at every opportunity! You have been rude to your mother, looked down your nose to me, and strutted around like you own the whole world since you drove up in your shiny Mercedes! I won't have it! Until you can respect us in our home and accept where you've come from, don't bother to come back home!"

"Enough!" Marian stood in the kitchen doorway. Tears streamed down her cheeks. "Stop it, both of you! I hardly ever have my family together, and I don't want to listen to arguing during the rare occasion. Just stop!"

Paul glared at his father. He pushed past his mother and stormed through the living room and up the stairs, two at a time, to his room. He sat on the edge of the bed. The fiery anger grew within him. He stood quickly and threw his things into his suitcase. He raged down the stairs and through the living room to the kitchen.

"Paul! Don't leave like this!" Steve shouted to him.

"Back off, Dad!" Paul turned quickly, pointing his finger at Steve as a warning to stay away. He went out the door, slamming it behind him.

"Let him go, Steve." Marian rested her hand gently on his arm as he rose to go after his son. "He has to figure this out for himself."

"I'll go to him, Mom," Jason said.

Paul tossed his bags into the trunk and looked up at Jason as he came out to the driveway. "Don't start, Jason. I really don't want to get into it with you right now."

"I wasn't planning to start anything. I just want to make sure you're okay before you leave."

"Why can't they just be happy for me, Jason? Why can't they just accept that I don't belong here anymore? I just can't stand the small-town, small-minded, keep it in the family way of thinking."

"I remember when we were kids," Jason smiled. "You had big plans to own that big Victorian two blocks away that's been empty since we could remember, make Dad's marina the biggest in Maine and marry Lilly

59

Shaffer. You never planned anything small, but you always planned it here – at least until the end of high school. I think that's what they remember, Paul. Dad had always believed you'd take over his business. Mom always believed you would marry Lilly Shaffer, or some other sweet church girl. They've had a hard time accepting the change in you."

"Sweet church girl. I wouldn't exactly give Lilly that label anymore." Paul stared off into the distance, turning Jason's words over in his mind.

"I'm sorry I brought up Lilly, Paul. I didn't realize those memories were still painful. You understand what I'm saying though, don't you?"

Paul still looked off in the distance. "Lilly...not painful so much anymore, just a shadow I guess." He turned back to his brother. "I know you're happy here, Jason. I don't mean to say that you're small-minded. You found your place here. You married a wonderful woman. You work the job you've dreamed of your whole life. You're content here. That makes Mom and Dad happy, too. I'm glad you're doing well. You've never disappointed them in anything you've done. I don't feel like I can do anything right, despite all that I've accomplished."

"Lydia and I started going to that interdenominational church right after Sarah was born. We love it there. Dad about had a stroke when he found out we were withdrawing our membership from the Baptist church and going over there for good. It took a while for him to accept that we weren't leaving God. We were going where we felt led to go. Dad gets pretty set in his ways. He and Mom will never stop praying for you and neither will Lydia and I. Give them time, though, where your career and lifestyle are concerned. They'll come around."

Paul nodded and shook his brother's hand. He opened the car door and paused before getting in. "Tell Lydia I'm sorry for leaving this way. I'd love for you and little Sarah to come visit. I have a spare room in the condo and a great view of the City from my balcony. I bet you guys would love Central Park. The zoo is great."

"Sounds good, Paul. We'll consider it. It might be a nice vacation for us." Jason waved as Paul closed the door and started the car. Jason stood with his hands in his pockets and watched as Paul backed out of the driveway and pulled away down the road.

Paul drove through town, angry with himself as much as with his parents. Why did it always happen like this? Why did he let them get to him? He spent the next 100 miles fuming and wringing the steering wheel. The drive helped him calm down, and exhaustion took over. He knew he needed to stop for the night.

He found a Bed and Breakfast in Biddeford on his GPS. He was pleased to find they had a room available with a private bath. He gave them his credit card and was quickly shown to a cozy room.

"Breakfast is from 7:00 to 11:00," the middle aged man informed him pleasantly. "If you need anything, don't hesitate to let us know." He handed Paul his room key and left.

Paul dropped his bags on the floor, sank to the bed and dropped back into the soft comforter with a sigh. It was a peaceful place, yet his mind and heart were in such turmoil he couldn't lie still for long. He sat up and went to the window. The moonlight revealed a large garden with a fountain and gazebo. Paul turned from the window, grabbed his room key and made his way outside.

It was a clear night. The moon, large and brilliant, cast its light over the little stone paths that twisted and turned through the garden. The fountain bubbled seemingly in time with the slight breeze. Wooden benches were scattered throughout the garden, under trees, next to bushes and bird feeders. The gazebo was an old lattice frame with vines spiraling up to the edge of its roof. Little buds were starting to appear, signs that spring had come.

Paul walked through the garden, his mind wandering to his parents, his home and his new life. He couldn't help thinking about his conversation with Jason and the dark shadow that crossed over his heart when he'd mentioned Lilly.

Lilly - the girl who'd broken his heart and given him a new image of "sweet church girl." She'd started the avalanche in his life that opened his eyes to the hypocrisy in his church and the town. It was during that time in his life that all of the questions about his faith had come to life. It had triggered the rift in his family.

He stared into the fountain, the water dancing in the moonlight. The breeze picked up, bringing a chill to the air. Paul shoved his hands into his pockets and scrunched his shoulders up to his ears to help against the cold.

"I know you're there, God. I've never questioned that. I just can't figure out What or Who You really are." Paul stood a few moments in the quiet darkness. Nothing. "Still not listening to me, are You? I guess I was a fool to think You would."

Shaking his head, he turned back to the house. A good night's sleep should clear his head and get him back on track. He made his way back to his room and went to bed. He stared at the ceiling for more than an hour before drifting off to sleep.

———————

Miles away in Rockport, his mother slipped out of the house in her slippers and robe. She walked in the moonlight toward the docks. The wind blew stronger the closer she got to the marina, making it necessary for her to hold her robe closed with one hand and push her hair out of her face with the other. The voice of her son had pulled her from her sleep and sent her into the chilly night.

Standing at the end of the pier, she stared over the moonlit ripples in the bay. "God, please take Paul back. Please Lord! He needs You desperately! Show him the truth, bring him back to You."

She stood for several minutes before wiping the tears from her cheeks and walking home. She knew God had heard her prayer. When the answer would come, she did not know. She only knew she had to trust Him with her son.

TEN

Paul was up early the next morning. He ate a light breakfast and was on the road by 8:00. He was pulling into his parking garage in New York by 2:00 that afternoon. It felt good to be home again, back in his comfort zone.

His phone was ringing when he entered his condo. Answering the phone, he noted the light flashing on his answering machine – ten messages in one day!

"Hello."

"Paul? It's Marshall. Pratt told me you were out of town, but I haven't been able to reach you on your cell."

Paul reached into his pocket and checked his phone. No missed calls. "I've had my phone with me the whole time. I don't have any missed calls, Marshall. Is everything okay?"

"Everything's fine. I was just wondering when you'd be home. Marcus is still in New York and wanted you to join us again for dinner. What are you doing back already, by the way?" Marshall sounded more relieved than concerned with Paul's early homecoming.

"Long story. I'm here to stay for the remainder of the weekend, Marshall. When do you think Marcus wants to get together?"

"I'll call him, but don't be surprised if it's tonight. I'm amazed you didn't have any messages from him when you returned home."

"I haven't had time to check my machine. I was coming in the door as you were calling."

"Well, I'll touch base with Marcus and let you know. Thanks for giving up your weekend. I appreciate it!" Marshall hung up before Paul had time to respond.

Paul put the phone back on the cradle and pushed the button on his machine. Four of his messages were from Marshall, two from Marcus and the rest were hang-ups.

63

He looked again at his cell phone. *"No missed messages. I guess I'll have to take this thing to be checked,"* he thought, noting that he hadn't had a call the whole time he was gone. A normal day yielded thirty or more calls. He hoped the problem with the phone hadn't cost him any of his clients.

He spent a few minutes unpacking and starting laundry. The cleaning lady had obviously not been there the day before and had neglected to call and let him know. Irritated, Paul dialed the agency and left a heated message about the lack of consideration on the part of both the cleaning lady and the agency. His cell phone chirped before he was finished leaving the message.

"Nineteen messages" appeared on the screen.

"What the heck?" Paul said to himself, hung up the landline and started checking his messages. Several were from the day before, including one from the cleaning lady, informing him of a death in her family.

Paul groaned. "Great. Now I have to call back and apologize!"

Most were from Marshall and Marcus. Two were from a potential client he'd taken to lunch the previous Wednesday. "This is perfect! If I've lost that account, I'm going to scream!" He grabbed his jacket and stormed out of the condo. He called and left another message at the agency, offering his apologies to the cleaning lady. He then called and left one for Marshall while in the elevator and marched straight to the wireless store.

The young blonde woman behind the counter smiled sweetly as she offered a scripted explanation for the trouble with his phone that included everything from possible exposure to excess heat, cold or moisture to having been dropped from an impossible height that would cause a "shock" to the phone's electronics. It seemed to Paul that the only possibility she didn't mention was that it had been trampled by a herd of elephants in the Amazon.

"It hasn't been washed, left in the car, tossed in a snow bank, dropped from a plane or accosted by violent thugs! It was working fine. Yesterday was the first time I've had any trouble with this phone. It never rang once yesterday! Not once! I received none of my messages until this afternoon. Nineteen messages came pouring in all at once, all from yesterday, and it may have cost me a client! I refuse to pay for an obvious defect," Paul informed the woman in as calm a tone as he could manage. "This is completely ridiculous."

"You do have insurance on your plan, Mr. Matthews," the clerk informed him. "It will replace your phone."

Paul calmed down and agreed to have his phone replaced. He perused the store as she entered the claim information into the computer. By the time she'd completed her entries, he had been convinced by another saleswoman to upgrade to the newest model. The upgrade cost him seventy-five dollars, "which, of course, will cancel the replacement fee associated with your insurance plan," she said with a smile.

The clerk transferred the information from his old phone to his new and sent him from the store with a new phone and accessories. He was barely out of the store when it chirped a message from Marshall, informing him of Marcus's desire to meet with him for dinner that night.

Paul met Marshall outside the Waldorf at 7:00. They entered the hotel restaurant together and found Pratt already seated at the table with Marcus. To Paul's surprise, Kevin Murphy joined them shortly after they'd been seated.

Kevin Murphy was an arrogant, self-indulgent sycophant who served little purpose in the company. Kevin's father, the previous VP, owned enough stock prior to his death to give him voting rights in the company. His death passed those shares on to his son. He had also passed his position on to him by resigning when he'd become ill and convincing the board to vote on behalf of Kevin.

It was a wasted position. Kevin spent most of his time trying to look busy while accomplishing little to nothing. Had it not been for the clients who felt a loyalty to Kevin's father and demanded his representing their accounts, the board of directors would have removed him from the position and turned it over to another. His presence at dinner that night added to the mystery surrounding Marcus Reed for Paul. Kevin never joined them for anything.

Much of the evening consisted of small talk - politics, business, family - the typical conversations. The dinner plates were finally cleared away, dessert ordered and coffee cups filled. Kevin excused himself, mentioning a prior obligation and left without apology.

"Why ever do you keep that man, Marshall?" Marcus inquired, stirring sugar into his coffee.

"His father, faithful clients, you know the story. We haven't figured out how to get rid of him without causing serious problems from the ignorant few who demand his retention. He gets paid $250,000.00 a year to sit at a desk a few hours a day and basically do nothing." Marshall shook his head. "One of these days, we'll have to figure something out."

Pratt cleared his throat. When Marshall turned to him, Pratt nodded toward Paul with an apprehensive look.

"Paul isn't a fool, Pratt. He knows exactly what Kevin is. He also understands discretion." Turning to Paul, Marshall continued, "He realizes the difficulty it would cause should the conversation be repeated."

Paul smiled and nodded his understanding. "I didn't hear a single word that I feel warrants repeating."

Marcus chuckled at the remark. "Well, gentlemen, shall we finish our dessert and move into the lounge? I believe we'd be much more comfortable there. I could certainly use a brandy and I am eager to hear what bonus was offered this young man to convince him to give up his weekend to entertain me."

Paul laughed. "No bonus was offered. I was more than happy to be back in New York. My little getaway didn't go as planned."

They were shown to a table in the lounge and drinks were soon delivered. Marshall excused himself, took his drink and went to the other side of the lounge to speak to a client sitting there. Pratt was soon distracted by a beautiful woman at the bar. Within minutes, Paul and Marcus were alone at the table.

"So, tell me what happed that brought you home so soon." Marcus reached for his brandy.

"Oh, I guess the best way to sum it up is to say that my parents and I no longer share the same vision." Paul shrugged. "It's been that way for some time now."

"I have the advantage of being a parent as well as someone's child, Paul. I have a view from both sides. Tell me what happened."

Paul took a deep breath. "This isn't a short story, Marcus. We could be here for a while."

"I don't mind. I'd very much like to hear your story. I can tell you aren't happy about the situation."

"I'm not. I care about my family, but they still want to influence my every decision, my father especially. I think he still believes that one day I will come to my senses, throw away my foolish ideas about wealth and power and come back home to run his marina and boat shop. At one time, I thought that's what I wanted. I worked side-by-side with my father for several years – from the time I was 11 years old until I graduated from High School. My senior year was strained, but I was still there. I even offered some ideas about how to make the business more profitable, but Dad never saw it the way I did."

"He wanted you to run his business, his way," Marcus said sympathetically.

"That's it, exactly. I was supposed to stay in Rockport for the rest of my life, marry the girl my mother picked out for me, attend church every Sunday, Wednesday and holiday. Alcohol was off-limits. I was never to question my father on anything. I was more or less on that path until the summer after my junior year. The worst fight we had, up to that point, was after a graduation party for a friend who was a year ahead of me in school. Dad was waiting up when I got home. It was past my curfew and he knew I'd been drinking. He yelled, screamed and preached at me until my mother had come downstairs, crying and reminding us that I had a younger brother upstairs trying to sleep. He accused me of abandoning my morals and dishonoring my parents."

Paul paused, finished his drink, and raised his glass in request of a refill. "Dad hardly spoke to me for about a week. My girlfriend's father, who happened to be our church pastor, dragged me into his office to counsel me on the dangers of visiting Sodom and Gomorrah. He also reminded me that his sweet little girl would be forbidden from seeing me if I didn't turn from my evil ways."

"I noted a bit of sarcasm when you referred to your girlfriend."

"She was the final trigger, so to speak. We were young, but I knew I loved her. I had planned to go to college, buy her the home she always wanted and marry her. At that time, my plan was to stay in Rockport. I was going to take over Dad's business and follow that scripted life my parents had for me. I guess at the time I didn't really know any better. I asked Lilly to marry me that summer, promising her father I wouldn't let myself be tempted again to fall into that 'pit of sin' I had fallen into before."

The waitress returned with another drink for Paul, her interruption allowing him a moment to compose himself before launching into the rest of his story.

"That summer was the best of my life. We started making plans right away. You would have thought the wedding was the next week the way we discussed the details and plans for our lives. We still had our senior year of high school and I still had college, but we KNEW that's what we wanted. Dad was happy. Mom was happy. I believed I was happy. Then, in August, everything came crashing down. Reverend Shaffer called me and asked me to meet him in his office one afternoon. When I arrived, Lilly was sitting against the wall, tears running down her face. Both of my parents were there as well, my mother's eyes red and swollen, my father's face pinched tight."

Paul furrowed his brow at the memory and stared into his glass. "I was hardly through the door when Reverend Shaffer boomed at me 'Did you think that because you were engaged, you could put your hands on my daughter?' I was shocked. We had never done what he was accusing us of. I looked over at Lilly. She just shook her head, refused to speak. When I denied ever having touched her, Reverend Shaffer and my father both called me a liar. Lilly finally spoke up and begged her father to stop, swearing that the baby wasn't mine. I was devastated. She was pregnant. She refused to reveal the name of the father. The Reverend and my parents finally gave up trying to get me to confess. Dad practically dragged my stunned body out of the office. I could hear Lilly weeping even after the door was closed."

Paul downed the last of his drink and waved his glass again in the direction of the waitress. "I had never, ever touched her. We had promised each other we'd wait, start our marriage Biblically. You know, 'do things the right way.' The baby was not mine. Because she refused to name the father, everyone – her father, my parents, half the town – believed it *was* mine. Not only was I dealing with having my heart ripped out of my chest by this girl I had planned to make my wife, but my own parents were calling me a liar. My father kept throwing the night of my friend's party in my face. He never forgot that and insisted that I had let myself be taken by the devil that night."

Paul waited for the waitress to return with his drink before continuing. He was feeling the alcohol going to work on him, relaxing him both physically and mentally. "You know what hurt the most, Marcus? What hurt the most is that God abandoned me that summer. I prayed He'd show my parents the truth. I prayed He'd work it out so that my name would be cleared. He never did. Lilly lost the baby a month later. She never revealed the name of the father. She let everyone believe I had abandoned her, left her used and damaged. It was then that I decided it was time to take charge of my own life. My mother has somewhat come around. My father still holds it all against me. Every time I go home, it gets worse." Paul shook his head, a vain attempt at clearing his mind of the painful memories. "I can't spend even one day at home without them asking about my church attendance or whether or not the woman I am dating is a good church girl. It makes me crazy."

Marcus sat back in his chair and crossed his arms, his eyes boring into Paul's soul. He motioned to the waitress for refills. He waited for Paul to take another drink before finally speaking.

"It's time to let it go, Paul. You're still trying to prove your innocence. You're still trying to win your parents' approval. You're still making excuses for your realization that your family religion is nothing more than a crutch and lie from the Middle Ages to keep people under control. Take control of your own life."

Paul swallowed hard. He wasn't sure he was ready to throw God out of the equation of his life yet. He fidgeted with his napkin and cleared his throat as he looked up at Marcus. "You don't believe in God? You don't believe there's something greater than us out there?"

Marcus laughed at Paul's discomfort. "You're doing some serious squirming over there! You aren't in Sunday School anymore, young man! You yourself just admitted that God abandoned you that summer. There's no shame in admitting what you now realize to be the truth – that this *god* you've had crammed down your throat your entire life is just a fairy tale. Yes, I do believe there's something greater out there, but it isn't some gray-haired old man sitting on a throne in the cosmos dictating the rules of life. It's a greater consciousness that we all share. I believe "god" is really a part of all of us."

Paul wasn't sure how to respond to Marcus. He wasn't sure what he believed about God, but he wasn't ready for what Marcus was suggesting either. He had this unexplainable feeling of warning deep in his soul. He was relieved when Pratt stumbled back to the table, the beauty from the bar on his arm.

"Paul!" Pratt spoke his name far too loudly and enthusiastically. "Bridget here has a friend. Care to double date with us? What's your friend's name again, Sweetheart?"

Bridget smiled at Paul seductively. "Brandi. Her name's Brandi, and you look just like her type of guy."

"No thanks. I appreciate the offer, but I wouldn't be very good company tonight." Paul had no doubt these young ladies were nothing more than high priced, well-dressed prostitutes. The thought of spending an evening in their company made his stomach churn.

"Suit yourself. I don't mind keeping all of the fun for myself." Pratt laughed as his companion whispered something in his ear and steered him away from Paul and Marcus.

"Gotta' love the man, but I never have understood his, shall we say, *appetite*," Marcus said with a smile, turning back to Paul.

"Are you married, Marcus?" Paul asked, finding it an easy way to change the subject.

"I'm a widower. My wife died, let's see, sixteen years ago. My daughter was only fourteen, so I've raised her by myself. My parents have been gone since I was twenty – car accident. My in-laws are also gone. I have no siblings and neither did my wife. So, it's just Lena and me."

"Marcus, if you don't mind my asking, where exactly are you from?"

"My father was from Canada, my mother from Norway. I grew up in Turkey. That's still my home-base, so to speak. My home office is there as well as my daughter and her fiancé. I still have the property in Canada that was owned by my father's family. In fact, I claim Canadian citizenship, though I don't spend much time there. I more or less live all over. I have homes in Italy, Spain and Ireland as well as Turkey and Canada." Marcus paused and took a sip of his drink. "Textiles – that's the answer to your next question. I deal in textiles."

"Textiles?" Paul looked over at Marcus in disbelief. "As in, wool, cotton – textiles of that sort?"

Marcus laughed at Paul's reaction. "Everyone is surprised at first when I tell them that. Yes, some of it consists of fabrics, yarn, etc. But I also deal in plexiglass, asbestos, and other textiles of that sort. I travel around the world procuring the highest quality materials. There's considerable profit in the industry. It's amazing how much people will pay for silk and cashmere."

Paul shook his head. "I'm sorry Marcus. I guess I pictured you as an oil sheik or automotive king. I can't see you sitting at a spinning wheel."

Marcus's laughter rang throughout the bar. "I can't see myself at a spinning wheel, either! Actually, I inherited the business from my late wife's family. My father's family had considerable wealth that allowed us to live wherever we chose, but my wife's family was of high regard in her region. As her father's only offspring, she was the only heir. The profitability of the company was far too great to sell off or dismantle."

Marshall returned to the table briefly. "I must be on my way, gentlemen. I apologize for leaving you alone tonight, but couldn't in good conscience ignore a client. Good night to you both. Thanks again, Paul, for joining us." He nodded in Pratt's direction. "I will leave him in your capable hands, Marcus."

"He's on his own, my friend!" Marcus laughed. "He's a big boy. He can take care of himself, so long as his wife doesn't find out, of course."

Marshall laughed at Marcus's comment and waved his good-bye.

"I should be on my way as well," Paul said to Marcus, rising unsteadily from his chair.

"You don't have your car tonight do you?" Marcus asked.

"No, I was a little more sensible tonight and took a cab. Getting home isn't a problem. The ride up the elevator to my condo might prove a little troubling, but I'll be fine." Paul shook Marcus's hand, waved good-bye to Pratt and stumbled out to a cab. He fell into the seat and gave the driver his address.

Paul rebuked himself for being stupid again. "Second time I've made a fool of myself in front of that man," he muttered to himself.

He was able to control his lurching stomach during the cab ride and successfully waited to throw up his dinner until after the cab had pulled away. He stumbled through the lobby and into the elevator. He leaned his head against the back of the car and groaned as it lurched to a stop at his floor. He staggered through his door and dropped onto the couch where he passed out for the night.

When he awoke the next morning, he was still fully clothed, including his tie and shoes. His whole body felt like it had been through a battle. He stood up, rubbed his eyes and dashed to the bathroom, his stomach protesting the abuse from the previous night. Most of his Saturday morning was spent sitting on his bathroom floor, his head pounding. "Never again," he said to himself. "Never."

By 6:00 that night, he was again seated in a cab, on his way to the Waldorf for another dinner with Marshall, Pratt and Marcus. "Never" lasted until they were again settled into the lounge for the evening. Once the drinks were poured, Paul forgot the misery from the night before and started another night drinking.

"What a great weekend," he said to himself at 1:00 AM when he was once again seated on the bathroom floor of his condo. He dragged himself into his bed around 3:00 Sunday morning, repeating the promise that it would be the last time he drank himself into oblivion. It wasn't long before he drifted off to sleep.

Paul slept fitfully well into the morning. He spent the afternoon at home and soon became restless. Feeling somewhat claustrophobic, he decided to go out for a simple dinner alone. He stood on the curb for a few moments, listening to the night sounds. *"I love this city,"* he thought. He took a deep breath, waved away a cab and walked the several blocks to the restaurant, enjoying the feel of the City's energy.

———

At noon Sunday, Brooke sat on the train, staring out the window at the scenery flying past. Her weekend with her father had been fun and relaxing. It had gone by so quickly, though, that she felt she had only spent a short time off the train.

She had boarded the train at 7:00 Friday morning and was in Syracuse by 12:30. Her father was waiting for her when she stepped off the train.

"Brooke! Over here!"

She hugged her dad and was surprised to see her grandparents standing off to one side. "Grandma and Grandpa Merriweather!" She hugged them and listened to them both talk to her at once.

They all left the station together and went to lunch at a little downtown café. It had been months since she'd seen her maternal grandparents. They lived in the Adirondacks, nearly six hours from her apartment in New York City. It seemed she never had the chance to see them.

They spent the afternoon together, visiting some of the downtown shops after lunch, and then returning to her father's home for dinner.

"Why don't you stay the night?" Brooke asked when her grandfather mentioned the need to get on the road.

"No. We're only here for the day. I had a doctor's appointment this morning and we decided to stick around to see you," he explained.

"Doctor's appointment? Here? You live two hours away! What's going on that required you to see someone in Syracuse?" Brooke looked at her grandfather, concern in her eyes.

"I'm fine, Honey. Just getting old. My regular doctor wanted me to see a specialist because of the back pain I've been having. We're going to try some special physical therapy that can be done close to home. That should fix me up. Don't you worry about me!"

Brooke hugged her grandparents and stood in the driveway with her father as they pulled out of the driveway. "Is he really okay, Dad?" she asked when they'd pulled out of sight.

"I think so. Your grandmother would have spoken up if there'd been anything to worry about. We'd have spent some considerable time in prayer if it had been serious." Martin smiled reassuringly at Brooke. "He's fine. Come on. Let's go in and spend some time together before the weekend is over."

They spent Friday evening eating junk food and watching movies. They got up early Saturday morning, had a leisurely breakfast and spent the rest of the morning working in her father's rose garden. Brooke felt like a little girl again, working beside her father and just enjoying the time together. She missed these moments.

Her father had planted the garden for her mother when they'd first moved into the house. There was a rose bush for each of them - a white one for her mother and a bright red one for him. When they were pregnant for Brooke, they'd planted a deep, red one. The pink bush for Brooke's baby sister had not been planted until after both her mother and the precious baby had been buried. The garden had been her father's therapy during the painful months following the loss. It had become a tradition for Brooke and her father to work in the garden together, nurturing the plants, pruning when needed. Each spring, when the first rose blossomed, it was picked and put in a special place on her mother's grave.

She finished picking the dead twigs and brown leaves from her own rose bush and then turned to work on her father's. It seemed to be behind the others in its growth. "What's wrong with your plant, Dad?"

"I'm not sure what's going on. I'll run to the nursery Tuesday and see what they can tell me. Probably just needs dusting for mites or fungus. It's survived over twenty-five years. I'm sure it'll come back. They're all running a little behind this year. I think the long, harsh winter has slowed them down."

Brooke wasn't sure. There wasn't a green leaf or bud on her father's bush anywhere. Many of the branches were solid, but others were dry and brittle. She hoped it would survive. She couldn't imagine the garden without the bright red roses.

They'd spent the rest of the afternoon working in the gardens together. They cooked out for dinner and invited their neighbor, Linda, who brought a salad and her famous chocolate lava cake. They sat in the yard and talked until the evening air became chilly, then moved into the kitchen for dessert and coffee. Linda helped wash the dishes and left when it started to get dark outside.

"You and Linda have been friends for years, Dad. Why haven't you two ever gone out?" Brooke asked her father.

"Oh, I guess we both always felt a certain loyalty to our spouses, despite that they've both passed. I could never love another woman the way I loved your mother. And I don't believe she could ever love another man the way she loved Jack." Martin squeezed Brooke's shoulder. "I don't mind being on my own. I have a good life."

Brooke and Martin went to the living room and spent another evening watching old movies and laughing over her childhood memories. Sunday arrived too soon. Brooke had to be back at the station by noon to catch her train home.

They attended the early church service and stopped for a light lunch before going to the train station. Brooke's father hugged her tight, kissed her on the forehead and promised to come to New York soon to visit. He was still standing on the platform when the train pulled away.

Brooke spent a few minutes watching towns and villages zoom by, then pulled out her sketch book and started working on sketches for the upcoming show. They had a lot of work ahead for 'Madame Butterfly' and she didn't want to let Meryl or Heron down. By the time her train pulled into the station in New York, she'd rough-sketched only three costumes. For some reason, her thoughts had turned to her father's withering rose bush, her pencil drawing petals and thorns instead costume designs.

———————

Brooke was home in time to attend the evening church services. She loved her childhood church in Syracuse, but this was her home church now. She slipped in just as the music was starting for worship. Rachel noticed her entrance and waved her over. Brooke smiled at Shaun standing next to Rachel with a look of pride in his face.

Brooke slipped into the pew, put her purse and Bible down and straightened back up to sing with the rest of the worshippers. Rachel squeezed Brooke's hand to get her attention and waved her left hand in Brooke's face, a diamond flashing in the light. Rachel had to stifle her laugh at the surprised look on Brooke's face. Brooke could hardly wait for church to let out.

As soon as Pastor Brian said "You are dismissed," Brooke grabbed Rachel and said "Start talking right now!"

Rachel and Shaun both laughed at Brooke's reaction. "Join us for dinner," Shaun said after he'd stopped laughing. "We'll tell you everything then."

The three of them walked the few blocks to an Italian Restaurant they all enjoyed. While they waited for a table to open up, Rachel shared her news with Brooke.

"I know it's sudden, but I know I love him. He asked me Friday night at dinner. We plan to have the ceremony in August and I want you to be my maid of honor."

"I'm happy for you both." Brooke looked over at Shaun who was standing with his hands in his pockets, his face beaming. "It took you months and months to finally ask her out and only two weeks to propose! You are one very confusing man!"

Shaun laughed. "I thought I'd better ask her while I still had some courage. You know me, I can't do anything halfway."

They were soon shown to a table and ordered their drinks and appetizers. Shaun asked a simple blessing before the waitress returned to take their dinner order.

Shaun sipped his water and nodded toward the entrance. "Looks like we got here at the right time. Look at all of those people coming in."

Brooke and Rachel glanced at the crowd waiting at the door. "This place is pretty popular," Rachel said.

Brooke looked over at the door again. "I know that guy. His name's Paul. He's the guy I told you about that I met at Papa's apartment."

"Which one?" Rachel asked, looking again at the group packed together at the door.

"The one in the black slacks and green sweater...who's now smiling and waving at me," Brooke said, embarrassment blooming on her face.

"Invite him over," Shaun offered. "He's welcome to join us."

Shaun stood up when Brooke didn't make a move.

"Shaun! No! I hardly know the guy!" Brooke wanted to crawl under the table as Shaun motioned for Paul to come over.

Paul spoke to the hostess and motioned toward Brooke's table. The hostess looked over and nodded. Paul made his way to their table and extended his hand to Shaun.

"Are you meeting someone?" Shaun asked after the introductions.

"No, I just didn't feel like staying in tonight." Paul spoke to Shaun, though his eyes were fixed on Brooke.

"Why don't you join us," Shaun invited.

"I don't want to impose."

"It may be time for breakfast before another table opens up," Shaun laughed. "Besides, I'm a little outnumbered here tonight. I would really appreciate another man at the table to help me with all of this female conversation. Too much more of it, and I'm afraid I'll leave here wearing pink!"

Rachel slapped Shaun's arm playfully. Paul laughed and accepted the invitation. Shaun waved the waitress over. "Please add one more to our party."

The waitress smiled at Paul, "A drink for you sir?"

"Cabernet and ice water, please." Looking at Shaun, Paul asked "Have you already ordered dinner?"

"Yes, but that's okay, take your time," Shaun nodded.

Paul looked quickly over the menu and ordered as soon as the waitress returned with his drink. "Are you celebrating something or is this just a friendly night out?" he asked.

"Celebrating!" Shaun exclaimed. He reached over and took Rachel's hand. "This beautiful woman has agreed to marry me!"

"Congratulations," Paul replied. He looked back over at Brooke and smiled. "This is a very good night, then, isn't it?"

The four of them fell into easy conversation, taking their time with dinner. Paul talked briefly about his occupation, explaining the international financial markets and how they affect the markets in the U.S. Brooke was impressed with his intelligence and his obvious devotion to his career.

"What do you do, Shaun?" Paul asked, reaching for his wine.

"Nothing as exciting as international finance. I teach art at one of the middle schools here in the city," Shaun replied.

"You don't think your job is exciting?"

"I love my job, and for me it's immensely exciting, but I can't imagine you'd consider my job exciting after what you just described."

"I don't know," Paul countered. "I think it takes a great deal of courage and dedication to be a teacher. And patience! I would never have the patience to be a teacher. Don't get me wrong, I love kids. But, to spend hours every day dealing with kids who likely could care less about their education, trying to make them do what they need to do, well, I could never do it. I give you a lot of credit."

"Well, thanks," Shaun said quietly. "I appreciate that. Not many people consider what a teacher has to endure. I enjoy it, though. I've always liked kids and have long wanted to try to make a difference in their lives. And, I have always loved art. In fact, that's how I first met Brooke. We took several of the same art classes together at NYU. We were like Siamese twins most of our time in college."

"Did you two date?" Paul asked, feeling a pang of jealousy.

Brooke and Shaun both laughed. "No," Brooke answered. "He was like my big brother, or guardian. We've always seen each other as 'just friends'".

Rachel looked at her watch and whispered quietly to Shaun. Shaun smiled and nodded. "Well," he said to Brooke and Paul. "We need to be going. I promised Rachel I wouldn't keep her out too late." Shaun waved to the waitress and requested the check.

"Oh, no," Paul said. "I'll get this - my engagement gift to you, as well as a 'thank you' for strong-arming Brooke into letting me join you for dinner."

Shaun tried to argue, but Paul refused to accept anything toward dinner. Shaun relented and shook Paul's hand. He kissed Brooke on the cheek and reached for Rachel's hand. Rachel hugged Brooke and whispered "I'll call you tomorrow." Shaun and Rachel left Brooke and Paul alone.

Paul cleared his throat after a few moments of silence. "Dessert and coffee?" he asked.

"Okay," Brooke agreed.

They spent the next hour laughing and talking. Brooke found it easy to talk to Paul. He laughed at her little jokes and showed a sincere interest in her work. He smiled when she spoke of her grandfather. Her affection for him and her closeness to her family was obvious. Warmth rushed over her when he reached over and covered her hand with his.

When they'd finished their dinner, Paul offered to walk her home. They continued to talk about their jobs and their shared love for the City. When they reached Brooke's building, they stood quietly looking into each other's eyes for a few moments.

"Well, this is it," Brooke said, her heart pounding so hard she was certain he could hear it.

Paul just smiled. "Can I call you? I'd like to do this again."

Brooke could only nod and smile shyly. Paul took her hand and leaned forward, kissing her lightly on the cheek. Brooke started to shake, the nervousness taking over.

"Why are you shaking?" Paul asked, his voice deep and husky.

"I'm cold."

Paul squeezed her hand.

"Good night, Paul." Brooke pulled away and rushed into the building.

She stepped into the elevator, pushed the "11" button for her floor and leaned back against the elevator wall. When the doors closed, Brooke hugged herself tightly, attempting to stop her violent shaking. She didn't know why, but the feelings that washed over her when Paul was near frightened her more than anything she'd ever felt in her life. Only one evening and she knew she was falling in love with him.

Outside, Paul watched her walk through the doors and disappear into the elevator. It wasn't until after she was out of sight that he turned to the street and hailed a cab. He spent the ride home thinking about the beautiful woman he'd just left. Her eyes and smile were etched in his mind. As the cab drove through the City to his condo, he smiled into the night, knowing that this woman was about to change his life.

ELEVEN

BEFORE 6:00 IN THE MORNING, Brooke was wide awake. She stared at the ceiling for several minutes, her mind filled with images of Paul and the conversations of the night before. Her heart fluttered when she remembered his smile and the delicate kiss he'd placed on her cheek. She hoped and prayed he would call her. She wanted to see him again.

"Last day of my long weekend and I'm awake at six," she said to the ceiling. "Might as well get up."

Brooke got up, turned on the coffee pot and started her laundry. She was meeting Ruth for breakfast, but not until 9:00. She sprayed cleaner on the bathtub and washed her face. She went back to the kitchen and poured a cup of coffee.

Taking her cup to the living room, she opened the doors to the outside, breathed the morning air and sat on the couch. Sipping her coffee, she opened her Bible and spent the next half hour reading God's Word and praying for her friends and family. She had trouble staying focused, thoughts of Paul flooding her mind.

"I need help here, God. I really like him, but I can't have my mind on him ALL of the time. I'd like to focus on You for a while." She was soon able to get her mind completely on her prayers.

It didn't take her long to clean the apartment and get ready for her breakfast with Ruth. By the time she left, her cleaning was finished, allowing her the rest of the day to do as she pleased.

Ruth was waiting at the café when Brooke arrived. "I left early and you're still here before I am! Are you ever late for anything?" Brooke asked, hugging her friend.

"I try not to be. I'd rather wait than expect someone else to wait for me. Besides, this way I get to choose the table!"

Brooke laughed at Ruth's humor. The waitress came to their table with coffee and juice and took their breakfast order.

"So, what has you so happy this morning?" Ruth asked with a smile.

"Well, let's see. I found out last night that Shaun and Rachel are engaged after only two weeks of dating. I think that's something worth being happy about. They are, after all, two of my best friends in the world."

"No, it's something more than that," Ruth replied. Leaning back in her chair, she looked closely at Brooke, pretending to inspect her. Suddenly, her face lit up with awareness. "You've met someone!"

Brooke looked over at her, surprised at Ruth's ability to read her so well. Shaking her head, Brooke smiled and told her about Paul and the evening they'd shared.

"Sounds like a great guy. The fact that your grandfather likes him is huge. I don't think he'd trust the pope with you unless he agreed to an interview!" Ruth reached over and patted Brooke's hand. "I'm happy for you, Dear. It's about time you met someone."

"Ruth! We've only been out once. I'm not making wedding plans yet! I hardly know him!" Brooke shook her head at Ruth. "I do like him, though. He's all I've thought about since he walked me home last night. I even prayed for him this morning!"

"Okay, Honey. I won't pick on you anymore this morning. Tell me what Shaun and Rachel have planned." They spent the rest of breakfast talking about the upcoming wedding and how happy Rachel and Shaun were.

Ruth turned the conversation back to Paul when the waitress had cleared their table and brought their check. "Does your grandfather know yet that you two went out?"

"No, I haven't seen him since I've been back. He went to Uncle Vince's and Rhea's house for the long weekend." Brooke laughed and shook her head. "I can picture his smug look, though, when he finds out we went out. He'll be awfully please with himself!"

Ruth paid the bill. They left the café together and continued their conversation outside.

"I want to meet this Paul, Brooke. You're like a daughter to me and I want to know what this guy is like."

Brooke smiled at her friend. "Don't worry. I won't start making my own wedding plans until I have your full approval!"

Brooke waved to Ruth and turned toward the subway. She smiled at her friend's protectiveness. Ruth was the mother Brooke never had, and she treasured their relationship. She couldn't wait for her to meet Paul.

Brooke found a seat on the train and decided to go to Central Park. It was a beautiful day and she didn't want to waste it inside. She wanted to stop by her apartment for her sketch pad on the way. She was on her street, heading toward her building when her cell phone rang.

"Brooke? It's Rachel. Are you busy?"

"Hi Rachel. No, I'm not busy. I thought you'd be with Shaun, planning your big day. What's going on?"

"We're good. We plan to have dinner tonight, but I wanted to see you today, if that's okay. Do you have some time?" Rachel's voice was strained.

"I'm available right now, Rach. What's wrong?"

"Let's meet at the coffee shop. I'll see you in a few minutes," Rachel replied and ended the call.

Brooke stared down at her phone, frowning at the conversation. She knew something was wrong. She turned back to the subway and went to *La Regina* to meet her, hoping everything was okay.

Brooke waited for Rachel outside the café. Rachel gave Brooke a hug when she arrived, but hardly looked at her. They went in, ordered espresso and sat at a table by the window. The shop was crowded, people coming and going incessantly. Rachel took a sip from her cup and looked over at Brooke, noting the worry on her face.

"I'm okay, Brooke. I just have some news I wanted you to hear from me."

"Well, tell me. You've got me pretty worried here Rachel. What's going on?" Brooke reached over and squeezed Rachel's hand. "Whatever it is, you know I'm here for you."

"I know," Rachel nodded her understanding. Taking a deep breath and letting it out slowly, she finally said "Brooke, I quit my job on Thursday."

Brooke slouched in her chair, shocked by the news. She and Rachel had worked together since they'd completed college and started as interns. They were each other's support when Heron made their lives miserable. They prayed together, worked on the same team and shared much. Brooke finally spoke, "What happened, Rachel? What did Heron do?"

Rachel shrugged her shoulders and wiped a tear from her cheek. "I was accused of being lazy, doing substandard work, even of insubordination. I was taken off Heron's team and put on Ruby's as a "repair person" for 'Shakespeare in the Park.' I heard about 'Madame Butterfly' and Heron told me she couldn't trust me to pull my weight. So, I was given to Ruby. I couldn't take anymore, Brooke. I'm sorry. I feel like I'm abandoning you, but I just can't do it anymore." Rachel looked over at her friend.

"Oh Rachel! I'm so sorry. I knew about 'Madame Butterfly,' and I knew Ruby was going to take over the Shakespeare costumes. Meryl invited me to be a part of some of the costume planning and Heron attacked your and my friendship. She accused me of letting our friendship get in the way of our work. I denied it and I think she took it out on you. I'm so sorry." Brooke felt terrible. She didn't know what else to say or do for her friend. She felt responsible for what had happened.

"I don't blame you. It isn't your fault, Brooke. I just wanted you to hear it from me, not from some blabbermouth at the studio. You know how this stuff works."

Brooke nodded her understanding. "What are you going to do for work? Do you have any leads? You can use me for a reference if you need one. I'll be glad to tell anyone how great you are at your job."

"Thanks, Brooke. I'm not sure exactly what I plan to do, but I do have something temporary lined up. I went to one of the bridal shops to get an idea of what I may want for a wedding dress and started talking to the owner. When she found out what I did for a living, she asked me if I would be willing to work with her for the summer. The shop gets so busy during June and July that she can hardly keep up."

Rachel shrugged her shoulders. "You know something Brooke? I have prayed for a long time about this. My dream has always been to have my own shop, to design and sew my own creations. Maybe it's time to figure out how to make it work."

"What does Shaun have to say about all of this?"

Rachel smiled, her affection for Shaun showing on her face. "He's so wonderful. He said we'd figure something out. He even offered to pay my bills until we're married and can find a place together. I told him not to worry about it. I do have some money saved and I know I can scrape by."

"You know you can stay with me for a while if you want to. I have a comfortable couch and I wouldn't mind at all," Brooke offered.

"I appreciate it. I was so worried you'd think I was weak and cracked under the pressure. Do you think I'm weak?"

"No way! I think it took a lot of courage to do what you did! I will pray for you, Rachel – and for Shaun."

Rachel and Brooke talked about the wedding, shifting the conversation to something pleasant. By the time they left the café, Rachel was smiling again. There was no doubt Shaun made her very happy. Brooke left her friend knowing that nothing could ruin Rachel's happiness. She longed to feel what Rachel was feeling and hoped she was going to find it soon, her mind drifting back to Paul.

———

Paul awoke Monday morning with Brooke's smile on his mind. He closed his eyes and the image became so vivid he felt he could reach out and touch her beautiful face. He wanted to see her again. But would he appear too eager if he called already, asking to see her again? He wasn't sure. Maybe he'd pay her grandfather a visit. He might get lucky and run into her there.

He spent the morning reading his emails and following up with a few clients. By lunchtime, restlessness took over. He sat down at the piano and played a piece. After he keyed the last note, the silence in the apartment was unbearable. He rose quickly from the piano bench, grabbed his keys and cell phone and walked to the subway. He just had to see her again.

Twice during his train ride, he started to dial her number and changed his mind. *"No,"* he said to himself. *"You'll look desperate. Just go to Nick's apartment."*

He rang Nick's bell several times. No answer.

"Now what?" He asked himself. He stared again at his cell phone. Shaking his head, he walked to *La Regina*. *"Maybe Gianna will have a suggestion."*

The café was crowded. Paul waited several minutes before Gianna was available. "You just can't go a day without my espresso, can you, Mr. Matthews?" she smiled at him.

Paul laughed. "I forgot my mug, so I guess I'll just have to settle for those great cookies," he said, pointing to the plate behind the counter.

Gianna filled his order and handed the box over the counter to him. "Are you working today?" When Paul shook his head, she asked "Then why don't you order a cup and relax here for a while. You're always in such a hurry."

Paul chuckled. "Okay, you got me. But only one cup." Paul moved over to a stool, put the pastry box down, and looked again at his cell phone.

"Waiting for an important call?" Gianna asked as she the cup in front of him.

"No, not really." Paul put his phone in his pocket, took a sip of his espresso and looked back over at Gianna. He waited for her to finish with another customer and asked "Do you know what Nick Barsanti is up to today? I went by his apartment to see how he's doing and didn't get an answer."

"He went to Long Island to visit his younger son and daughter-in-law," Giannia responded. "Don't worry about him. He's fine – stubborn as ever."

Paul was disappointed by the news. If Nick wasn't home, then Brooke wouldn't be there either. "Oh. I'm glad he's doing okay." He took another sip and smiled up at Gianna. "I just wanted to say 'Hi.'"

Finishing his espresso, he waved to Gianna and left the café. He stood for a long moment and stared up at the buildings stretching into the sky above the City. He didn't want to go back to his condo. Shaking his head, he turned toward the Park. Maybe a long walk would do him some good.

Brooke carried her sketch pad to a bench overlooking one of the many ponds in the park. She had stopped momentarily to watch some of the 'Shakespeare in the Park' Festival, but couldn't bear the heartbreak she experienced when she considered someone else was working on her costumes. Despite the entire team having been moved from the show, she still felt a sense of loss. She'd never been taken out of a show before. The fact that she was removed for disciplinary reasons made it worse.

She sat down on the bench, took a deep breath, and smiled up at the sun shining bright and strong. It was a beautiful day. There were birds singing in the trees and the flowers were starting to bloom. The voices of happy children laughing could be heard in the distance. She enjoyed the fresh air and scenery for a moment before getting to work on her sketches.

She wanted to complete the three she'd started on the train. She realized that most of the other team members would wait until the next day to get to work, preferring to enjoy their time off, but Brooke wanted to be ahead, to impress Meryl and Heron. The more she completed now, the more time she'd have to make adjustments if necessary.

It didn't take her long to finish the sketches, even making some smaller drawings of some alternative ideas. She packed up her kit and looked out at the pond. She watched the ducks swimming around and wished she'd brought some bread to feed them. "I should have brought a snack for myself," she said, noticing her hunger for the first time. She looked at her watch and was surprised at the time. "No wonder I'm hungry. Deli sounds good, and it's close!"

The line into the deli was long. Brooke hadn't considered that it was a holiday and that everyone in New York was probably out enjoying the first real weekend of the summer. She noted that there were a few tables available outside, but she doubted she'd find anything inside. "I guess I'll have to take it to go," she decided.

She hadn't been in line long when she felt someone standing behind her. The line inched forward the slightest bit, but the person behind her seemed to move a foot, getting so close to her that she could feel his clothes.

"This person has no sense of personal space," she thought, moving forward enough to give her some space between them. He moved as well.

Brooke resisted the urge to turn around and tell him to back off, fearing that it might trigger some negative reaction. She took a deep breath and moved enough to brush against his sleeve, hoping he'd realize how close he was and step back a little. Instead, he moved closer.

He was so close now she could feel his breath in her hair. She was certain he was doing it on purpose and it made her nervous. She let out a little involuntary shiver and prayed silently that the line would move faster so she could get away from this person.

He moved closer to her and whispered in a deep, familiar voice. "Are you cold again?"

Turning quickly, Brooke found Paul standing behind her, a big smile on his face. She couldn't hide her shock. Finally she laughed.

"You scared me, you know! I thought you were some nut!"

Paul laughed. "I could feel you shaking. Sorry about that, but I couldn't resist. Care to have lunch with a nut? I already have a table if you don't mind sitting outside."

Brooke laughed and followed Paul to his table. "I think I need to start worrying about you," she said with a smile as she sat down. "Not many normal men would invade the personal space of a woman they'd just met."

Paul gave Brooke an innocent look. "I kissed you on the cheek last night. That was more personal than breathing on your hair," he said with a laugh.

Brooke smiled at him, feeling her face turn a shade of red. "Well, the kiss was very nice – and normal! The breathing in my hair thing was a little creepy until I found out it was you!"

"I didn't mean to scare you. I saw you get in line and had planned to just walk up and talk to you, but then I didn't know what to say. When someone came up behind me and I had to get close to you to get away from them, well, it kind of started out as an accidental brush up against you. I couldn't help myself after that."

Brooke shook her head, laughing at his attempt at humor. "Believe me! Talking to me would have been more effective!"

The waitress came to the table with Paul's drink and took Brooke's order. "Can you wait to deliver my order until hers is ready?" Paul asked.

"Of course," the waitress smiled. "I'll be right back with your iced tea," she said to Brooke.

"Gianna told me your grandfather was visiting his son on Long Island. Is that your father?" Paul asked Brooke.

"No, that's my Uncle Vince. Dad lives in Syracuse."

"Syracuse? What took him there?"

"School. He went to Syracuse University and studied business management and met my mother. That's where they got married and bought the house."

The waitress returned with Brooke's tea as well as their lunch orders. Paul watched Brooke as she sipped her tea. Her long, brown hair spilled down over her shoulders in thick waves down to her waist. She seemed to glow from within. She was the most beautiful woman he'd ever seen.

They fell into easy conversation during lunch. They talked about the City, the places they both enjoyed. "La Regina is my all-time favorite café in the City," Paul told her.

Brooke laughed. "Mine, too! Of course, my grandfather has known the family that owns it since he and my grandmother came to America. Gianna is the granddaughter of the original owners. I've known them since I was a child."

"Is your mother from Italy, too?" Paul asked.

"No. Her family can be traced back to the Civil War. Her father is a retired pastor and her mother was a seamstress. They live in the Adirondacks now. They've lived Upstate forever, I think."

Paul cleared his throat. "You don't talk about your mom. Are your parents divorced?"

Brooke shook her head. "No, Mom died in ninety-one during childbirth. My baby sister died four days later. Mom had a difficult pregnancy and a long hard labor and delivery. I don't know all that happened, but Dad said that she was gone before she even had the chance to see her newborn daughter. Rose, my baby sister, was ill from birth – underdeveloped lungs and a heart problem. She was full-term but weighed only 4 pounds."

"I'm sorry I made you go through that pain, Brooke," Paul said, reaching over to take her hand. "You didn't have to tell me all of that if you didn't want to."

Brooke smiled over at him. "That was nineteen years ago, Paul. I will never forget it, but the pain isn't nearly what it was then. My father is a strong man, always has been, and despite all he went through, he never let go of his faith. He raised me, loved me and gave me the childhood that he and my mother had planned for me. My life has been blessed."

He looked into her eyes again, marveling at her strength. Squeezing her hand, he rose from the table. "Come on. I'll pay the waitress, if I can find her, and we'll figure out how to spend the rest of the afternoon."

Paul took Brooke's hand as soon as they'd left the deli. Brooke talked more about her home in Syracuse and her childhood. "Dad wanted me to have as normal a childhood as possible. He didn't want me to miss out on "being a girl," as he put it, just because I was being raised by my father. So, I took ballet and tap. Our neighbor, Linda, taught me to sew. I spent a lot of time there when Dad was working. Her husband died a year after my Mom. She has a son and a daughter, so our families got together a lot. My dad did "guy" things with her son Jeremy, and Linda would do the "girl" things with Rebecca and me. We went to the same church and same schools. We were just like brother and sisters."

"What does your father do? You mentioned that he studied business management in college. What kind of business?"

"Dad took basic business management to help him manage his carpentry business. He does mostly cabinetry, but he also does some furniture, wood restoration, that kind of stuff. He's quite talented. Papa taught him and Dad always loved it. I guess Papa had hoped that Dad would take over his business one day, but Dad hated New York." Brooke looked at Paul. "My Mom wasn't Dad's only reason for staying in Syracuse."

Paul nodded his understanding. "I can relate to that. My father had always hoped I'd take over his business, too."

"What does your father do?"

"Boats – building, repair, storage, everything. He also owns a marina." Not wanting to dwell on his recent disagreement with his parents, Paul quickly asked "So, how'd your grandfather take it when your Dad left?"

"I think there was some tension between Dad and his parents when he moved. It went beyond Dad leaving the City, though I don't know all of the details. He and his parents went through some differences of opinion, but Dad has never told me all of it. I don't think he wants me to have a negative opinion of Papa and Nonna."

"Your father hasn't had an easy life, has he?" Paul asked Brooke, leading her to a bench to sit down. "To lose a wife and daughter so early in his life couldn't have been easy. I know your grandmother died when you were a child, too." Brooke looked at him with surprise. "Your grandfather told me about her cancer, that she died when you were only six."

Brooke nodded. "She had breast cancer when I was a baby. They did a mastectomy and she beat it. Or, so everyone thought. The cancer showed up in the other breast while my mom was pregnant for Rose. They did another mastectomy and started treatment. We didn't know that it was also in the lymph nodes – she never told anyone. She came to spend a few weeks with us while Mom was pregnant and then again for awhile after Mom died, not once hinting that she was terminal. I treasure those weeks with her."

"I've always been close to my grandparents, too. I spent a lot of time with them. My grandmother was a music teacher. She still teaches piano to a few of the kids in our town. She started teaching me to play as soon as I was able to reach the keys. My grandfather was the one who started the boat business my father has now. He died about ten years ago. He was much older than Grandmother and died peacefully in his sleep one night."

"How about your mother's parents?" Brooke asked.

"They both died when I was a kid. Grandpa was an engineer. He died when I was five or six. Grandma died only a year or two later. I don't really remember them."

Paul and Brooke sat in silence for a long time. Paul took Brooke's hand again. "Have dinner with me tonight," Paul asked, finally breaking the silence.

Brooke looked into his eyes, wondering about the feelings that had taken hold of her. "I'd like that."

She leaned her head against his shoulder and felt his arm come around to hold her close. She closed her eyes and said a silent prayer for guidance. She was in love with Paul, despite knowing very little about him. "Help me, Lord, to know what to do," she prayed silently, hoping and praying that what she was feeling would last forever.

TWELVE

SPRING GAVE WAY TO SUMMER seemingly overnight. The chill that had clung to the early morning breeze was replaced with a gentle warmth, a promise that summer had truly arrived.

In Syracuse, the bluebirds were nesting. The snow had finally melted, leaving behind brown patches in the grass as a reminder of the freeze that had gripped the city. Martin spent his mornings in the garden, pruning and tending the rose bushes, sprinkling powder on the dying bush with great care. He smiled when he noticed the first rose blooming was on Brooke's rosebush. His afternoons were spent with his faithful neighbor, Linda, planting the shared vegetable garden that they would harvest together in the fall.

In Rockport, the marina was alive with the seasonal tourists and busy fishermen. The ice had broken up and drifted away, leaving clear waters for the boats to come and go without worry. The warm breeze rocked the boats gently in the harbor, promising a pleasant day. Steve was busy having the cabin cruiser lifted from the supports in the shop and into the water. Senator Maxwell stood close by, his smile broad as he waved to the media surrounding him.

Central Park was alive with birdsong and laughing children. The leaves on the trees rustled with the caress of the breeze and the flittering of the birds. The blossoms in the Conservatory Garden sprung forth in a breathtaking array of color. Cherry blossoms bloomed, azaleas flowered, leaves spread out in shades of green. Life was renewing in every corner.

The breeze fluttered the curtains on Brooke's open windows as she readied for work. It carried with it the sounds of horns blowing and traffic zooming on the street below. The warm breeze reminded her of Paul, making her smile as she thought of his handsome face and blue eyes.

A few blocks away, Paul chose a longer walk to a more distant subway terminal. His briefcase was gripped in one hand, his travel cup in the other.

While waiting to cross the street, he closed his eyes and breathed deeply of the summer air. He thought of Brooke's beautiful face, every detail painted clearly in his mind.

People everywhere felt the warmth of the same sun, were kissed by the same breeze, and despite the distance between them, witnessed the same newness that had come to life during the spring. With unbiased generosity, God poured out His love in the beauty and wonder of nature on the earth. Summer had arrived and brought with it many changes.

———————

Brooke sat at her workstation, her chin resting in her palm as she doodled in her sketch pad. Friday morning and she had already completed her costume sketches, including some revisions requested by Heron, and was waiting for final approval. Most on the team were still working to complete their first drafts.

Two hours had passed since Brooke had checked with Heron for additional work. "Just wait," had been Heron's response. So she waited at her workstation, her mind alive with images of Paul from the past several days.

Wednesday had been the only night they hadn't had dinner together. Paul had a business dinner. Brooke had Bible study and a dinner date with Papa. She smiled, remembering Papa's reaction when she'd told about her going out with Paul.

"I knew he was right for you!"

Brooke had laughed. "We're still getting acquainted, Papa. Don't start making my wedding plans yet!"

Brooke shook her head at the memory. Her grandfather was not easily impressed. He was also very protective of her. His approval of Paul was voluminous, not something Brooke would dismiss.

Brooke rose from her worktable and stretched. She took her cup to the water cooler, drew hot water for tea and returned to her table. She was growing impatient. She didn't like to be idle, and not having something specific to do grated on her.

Her wait had been spent sketching a garden scene from 'Madame Butterfly.' She had overheard some discussion that the company had been given the scene and prop contracts in addition to the costumes. Brooke had never designed a theatre scene before. Despite not being on either of the teams assigned those tasks, she drew the garden behind the home of Cio-Cio-San, the main character in the opera.

Gazebos and trellises filled the page. Japanese lilacs, bleeding hearts and several other blossoms hung like a canopy over the garden. Bonsai trees and bamboo dotted the scene. Various flowering shrubs filled the space with color. Shepherds hooks were placed throughout with Japanese lanterns hanging from the crooks. Flat stones created winding paths to benches and fountains.

In the midst of the garden, Brooke had sketched Cio-Cio-San and her servant, Suzuki, facing each other. Suzuki cradled a bouquet of Japanese lilacs in her arm, and she wore what appeared to be a simple kimono. Further inspection of the garment revealed a delicate floral pattern running through the material, the color the same as the lilacs.

Brooke sat back in her chair and looked over her drawing, pleased with the results. *"Not bad,"* she thought, selecting a shade of purple to add to Suzuki's kimono.

She looked up when she heard Heron's voice. Heron and Julie entered the room and stopped inside the doorway. Heron spoke again briefly to Julie, handed her a sketch and sent her back to her workstation. She approached Brooke's station with sketches in her hand.

"These for the wedding scene are great, Brooke. The only change I think needs to be made..." Heron paused and stared down at the garden sketch on Brooke's table.

"What is this?" she hissed. "Did Meryl assign something to you without telling me?"

Brooke shook her head. "No, Heron. I was just doodling. I heard about the scenes and just sketched what I thought the garden might look like."

Heron picked up Brooke's sketch pad and examined the sketch further. Her eyes opened wide when she saw two of the main characters in the scene. *"I* am doing the wardrobe for Suzuki! How dare you!"

Brooke stood up quickly, her heart pounding in her chest. "Heron. I never planned to submit these. I was only doodling. I couldn't just sit here and stare at the wall for the past two hours. Please don't get upset with me over this. It's just a drawing."

Heron slapped the pad back down on Brooke's table. "You will not overstep me! I am the team leader and I refuse to have you doing things behind my back!"

"Heron! I'm not doing anything behind your back! It's just a drawing!"

Heron glared at Brooke. "You will give that to me! I will not have you doing this!"

Brooke picked up her sketch pad and started to tear out the page. She stopped. She had always given in, even when it was Heron who was wrong. Not this time. Shaking, Brooke looked at her. "No, I won't. This is *my* sketch pad and what I draw in it is up to me! Heron, I never planned to turn this sketch in any more than I planned to turn in any of the other drawings in it. This is MY sketch pad, for my own personal use, not the one I use for work. I will not give it to you!"

Several of the other girls on the team had moved from their stations to see what was happening. It was rare for anyone to go against Heron and they all looked at Brooke with surprise. Julie turned toward the door and left quickly down the hall.

Heron's face turned red with fury. She shook her finger in Brooke's face. "You will regret this! Have you forgotten what happened to Rachel? Don't for a minute think that Meryl won't hear about this! You have no right…"

"Heron! What is going on in here?"

Everyone turned to see Meryl standing in the doorway. Julie stood behind him, looking sheepish. She glanced over at Brooke and smiled faintly.

Heron grabbed the sketch pad from Brooke and stormed over to Meryl. "Did you know anything about this? Did you know she was sketching scenes? And characters that *I* was assigned?"

Meryl looked at the sketch and looked at Brooke. "Did someone assign this to you?"

Brooke shook her head. "No, Sir. I didn't have anything to do while I waited for my approvals. I was just doodling. I never planned to turn them in. This is my own sketch pad, not my work pad."

Meryl looked at the others standing around the room. "Get back to work, Ladies. There's nothing to worry about." Once everyone had gone back to their stations, Meryl looked over at Heron. "What's this about, Heron? Why are you so upset? Is her work done?"

Heron looked between Meryl and Brooke. "No. I mean yes. Her work was finished. I am upset because she has no business assigning herself projects! Look what she's done here! She isn't even part of the scene crew! I refuse to have her overstepping her place!"

Meryl nodded. He started turning the pages of Brooke's sketch pad. "Do you mind?" he asked, looking at Brooke.

"No, Sir," she replied, sitting back down in her chair.

Meryl turned back to the first page. "Hm. I can see what you're so upset about," he said to Heron, a note of sarcasm in his voice. "A robin perched on a feeder; a woman's hand." He flipped a few more pages. "A bench in the Conservatory Garden in the Park." He raised his brows. "A young man." He smiled and nodded toward Brooke. She could feel her cheeks turning red as he looked over her drawings of Paul.

He turned back to the garden scene and looked at Heron. "Yes, I can certainly see why you're so upset. Heron, come down to my office. I think we need to talk."

Heron looked at Brooke and then back at Meryl. She shook her head and clenched her fists. "You're going to let this go?"

"There's nothing to let go. She wasn't doing anything wrong," Meryl said, turning to leave the room and motioning for Heron to follow.

Heron didn't move. She glared at Brooke and turned again to Meryl. "What's going on between you two? Why are you defending her?" her voice low and accusatory.

Meryl turned back to her, anger etched on his face. "What did you just ask me? How dare you accuse me of any impropriety! Okay, Heron. I wanted to talk to you in private, to save you any embarrassment in front of your team, but here goes! I think you've forgotten where you were once. I think you've forgotten that you were just like Brooke a few years ago, a young woman with great promise and talent. You had a team leader who took you under her wing and helped you develop your talent and gave you opportunity. That is part of your responsibility now that you are a team leader. You're failing to do that. Brooke has great potential and extraordinary talent and you should be encouraging her, not stifling her because of your jealousy!"

"Meryl," Heron tried to interrupt.

"I'm not finished! Furthermore, I, not you, am the owner of this company. You are my employee and it seems you've forgotten your place. I have half a mind to fire you on the spot. You have no right accusing me, a happily married man, of improper conduct with one of my employees. Now, since you are obviously not yourself today, I want you to go home." Meryl held up his hand when Heron again tried to speak. "I'm still not finished. You will take a few days off to consider your position in my company. I don't want to see you back here until Wednesday, and when you do return, you will report directly to me. We have much to discuss. Leave now."

Heron stared at Meryl for a long moment before turning on her heels and storming into her office. She returned quickly with her purse and portfolio, glared again at Brooke, and fumed out of the work room.

Meryl stared after her. He shook his head and turned back to Brooke. He took the sketchpad from her table and turned toward the door. "Come with me please."

Brooke followed quietly, afraid that she was about to be fired. Her heart pounded in her chest. She should have just given Heron the drawing and been done with it. It would have saved a lot of trouble.

Meryl closed his office door behind them, motioned for her to sit near his desk and sat down in his own chair. He was quiet for a long time as he studied the sketches.

He put the pad down on his desk. "I really like this," he said nodding toward the drawing. "I want you to draw the garden scene again, without the characters. I also want you to draw Suzuki in that costume with every detail needed to design it. I really like it, Brooke."

Brooke was afraid to speak. She was excited and nervous at once. "What about Heron?"

"What about Heron? I'm the owner of this company, Brooke. I've been keeping an eye on your work for some time. I've noticed Heron's growing jealousy. She is one of the best in the industry, but she isn't perfect, and she isn't indispensable. Part of her job is to notice talent and help to develop it. She has forgotten where she came from and what her responsibilities are. She needs reminding."

Brooke looked down at her hands. "Thank you," she said, looking up at Meryl. "I appreciate your standing up for me. I also appreciate your compliments."

"You're welcome. Now, get to work on those sketches and turn them in to me. Not Heron, but to me." Handing her sketch pad back over to her, he added, "I have your other approved drawings, You have done an excellent job, Brooke. I think it's time for you to be given more responsibility. Come see me when you get in Monday morning."

Brooke smiled and left Meryl's office. She felt like she was flying all the way back to her work station. "Thank you, Jesus!" She said under her breath. She never dreamed Meryl would notice her work, but he had. What a perfect week it had turned out to be!

––––––––

Brooke stopped to see her grandfather on her way home from work. She and Paul were having dinner, but she wanted to share with Papa what had happened that day.

He smiled at her after she'd told him about her day. "That's wonderful news, Sweetheart! It's about time that woman was put in her place!"

"I was so nervous, Papa. I thought for sure he'd take her side. I never dreamed it would turn out like it did."

"Would this promotion put you in a position to help Rachel get her job back?"

"I doubt it, Papa. First of all, Rachel left on her own. Granted, Heron's treatment of her pushed her to quit, but if she were to go back to the company, she would still have to work with Heron. I don't think Rachel would want that."

Papa nodded his understanding. "Has Rachel decided what she's going to do?"

"Not really. She told me she believed it was God's way of opening the door for her to follow her true dream of starting her own design business. That's what she's always wanted. She just needs a location and the money to get started. Shaun supports her completely." She filled Papa in on all that Rachel had shared with her about their plans.

Papa sat a long moment, his brow furrowed in concentration.

"What are you thinking, Papa? You look puzzled."

He shook his head and smiled at Brooke. "Nothing's wrong. I was just wondering about the two of them." He sat another moment in silence then asked, "Brooke, have you ever considered starting your own company?"

"No, theatre work is all I've ever wanted. I wouldn't mind having my own team or even working with a travelling company someday, but what I'm doing right now is exactly what I want."

Papa smiled and nodded. "God certainly has wonderful plans, doesn't He?"

"Yes, He does," Brooke agreed. She looked at the clock and stood to leave. "I need to get home and change. Paul's picking me up at 6:45!" She kissed him good-bye and rushed home to get ready for Paul.

Brooke changed her clothes and touched up her make-up and hair. She gave a critical look at her image in the mirror. She felt so plain. What could someone as attractive and successful as Paul see in her? The buzzer sounded before she had time to really think about it.

She met Paul in the lobby. She blushed as his eyes moved over her body and stopped to gaze into her eyes. "You are very beautiful, Brooke."

She dropped her eyes to the floor and spoke quietly. "Thank you."

Paul moved forward, cupped her chin in his hand and lifted her head so her eyes met his. He leaned forward and kissed her gently on the mouth. He pulled away and smiled. "Don't be embarrassed Brooke. You are a very beautiful woman. That's nothing to be embarrassed about!"

She smiled up at him as she accepted his hand and let him lead her out into the City night. No one had ever made her feel the way he did. She felt safe with him. He made her feel beautiful and appreciated.

Paul rested his elbows on his balcony railing and watched the activity below. After midnight and the city was still alive. It was the first Friday night he'd been home by midnight in weeks. Marcus had kept him busy until his departure Tuesday afternoon. It was a strange feeling to be home so early.

He was grateful for the time with Brooke. Had Marcus still been in town, he wouldn't have been able to see her as much. He was developing strong feelings for her and he suspected she was for him as well. He wanted as much time with her as possible. He was even considering asking her to be his dinner companion for some upcoming business dinners.

He thought back over their evening together. She spoke easily about her childhood, her faith and her goals. She laughed at his jokes and seemed genuinely interested in his work. She accepted his hand when he reached for hers while they strolled through the park and let him hold her close while enjoying the jazz concert on the Great Lawn. It had been a perfect evening.

It was her faith that kept invading his otherwise pleasant thoughts. She wasn't the least bit superficial. She truly believed in her faith and lived what she believed.

How in the world could he blend Brooke into his life? Would she be comfortable in the atmosphere he often found himself in when dining with business partners and clients? He was falling in love with her and wanted to share it all with her, but was he crazy to think she would want to?

He shook his head at the thoughts and laughed. He had spent the past eight years trying to forget the life he had run from in Rockport. He had wanted to run away from his parents' strict religious beliefs and the hypocrisy he had seen in his church. His relationships since then had been shallow. He had purposely sought beautiful, worldly women – women who would make him look good, women who would fall easily into his arms, women who would make no demands of him.

Brooke was completely different from those women. She was incredibly beautiful, but that's where any similarity ended. She was intelligent and modest. She was obviously a woman of strong morals. Susan had invited him into her apartment on the second date. He and Brooke had been out all but one night in the last week and he hadn't been any further than the building lobby.

Paul stood up and raked his fingers through his hair. How did he end up with a woman like this? How could he be falling in love with her? He had much to think about. His world was completely different from hers. Someone was going to have to compromise. He wasn't ready to alter his life, but he knew from his church years that she wouldn't likely be willing to alter hers either.

He looked down once more at the activity in the City. He felt restless, like he was missing something. He couldn't stay in, he had to get out. Grabbing his keys and phone, he left the apartment.

He raced out of the parking garage, not sure exactly where he was going. He drove several blocks before pulling up in front of the Waldorf. He handed his keys to the valet and made his way to the bar.

He settled onto a barstool. He sipped his drink and stared at the continuous newsfeed on the television screen above the bar. He hardly heard what the reporter was saying. He felt more restless than he had in his condo. He just couldn't sit still.

He rose to leave and waved good-bye to the bartender. He turned toward the door and stopped. Susan was standing with a small group of people near the door. She smiled at him, excused herself from the group and moved seductively toward him.

She drew close to him and kissed him on the cheek. Her lips brushed his ear as she whispered "I've missed you. You haven't called me." When she pulled away from him, she smiled again, looking up at him through her lashes.

Paul could feel her closeness. Warmth flooded his body as memories of the passionate nights they had shared raced through his mind. The feeling didn't last long, however. He stepped away from her and smiled disdainfully.

"I haven't called because we aren't a couple anymore, remember?"

"That could change, Paul. We could be a couple again. I miss you. What if we spend tonight together – just one night, a little reliving of our time together." She moved toward him again, her deep red lips curving into a knowing smile. "Maybe it would remind you that we were a great couple."

Paul felt a sudden repulsion. He looked at Susan and wanted to get away. He thought of Brooke and her sweetness. He looked again at Susan and felt dirty. "I can't, Susan. We aren't together anymore and that's that." He turned away from her and left the bar.

He didn't wait long for the valet to bring his car around. Paul tipped him generously, jumped into the car and drove off. Once again, he found himself driving around without a destination. He shook his head in dismay. A week ago, he would have accepted Susan's offer and sent her on her way in the morning without the least bit of conscience. Tonight, confusion gripped him. He drove aimlessly for nearly an hour before returning to his condo and the balcony. He stared out again at the night. He dropped his head into his hands. What was this new woman doing to his life?

THIRTEEN

SOMETIME IN THE EARLY HOURS of Saturday, Paul again felt the gentle rocking of the boat and heard the sounds of the waves lapping against its side. Even the sound of the buoy ringing in the distance was the same. Everything about the dream was the same as before, except this time he wasn't alone.

He strained his eyes into the sun in his attempt to make out the figure at the stern. The sunlight engulfed the man, making it impossible for Paul to see any more than his silhouette. The man leaned forward. He smiled a broadly and offered him something. Paul reached forward to take the package. In his hands he held a loaf of bread.

"You have to eat it," the man said.

Paul looked down at the loaf of bread and looked back up at him questioningly. The man started to lean back. Paul was able to catch a quick glimpse of him before he was again bathed in the blinding sun. It was Herbie, smiling his huge, child-like smile. He nodded once at Paul and disappeared.

Paul was startled awake by the ringing of his telephone. He looked at the clock – 7:00. Paul groaned and reached for the phone. Only Pratt or Marshall would be calling this early on a Saturday morning. That meant that either Marcus was back in town and Pratt needed him to entertain, or the market had taken a dive and he was needed for damage control with the company's clients. Either way, his day would be shot.

Paul pressed the phone against his ear. "Hello?" It was more a question and a mumble than a greeting.

"Good Morning, Paul." It was Jason's voice on the other end.

Paul sat up abruptly and swung his legs around the side of the bed, now fully awake. "Jason, what is it? Are Mom and Dad alright? What about Grandmother? What's happened?" He was speaking too quickly for Jason to break in.

Jason chuckled. "Hey, big brother, slow down! Nothing's wrong! I guess I should call more often if you think the only reason I'd be calling is if something's wrong!"

"Sorry." Paul ran his hand over his chest and took a deep breath, trying to steady his heart and his breathing. "I didn't mean to sound so frantic. I just don't often get calls at 7:00 on a Saturday morning. Just caught me off guard. So, what's going on?"

"I have to take my summer vacation now if I plan to take one. There are two guys in my platoon who have babies coming near the end of summer and they want to save their time for then." Jason paused. "I was wondering if your offer to come see you was still open? Lydia and I thought it might be nice to come to New York and see you for a change."

"Yes! Definitely! That would be great, Jason! I won't be able to take any real time off work and I do have a business dinner next week, but if you don't mind having to entertain yourselves while I'm working, it would be great to have you here. Sarah's still little, but you would love the zoo at the park. We could go to the museum, whatever you guys want! When do you think you'd get here?"

Jason laughed. "Well, we were planning to leave in a few minutes. We can be in New York around 2:00 this afternoon. Would that work okay?"

"Yes, it does. I have a date with Brooke tonight, but I know she'll understand if I have to break it." Paul was excited about finally being able to show his brother what his life was like in New York.

"How about inviting her to join us, Paul? I'd really like to meet her. Or aren't you ready to subject her to the family yet?" Jason teased.

"No, actually that sounds good. She's very family oriented and I know she'd like to meet you. Call me when you're close. I'll have a parking space reserved for you in the parking garage and I'll let building security know you're coming so they don't make you wait in the lobby for me."

"Hey, don't get too crazy! We aren't moving in, just staying a few days. I don't think it would kill us to park on the street."

"Believe me, Jason. You don't want to park on the street. You'd either have to deal with parking meters or limited time parking. Either way you'd have to run down and feed a meter or move the car every four hours. And despite my living in a good neighborhood, you may wake up in the morning and find your car stripped clean or gone completely. You definitely want to park in the garage!"

"Okay, I guess the garage it is!" Jason agreed. "See you in a few hours."

When Paul hung up the phone, he ate breakfast and drank his coffee while he quickly straightened up the condo. He put clean sheets on the bed in the guest room and put fresh towels and washcloths out for his brother and sister-in-law. He looked around the room. "I wonder what Sarah will need to sleep on. She isn't old enough for a roll-away." He considered running to a nearby children's store and asking someone there, but then thought better of it. "I guess I'll wait and see what Jason and Lydia want to do."

He checked the refrigerator and cabinets and made a shopping list. He wanted to have all of his errands finished early so he could talk to Brooke and be ready for his brother's arrival.

By 11:00, Paul had finished his errands. He set a vase of flowers on the table in the guest room for Lydia. He looked around the condo, satisfied that Jason and Lydia would be pleased and comfortable while visiting.

He dialed Brooke's cell number, a little concerned about having to change their plans. He didn't want to do anything that would damage, even a little, the relationship they were developing. He cared deeply for Brooke. But Jason was his brother and he hoped she'd understand.

"Good morning, Paul."

Brooke's voice sounded so sweet to him, his heart skipped a beat. "Good morning. Have my number programmed into your phone already?"

Brooke laughed. "Even if I didn't, we've talked so much over the past week, I recognize your number! So, how are you this morning?"

"Good. I didn't interrupt anything did I? I hear traffic in the background."

"No, I'm on my way to see Papa. We're having lunch. Then, I have to get home so I can get ready for my date with this incredible guy I met." Paul could hear the smile in her voice.

"About that date." Paul took a deep breath. "My brother called me this morning. He and his wife decided at the last minute to spend their vacation here this week. They'll be her around 2:00. I'm sorry, Brooke. I had to cancel our dinner reservations. I hardly see my brother."

Disappointment filled Brooke. She understood. She couldn't expect him to give up time with his brother just to have dinner with her. He could see her anytime. That little doubting voice in her head tried to tell her that he just didn't want to see her, but she quickly put the thought out of her mind.

Clearing her throat, she quietly responded, "I understand, Paul. He's your brother. So, um, when do you think I'll be able to see you again?"

"You sound unhappy, Brooke. I'm sorry. I want to see you again soon, too. How about tonight?"

"Okay, Paul, I'm confused. I admit I'm disappointed, but I understand. I don't want you to give up your time with your brother to take me to dinner. I'm not that selfish."

Paul laughed. "I'm not giving up time with my brother, and I know you aren't selfish. He's the one who suggested that you join us. They have a one-year-old, so dinner may not be anything more than pizza here at my condo, but they want to meet you and I would love to have you here."

"Oh," Brooke smiled. "I'd like that Paul! What time?"

"I'll call you after I hear from them, but it will probably be around 5:00 or 5:30. Will that be okay?"

"Sounds good, Paul. I'll see you then."

She tucked her phone back into her purse and went into the deli to wait for Papa. She thought about meeting Paul's brother and sister-in-law. She was excited about finally meeting some of Paul's family. He didn't talk much about his family or his childhood. What little he did say sounded more like he was reading a script than sharing information about his life.

Despite the excitement, she was a little nervous. What if they didn't like her? One wrong word could ruin what she believed to be the beginning of a wonderful relationship. She didn't want to do anything that could do that.

"You look like you've had a difficult morning. What's the matter, Sweetheart?"

Brooke jumped. Papa stood before her, looking concerned.

"Papa, I didn't see you come in."

Papa kissed her cheek and sat down across from her. "I know. I walked right by the window, smiled and waved, and you never saw me! You were off in Never-Never land. Looks like you have something pretty serious on your mind. Something happen at work again?"

Brooke laughed. "No, nothing new since yesterday. Paul had to change our date for tonight and it's made me a little nervous." She told him about Paul's brother coming into town, the plans for dinner at Paul's condo and her concerns about meeting his family.

Brooke took a sip of her water and shrugged. "He seemed pretty excited about seeing his brother. He hardly talks about his family. I just don't want to make a bad impression."

"Sweetheart, you worry too much! You will be just fine." Papa patted her hand.

After the waitress had taken their orders and returned with water for Papa and iced tea for them both, Papa cleared his throat and looked at Brooke. "I have some important news for you."

Brooke felt panic wash over her. Papa looked serious. "What's the matter Papa? You aren't sick are you?"

"No, Sweetheart, nothing like that. I've just made a big decision this morning. I've decided to sell the shop and the apartment."

"What! Papa, you said only a couple of weeks ago that you wouldn't sell to just anyone! Did Paul talk you into it? I will wring his neck if he pressured you into selling! I can't imagine just anyone having your shop and where will you go?" Brooke's words seemed to tumble over each other. She was shocked.

"Calm down, Brooke. Paul hasn't said another word about it, though his words have stuck with me. Actually, you are the one who convinced me to sell, in a round-about way."

"Me? What did I say to convince you to give up your home?" Brooke was shocked that he would believe she'd want him to sell.

"Honey, I don't know why, but I had always thought you wanted your own dress shop. I had planned to pass it on to you. Yesterday when we were talking about Rachel, you said you never wanted your own shop — that made me decide to sell. There's no reason to keep it now."

"Papa, I never knew you'd wanted me to have your shop. I guess I always saw it as a carpentry shop. Silly, I know, since you can change it into anything you'd want. I'm sorry if I disappointed you."

"Sweetie, I'm not disappointed. I'm proud of you. It just made things clear to me. I'm getting old. It's time to start getting things in order. I looked at an apartment in an assisted-living facility this morning.

It's not a nursing home and there are several different levels of care. I require no care, so I can have a real apartment with a living room, kitchen, bedroom, bathroom – just like I have now. The only difference is that I have priority if I ever need a place that offers more assistance. It's perfect. The only thing I will have to give up is the furniture in the spare bedroom."

"How far away is it, Papa?" Brooke was afraid she wouldn't be able to see him as often.

"One whole block away from where I am now. I know that will make it harder for you," he said, mimicking sadness. He then laughed. "I will still be able to go and harass Gianna, and you will be able to come see me as often as you do now."

Brooke smiled. "Sounds like you have your mind made up. When do you plan to put the building on the market?"

"I'm not. I already have a buyer and I can move into my new place the end of June." Papa laughed at Brooke's shocked expression. "Rachel and Shaun are going to buy the building. I talked to them this morning. Rachel got so excited about having her own shop, I thought she'd just burst! They plan to talk to the bank Monday morning, but Shaun's sure they'll have no trouble getting a loan. And, if they do have any trouble, I'll offer to carry the note until they get settled."

Brooke felt tears coming to her eyes. She got up and hugged her grandfather. Her voice choked in a whisper, "Thank you, Papa. Rachel is like a sister to me. Thank you for doing this for her and Shaun."

Papa patted Brooke's arm and pulled her away from him. "You're welcome, Sweetheart! I know you feel responsible for Rachel leaving the company. It isn't your fault and it isn't your responsibility. This helps me as much as it helps them." Patting her arm again, he nodded toward her chair. "Why don't you sit down and eat your lunch! It will be dinner time if we don't stop gabbing and eat."

———————

Jason and Lydia arrived at 2:30. Paul met them in the lobby to help them carry their luggage up to the condo. He could have let one of the building staff do it, but he knew it would make Jason uncomfortable. Paul gave Lydia a kiss on the cheek and tweaked Sarah's nose. She giggled and buried her face in Lydia's chest.

Jason hugged Paul and clapped him on the back. "You look much better than you did the last time I saw you!"

Paul smiled and nodded his agreement. "I'm in my comfort zone here. Come on, let's get you upstairs. Brooke is coming over around 5:00 for dinner to meet you. I thought you might like to relax a little before she gets here."

Jason and Lydia gasped when Paul let them into the condo. "Good heavens, Paul. You could put our whole downstairs in your living room!" Lydia exclaimed as she looked over the room.

Paul laughed. "I like my space. It's hard to find in this city!"

Paul gave them a tour of the condo. Jason commented on the entertainment center. Lydia fell in love with the kitchen. Both were surprised by the view from the balcony. "Wait til you see it tonight. Nothing compares to the lights and activity in this city," Paul said, nodding toward the view.

They spent the rest of the afternoon talking and laughing. Jason set up a travel crib for Sarah. She was learning to walk and it didn't take her long to find things to get into. "Not used to having an explorer in the house," Paul joked, moving everything she could reach to a safer location.

Brooke arrived at 5:00, a pastry box in one hand and stuffed giraffe in the other. Paul kissed her lightly and introduced her to his brother and sister-in-law. Sarah squealed and clasped the giraffe.

"You have a friend for life," Lydia said, smiling at Brooke.

It didn't take long for Brooke to relax with Jason and Lydia. They were just everyday, down-to-earth people. Jason talked about his work with the Coast Guard. Lydia loved being home with Sarah. They both loved living in Rockport. The way they described living in the seaside town made it sound like paradise.

"Nothing compares to the salty breeze that greets you in the morning," Jason told her. "You'll have to come up some time when Paul visits. Mom and Dad have an extra room and so do we. You'd love it there."

Paul laughed at Jason. "Hey, take it easy! You'll scare the poor woman away. We haven't been dating long enough to plan weekend getaways!" Paul smiled at Brooke. "How about we just start with dinner? I'd better order if we want to eat at a reasonable time."

It was an hour before dinner arrived. Brooke answered questions about her job and the theatre. "Sounds exciting," Lydia exclaimed when Brooke mentioned some of the Hollywood celebrities who were a part of 'Shakespeare in the Park.'

"It's funny," Brooke said. "They are just people. They laughed with us and had conversation with us. The extras that haven't made it yet to Hollywood are the ones who seem to have the attitude problems and unfortunately, I typically costume the extras. I spent A LOT of time praying for patience!"

Sarah started to get fussy. Lydia fed her and changed her for bed. Sarah, still clinging to the giraffe, curled up in Brooke's lap. She put her fingers in her mouth and looked up at Brooke. Her little eyelids would droop for a second and then she'd quickly pop them open again.

Brooke smiled down at her. "I think somebody's fighting sleep."

Lydia chuckled. "I'd better take her and tuck her in. She'll never go to sleep as long as she's snuggled up and trying to impress you." She took Sarah from Brooke's arms and went into the spare room.

Brooke helped Paul set out the dishes for dinner. By the time Lydia came back to the living room, the pizza had arrived and they settled down to eat. "Mind if I say grace?" Jason asked, taking Lydia's hand and reaching for Brooke's.

Brooke smiled, put her hand in Jason's and reached for Paul's. Paul just shrugged and took her hand. Jason blessed dinner and they resumed their conversation.

Jason and Lydia talked easily with Brooke. She was comfortable with her faith and they noticed. Before long, the conversation turned to church and religion.

"Do you attend the same church as Paul?" Jason asked, reaching for another slice of pizza.

"No. I attend an interdenominational church a few blocks from my apartment. It's on a street that's close to the not-so nice part of the City, but Pastor Brian and Lauren have done a lot to reach out to the people in need in the area. It's amazing what they've accomplished in the time they've been here."

"Sounds like a nice church," Lydia said. "We had planned to go to church in the morning." She looked over at Paul. "Unless you wanted us to meet your church family, I'd really like to visit Brooke's church."

Paul looked at Jason. He wasn't sure what to say. Church family? He didn't want to admit that he hadn't walked through the doors since Easter and that was only so he could tell Mom he'd been there. He felt guilt wash over him.

"Well," he laughed, trying to cover his discomfort. "Honestly, I've been so busy these past weeks, I haven't really had time to go. I don't think they'll miss me if I miss tomorrow."

Brooke sat up straighter in her chair, excitement rising up in her. Reaching for Paul's hand, she asked "You'll come with us tomorrow? I can't wait for you to meet Pastor Brian and Lauren!"

Paul's heart sank into the pit of his stomach. He hadn't planned to volunteer to visit Brooke's church. He had merely been trying to tell Jason and Lydia that he didn't mind *them* going with her. Now he felt trapped.

"Sure. Sounds great!" he lied, squeezing Brooke's hand. "How about lunch at the deli in the park and then a walk through the zoo after church?"

"What the heck," he thought. *"Might as well make the best of it."* He spent the rest of the evening dreading Sunday morning.

FOURTEEN

PAUL FOLLOWED BROOKE INTO THE church Sunday morning as she and Lydia talked about their afternoon plans at the park. By the time Brooke left his condo the night before, it had been decided that a picnic was the perfect idea. Jason agreed it would be good for Sarah to have plenty of room to move around after spending the morning in church.

Jason turned back to look at Paul. "You okay? You're like a dead man walking. This isn't death row, you know."

Paul took a deep breath. "I know, Jason. I admit I'm a little nervous. I've never been here before."

Jason shook his head and laughed. "Neither have we, remember? You have the advantage of knowing at least one person in the place. We don't know anyone!"

Paul pulled Jason away from Brooke and Lydia and spoke in a whisper. "Jason, I haven't been to church in months. You know how I feel about all of this. You and Lydia go every week. I feel a little out of place here."

Jason clapped Paul on the back. "Come on, big brother. You'll be fine. Just try to relax and give it a try. I'm sure there's a reason God pulled you through those doors."

Paul looked away from Jason and mumbled, "That's what I'm afraid of."

Shaun and Rachel greeted them shortly after they'd entered the church. Shaun shook Paul's hand and smiled. "I wondered how long it would take Brooke to get you to visit us! Good to see you, Paul."

"Thanks," Paul replied. "Shaun, Rachel, this is my brother Jason and his wife Lydia. The little wiggle worm is Sarah. She's only a year old and has trouble holding still."

Rachel smiled at Lydia and took hold of Sarah's little hand. "She's adorable. Is she going to sit with us or are we taking her to the nursery?"

"Nursery! Definitely!" Jason said without hesitation. "I want to enjoy the service, not chase her all over the place!"

Rachel laughed. "Here, let me show you the way. I'm sure Brooke wants to show Paul off to a few more people before the service starts." Turning to Brooke, "You guys go ahead. Shaun and I will make sure they find you okay."

Brooke smiled up at Paul. "Ready to meet a few more people before the service starts?"

Paul took Brooke's hand and let her lead him into the sanctuary . He felt like he was being taken before a firing squad. He was uncomfortable enough without being dragged all over the church meeting people for the first time.

He couldn't help looking around at the variety of people. There were old and young, black and white, rich and poor. The mix surprised him. His parents' church was made up mostly of middle class, white families who had been a part of the church for years. The church he occasionally attended near his condo was all upper class. No way would you see people in ratty jeans and beat up sneakers in either church.

"Ruth is right over there, Paul. I really want you to meet her," Brooke said, interrupting his thoughts.

Brooke had told Paul about Ruth. He had pictured an overweight, grandmotherly woman with grey hair and wire-rimmed glasses. He was shocked when he saw her. She was an attractive woman in her fifties. She was almost as slim as Brooke with auburn hair that had a few streaks of silver. She had a bright smile.

"Ruth, this is Paul," Brooke smiled.

Paul took Ruth's hand. "It's so nice to meet you. Brooke talks about you often."

Ruth smiled at Paul. "It's nice to meet you, too. Brooke has talked about you non-stop since she met you. I was starting to wonder if you were some figment of her imagination!"

Paul laughed. He was surprised at how comfortable he was with her. Brooke loved this woman like a mother. He wasn't sure what he had expected, but he hadn't expected to feel so at home with her.

Ruth hugged Brooke and smiled again at Paul. "I hope to see you again soon, Paul. Enjoy the service." She patted Brooke's arm and walked to the front of the church and up into the choir.

By the time Brooke led Paul to their pew, Rachel and Shaun had returned with Jason and Lydia. Everyone filed into their seats in time for the service to start.

"Good morning! I hope everyone is ready to shout out to our Lord this morning!" the choir director said into the microphone. Within seconds, the band started to play and voices blended in an upbeat song. Hands clapped to the music, palms were lifted up.

Paul had never experienced this in church before. He wasn't sure what to do. He looked over at Jason and Lydia and was surprised to see them keeping up with the music - Jason smiling and clapping, Lydia waving a hand through the air and swaying to the music. They looked like they belonged. Paul felt awkward and out of place.

The music came to an end. A woman stepped from the choir and stood to one side as the rest of the singers filed down into the main part of the sanctuary.

The pastor stepped to the microphone. "Be seated," he said, smiling to the congregation. "Sister Marcia is going to bless us this mornin' as we make our offering to the Lord. If you're a visitor this mornin', welcome. Your presence is your offering, so don't put anything into the collection plate. Just enjoy being here with these saints of God." Bowing his head, he prayed "Lord, bless this offering we give to you. Help us, Lord, to use it for Your service and to further Your kingdom. Amen."

The ushers took the offering plates to the congregation. The soloist moved closer to the microphone as the music started. Her soulful voice resonated throughout the church. People raised their hands toward heaven and waved in time to the music. Sniffles could be heard throughout the room as she finished the song and stepped down from the stage.

The pastor returned to the podium. "Thank you, Sister, for blessing us. God has breathed His Spirit into your voice."

"Amens" could be heard around the room.

"The title of my sermon this morning is 'Where Your Heart Is.'"

Paul sunk deep within himself as he listened to the pastor preach about the dangers of seeking wealth and position before seeking God. He felt something reaching into his soul and tugging at some deep place. Resentment built as he considered the years of guilt that he had endured while growing up in his parents' legalistic church.

He believed that Jason and Lydia had some how planned this, their bringing up the "church on Sunday" topic to Brooke as a way to drag him back into the pit of guilt and control he had escaped when he'd moved from Rockport.

By the end of the service, his anger at having been dragged through the doors was hardly containable. As the people around him were shaking hands and gathering their belongings, he excused himself and made his way to the restroom. He needed a minute to compose himself, fearing he would lose his temper with Jason. He didn't want to lose it in front of Brooke.

The restroom was empty. He stood for a moment, staring at his reflection. He had to make an effort to calm down. Jason could read him like a book and he didn't want him asking questions in front of Brooke. The door opened and he looked quickly down at the sink and turned on the water. He washed his hands and looked again at his reflection.

"Smile, Paul," he told himself. "Pretend everything is just wonderful." He took a deep breath and went back out to find his companions.

Jason and Lydia had already claimed Sarah from the nursery. She still clutched the giraffe Brooke had given her the night before. She had her fingers in her mouth and rested her little head on Lydia's shoulder. As soon as she saw Paul, her eyes lit up and she wiggled to get out of Lydia's arms.

Paul relaxed as he held his niece in his arms. She was so innocent. She snuggled up close and rested her head against his chest. He felt the anger leave him, at least for the moment.

"She does love her uncle," Jason said to Paul. He winked at Brooke. "At least you know he's good with kids!"

Paul shook his head and laughed uneasily. "Don't even go there, Jason," he said, handing Sarah back to Lydia.

Brooke took Paul's hand as they approached Pastor Brian and Lauren. "Pastor, Lauren, I would like you to meet my friend Paul Matthews."

Paul smiled and shook their hands. "Good to meet you."

"Glad you're here. I hope you'll come back and visit sometime. Do you have a home church?" Pastor Brian asked.

"Yes, I do. When I'm able to make it, I go to the Baptist church near my condo."

"Well, it's good you have a church. It's important to make time for God." Pastor Brian looked back at Brooke and took her hand. "We love you, Sister. Lauren and I would like to have coffee with you real soon. Call me."

Brooke hugged Pastor Brian. "I will, Pastor. Thank you."

He held her close for a moment and spoke quietly, "Be careful, Brooke. Keep your guard up." He pulled away and squeezed her hand before letting go. He nodded at her and turned to the next parishioner seeking his attention.

Paul ordered lunch to go from the deli. Brooke had thought ahead and packed a bag with a change of clothes. They stopped by Paul's condo long enough for everyone to change clothes and pick up a blanket and toys for Sarah.

The afternoon was warm and sunny. They found a nice picnic spot on the Great Lawn where they could spread out and enjoy their lunch. Sarah was fast asleep on the blanket within a half hour. She had, as usual, her fingers in her mouth and the giraffe clutched close. It wasn't long before her hair was stuck to her forehead with perspiration.

The four of them fell into easy conversation. Brooke shared more about her growing up in Syracuse. Jason and Lydia talked about their family in Rockport. Paul hardly spoke until Jason mentioned their father and the marina.

"Dad had always hoped that either Paul or I would take over the business. Paul had this New York dream of his, and all I ever wanted to do was join the Coast Guard. I don't know what Dad will do with it now unless he sells it. The only employee he's had for any length of time is Herbie and he's hardly qualified to take over a business," Jason explained.

"Surely with some guidance and training, he could figure it, couldn't he?" Brooke asked. "If he's been with your father that long, I can't imagine he isn't capable."

Paul jumped in. "Herbie has a mental disability. He has the mentality of a 12 year old. He's a hard working, teachable man, but definitely not capable of running a business. Who knows what will happen to him when the time comes."

"That's too bad," Brooke replied. "Not only for the business but also for Herbie. It sounds like your father is a kind, patient man."

Paul grunted. "Depends on who you ask."

Brooke looked at Paul with surprise. His face was filled anger. She looked at Jason, hoping for some explanation. Jason cleared his throat, "I think it's time to check out the zoo. This conversation is getting far too serious."

Brooke glanced at Lydia who simply shook her head and picked Sarah up from the blanket. Jason and Paul threw the trash into the receptacle while Brooke packed the blanket and toys. Nothing more was said about Paul's family.

Brooke walked into her apartment and sighed. She kicked off her shoes by the door, and dropped her purse and keys onto the table. It had turned into a long day, and she was glad it was over.

She pushed the button on the answering machine and booted up her laptop. There were only two messages – one from her father telling her to check her email. The other was from Ruth, asking when they could get together.

She filled the tea kettle and changed into her lounge pants. She wanted nothing more than to have a relaxing cup of tea while she checked her email and then spend a little time in prayer before going to bed. Too many of the day's events left her puzzled, if not confused.

Pastor Brian's words had echoed through her mind all day – "Be careful, Brooke. Keep your guard up." She knew it wasn't Paul's religion. Pastor Brian had spoken many times on the dangers of letting religion divide the children of God.

It didn't matter what denomination you belonged to so long as your church was a Bible-believing, salvation-preaching, Jesus Christ exalting church. The only time he had spoken out against a specific religion was when it was a cult or one that worshipped some deity other than Jehovah God.

No, she was certain that had nothing to do with it. Did he see her getting too close too soon? Or was there something in Paul that he had been able to detect? Paul had acted strangely all day. In fact, his odd behavior troubled her more than Pastor Brian's words.

Brooke quieted the whistling tea kettle and poured the boiling water into her cup. Dunking the tea bag up and down in the steaming water, she thought about the odd day. "God, please help me to make some sense of this day. I am so confused, and I know you aren't a God of confusion."

She settled onto the couch, her Bible in her lap. She had her laptop open on the coffee table, music streaming from its speakers. She closed her eyes and tilted her face toward heaven. "Please, God."

Her thoughts returned to the afternoon. Paul had hardly spoken after the discussion about his father. It was as though she'd violated some unspoken rule by mentioning his father's apparent kindness. She had asked Lydia about it when they'd taken a break at the zoo. Jason and Paul had gone for cold drinks, leaving them alone for a minute. Lydia's response had only added to the mystery.

Lydia had replied with a shake of her head, "That's a question you need to ask Paul. I wouldn't feel comfortable about revealing any of that to you."

Brooke took a deep breath and tried to get the thoughts from her mind. She was in love with Paul. She knew that without a doubt. She was hurt by his silence throughout the day, but she also ached with compassion for him and his obvious pain that was rooted to some past event with his family. She didn't want him to be in pain.

"God, please," she prayed again. She opened her eyes and searched her Bible for direction. *"The Lord is near to all who call on Him, to all who call upon Him in truth,"* she read in Psalms. "Thank you, Lord. I know You are near me."

She closed her Bible and checked her email. One was from Meryl, telling her to meet him in the prop room instead of his office in the morning. "Be ready to do a quick sketch of the trellis and gazebo for the team – not tonight, but tomorrow morning."

The email from her father was the perfect end to her day. She smiled at the beautiful picture he had attached and the peace she felt in her spirit. It was a picture of her rose bush, the deep red blossom filling the screen. A little bud could be seen in the corner.

"Your bush has given us the first rose this summer, Sweetheart. I hope you enjoy the picture and that it brightens your day."

She typed her response, "It's beautiful, Daddy, and it's just what I needed. Thanks and I love you."

Brooke closed her eyes and thanked God for His wonderful timing. That email was just the encouragement she needed. It was as if God was telling her to just trust Him. If He can keep the roses blossoming perfectly every year, He could certainly make sense of the events in her life.

She closed her laptop and went to bed. She slept peacefully, knowing God was in control of it all. Whatever happened, whether in her job or her relationship with Paul, it would work out according to His plan.

FIFTEEN

THE WEEK FLEW BY IN a blur. It seemed to Brooke that one minute she was in the prop room doing scene sketches on Monday morning and the next minute, she was walking into Wednesday night Bible study. For that, she was extremely grateful. She felt the need for her Christian family and God's Word like a desert begged for rain. The week had been both busy and stressful. Despite her daily Bible reading and prayer time, she felt empty.

Brooke was early. She went to her classroom, took one of the seats and sighed. Closing her eyes, she tipped her head back and tried to clear her mind. It seemed like every event from Sunday forward was replaying in her thoughts.

She was still processing the changes that had taken place at work. She had spent all of Monday morning working with the prop team on the garden scene. Brooke was thankful for the team members. They were knowledgeable and willing to offer their suggestions and accept hers. She had never designed a scene before and was grateful for their willingness to work with her.

She finished the sketches and her work on the scene in time for lunch. She didn't make it out of the building, however, before Meryl stopped her and asked for a quick meeting in his office. The meeting was short and to the point.

"I'm giving you a trial-promotion, so to speak. I want you to take over the supervision of the costumes you've designed for the extras. The sewing and fitting of those will be turned over to Julie and Vic. You will work on the one costume for Suzuki – remember Heron will do the rest for that character. You will also continue with the supporting characters you've designed. You and Heron will have to work together, but I want you to report directly to me. Once this show is finished, we'll see if the promotion is permanent." Meryl smiled at Brooke.

Brooke had been stunned. Although she was thrilled with the opportunity, she was concerned about Heron's reaction. She would have to work *with* her rather than for her. Meryl must have sensed her hesitation and reassured her that there would not be a problem

Heron had come out of Meryl's office Wednesday looking wilted. She glared at Brooke, but said nothing. Most of the day, they had worked in silence. The only time Heron had said anything was to remind Brooke of the fittings at the theatre on Thursday morning. The tension had been unbearable.

She was thankful that the day was finally over. She was also thankful for the refreshment the Bible Study would offer.

Brooke sat up in her chair and looked around the room. She was still the only one present. She felt alone. She and Shaun had once sat together for these Bible studies. He had been like a brother to her since she'd moved to the city. Now he was moving on to another stage in his life that didn't include her, at least not the way it once had.

Since becoming engaged, he and Rachel had joined the study group on marriage. They were the only unmarried couple in the group, but they both felt it important to be with other couples from whom they could "glean relationship wisdom," as Shaun described it. Brooke knew that to be a wise decision. Still, she felt some jealousy at the way things had shifted over the past several weeks. Shaun and Rachel were busy planning a wedding, attending Bible study and pre-marital counseling, leaving little time for socializing. Rachel had called the night before to share her excitement over the bank granting them the loan to buy Papa's building. She was excited for them, but still felt some loss at her grandfather giving up his building. She did her best to put those feelings aside and instead prayed God's blessing on her friends.

She tilted her head back again and closed her eyes. This time, her thoughts drifted to Paul. She hadn't seen him since Sunday afternoon. They'd spoken Monday night, but it was a quick, almost dutiful phone conversation. He was taking Jason and Lydia to dinner and to see some sights. He hadn't invited her to join them or asked her if she would be able slip away for even a few minutes.

Tuesday he had a dinner meeting for work, and she had Bible study on Wednesday. Jason and Lydia were going back to Rockport Thursday morning. Paul had another business dinner Thursday night. She was hoping to see him over the weekend. A voice in her head kept trying to convince her that he was already growing tired of her.

She was disappointed that she wouldn't be able to see him. She was also disappointed at not having another opportunity to see Lydia and Jason. They had only spent a few hours together over the weekend, but she felt a bond with them. She knew it was their shared faith that drew them together, but she also genuinely liked them and believed they could be closest of friends if not for the distance between them. She felt she could easily fit into Paul's family.

"I love him, Lord. What am I going to do?" They had only been together a short time. They hardly knew each other. But, somehow, she had already fallen in love with him. "Please, God," she begged. "Show me what to do."

She sat up in her chair again. She wanted to leave. She wanted to talk to Papa. She reached for her Bible and purse and started to get up. Lauren and Ruth entered the room and smiled at her. Others followed, quickly filling the seats. She sat back down and tried to clear her mind. The clutter in her head, however made it difficult to concentrate.

When the class ended, Ruth walked over and hugged her. She pulled away to look into Brooke's face and furrowed her brow. "Dear, are you okay? You look ready for tears. What's going on?"

Brooke shook her head and gave a weak smile. "Long week. Work has been crazy and I haven't seen Paul since Sunday. It would take a while to get into it all."

"Have dinner with me tomorrow night, Sweetie. You look like you need a change of pace. I'd take you out tonight, but I have a girl coming by who may be interested in renting a room when she starts classes in the fall. I won't take no for an answer, though, for tomorrow night!"

Brooke gathered her things and decided to skip seeing Papa and go home. Maybe what she really needed was some alone time and a good night's sleep. She spoke briefly with Lauren on her way out of the church. She waved down a cab and rode home in silence.

She was in bed early, but found it difficult to sleep. It wasn't until sometime after 2:00 AM that she finally drifted off, her dreams filled with the anxious thoughts she'd carried with her into sleep.

Paul left for work Thursday morning before Jason and Lydia were awake. He was able to honestly tell them the night before that he had a packed day ahead. Marcus had flown in Wednesday afternoon and his presence always added extra hours to Paul's days. He explained his need to get an early start and said "good-bye" before going to bed.

He was ready for them to be on their way. Jason had been on his back since Sunday evening. Every day, his brother had sounded more and more like their father. Paul had enough. He couldn't take another minute of his brother's self-righteous attitude and preaching.

The first thing Jason had said after Brooke had left on Sunday was "Paul, you need to be careful. She's falling hard and you aren't ready for this, big brother."

The anger boiled up in Paul like lava. "Exactly what do you mean by that, *little brother*? In case you've forgotten, I'm a bit older than you are and have far greater financial stability to offer a woman than you ever will. Besides, we've only been dating for a week and a half – too soon to be talking about anything permanent."

"Don't get defensive, Paul. I'm just saying that you need to take a step back and look at the whole picture. Lydia and I could see the way she looked at you, the way she escorted you around the church, introducing you to the people that mean the most to her. She is proud of you. She definitely loves you. It's written all over her. I just don't want you thinking this is just some casual acquaintance. She doesn't see it that way."

"Okay, fine. What if you're right? How do you know I'm not in love with her? How can you sit there and say that I don't know what I'm doing? I have strong feelings for her. I don't, despite your accusation, see her as some casual fling. I happen to care about her." Paul shoved his hands into his pockets and looked out the window.

"So you care about her. Have you thought about the differences in your lifestyles, the differences in your faith? She's devoted to hers. You rejected God years ago." Jason walked over to stand by Paul. "How will you ever work that one out?"

"Jason, this isn't the Dark Ages. I would never force a woman to give up what she believes. I'm sure we could come to some compromise."

Jason put his hand on Paul's arm. "You may be willing to compromise, but she won't. Believe me, Brother. If she has to choose between her faith in Christ and you, you're gonna lose!" Jason pulled his hand away and went into the spare room, leaving Paul to consider all that he'd said.

Paul had spent the rest of Jason and Lydia's stay making excuses for not including Brooke. In reality, he wanted to keep her as far away from them as possible. He didn't want them to say or do anything that would jeopardize his relationship with her.

Thursday morning he was still thinking about it. Brooke had definitely done something to him. He wanted her to be comfortable and happy with him. He wanted her to be able to be herself. But he also wanted her to respect his feelings and convictions.

He walked into *La Regina* to get his morning coffee. The place was crammed tight with the usual morning crowd. Paul squeezed between a table and the person in front of him in line. He felt the need to hold his breath so as not to invade the guy's space.

He turned slightly to look around and noticed Nick sitting near the window. "Good morning, Mr. Barsanti."

"Good morning, Paul. Please, just Nick. Haven't seen you in a while. Doing okay?" Nick stood up and walked over to Paul.

"Fine. Just really busy. My brother and his family were here for the week. They leave this morning. And I've had to work while they've been here. I feel like I need a vacation from my brother's vacation! I haven't even seen Brooke since Sunday."

"She mentioned that you've been a busy man this week. I think she understands, though. She stays pretty busy on her job as well." Nodding toward the line, he said "I think you're up. Good talking to you, Paul. Stop by and see me soon." Nick smiled and left the café.

Paul thought of Brooke all the way to the office. He realized he needed to talk to her. By the time he reached his floor, he'd made up his mind that regardless of the demands Marcus would put on his time, he would call Brooke that night. He couldn't let another day pass without learning what he could about her feelings for him. Only then could he truly face what he was feeling for her.

Brooke spent the morning at the theatre helping Heron with the fittings. Heron hardly spoke. Her attitude wasn't as hostile, though, as it had been the day before. Brooke took it as a good sign that she was accepting the situation.

Meryl was waiting by her work station when she returned to the studio. "How'd it go?" he asked before she had time to put her purse away.

"Surprisingly, not bad. We aren't best of friends yet, but we were able to work together without killing each other," Brooke replied.

Meryl chuckled. "Well, good. I'm glad there wasn't any blood shed! Keep up the good work, Brooke." He slapped his hand on her table and smiled at her before he left.

The words of encouragement were just what she needed. She spent the rest of the day working with Vic and Julie on the costumes assigned to them. They accepted her promotion happily and worked hard to follow her designs. By the time she left for the day, Brooke felt more confident in her new position.

She called Ruth when she was on the subway to make sure they were still having dinner.

"Of course. I need to see my girl. I've hardly seen you since you moved out. Now I understand what mothers mean when they say that their children never call."

"Very funny! I talk to you all the time!" Brooke laughed. "Oh, Ruth, could you do me a favor please? I forgot my mother's jewelry box when I moved out. It's on the shelf in my old closet. Do you mind bringing it with you tonight?"

"I'll bring it along. See you at seven, Sweetie."

Brooke couldn't wait to see her friend. Ruth was right. They hadn't spent much time together recently. Ruth was the mother she'd never had and she missed her. She knew that she could share her feelings with Ruth about the changes in her life, and she would give her honest opinion and offer sound advice.

Brooke reached her apartment with enough time to change her clothes and check her phone messages. One was from Papa, asking her when they could have lunch or dinner again. The other was from Paul.

"Hi, Brooke. I'm sorry I haven't had the chance to see you this week. I'd like to see you later, if possible, after my business dinner. I'll call again later."

"Guess I'd better call him," she said to herself as she deleted the messages. She grabbed her purse and turned to leave. The phone rang. Brooke reached to answer it and felt her stomach quiver. A sense of dread swept over her as she picked up the receiver.

"Hello?"

"Brooke?" The voice on the other end was frantic.

"Yes, it's Brooke. What's the matter? Who's this?"

"Brooke, it's Heather – you know, Heather from Ruth's. Brooke, you've got to come over now. Something's happened to Ruth. Please, come fast!" Heather hung up the phone before Brooke could respond.

"Oh dear God! Please, Lord let her be alright!" Brooke prayed as she left her apartment and dashed to the elevator.

Brooke ran out of the building and stepped to the curb to hail a cab. Tears stung her eyes as she tried to get first one then another cab to stop for her. They were all either busy or out of service. She had to get one to stop for her soon. She was shaking all over. "Please God, be with my friend."

She was about to wave at the next cab when she heard "Brooke?" and felt a hand on her arm. She jumped and turned toward the voice. "Oh thank God! Paul, it's you!" She wept and fell into his arms.

Paul was bewildered by her reaction. He pulled her away from him and saw the tears streaming down her cheeks. "Brooke, what on earth is the matter?"

Brooke choked, "It's Ruth-something's wrong. One of the girls from her house called me - something's happened. I've got to get out there. Please Paul." Her words ran together in one long breath.

Paul nodded. "Don't worry. I'll get you out there." He waved down a cab and helped Brooke in. She gave the driver the address and buried her face in Paul's shoulder. He held her close and kissed the top of her head. Knowing there was nothing he could say, he sat helplessly and let her cry as they rode through the City.

SIXTEEN

THE CAB HAD TO LET them out nearly a block from Ruth's house. The street in front of her house was blocked by NYPD, rescue and an ambulance. News crews were set up a short distance from the police barrier, their cameras pointed in the direction of the activity. Police tape cordoned the area in front of the house. Several men in uniform were keeping people away. Others were questioning the neighbors.

Brooke felt like she'd stepped into a bad movie. People were loitering around, craning their necks in hopes of even a glimpse of something tragic to feed their morbid curiosity. Paul kept a tight hold of her arm as they passed through the onlookers. She had stopped crying, but the shaking was getting worse as they moved closer to Ruth's house.

Paul reached for her hand. "Try to calm down. Don't assume the worst."

Brooke choked, "I can't help it, Paul. Look at the police and crime scene tape. I could hear it in Heather's voice. Something terrible has happened to Ruth."

Paul squeezed her hand. "Come on. Let's see if someone can tell us what's going on and if they'll let you get to Heather."

They had to push their way through the crowd of people standing around to get to one of the police officers. "Can't go through there. This whole area is a crime scene," the officer said as they approached him.

"This is Brooke Barsanti, Officer," Paul spoke. "She was very close to Ruth. One of the girls who lives here, Heather, called her and asked her to come down. Please, can we at least get to Heather?"

The officer looked around and signaled for another officer to come over. "Can you take these folks to the house? She's a friend of one of the girls who lives at the house."

"Officer Marks," he said, shaking Paul's and Brooke's hands. "How do you know the young woman who called you?"

"I lived here for six years. Ruth was like a mother to me. Heather moved in last fall. That's how we knew each other," Brooke responded in little more than whisper.

"Did you remain close to Ruth?" He stopped in front of the house, making sure that Paul and Brooke faced away from the activity.

"Yes, Sir, I did. We are very close. We were planning to have dinner tonight. I just talked to her a couple of hours ago." Brooke choked back a sob. "Please, was she hurt bad?" Brooke knew the answer from the expression on the officers' face.

"Ma'am, let's find your friend. Don't go anywhere. We may have some questions for you." He left briefly and returned with Heather.

"Oh, Brooke! It's so awful!" Heather threw her arms around Brooke's neck and sobbed. "I don't know what we're going to do!"

"Heather, please, tell me what happened." Brooke walked Heather to the curb where they sat down.

Paul left them to talk and called Pratt to change his dinner meeting. Pratt seemed irritated, but agreed to reschedule. He then called Marcus to postpone his later meeting with him. Marcus was very accommodating and agreed to wait to hear from Paul the next afternoon.

When Paul returned, Brooke and Heather were hugging each other, sobbing uncontrollably. He sat next to them on the curb and took Brooke's hand. He knew from the activity and the way the police were avoiding their questions that Ruth was dead.

An hour passed before the scene started to calm down. The onlookers finally broke up and went to their homes, their sadistic hunger satisfied. Heather's parents arrived to take her home. Brooke stood on the sidewalk in front of Ruth's house, hugging herself, staring up at the door.

The coroner arrived and Ruth's body was taken from the house. Brooke could see through the open door that the table in the front hallway was tipped over, the vase smashed on the floor. The flowers that had been in the vase were scattered across the hardwood, the petals crushed from the foot traffic. Brooke shook her head in disbelief. How could anything like this happen?

Paul stood close to her, his hand resting on the small of her back. "What did Heather tell you, Brooke?" he asked quietly.

Brooke reached up and wiped the tears from her face with the back of her hand. She choked down another sob and cleared her throat. "She got home from work and found the front door kicked in. The hall table was overturned. Ruth was lying, face-down, in a pool of blood at the end of the hallway, near the kitchen. Her purse was dumped out."

Brooke took a breath and continued, "Heather called 911. When they arrived, they had her go with them through the house. Heather's laptop was missing. Melissa's T.V. and DVD player were missing from her room. The T.V. and DVD player were taken from the living room. The stereo was taken. Ruth's wallet was gone. I guess they cleaned the place out." Brooke stopped and furrowed her brow, her attention drawn to the yard.

"What is it?" Paul asked, looking in the direction of Brooke's gaze.

Brooke walked over to the flower bed by the steps leading into the house. She bent down and pointed to a box that had been dropped in the grass. "That's my mother's jewelry box!" She exclaimed.

She reached to pick it up. "Wait, ma'am! Don't touch it!" Officer Marks called to her. "Just a minute. You have to let us do that." He motioned for another officer to come over and retrieve the jewelry box. Turning back to Brooke, he asked "Was there anything in it?"

"Yes, Sir, there was," Brooke tried to control the tears. She had so many memories in that box. When the officer picked it up, the only thing that remained was her graduation tassel from High School. The top had been broken off, the hinges dangling carelessly. "Is there anything on the ground?" she asked.

"No, ma'am. This is it," the officer replied.

Officer Marks nodded to the officer to take the box away and then turned to Brooke. "I know this has been a rough night, but do you think you could come down to the station and answer a few questions? I'd like to know what was taken from your box, though I doubt we'll ever be able to recover the items. I'd also like to ask a few questions about the other young women who lived in the house. We haven't been able to locate this Melissa that your friend mentioned."

Brooke nodded her agreement. She had no idea how to find Melissa. She knew very little about her, but she'd do whatever she could to help them find the person who did this to Ruth.

———————

Paul and Brooke rode in one of the squad cars down to the police station in silence. Brooke watched the people on the street, going about their lives like nothing had happened. Ruth was gone. She was such a special woman. She had touched so many lives. Any of those people out there could be the person who'd taken her life.

When they reached the station, Paul and Brooke were taken to a room to wait for Officer Marks. Coffee was brought in for them. They waited nearly an hour before Officer Marks arrived. He entered the room and closed the door firmly behind him. "I apologize for the wait. I couldn't leave the scene until everything was taken care of. Do you need anything? Water? More coffee?"

"No, thank you," Paul replied. Brooke could only shake her head.

The officer sat down and opened a folder. He scribbled notes on the paper and looked up at Brooke and Paul. He handed them both a form to fill in their full names, addresses, phone numbers, even their place of employment. "Just makes things easier later if we need to get in touch with you for any reason," he explained when Paul looked at him questioningly.

"Now," he said, turning to Brooke. "Please tell me again how you are related to the victim."

"Well," Brooke began, "we aren't really related. She boards young women who attend the local colleges. I'm from Syracuse and needed a room when I came to NYU. My grandfather lives here in the city and had heard about her. I moved in the summer before my freshman year and stayed until this May when I found my own apartment. Ruth treated me like a daughter."

The officer nodded. "So, you've remained close to her. Do you know any of the other women who live there?"

"Heather has been there since last September. Melissa moved in around Thanksgiving. Pam has been there for two years. I know Heather pretty well. She's taking some of the same classes I did. I know Pam only from what I saw at Ruth's and I can't really say that I know Melissa at all. She kind of keeps to herself," Brooke shrugged her shoulders. "I can't really think of anything else to tell about them."

Officer Marks cleared his throat. "Did Miss Howell have a boyfriend, a lover?"

Brooke had to laugh. "Ruth? No. She jokingly called herself a Protestant nun. She never, as far as I know, dated or expressed interest in anyone. She believed God had called her to take care of us, the young women who came into the City and needed a guardian. She volunteered at our church and did a lot of community service. Ruth was married to God."

"Well, thank you for your time, Ms. Barsanti." Officer Marks handed Brooke a form. "If you could please fill this out with the contents of the jewelry box, it would be helpful. Please be as detailed as possible. If you had a necklace with a broken clasp, for example, be sure to mention the broken clasp, etc. Be thorough. As I said earlier, the chances of finding anything are slim, but we'll do what we can." He turned to leave the room then quickly turned back to Brooke. "Oh, by the way, Melissa has been located. She was apparently with her boyfriend. So, she's safe and accounted for." He smiled at Brooke and left the room.

"Well, that's good news," Paul said, squeezing Brooke's hand. "At least we know she's okay. What about the other girl, Pam?"

"She went home to see her parents for the summer. I guess someone needs to get in touch with her, too, don't they?"

Brooke looked down at the form. The items in that box were precious to her. The box had been her mother's. It had held an ivory-set-in gold brooch with roses carved in it that her father had purchased for her mother as an engagement gift. It had her mother's initials, a heart and her father's initials engraved on the back.

Papa had given her grandmother a bangle with ivy engraved on it before they'd emigrated from Italy. Inside he'd had engraved "To Sophia – Love, Your Nicholas." Papa had given it to Brooke on the day of her high school graduation.

The rest of the contents were some old costume jewelry, some old hat pins and a pocket watch that didn't work. Her grandfather Merriweather had purchased the watch for her at a yard sale when she was in her early teens because she'd liked the roses carved on the cover.

When Brooke had completed the list, she and Paul sought out Officer Marks. "Sir, the only things that were worth anything are the brooch and the bangle. Every thing else was only sentimental in value."

Officer Marks took the form from Brooke. "It doesn't matter what the monetary value is. We still like to know what you've lost. Thieves don't know whether or not a piece of jewelry is worth something. Not until they try to pawn it. If we can get a good description of these items to the pawn shops, we may be able to find out who did this. It doesn't always work, but it's a shot. Thank you both for your time." He shook their hands again and directed them to the exit.

Paul led Brooke out into the night air. It was late, nearing midnight. He hailed a cab and gave the driver Brooke's address. Once on their way, he reached over and took her hand.

"I don't want you to be alone tonight, Brooke. I'm worried about you," he said, reaching up and gently moving her hair away from her face.

"I'll be alright, Paul. I can always go to Papa's if I have to. Rachel would probably come over, too, if I called her. I'm okay, really."

The cab pulled up in front of Brooke's building. Paul paid the driver and walked Brooke to the door. She stood up on her toes and kissed him on the cheek. "Thank you for being there for me tonight, Paul. It means a lot to me."

Paul reached for her hand, pulled her close and kissed her firmly on the mouth. He ran his fingers across her cheek and looked into her eyes. "I'm not leaving you until I know you have someone to be with tonight, Brooke. If I have to sit in the lobby all night, I will," he whispered.

Brooke sighed and nodded. "Okay, you can come up with me, but only until I can reach either Rachel or Papa."

Paul smiled at her, "Agreed."

Brooke led Paul through the lobby and into the elevator. She checked her cell phone on the ride up to her apartment. She had silenced it when they went to the police station. "Twenty messages," she said, shaking her head. Most were from people from church. Pastor Brian and Lauren had left one, so had Rachel and Shaun. There was also one from Papa.

"See?" she said, holding her phone up for Paul to see. "I have lots of people looking out for me. You have to work tomorrow. You should go home and get some rest."

"No way! Not until I'm satisfied that you're taken care of." Paul crossed his arms and gave her a stern look.

Brooke gave a weak laugh. "You are a very difficult man!"

"You're pretty stubborn yourself! And you smiled for the first time in hours."

Brooke smiled back at him and took the apartment key from her purse. She unlocked the door and let Paul in. "Not quite as elegant as your condo, but I like it."

"Not bad," he said to her. "You've really done a great job in here."

He spent a few minutes looking around while Brooke put her purse away and excused herself to the bathroom. He opened the doors on the living room window and looked out at the City. Despite the traffic that never ceased, the City seemed peaceful. He couldn't explain why. After the tragic evening he and Brooke had just shared, he would have thought he'd feel more anxious. But, he didn't. He couldn't explain the peace he felt when he was with Brooke.

Brooke came out of the bathroom and walked over to him. "This was one of the big selling points for me on this apartment. I love the view." She looked up at Paul. "Thanks again for everything tonight. I hope your boss isn't too upset with you for missing your meeting."

"Oh, he'll get over it." Paul touched Brooke's cheek gently. "You've been crying again," he said, rubbing his thumb over the tear streaks on her face.

Brooke cleared her throat and nodded. "I just can't believe she's gone, Paul. I loved her. She was my best friend."

Paul held her close and let her cry. When the tears slowed down, he led her to the couch and had her sit down. He kissed her on the forehead. "Sit still. I'm going to put your tea kettle on, if you don't mind my rummaging through your kitchen. And I need to make some phone calls."

Brooke nodded and pulled her knees up to her chest. She rested her head on her knees and prayed quietly that God would help her through this. She couldn't imagine not having Ruth to talk to.

She could hear Paul in the kitchen filling the kettle with water and setting it to boil on the stove. She heard him opening and closing the cabinets several times. She heard his voice speaking softly, though she couldn't make out what he was saying. The kettle whistled, his conversation ended, and she heard him moving again in the kitchen.

Paul came back to her with a cup of tea and sat down beside her. He combed her hair away from her face with his fingers. "I called Nick. He was still awake. What happened to Ruth was on the news, and he's relieved that you're okay. He's on his way over to spend the night with you."

"Paul, he's seventy years old! I should be going to his house!" Brooke started to get up. Paul took her wrist and pulled her back down.

"I asked him if he wanted me to bring you over to his place and he insisted on coming over here. He said he slept on this couch many times when your grandmother was still alive and he could handle it tonight. Brooke, he wants to be here for you. Let him."

Brooke nodded and settled back down on the couch. She took a deep breath and sipped her tea. Paul got up and found a blanket to wrap around her shoulders and sat back down beside her and held her close. By the time Nick arrived, Brooke was asleep, her head resting on Paul's shoulder.

Brooke awoke to the smell of coffee and the sound of soft whistling. She sat up and winced at the crick in her neck. Her clothes were stuck to her, wrapped around her like a straight jacket. She remembered drifting off with Paul next to her on the couch and realized she'd remained on the couch all night.

She dropped the blanket onto the couch and went into the kitchen. Papa was taking eggs and bread from the refrigerator. The coffee pot was gurgling its final drops of into the carafe. Papa had already set the table.

"Good morning, Papa," Brooke said, sleep still heavy in her voice. She squinted against the light.

"Buongiorno, Sweetheart," Papa responded, walking over and hugging her. "Are you okay this morning?"

Brooke shrugged her shoulders. "I'm not really sure, Papa. I feel numb. I cried so much last night. I don't think I have any tears left. Paul must think I'm a wreck."

"No, he doesn't. He's worried about you. He stayed with you last night until I arrived. You were sleeping so well that we didn't want to wake you to move you to your bed. I hope you don't mind – I slept there instead. I don't think I could have managed the floor."

"No. I'm glad you did take the bed. I don't know how you would have managed the couch. My neck is killing me," Brooke said, rubbing the back of her neck.

"It'll relax when you've been up awhile."

"What time is it, Papa?" She looked up at the clock. "Great! I have to be at work in half an hour. I'd better call Meryl and tell him I'll be late."

"Brooke, I think you need to tell him you need the day off. You've had a tragic night."

"Papa, I can't call in…"

"Don't argue! And don't give me that look! If he can't understand what you've just been through, then you don't need that job! Now, get on the phone and tell him you won't be in. I've already called Martin. He's on his way. You know he'll agree with me!" Papa gave her his "no-arguments" expression.

Brooke sighed and shook her head. "Okay. I'll call in. I think I'd be better off keeping busy than sitting around and thinking about it, but I know you won't take no for an answer."

"You're right! I won't!" He muttered under his breath in Italian as he turned back to the counter and cracked eggs into a bowl. Brooke knew that meant the discussion was closed.

Brooke took her phone to the living room and opened the doors to the outside. She dialed Meryl's number. Her heart pounded in her chest as she waited for Meryl to answer. She'd just gotten her promotion. There was so much work to be done. She knew it was a bad time to be calling in. She was afraid of what Meryl would say.

"Hello," Meryl finally answered.

"Meryl, it's Brooke. I'm afraid I have an emergency and need to ask for the day off." Brooke held her breath.

"Good morning, Brooke. I was expecting your call. I saw the news last night and recognized your old address. I'm sorry about what happened to your friend. Don't worry about a thing. Call me sometime over the weekend and let me know if you need Monday off for funeral arrangements." Meryl's voice was full of compassion. "If you need anything, give me a call. You know we're here for you."

"Thank you, Meryl. I appreciate it. I'll keep you posted on everything." Brooke hung up and choked back a sob. She was grateful for his understanding. His concern brought the previous night back and caused the tears to well up. She shook them off. Taking a deep breath, she went back to help Papa in the kitchen.

"I'm all set. He told me not to worry."

"I thought he might. Let me take care of breakfast. Get your coffee and sit down. You need to just sit for a bit." Papa handed her a coffee cup and motioned toward the table.

Brooke sat down and sipped her coffee. Papa scrambled eggs and buttered toast. He brought the plates to the table, set one before Brooke and took the seat across from her. He bowed his head and offered a simple blessing.

Brooke stared at her plate. She wasn't hungry. All she felt was sadness and exhaustion.

"You need to eat, Brooke."

"I know Papa. I'm not hungry, though. I'm more tired than anything else."

Papa shook his head and sighed. "Won't do you any good to get sick. You've got to eat something."

She nodded and forked a few bites into her mouth. She choked down some toast and pushed her plate away. "Sorry, Papa, but that's going to be it."

He shook his head again and took Brooke's plate to the sink. "I made the mess, I'll clean it up. You just relax. I think you need more rest."

Brooke poured herself another cup of coffee and went to the living room. She picked up her Bible and started to sit down when the phone rang. "I get the feeling this is going to be a long day," she said, reaching for the phone.

"I told you to rest. I'll get it," Papa said, picking up the phone. "Good morning, Paul." Papa walked over and stood before Brooke. "She's okay. She's tired and she refuses to eat, but other than that, I think she's about as good as can be expected." Papa paused. "Yes, she's awake and, as a matter of fact, giving me an evil look. Hold on and I'll let you talk to her." Papa handed Brooke the phone and went back to the kitchen.

"Good Morning, Paul. Thanks for everything last night. I appreciate it more than you know," Brooke said.

"No need to thank me, Brooke. I wanted to be there for you. I'm on my way to work, but I wanted to make sure you were okay. I'm not sure what Pratt has in mind as far as the cancelled business dinner. I may have to make it tonight. I'll let you know, but I may not be able to get to you tonight. Will you be okay?"

"I'm fine. Papa is here. He called my father this morning. He's on his way from Syracuse. I won't be alone, I can guarantee you that. Between Papa and Daddy, I'll probably be under constant supervision."

"Well, I'm glad you won't be alone. If I can get away, I will. I just don't know how late I'm going to be. Promise to call me if you need anything."

"I will, Paul. Hope your day goes well." Brooke hung up the phone and went to the kitchen.

Papa smiled at Brooke. "I think that boy really cares about you."

"Okay, Papa. You've already played matchmaker," Brooke playfully scolded. "You've done your part." Brooke reached for the dishtowel and stopped as the door buzzer sounded. "See? I told you it was going go be a long day"

By lunchtime, Brooke's apartment was full of people. Pastor Brian and Lauren were the first to arrive, the tears flowing the moment Brooke opened the door. Shaun and Rachel arrived shortly after, followed by a couple of women from her Bible study, two deacons and their wives. They pulled chairs into the living room and drank the coffee that Papa kept brewing. They cried together for a long time over what had happened. When the tears finally ceased, Pastor Brian took control of the group.

"I think we need to spend some time in prayer. Not for Sister Ruth, obviously. She's in the arms of our Lord. We do need to pray, though, for those who are hurting right now from this loss." Pastor Brian looked around the group as he spoke. "Hard as it is, we also need to pray for the ones who did this terrible thing. They are lost souls."

Everyone stood together and joined hands as Pastor Brian's powerful voice filled the air in prayer. "Father God," he prayed. "We thank You for the blessing of Sister Ruth. We miss her already, Lord. Be with us as we come to terms with what has happened…" His voice grew stronger as he prayed, the words of comfort for the hurting and the prayer for the ones lost reached heaven in a steady rhythm.

"Lord, we also ask that the police find them that did this terrible thing. Bring them to justice, dear God." His voice cracked as he presented those words to the Lord. The others in circle began weeping again. He cleared his throat and whispered a choked "Amen."

"Amens" were said around the circle. The room remained quiet. It seemed no one wanted to interrupt the peace. Lauren began to hum softly. Whispers of praise started to rise. Pastor Brian took up the song, his deep voice bringing the song to life. One and then another voice joined in until the entire group was in harmony before the Lord.

When the song came to an end, sniffles replaced the melody. Pastor Brian again said "Amen." He cleared his throat and quietly said "Our Comforter is here. Let this peace be with you. Don't weep for Sister Ruth. She is with our Lord, and her life was a beautiful picture of God's love for us to hold on to."

Brooke's father arrived late Friday afternoon. Brooke cried again when he entered the apartment. Papa made more coffee and the three of them sat around Brooke's table discussing what had happened.

"Ruth doesn't have any family, does she?" her father asked, reaching for the sugar bowl.

"No, she didn't," Brooke answered quietly.

"How does all of this work? Who takes care of funeral arrangements, burial? What about her home and its contents? I'm sure she had to have a will, but how does anyone find this stuff out?" Martin shook his head.

"Pastor Brian called just before you arrived. The officer in charge of Ruth's murder investigation called and asked him to go to the police station. Apparently, Ruth's lawyer was watching the news last night just like everyone else and saw what happened. He showed up at the police station this morning with a will, of sorts, that explained what Ruth wanted," Brooke said.

Brooke took a sip of her coffee before she continued. "It was Ruth's wish that Pastor Brian perform the funeral service. She wanted to be buried in the cemetery outside of the City. He has been entrusted with taking care of everything relating to her funeral and burial. She even left enough money to cover the costs."

"Well, that's good news. I guess I shouldn't be surprised that she would have everything in order. She was a special woman," Martin said.

"I guess there's more to the will. Pastor Brian and Lauren, one of the church elders, a woman named Shannon who was one of her first boarders, and I have all been asked to meet at the lawyer's office Tuesday morning," Brooke said, staring into her coffee cup.

"When's the funeral?" Martin asked.

"Sunday afternoon at 2:00. Ruth wanted a short, closed-casket service and then a party celebrating her life in the fellowship hall. The burial is to be quiet – Pastor Brian and Lauren, Shannon, the girls currently living at her house and me. That's it."

Martin nodded. "I can understand that. I don't want anyone making a big fuss over me either."

"I'm not ready to talk about that, Daddy," Brooke said, giving her father a stern look.

"Got to talk about it sometime. I'm not getting any younger, you know."

"Martin, I don't think this is the right time," Nick said, looking over at his son. "Better left for another time." He looked at the clock and stood up from the table. "It's getting late. Let's get some dinner, my treat." He looked over at Brooke and wagged a finger at her. "No arguing! You have to eat and that's that!"

Brooke looked over at her father and shook her head. "I guess I don't have a choice, do I?"

The sun shone bright and clear Sunday. A light breeze kept the City heat at bay. Lines of people waited to enter the church. The sanctuary was standing room only, with an hour still to go before the funeral would start. Paul found Brooke sitting in the front row, holding tightly to her father's hand.

Paul walked over to where she sat. He offered quiet greetings to Nick, accepted the introduction to Brooke's father and squeezed in next to Brooke. He kissed her on the cheek and took her hand. "How are you holding up?"

Brooke shrugged her shoulders. "Mixed emotions, I guess you could say." She looked up at him and whispered "I am so glad you're here."

"I'm sorry I haven't been able to stop by to check on you. Marcus has kept me busy. I wouldn't leave you to handle this alone," Paul said to her, nodding toward the casket.

Paul hardly had time to call her. There hadn't been even a minute to stop by and check on Brooke. He'd had to attend the dinner meeting Friday night that Pratt had rescheduled from Thursday. He'd entertained Marcus well into the early morning hours Saturday and then joined him again for lunch.

Saturday night was more or less a replay of every other night that Marcus was in town – dinner at the Waldorf, drinks in the bar, Paul not getting home until after midnight. At least he had used some sense and kept the drinks to a minimum. He wasn't sure how he could have handled a funeral with a hangover.

Brooke looked more in control than Thursday. She was definitely mourning her friend, but she had a serenity he couldn't explain. He envied her ability to be so calm. He wanted to ask her how she did it, but before he could speak, Pastor Brian stepped up to the podium.

"Good afternoon, friends," Pastor Brian began, his hands gripping the sides of the podium. "For those of you who are visiting and don't know me, I am Reverend Brian Jefferson. We are here today to honor the life of our precious sister, Ruth Howell. Please bow your heads and join me in prayer for our time together."

The room was silent as Pastor Brian prayed for those feeling the loss of Ruth. He prayed, just as he did at Brooke's apartment, for those responsible for taking Ruth's life, pleading with God to show them their need for His mercy and salvation. When he finished, a few "Amens" were heard, but the room remained mostly silent.

The choir stood and Lauren moved to the microphone. She nodded to the pianist and began to sing "What a Friend We Have in Jesus," her voice touching the heart of each person on the sanctuary. Sniffles were heard throughout the room when she and the choir completed the song.

Pastor Brian stepped back up to the podium. "Sister Ruth requested that this service be short and that it glorify Jesus more than her. Glorifying Christ is going to be easy. He was the center of her life. Not talking about her, and keeping this short – well, friends, that won't be easy. She lived her life for others, dedicated every part of her being to her Savior and Lord. She gave more than she took, praised more than she complained, laughed more than she cried. She lived a life that mirrored Christ. Her life was a picture of the power and grace of our Lord."

Despite his attempt to keep the service short, it lasted an hour. At the close of the service, Pastor Brian made a plea to those in the room who didn't have Christ in their lives to follow Ruth's example and let Him into their hearts. He closed in prayer and the choir sang "Amazing Grace" as the congregation made their way to the fellowship hall for refreshments.

Brooke was surprised to see Meryl and his wife approaching her after she entered the fellowship hall. Meryl expressed his condolences again as his wife hugged Brooke. "How are you holding up?" Meryl asked.

"Okay, I think," Brooke replied. "There are a few of us who have been asked to meet with Ruth's attorney Tuesday morning. Ruth didn't have any family left, so it's just a few of us from the church."

"Well, I want you to take tomorrow and Tuesday off. Come back Wednesday. We still have time on 'Madame Butterfly,' so don't worry about anything. I want you to take a little time to come to terms with what's happened. I think you need it."

"Thank you. I appreciate that. Thanks for coming. It means a lot to me." Brooke smiled at them as they left.

The "Life Celebration," as Pastor Brian called it, lasted until after 5:00. Many lives were touched by Ruth. Brooke looked around the room at the people lingering. Ruth dedicated her life to feeding the poor, sheltering the vulnerable, teaching the uneducated, and loving the unloved. Her life truly was an example of Christ, and the people gathered to remember her were proof of it.

Brooke walked into the lawyer's office Tuesday morning, glad her father was with her. He had remained in the City after the funeral Sunday and spent all day Monday with Brooke. He was a great comfort to her. Pastor Brian and Lauren, Deacon Taylor, and Shannon were already waiting in the office.

Brooke said a quiet "Hello" and took the empty seat next to Pastor Brian. Her father had been asked to remain in the outer office during the meeting.

The lawyer entered the room and took his seat. "Thank you all for coming. Ruth Howell asked me to oversee the reading of her will and see to the distribution of her effects. Each of you is, in some way, included in her last requests." He cleared his throat, put on his glasses and opened the blue folder that lay before him.

"My dear Brothers and Sisters," he read. "Each of you has been the family in my life. The Lord has blessed me greatly by giving me such wonderful people to share my life with. I don't have much in the way of earthly treasure, but the treasure that awaits me is greater than any of us can imagine. What I have been blessed with on this earth, I leave to you as follows:"

Looking up from the folder, the attorney looked at Shannon. "To you Shannon, my first sweet adopted daughter, I leave the dressing table in my room, the painting above the sofa and this box." The lawyer stood up and handed Shannon a green box and sat back down. "You have remained close to me since I first opened my doors to young women. God bless you always."

He turned then to Brooke. "Brooke, my other sweet adopted daughter, to you I leave the rocking chair and round pedestal table in the living room, and this box." The lawyer handed Brooke a wooden box with roses painted on the cover. "Hold on to the Lord, my dear. Never let go. Much love to you and God bless you."

Brooke held the box close and felt the tears run down her cheeks as the lawyer continued the reading. "To Pastor Brian and Lauren, I leave the house and the remainder of my belongings to be sold, the funds to be used to further the ministry of the church. Deacon Taylor, I have asked you to be here as a witness to this. Christ has instructed us to sell all we have and give to the poor. There are many in need, my Brother and Sister. Please take care of them."

Pastor Brian and Lauren wept quietly as the lawyer handed them an envelope and said simply "This is for you personally."

The lawyer again took his seat. "I've spoken to the investigator at the police station. The items left to you young ladies are not considered part of the crime scene. He is willing to meet you at the house when we leave so that you may take possession of those items. He will photograph them for the police records. I will provide copies of the will to be included for their use. Pastor and Deacon, the items left to the church – the home, her automobile and the other contents of the house *are* considered to be part of the crime scene. Nothing can be done with those items until such time as the case is disposed of or if a judge permits the use of photos as a substitute."

He rose from his seat and nodded to the door. "If you are willing, I would like to regroup at Miss Howell's home."

Officer Marks met them there to take the photographs of the items being removed. He also got signatures from Brooke and Shannon on the documentation of the items being removed from the house.

Martin loaded the chair and table into the back seat of Brooke's car. They drove to her apartment in silence. Martin parked Brooke's car in her space in the parking garage. They put the chair and table in Brooke's living room and stood quietly for a few minutes.

"I miss her, Daddy," Brooke finally said.

"I know, Honey. She was good to you." Martin kissed Brooke on the forehead and held her for a few minutes. "Do you want me to stay another night?"

"No, I'm okay. I have to work tomorrow and I'm sure you have things to do, too."

"If you need me, just call." He hugged her again and left the apartment.

Brooke sat down in the rocking chair and opened the box that Ruth had left her. Inside was an envelope with some cash, a gift book with poetry that had belonged to Ruth's mother and a small porcelain angel, its face lifted toward heaven. There was also a card with a note of encouragement.

Brooke let the tears flow. She knew why Ruth had given her the rocking chair and table. Brooke had spent many hours sitting in that chair in Ruth's living room, listening to Ruth read Scripture to the girls or just spending time in conversation with her friend. What Brooke didn't understand was how Ruth knew it was time to put the items into the box for her. The date on the card was from two weeks prior. It was as if Ruth knew something was going to happen and wanted to be prepared.

Brooke tucked the card inside the book of poetry and put it on the pedestal table. She looked up at the curtains that Ruth had given her the week she'd moved into the apartment. Ruth was a precious woman of God. Brooke missed her friend deeply, but she knew she was in the arms of the Lord. That truth would carry Brooke through the pain and loss.

SEVENTEEN

Brooke found a floral arrangement and fruit basket at her workstation when she arrived at work on Wednesday. She put her purse away and pulled the cards from their holders. The floral arrangement was from Meryl and his wife.

She opened the card from the fruit basket and caught her breath. It was from Heron. It was a simple note: "Brooke, sorry for your loss. I know you were close to your friend. Heron." Brooke was stunned. Heron had never shown any kind of warmth. The simple act of kindness was completely out of character.

Brooke went to the break room for a cup of coffee and returned to her workstation to sort through her messages and the stack of drawings and instructions that awaited her. Meryl had approved all of her remaining sketches, freeing her to move on to the costume productions. She took her portfolio to the prep room and started the pattern designs for the costumes. Heron entered shortly after Brooke and started work on her own projects.

"Good morning, Heron," Brooke greeted her.

Heron looked up. "Good morning."

"Thank you for the basket and the card, Heron."

"You're welcome. I know how much your friend meant to you." Heron's voice was strained. She turned back to the table and continued to work in silence.

Brooke watched for a moment, hoping that the conversation might continue. Heron said nothing more. Brooke sighed and went back to work. *"It wasn't much, but at least it's a start,"* she thought, arranging the drawings on her table. *"We might be able to figure out how to work together yet."*

Several other designers joined them in the prep room. A few offered their condolences to Brooke. Only one person spoke to Heron. Quiet conversation went on during the course of the morning, but Heron and Brooke continued to work in silence.

By lunch time, Brooke had given up on any further conversation with Heron. She left the unfinished patterns on the work table. She put the completed patterns away and returned to her workstation to retrieve her purse.

She had two messages on her cell phone from Paul. The first was a simple "hope-you're-doing-okay" message. The second was an invitation to lunch. "I'll be at the café around the corner from your studio at noon if you can get away."

She grabbed her purse and hurried to meet him. She hadn't seen him since Ruth's funeral. He'd called Monday to check on her and Tuesday he sent flowers, but his work responsibilities had kept him away. She missed him and wanted to see him, even if only for an hour.

Paul sat a corner table, one hand wrapped around a coffee cup, the other flipping the pages of a file. She ordered her lunch at the counter, accepted the small, plastic ring with the order number on it and filled a glass with tea from the beverage station. She elbowed her way through the lunch crowd and smiled at Paul as he looked up from his pages.

"Brooke!" Paul stood and pulled out the vacant chair for her. He kissed her lightly before she took the seat. He sat back down, gathered up his papers and put them into his briefcase. "I was afraid you wouldn't be able to make it. I know if I miss a couple of work days, I end up confined to my office for the next week, just trying to catch up."

Brooke reached up and slipped the order ring onto the hook on the wall so the waitress would know where to deliver her lunch. "We're ahead of schedule. It isn't often we have to sacrifice lunch. Now, the closer we get to opening night, we may find ourselves working until 8:00 or 9:00 at night, but we usually still take a lunch break, just to keep our sanity!"

"Well, I'm glad you made it. I've been concerned about how you're doing."

"I'm okay. I have moments when I feel the tears creeping up on me, but for the most part, I'm not doing too bad."

"I don't know how you're doing it, Brooke. I have lost people close to me, and it took me weeks just to come to grips with the loss. You seem so, well, relaxed about it."

The waitress delivered their lunch plates and refilled their drinks. Paul felt his face grow warm when Brooke bowed her head and blessed their lunch. He was having a hard time getting used to her openness with her beliefs.

"I know where she is, Paul. I can be at peace because I know, without a doubt, that she's in heaven right now. Yes, I miss her – terribly. I have this empty place in me now because I know I can't just pick up the phone and call her, or join her for lunch, or cry on her shoulder if I'm having a bad day. Any sadness I feel is for myself. She is in a far better place."

Paul searched Brooke's face. He knew she was sincere. He used to believe the way she did. He used to have that confidence. Not anymore. He still believed that God was there, that Christ was real, but any real depth of involvement in people's lives, well, he had a hard time with that.

He smiled at Brooke and said simply "I'm so glad you aren't depressed about it. I've been worried about that."

"Thanks for that, Paul. It means a lot to me."

They spent the rest of their lunch talking about their jobs. Brooke filled him in on her "promotion." It was the first opportunity they'd had to talk in a week. "Heron isn't taking it very well." She paused to finish her sandwich and sip her tea. "She has this terrible control issue. While I was still an intern, she was fine. She was helpful and very good at teaching me what I still needed to learn. Once the internship ended and I became a full-time designer, things changed. I still don't understand it."

"She probably feels threatened. From all that you've told me, it sounds like your boss is impressed with you. Heron is probably afraid that you're going to oust her." Paul pushed his plate back and picked up his coffee cup.

"Well, there's no danger in that. She's one of the best in the industry. I can't imagine Meryl letting her go for anything." Brooke looked at her watch. "I have to get back. I still have a few more patterns to complete and Meryl wants to meet with us before we leave for the day."

Paul swallowed the last of his coffee. He rose from the table and picked up his briefcase. "I have a meeting tonight with a potential client. So far, I'm open tomorrow night. Can we have dinner?"

Brooke smiled. "I'd like that."

They walked out of the café together. Paul kissed her good-bye and waved as he headed off to the subway. Brooke turned and walked back to the studio, feeling like she was walking on air. She spent the rest of the afternoon trying to ignore the fluttering in her stomach.

———————

Paul was in Brooke's lobby before 6:00 Thursday night. Brooke exited the elevator wearing light-weight white slacks and a simple, short-sleeved blue silk top. Paul's heart beat against his chest when he pressed his lips against hers. "You are beautiful, Brooke," he said quietly.

Brooke smiled and dropped her gaze to the floor. David, the security guard, was sitting behind the desk in the lobby, watching the two of them. She could feel her cheeks turning red. "Thank you, Paul. Are you ready?"

Paul took her hand and led her to the cab he had waiting by the curb. "So, what are you in the mood for? Elegant, casual? You name it."

"You know, I think I'd like Chinese. Papa has cooked for me so much lately, I think it would be nice change of pace."

"Chinese it is." They took a cab to a little family-owned restaurant in China Town.

It was a simple place that catered to the locals rather than the tourists. The entrées were all made from family recipes. An elderly woman greeted Paul with a smile and a bow when they entered. She showed them to a table and handed them menus. She filled their water glasses and left them to look over the menu.

Brooke noticed only one other couple in the dining room. "Not too busy are they?"

"One of the advantages of going out in the middle of the week and getting here early. Just give it a little bit and it will start to fill up. On Fridays and Saturdays, it's impossible to get a table."

The woman returned and took their orders. She returned with fried noodles, soup and egg rolls. She stood by the table until Paul had tasted the soup. He smiled at her and nodded "Tastes very good, thank you." She nodded, bowed and returned to the kitchen.

Brooke watched her go into the kitchen. "You must eat here a lot."

"I do, but she does that with everyone. If it isn't to your liking, she'll take it back and bring you something else. She'll do the same thing when she brings the entrées."

Brooke and Paul finished the soup and egg rolls in time for their hostess to bring out their orders. Again, she stood by the table until they'd both tried the dishes and were satisfied.

Paul sprinkled soy sauce on his noodles and asked Brooke about her day.

"Not much to tell. Pretty much the same as yesterday. I finished the patterns for the rest of the costumes and started pulling fabric, but that's about it. How about yours?"

"Hectic. I had to finalize the contract with the client I gained last night. I was afraid I was going to have to cancel our dinner. One of the stocks we frequently purchase on behalf of our clients started to slip late today because of a sexual harassment suit that goes to court next week. It has some of our clients worked up. I was afraid I was going to have to either spend the night on damage control or attend another dinner meeting with my boss."

"How'd you get out of the dinner meeting?" Brooke asked before taking another bite of her dinner.

"Marcus and Marshall were invited to a black tie, invitation only, dinner with a senator. They couldn't have smuggled me in if I'd been the President of the United States. Pratt already had some prior engagement. So, I was off the hook."

"Well, I'm glad. I was starting to think we were becoming lunch-only companions!" Brooke laughed.

They finished their dinner and made their way to the door. "It is getting busy, isn't it?" Brooke remarked, noting the people waiting at the door to be seated. The hostess smiled and bowed when they left.

Paul took Brooke's hand and walked to the edge of the sidewalk. "Feel like a stroll through the Park? It's still early and I'm not ready to say good night."

Brooke smiled and nodded. Paul waved to a cab. Once they were on their way to Central Park, Paul turned Brooke's face to him and kissed her on the mouth. "I've wanted to do that since we sat down to dinner," he said, his voice hoarse, after he released her.

Brooke dropped her eyes to her lap. He reached over and took her chin gently between his thumb and forefinger. "Don't go getting shy on me now," he laughed and playfully tweaked her nose.

Brooke laughed uneasily. "I'm not used to all of this, Paul. I've never felt like this before. It's just a little unsettling for me."

"I understand. I'll try not to push too hard, Brooke. I care a great deal for you. It's hard for me to not show you those feelings."

The cab stopped, Paul paid the driver and they walked hand in hand down the path through the Park. Neither spoke as they listened to the night sounds and watched other couples enjoying the summer breeze. They soon left the path and sat on a bench near the pond by Belvedere Castle.

"This is my favorite spot," Brooke said softly, leaning her head against Paul's shoulder.

Paul leaned down and kissed her on the top of her head. "I like it here, too." He put his arm around her and pulled her close. They spent the next hour sitting on the bench, watching the ripples in the pond. It wasn't until the street lamps started to cast their yellow glow that Paul stood and took Brooke's hand in his, pulling her gently from the bench.

"I think it's time we go," he said to her, nodding in the direction of a disheveled man stumbling along the path.

"I think you're right." She let Paul lead her to the street. They got into a cab and settled into the seat, Brooke leaning against Paul. She didn't want the evening to end.

When the cab stopped in front of Brooke's building, Paul asked the driver to wait.

The driver nodded and Paul helped Brooke from the car and into the building. Brooke pushed the button for the elevator. Paul pulled her close and kissed her on the mouth. "Do you want me to send the cab away? I could stay a while if you'd like?" He looked deep into her eyes, tracing her cheek with his fingertips.

"I don't think that's a good idea tonight, Paul. I'd better go up alone." Brooke smiled up at him, trying to ignore the quivering in her stomach.

Paul kissed her again. "Okay, Brooke. I'll call you tomorrow."

Brooke smiled and watched him leave the building and get into the cab. He rolled the window down and waved to her as he pulled away from the curb. Brooke got into the elevator and pushed the button for her floor.

"Now I know how Rachel feels," she thought with a smile as the elevator doors closed. She closed her eyes and relished the feeling all the way up to her floor.

———————

Heavy rain greeted the City Friday morning. People used whatever they could to shield themselves from the downpour. The wind blew hard, turning umbrellas inside out. Brooke's umbrella fell victim to the gusts the minute she walked from the shelter of the subway platform. By the time she reached the studio, she was soaked to the skin.

"You're the only woman I know who can get completely drenched and still look nice!" Julie laughed when Brooke walked into the prep room.

"I wish I could believe you! I feel like a drowned mutt!"

"I have a question about the servants' costumes I'm working on," Julie said after Brooke put her pattern book on the work table.

Brooke helped Julie with the costumes most of the morning then returned to her own patterns. She was pulling bolts of fabric and noting the yardage when Meryl came into the room. He approached Brooke quietly.

"I need to see you in my office, Brooke," he said. "Right now. It's important. Leave what you're working on."

Brooke was filled with dread as she followed Meryl from the room. She realized she hadn't seen Heron all morning. *"Great! I wonder what she's complained to him about today,"* she thought as she and Meryl made their way to his office.

Brooke stopped in the doorway when she saw Officer Marks sitting in one of the chairs near Meryl's desk. He stood quickly and walked over to Brooke. "Ms. Barsanti," he said, shaking her hand.

"Officer," Brooke said.

"I'll let you use my office if you need to," Meryl said to them.

"No need," Officer Marks said, stopping Meryl before he could leave. "I would like to take Ms. Barsanti to the station, if this is a convenient time."

"I don't understand," Brooke said, looking at the officer questioningly.

"We may have a lead in the death of Ruth Howell. We need you to identify some of the items we've recovered," he replied. "Would you be able to come now, or is there a better time?"

Brooke looked at Meryl. "This is important, Brooke. Go ahead. If you aren't back by the end of the day, I'll gather your work and put it at your work station. Do what you need to do."

"Thank you, Meryl," Brooke said. She looked at Officer Marks. "Let me get my purse."

Brooke and Officer Marks rode down to the lobby in silence. It was still raining when they exited the building. Brooke was again wet by the time they reached the police car. Once inside, Brooke turned to him and asked "What's happened? What am I identifying?"

Officer Marks checked his mirrors and pulled into traffic. "We sent the detailed descriptions you provided for us to the local pawn shops. A brooch and bangle that fit the description of your stolen items, right down to the inscriptions inside, were pawned this morning. We just need you to look at them and positively identify the items and give a written statement verifying the fact."

Brooke was stunned. She never thought to see them again. She certainly didn't expect them to turn up so soon. "Does anyone know who the person is that sold them to the shop owner?"

Officer Marks nodded. "The pawn shop has a good surveillance system. The video shows both of them clearly."

"*Both* of them? You mean there's more than one person?"

He nodded again and looked at Brooke. He was quiet as he turned the car into the station parking lot. He got out of the car and walked around to open the door for her. When she rose from the car, he shut the door and looked her in the eye. "There's a man and a woman."

Brooke followed him into the station. Officer Marks led her into the same interrogation room she and Paul had sat in the previous week. "Have a seat," he said. "I'll be right back. Would you like coffee?"

"Please," Brooke answered, putting her purse on the table and sitting down.

A few minutes passed before a female officer entered the room with a cup of coffee for Brooke. She put the cup on the table before Brooke. "Officer Pike," she introduced herself. "I'll be sitting in with you and Marks. We don't like to leave a woman alone with a male officer."

"I understand," Brooke replied. She sipped her coffee and prayed her nervousness wouldn't show.

Officer Marks returned to the room, a blue, plastic bag in his hand. "Did Officer Pike introduce herself?" he asked, taking the chair across from Brooke.

"Yes, she did. Thank you," Brooke answered.

Brooke's heart started to pound when the officer took the items from the bag. The brooch and bangle were in separate bags. Both were tagged and labeled with Ruth's name, Brooke's name and a series of number. She stared at them on the table.

"Go ahead and pick them up, Ms. Barsanti. Just don't remove them from the bags. We don't want your finger prints on them," he explained.

Brooke felt the tears come to her eyes when she picked up the brooch and turned it over. The engraving was there, leaving no doubt. She put it back down on the table and picked up the bangle. She stretched the plastic over the surface so she could see the inside of the bangle. The tears streamed down her face when she put it down.

"Are you okay, Ms. Barsanti?" Officer Pike asked, handing Brooke a tissue.

"Thank you," Brooke answered with a nod, taking the tissue from the her. She wiped her eyes and her nose and looked up at Officer Marks. "These are from my jewelry box," she whispered.

"Thank you, Ms. Barsanti." He handed her the form she needed to fill out to complete her statement.

Brooke completed the form and handed it back to Officer Marks. "What now? Will I have to testify? How long before I can have my jewelry and the box back?"

"We have to keep them in evidence until the case is closed. Unfortunately, that could take some time." Officer Marks made a notation on the form and put it into the file folder on the table. "As far as whether or not you'll have to testify, that depends on the DA and the defense attorney. Testimony isn't typically required from someone in your situation. Your identification of the stolen property is enough."

He folded his hands on the table and looked at Brooke. "I know this has been difficult for you, Ms. Barsanti. We would like one more thing, if you think you're up to it."

Brooke looked at Officer Pike first and then Officer Marks. Both were looking at her with sympathy. "What else can I do?" she asked.

151

"We'd like you to take a look at the surveillance footage. We think you may be able to identify one of the suspects. Would you be willing to do that, Ms. Barsanti?"

Brooke followed the two officers from the interrogation room to a bank of computers. They seated her before one of the computers and clicked the "video" icon. The disk whirred to life inside the computer terminal. The dark screen lit up and the backs of two people could be seen standing at a counter.

The image flickered and offered the view from behind the counter, the faces of the two clear on the screen. Brooke gasped. "Oh, dear God!" She felt her throat tighten.

She looked up at Officer Marks. "Sir, the woman is Melissa!"

Brooke didn't return to work. By the time she was finished at the police station, her work day was over. Officer Pike offered to drive her home. Brooke asked to be taken to Papa's. She didn't want to go home. Brooke watched the City activity from Officer Pike's police car in silence until she pulled up to the curb in front of Papa's building.

Officer Pike walked around and opened the door to the car. "Will you be all right?" she asked as Brooke exited the car.

"I will be. Thanks for the ride." She shook the officer's hand and went up the stairs to Papa's apartment.

"Papa," Brooke called in as she opened the door.

"In here," he called from the kitchen.

Brooke closed the door and looked at the boxes stacked around the living room. She felt like she was in an obstacle course as she wound her way around the piles.

"Getting an early start on moving, I see," she said when she got to the kitchen.

"No point in waiting 'til the last minute. Sit. I'll make coffee."

Brooke put her purse on the table and sat down. She took a deep breath and closed her eyes. She felt the tears welling up again. *"I'm sick of crying,"* she thought. She took another breath and opened her eyes.

"Talk," Papa said, taking the seat across from her.

Brooke wiped the tears from her face and fidgeted with the napkin on the table. "The police showed up at work this morning."

"Ruth?" Papa asked, folding his arms.

Brooke nodded. "They found the brooch and bangle that were taken from my jewelry box and wanted me to come to the station to identify them."

Papa rose from his seat, poured the brewed coffee into cups and set one before Brooke. "Keep talking," he said. He put cookies on a plate and brought them to the table while she recapped the afternoon.

"Papa, I couldn't believe it when I saw Melissa's face on the security tape." She turned her coffee cup back and forth on the table before finally taking a sip.

"Sweetheart, I know that was hard." Papa reached over and took Brooke's hand. "What did they say when you identified her?"

"The guy in the video is her boyfriend. They picked them up right after they got the call from the pawn shop. I guess they were able to get his license plate number. That's how the police tracked them down. Melissa tried to deny any involvement. She gave a false name, didn't have her identification with her. She claims that he came home with the electronics and jewelry the day Ruth was murdered. She said he told her it was from a buddy who owed him money and that they would have to pawn the stuff to get back what the guy owed."

"She believed him?" Papa asked with disbelief.

"I don't think that's what happened at all, Papa. How could she not know what had happened? I mean, she was told what had happened to Ruth. She had lived at Ruth's for months. She had to have known. She had to have recognized the stuff he brought in. Besides, why would she give a fake name if she wasn't guilty?"

"You're right, that wouldn't make sense."

"The boyfriend sounds like a real prize. I guess he has quite a record. He's on probation right now for a burglary from a couple of years ago." Brooke shook her head. "She had to have helped him somehow. He knew when no one else was going to be there. He knew where to find everything. He couldn't have done it alone. I just don't understand how anyone could hurt someone like Ruth, especially someone who knew her."

Papa nodded. "It's amazing what people will do when they're driven by greed, Sweetheart. It happens all of the time, I'm afraid. You see it in the paper every day. Money will drive people to commit the most terrible crimes – even murder."

EIGHTEEN

PAUL'S FRIDAY FELT MORE LIKE a Monday. Stock prices slipped further as the news reported more details of the sexual harassment lawsuit against the retail giant. Paul's extension stayed busy all morning, clients calling with concern over the losses they were sure to be facing.

By lunchtime, he had convinced all but two clients who held stock in the seemingly doomed company to wait to make a decision on their shares until he'd had the opportunity to speak with Pratt and Marshall. The two who insisted on selling threatened to pull their accounts and take their business elsewhere.

Paul leaned back in his chair and combed his fingers through his hair. He was the expert in this area. Why couldn't these people just trust him? Clients had agreed to purchase stocks that they knew were risky, but as soon as a dependable company experienced a setback, they all raced to liquidate whatever shares they had in that company. It didn't make sense.

Paul looked at the clock on his desk. "No way I'm getting out of here for lunch today," he thought. He pulled a delivery menu from the drawer and called in his lunch order. He rose from his chair. He stretched and grabbed his suit-jacket. What he needed was a few minutes of air.

Paul left his office and stopped at his secretary's desk. "I'll be right back, Kelly. I've ordered lunch, so…"

Kelly's phone rang, interrupting Paul. "Yes, Mr. Young?" Kelly said into the receiver. "Yes, sir. He's right here. Okay, yes sir." Kelly hung up the phone and turned back to Paul. "Mr. Young wants you to meet him in his office. Mr. Murphy and Mr. Appleton are there as well."

Paul sighed and shook his head. "So much for a little air," he said, more to himself than to Kelly. He pulled a $20 bill from his wallet and handed it to her. "When my lunch gets here, can you please pay the guy and just put the bag on my desk?"

Kelly nodded and set the money on the corner of her desk. Paul turned and made his way to Pratt's office, shrugging into his suit jacket as he went. He knew before he got to the door it was about the stock crisis. What else would make these guys barricade themselves in Pratt's office during lunch hour – especially Kevin Murphy? Kevin was out most of the time. He certainly wouldn't stay in for lunch unless there was a serious problem demanding his attention.

Paul knocked lightly and opened Pratt's door. "You wanted to see me?"

"Yes, please come in, Paul," Marshall answered.

Paul entered the room and closed the door. Kevin sat in the corner with his arms crossed, looking bored and bouncing his leg nervously. Pratt sat in front of his desk next to Marshall.

"Please, Paul, have a seat," Pratt motioned to a vacant chair.

"Thanks," Paul said, taking the seat closest to Pratt.

The room was quiet for a moment before Kevin spoke. "Good God, Marshall. Let's get on with this. It's lunchtime and I have an appointment!"

Marshall looked at Kevin, who sank further back into his chair. Pratt cleared his throat and turned to Paul. "A few of our clients have called this morning with concern over the falling stock prices on our retail friend. We need to make some decisions on this situation. We have some very nervous clients and frankly, I don't blame them."

Kevin stood up and paced, stabbing the air as he spoke. "We should sell now before it bottoms out and our clients lose a ton on their shares."

Pratt nodded and looked at Marshall. "I'm inclined to agree with Kevin. They've dipped two days in a row. If we wait much longer, the losses will be astronomical. If we sell now, we may be able to minimize the damage."

Marshall looked at Kevin, who was still pacing. He looked in Pratt's direction briefly and then turned to Paul. "What is your opinion on this little situation?"

Paul looked nervously at Pratt and Kevin. He turned back to Marshall and cleared his throat. "I think we should wait to sell until after the hearing on Tuesday."

"Good God, Marshall!" Kevin interrupted. "Why in the world are you wasting time with this? It's clear what needs to be done! Listen to this kid and we'll have clients pulling their accounts so fast, we won't know what hit us!"

Marshall glared at Kevin and turned back to Paul. "Please go on, Paul. I would like to hear your opinion on this."

Kevin started to protest, but Marshall held his hand up for his silence.

"Well," Paul began. "I've been watching this lawsuit closely since it first showed up in the news. I don't think there's any real wrong-doing on the part of the retailer. From what I've seen in the news and in their corporate reports, I think this is nothing more than a few disgruntled employees who are trying to get a piece of the retailer's millions."

"This is ridiculous, Marshall. Is this guy psychic now, or something? How could he possibly think this?" Kevin gestured toward Paul. "There's no way of knowing this. We can't chance it!"

"Kevin, sit down. For once in your life, be quiet and let the man finish what he's saying!" Marshall shook his head and turned back to Paul. "What's your basis for this theory?"

"Several women have come forward on behalf of the company, claiming that the plaintiffs were either dismissed for documented wrong-doings or have had previous disciplinary issues. It sounds like they are looking for revenge and the company has a sound defense." Paul sat forward in his chair and looked first at Pratt and then at Marshall. "I truly believe that selling now would be a big mistake."

Marshall sat for a moment. He looked at Pratt who nodded, then at Kevin who was fuming in the corner. "Thank you, Paul. Excuse us, please."

Paul nodded to them and left the room. When he returned to his office, Kelly was waiting for him, a questioning look on her face. "Nothing to worry about," Paul said with a smile.

Paul found his lunch on his desk, the change on his chair. He took a seat, opened the lunch bag and clicked on his email. His cell phone vibrated a message from Brooke. He sent her a quick text that he'd call her later and turned back to his email.

He looked up from his computer when Kevin stopped in his doorway. The man opened his mouth to speak, closed it again quickly and waved his hand in Paul's direction as if to swat away an irritation. He stormed toward the elevators, mumbling under his breath.

Paul shook his head. "I will never understand that man," he said to himself.

Marshall tapped on Paul's door and entered before Paul could speak. He pulled a chair close to Paul's desk. He crossed his legs and folded his arms. He leaned back and studied Paul before speaking. "Pratt and Kevin think I'm nuts to take your advice. I could care less what Kevin thinks. Pratt on the other hand has a strong grasp of the market. If the lawsuit proves legit on Tuesday, we could find ourselves with a mess."

Paul nodded. He didn't speak. He looked at Marshall and waited for him to continue.

Marshall stood from the chair and adjusted his jacket. "I hope you're right about this, Paul. I'm trusting your instincts. You've proven yourself many times." He paused outside of Paul's office and turned back to him. "I'm having a formal dinner party at 7:00 tomorrow night for Marcus. It would be nice if you could bring a date."

"Thank you, Marshall."

"I'll leave an invitation with Kelly, then." Marshall turned away and went down the hall to his office.

Paul shook his head and leaned back in his chair. "God, don't let me be wrong." It was more a comment to himself than a prayer.

Paul left his office after 8:00 that night and tried several times to reach Brooke at home. He dialed her cell and got her voice mail. He wanted to know what her message was about earlier, but he also needed to talk to her about the dinner party Saturday night. Marshall had a reason for wanting Paul to bring a date. This was the first time he had ever made that request.

Paul hailed a cab and settled into the seat with a sigh. It had been a long day. All he wanted was take out and a quiet night with the TV remote.

The cab pulled up in front of his building. His cell phone chirped as he stepped out onto the sidewalk.

Paul closed the door and the cab pulled away. "Hello," Paul said into the phone.

"Good evening, Paul. Marshall still have you at the office or have you been released for the night?" Marcus asked.

Paul closed his eyes. This could only mean a late night. "Good evening, Marcus. I've been released. Actually, I've just arrived home."

"Wonderful! I need a dinner companion tonight and you came to mind. I'm going to that little French place that Pratt introduced us to a few weeks ago. If you'd meet me there, I'd be most grateful."

"I'll meet you there, Marcus. Just give me a few minutes to run up and change."

Paul ended the call and went into his building. *"So much for a quiet night,"* he thought.

His cell phone chirped again before the elevator reached his floor. Taking a deep breath, he looked at the display, expecting it to be Pratt or Marshall. It was Brooke's cell number.

"Brooke, I've been trying to reach you all evening. Are you okay?"

"I'm fine, Paul. Just a long day." She spent a few minutes filling him in on her trip to the police station.

"I think that's good news, Brooke. They've caught them – in record time, I must say." Paul rested his phone on his shoulder and slipped the key into his door lock.

"I know, Paul. But, one of them is Melissa. I just don't understand it all".

"I'm sure it's been hard to take that news, Brooke. I wish I could have been there for you." Paul dropped his briefcase on the sideboard and shut his door.

"Are you home, Paul?"

"I am for about five minutes. I have to meet Marcus for dinner. Which – while I'm thinking about it - Marshall is having a formal dinner party tomorrow night for Marcus. Would you like to come with me? It's at 7:00 if you think you'd like to come along."

"I would like that very much."

"Great! I'll pick you up at 6:00 tomorrow night. You'll need a gown."

"I have a few, thanks to the cast parties I've attended these past few years. I'll be ready at 6:00. Good night, Paul."

Paul tossed the phone on the table. He went to his bedroom and stripped off his suit. He washed quickly and pulled on a pair of casual cotton slacks and a golf shirt. He shoved his wallet and phone into his pockets, grabbed his car keys, and left to meet Marcus.

He maneuvered the Mercedes through the usual Friday traffic, found a parking place off the street and went into the restaurant. The entrance was crowded with people waiting for tables. Paul forced his way to the hostess. "I'm meeting a business associate – Marcus Reed."

She smiled at him. "Right this way."

Paul followed her to the back of the restaurant. As usual, Marcus was seated at the best table, a bottle of Sicilian Red wine, uncorked and chilling, near the table.

"Ah, Paul. So glad you could make it," Marcus said, rising from his chair. He reached to shake Paul's hand. "I hope you didn't change any plans just to accommodate me."

Paul shook Marcus's hand and sat down. "Ice water, please," Paul said to the hostess and turned back to Marcus. "No plans tonight. I'm glad you called. Gave me something to do tonight!" he lied, picking up his menu.

The waitress brought Paul's water glass and an empty wine glass. She took their dinner orders and poured the chilled wine into Marcus' glass. He took a sip and nodded to the waitress who then poured a glass for Paul and returned the bottle to the ice bucket.

Marcus raised his glass to Paul. "$170.00 a bottle. I had to pay the manager to track it down for me." Marcus leaned forward and chuckled. "The best they have on the menu here is only $50! Couldn't quite stomach that!"

Paul laughed and sipped the wine. "This is excellent, Marcus." Paul didn't drink enough to tell one wine from the next. He could probably drink a $10 bottle and not know the difference. He wouldn't even consider admitting it to Marcus, however.

"So," Marcus began. "Marshall tells me you've made a rather daring stock prediction again today. Tell me about it, why don't you."

Paul recapped his meeting from earlier. "Marshall trusted my theory, though it doesn't sound like Kevin or Pratt agreed with him," he said in conclusion.

"Pratt is a little more conservative than Marshall when it comes to dangers in the market. Kevin is just a fool, concerned only with his own comfort. It's obvious Marshall trusts your intuition. You've proven yourself repeatedly."

Their dinner arrived and they turned the conversation to politics and the world market. Marcus agreed with Paul's concern that the current administration was going to damage the established trade relationships.

"Your wisdom far advances your years, young man," Marcus told Paul as they finished their dinner. "I would welcome your input on a few of my own business deals, when we have the opportunity."

"I would be glad to, Marcus. Just say when."

The waitress returned to remove their plates, took their dessert order and returned with coffee. Marcus excused himself briefly to take a call. The man from the neighboring table rose when Marcus did and followed him outside. Paul recognized him as Marcus's bodyguard from the party at the Waldorf where he first met Marcus.

"I apologize," Marcus said when he returned to the table. "Business never stops, I'm afraid."

"I understand completely."

Marcus chuckled. "I suppose you would, wouldn't you? I have yet to call you and hear that you have plans." Marcus leaned forward. "Don't work so much you neglect your personal life. You'll regret it later!"

Marcus sat back to allow the waitress to set the dessert plates on the table. "Marshall tells me you will be joining us tomorrow night. Will I have the pleasure of meeting your lady friend, assuming you have one?"

Paul laughed. "Funny you should mention that. Yes, you will be meeting Brooke tomorrow night. I found it odd, though, that Marshall would be adamant about my bringing a date. He's never done that before. Any idea why?"

Marcus smiled. "I think he wants it all to be very sociable, especially for Pratt. It seems that Marjorie is starting to grow concerned with Pratt's endless dinner meetings and nights away from home. Marshall believes that if Marjorie sees Pratt's co-workers with dates, she will be more relaxed and less suspicious of Pratt. I don't know whether or not it will work, but it's worth a try to keep his *marital bliss* intact."

Paul nodded his understanding. Pratt was more concerned with keeping his marriage intact to protect his image than for the marriage itself. His affairs were endless. Paul was surprised that he'd been able to keep them a secret from his wife as long as he had.

"Marjorie is a beautiful woman," Paul said. "I guess I don't understand his need to wander. I have to remind myself that I don't live with her, but it's still beyond my comprehension."

Marcus pushed his dessert plate back and sipped his coffee. "I never once cheated on my wife in all of the years we were married. I won't deny, however, that there were times that it crossed my mind."

"What kept you faithful?"

Marcus smiled at Paul. "I did love her, very much. But, frankly, I never wanted that blemish on my record. Her family was very important. We were watched very closely. It would have been discovered, had I chosen to follow my desires rather than my obligation."

Paul looked at Marcus. Why he was shocked at this admission, he didn't know, but he was. "So, it was a business decision rather than a moral one?" Paul tried to keep the accusatory tone from his voice.

"I guess you could call it that." He leaned forward. "Paul, you still see things through your ancient magnifying glass. Each man is responsible for his own life, his own pleasure, his own success. Stop looking at things in black and white. If you want something, reach out and take it. Unfortunately for Pratt, we live in a society that has yet to embrace the fullness of personal gratification. His only real guilt in this is his indiscretion. He really does need to be more careful."

Marcus's words replayed in Paul's mind as he drove home. *"If you want something, reach out and take it."* It triggered thoughts of Brooke. He couldn't deny his love for her. She was the most incredible woman he had ever known. He wanted her in a way he'd never wanted another woman before.

Jason's warning, however, invaded his thoughts. What would he do if their relationship reached the point where she did have to choose between her faith and Paul? How would he convince her that a she didn't need to choose? How could he convince her that what she embraced so fiercely only restricted her ability to really enjoy her life?

——————

Paul handed his keys to the valet and reached for Brooke. She smoothed her skirt nervously and accepted his arm. She took a deep breath as he led her up the walk to Marshall's front door.

Paul stopped and turned to her before they reached the door. He studied her for a moment, taking in the way her gown fit to her curves. Its copper color made her eyes seem darker and more intense. Cupping her cheek in his hand, he leaned down and quietly said, "Relax. You are beautiful – you look just fine!"

Brooke smiled back at him. "Thank you, Paul. I'm just a little nervous about what your friends will think of me. I don't want to embarrass you."

Paul chuckled. "Embarrass me? Not a chance! I will be the envy of every man in that house. Ready?" he asked, nodding toward the door.

Brooke nodded and let him lead her up to the house. Paul had their invitation in hand when the door opened.

"Your names, please?" the butler asked.

"Paul Matthews and Brooke Barsanti."

The butler stepped aside and allowed them to enter. He closed the door and announced their arrival to Marshall, who walked over and shook Paul's hand. "Glad you could make it, Paul." Turning to Brooke, he took her hand and squeezed it gently. "You must be Brooke. Marshall Appleton."

Brooke smiled. "Pleased to meet you, Mr. Appleton."

"Please, please. Just Marshall. Come, let's find you two some champagne." Marshall led them through the room to the bar, put glasses in their hands, and motioned toward Marcus.

"Paul, who is your lovely friend?" Marcus asked. He took Brooke's hand and kissed it, his eyes locking with hers.

"Marcus Reed, this is Brooke Barsanti. Brooke, this is Marcus," Paul said.

"Better keep her away from Pratt," Marcus said with a laugh. Brooke felt a shiver run up her spine as he leaned toward her, his eyes never leaving hers. "You are just perfect!"

Paul stepped forward to take Brooke's hand. "Do I need to keep her away from Pratt or from you, Marcus?" he asked jokingly.

Marcus smiled at Brooke. "Nothing to fear, my dear. I am only teasing you. I am not in the habit of finding companionship with women who are younger than my daughter!" He slapped Paul on the back. "She's quite lovely, Paul."

Marshall chuckled. "He's harmless, Brooke. Don't let him get you flustered!"

"I am in the theatre business, Sir. It takes a lot to get me flustered," she assured Marshall. Her stomach, however, was tightly knotted. There was something about Marcus that made Brooke uneasy. She had felt his eyes boring into her, as if he could somehow see into her soul.

Paul didn't notice her discomfort. He spent several minutes taking her around the room, introducing her to everyone he knew. He was relieved that Marjorie was on Pratt's arm when they approached. Pratt smiled at Brooke and took her hand at Paul's introduction. "I see why Paul has kept you hidden," Pratt said, an unmistakable hunger in his eyes.

Marjorie smiled weakly at Brooke. "Nice to meet you, Brooke. Paul, it's good to see you again." She moved closer to Pratt and put her hand on his arm, steering him away.

Paul watched them walk away and shook his head. He looked at Brooke. "Sorry about that. I had hoped that having Marjorie next to him would make him behave himself. I guess I overestimated him."

Brooke took a deep breath. "As long as you stay close, I'll be fine, Paul. Just don't run off and leave me for any length of time." She smiled at him and looped her arm through his. "Come on. Let's meet the rest of your friends."

Brooke remained quiet during the drive back to her apartment. Much of the evening's conversation had been shallow.

Never in Brooke's life had she seen so many self-indulgent, arrogant people in one room. The men had talked money and the stock market. The women seemed intent on outdoing each other with what they'd spent on jewelry, clothes, lessons for their kids.

"How old are your children?" Brooke had asked one of the women.

"Nine and twelve," she'd snapped, turning her nose up to Brooke. She then turned back to her friends, moving slightly so as to exclude Brooke from the conversation. Brooke had excused herself and walked away. She'd spent the rest of the evening shadowing Paul.

Even Paul had seemed like a different man. He too had spoken mostly of finance and wealth. He had fit right in. The only time he'd seemed sincere in anything he discussed was when one of his friends asked about Brooke. He had taken great pride in her, treating her like some great treasure.

Marjorie had been the only pleasant, genuine person she'd met. She'd lit up when she told Brooke about her daughters, and had seemed truly interested when Brooke shared a little about herself. Too bad the poor woman had spent most of the night keeping her husband out of trouble.

"You're quiet," Paul said, interrupting her thoughts.

"Just tired, I guess," she replied.

"Did you have a good time?"

"I felt a little out of place." She smiled and shrugged her shoulders. What was she going to say? *"No, I had a terrible time with all of those snobbish, immoral, sycophants? Better to keep that opinion to myself,"* she thought.

"It's hard when you don't know anyone. Maybe next time you'll feel more at ease," Paul said, reaching over to squeeze her hand.

"I really like Marjorie. She seems like a very pleasant woman. I felt comfortable enough with her to give her my phone number. She seems like a very lonely woman."

"Pratt's gone a lot. I think she is lonely. I'm glad you two hit it off." Paul pulled his car up to Brooke's building. "Is there someplace I can park, Brooke?"

Brooke smiled at him. "You can park here, Paul." She pointed out the windshield at the sign. "Two-hour parking."

He leaned over and kissed her hard on the mouth. "What if I want to stay longer than two hours?" His voice was a whisper.

Brooke looked down at her hands and then into Paul's eyes. "Then I think you should say good night here, Paul." She leaned over and kissed him. "Thank you for taking me with you tonight." She opened the car door and stepped out onto the sidewalk.

"Can I call you tomorrow?" The disappointment was evident in his voice.

"I'd like that. I'm having lunch with Rachel after church, so call later in the day. Good night, Paul."

Paul watched her walk up the sidewalk and into the building. Frustration washed over him. He gripped the steering wheel and cursed at the windshield. He wanted her desperately. He loved her beyond what he had believed possible.

Paul signaled and pulled out into traffic. Why did she keep shutting him out? How would he be able to show her what he was feeling if she never allowed herself to be alone with him? Somehow, he had to find a way.

NINETEEN

"MR. APPLETON WANTS YOU IN the conference room. He said 'immediately'," Kelly said from Paul's office doorway.

"Thanks, Kelly." Paul jumped up from his chair and walked quickly to the conference room.

It had been a hectic two days. Stock prices had dropped again slightly Monday, causing another panic among the stockholders. It was Tuesday and the stock value was so low that Paul believed that the only way it could go was up. Several clients had called that morning, filled with rage at Paul for not selling before the bottom fell out of the troubled corporation's value.

Everyone was holding their collective breath, awaiting the outcome of the court proceedings. Paul was especially nervous. He was still confident in his prediction, but if the retailer was found guilty, he was certain he'd be out of a job.

Paul entered the conference room and closed the door. "Good afternoon," he said, moving toward the table.

"Paul, have a seat. It looks like they're about to wrap things up," Pratt said motioning toward the flat TV screen on the wall.

Paul took a seat next to Marshall. Kevin, as usual, was pacing, his hands tugging at his loosened tie. Paul looked up at the screen on the wall. The market standings scrolled along the bottom of the screen. Most of the stocks were up for the day. The retailer, to his surprise, had dropped even lower.

"Marshall," Kevin began to speak.

"Just keep quiet, please," Marshall said impatiently and turned back to the screen.

"Finally!" Pratt said, leaning forward in his seat and folding his hands on the table.

The TV screen showed the steps leading up to the courtroom, a podium and cluster of microphones positioned at the top of the stairs. Members of the press were rushing from all directions, jockeying for a better position near the podium. The doors opened and a group of men and women exited, smiling in triumph.

A man approached the podium. The caption at the bottom of the screen identified him as the lawyer for the defense. "Ladies and Gentleman," he said into the microphones. "America's legal system has once again proven fair and impartial. After many hours of testimony from both sides of this issue, my clients have been found not guilty!"

"Thank God!" Pratt said, jumping up from the table. He reached down and shook Paul's hand. "You did it again! I'm sorry I ever doubted you!" Pratt opened the door and yelled out to whoever was in earshot. "Wine! We need wine!" He returned to Paul's side and slapped him hard on the back.

Marshall stood and smiled. "Good work, Paul."

Pratt's secretary entered the room with a bottle of wine. She smiled at the men, uncorked the bottle before putting it on the sideboard, and left the room quietly. Pratt poured the wine into four glasses and passed them out.

Kevin declined his glass and walked over to Paul. He sighed and shook Paul's hand. "Good job." He mumbled something about a meeting and left the conference room.

Marcus entered as Kevin left. He watched Kevin go down the hall. "I thought the news report was positive. He just left here like it was doomsday!" Marcus shook his head as he walked over to Paul and shook his hand. "Great job, young man!"

"Thank you," Paul said, rising from his chair. "Now I might actually be able to sleep tonight!" he said with a laugh.

"Yes, you'd better!" Marcus chuckled.

"Have a seat, everyone," Marshall said, motioning toward the table.

Paul sat back down. Once they were all seated, Marshall leaned forward and folded his hands on the table. "You've surprised us all, Paul. Most men in this business with your insight and ability are much older. They've been around the block a few times. You, on the other hand, just seem to have this natural ability."

Marshall paused and looked at Pratt and Marcus before continuing. "We think it's time for you to move to the next level with this company. It would take you one step below a partnership. Do you think you're up to the challenge?"

Paul sat back in his chair, stunned. He looked at the three men sitting in the room with him. Marcus reached over and squeezed his shoulder encouragingly. "I think I am," Paul replied, his head swimming with excitement.

Marcus looked at Marshall with a smile. "I knew he wouldn't let us down!"

Marshall looked back at Paul. "I had a feeling you wouldn't pass up this opportunity! When you get back from your first assignment in your new position, we'll have your new office ready."

"Get back? Get back from where?" Paul asked.

Marcus leaned toward Paul. "Greece."

"Greece? What would you be doing in Greece?" Brooke asked when Paul phoned her with the news.

"Marcus has a business associate there who would benefit from our international management. Marshall and Pratt want me to fly over and present our package to him. Marcus will be there for the initial introduction, just to make everyone comfortable. I'm so sorry, Brooke. I know I promised to help you move Nick into his new apartment, but I won't be back until Fourth of July weekend."

"It's okay, Paul. You can't *not* go where your boss sends you. Besides, you'd be crazy to pass up an opportunity like this.'

Paul chuckled. "I admit I'm not the least bit upset about going; it is a chance of a lifetime."

"Just be careful and take care of yourself. Don't worry about Papa. I already have Shaun and Pastor Brian, and Daddy is coming down to help. I'm sure we can manage."

"I'll be in touch, Brooke. Try not to miss me *too* much," Paul added, jokingly.

"Oh, I'm sure I will make it through somehow. Rachel needs my help with bridesmaids' dresses, and I have some finishing work to do for 'Madame Butterfly.' I've no doubt I can keep myself occupied," Brooke laughed.

Brooke sat for a moment after the call ended, considering the conversation. She didn't know how to feel. She was in love with Paul. She would miss him while he was away.

She also experienced a sense of relief. Since the night of the dinner party, she had been filled with confusion over their relationship. She was worried about him – not only for his safety, but also because of the world he seemed to be a part of. His main focus seemed to be on wealth and prosperity. While she knew there was nothing wrong with having either, Paul seemed to place them above anything else. He worshipped money and status like an idol on a shelf. That caused her great concern. She needed this time apart to think.

"You seem to be off in your own little world, Brooke," Rachel laughed as Brooke looked up from her work.

"Why? What do you mean?" Brooke asked, reaching for the scissors and cutting the thread from the hem on the flower girl's dress.

"I just asked if you wanted to take a break and get some dinner. Your answer was 'maybe just one cup!' Let me guess – your head is somewhere in, oh Greece, maybe?" Rachel laughed again. "Come on, you REALLY need a break. We've worked for hours. Let's get some dinner!"

Brooke hung the garment with the other completed dresses. She ran her hands over the four gowns on the rack. She and Rachel had worked on the dresses for the wedding party all but one night that week. Rachel had worked on her own gown while Brooke finished the bridesmaid dresses. The only one that remained was the dress Brooke would wear.

Brooke picked up her purse and smiled at Rachel. "I guess I do need a break. I thought you were asking me if I wanted coffee. I didn't even realize it was dinner time!"

They walked the block from Rachel's apartment to a corner café. "Not bad for a Saturday night," Rachel said when they were seated without a wait.

"Where's Shaun tonight?" Brooke asked after the waitress delivered their water glasses and coffee cups and took their orders.

"He's working on the shop. He wants to have that finished so that he can get right to work on the apartment when your grandfather moves into his new place." Rachel took a sip of her water and shook her head. "Shaun is so worried it won't be ready in time for us to move into. I keep telling him, we still have six weeks for goodness sake! I think we'll make it!"

Brooke laughed. "He just wants everything to be perfect for his bride!" She reached over and squeezed Rachel's hand. "I am so happy for you guys!"

Rachel smiled back at Brooke. "Thanks, Brooke. He really is wonderful."

The waitress returned with their dinner plates, refilled their water glasses and topped off their coffee cups. "Let me know if you need anything else," she said with a smile before moving on to the next table.

"Speaking of wonderful men, did you talk to Paul last night?" Rachel asked before biting into a French fry.

"He called last night. He wanted to make sure I'd received the flowers he'd sent to me at work."

"Ooh, flowers *and* a phone call! He must really miss you! Did he have anything interesting to tell you about Greece?"

Brooke squeezed ketchup onto her burger. "Not too much. He's already gotten the company he was there to see to sign a contract. I guess over the next week, Marcus plans to show Paul around."

Rachel sat back in her seat and looked at Brooke. "I sense a little bitterness in that. Are you jealous that he isn't flying home or is there something else?"

Brooke looked at Rachel over her burger as she took a bite. She dabbed her lips with her napkin and shook her head. "It isn't jealousy. I don't like this Marcus. There's something just weird, creepy about him. I can't explain it. The night I met him at the dinner party, all I could think of was some kind of, oh, I don't know, snake, slithering around. The problem is, he's polished and very charming. He has perfected the art of deception. I just don't trust him. He gives me the willies."

"Brooke, Paul is a grown man. I'm sure he realizes what this guy is if there's anything for him to worry about. I wouldn't let it get you upset."

"I feel it in my spirit, Rachel. I know that all I can do is to pray for him." Brooke paused. She was no longer hungry, her appetite lost as she considered her relationship with Paul. "I'm quickly realizing that Paul doesn't share our faith. I love him. I love him like I never knew was possible, and I'm afraid God is going to ask me to make a choice." Tears filled her eyes as she continued, "A choice between my love for this man and my love for God."

TWENTY

PAUL WAITED AT THE BAGGAGE claim for his luggage to appear on the conveyor. It had been an hour since his plane had landed, but according to an airport attendant, "due to mechanical difficulties," the luggage hadn't been unloaded from the plane.

He was growing impatient. He glanced at his watch for the dozenth time since landing and took a deep breath. His trip had been a huge success, but he was tired and irritable. Athens was seven hours ahead of New York and the flight was eleven hours. His mind was having trouble with the fact that, because of the time difference, the clocks read only four hours later than his departure from Greece. He needed sleep – desperately. Pratt had asked him to stop by the office before going home, which meant he wouldn't get any of that precious sleep for several hours.

Paul took another look at the bags spilling onto the conveyor – still none from his flight. He rubbed his eyes and walked over to the waiting area. He slipped his briefcase under a seat. Sitting with his arms crossed, he leaned his head back and closed his eyes.

Paul jumped when his cell phone rang. He hadn't meant to drift off and was relieved when he looked at his watch and saw that it had only been a few minutes.

Paul cleared his throat before answering. "Hello."

"Paul! It's Pratt. Where are you? Your plane landed an hour ago! Aren't you coming by the office?"

"I plan to. The luggage still hasn't been unloaded, some sort of mechanical problem." Paul could hear laughter in the background. "What am I missing? Sounds like a party."

"No party. Marshall's on the phone with Marcus. It appears you had a successful trip. We're having dinner when we leave here. If you don't make it back by the time the office closes, come to our favorite French place. Don't worry, we won't keep you late. I'm sure you're ready for sleep."

"Okay, Pratt. Sounds good. Hopefully, I won't be too much longer." Paul ended the call and closed his eyes again. *"Not late,"* he thought. He knew better. Pratt didn't believe in early nights.

It was finally announced that the luggage was starting to make its way to the baggage claim. Paul retrieved his bags and left the terminal in search of a cab. By the time he was seated and on his way from the airport, it was too late to go to the office. Paul had the cab take him home and wait for him to drop his bags and wash up. He was back within a few minutes and gave the driver the address to the restaurant.

"Driver, do you mind waiting for me at one more stop? I need to drop something off before you take me to the restaurant," Paul asked.

"Sure, no problem," the driver answered. "Where do you want to stop?"

Paul gave the driver Brooke's address then sat back and watched the people passing by. The cab pulled up to the curb in front of Brooke's building, and Paul got out.

"I'll be right back." He went quickly into the building and left a package for Brooke with the security guard.

"Okay, all set," he said, getting back into the car. He smiled when he thought of Brooke opening the package and couldn't wait to talk to her later. He hoped she'd missed him as much as he'd missed her.

Brooke pushed the button for the elevator and looked up to watch the numbers light up as the car made its way down to the lobby. Her day had been long and tiring. She and Heron had disagreed on one of the costume adjustments. Brooke had given in, trying to keep peace between them. She'd also received a phone call from the detective investigating Ruth's murder. He had more questions about Melissa. She had spent her lunch hour answering those questions. She was glad the day was over.

"Miss Barsanti," David, the security guard called to her.

Brooke turned to see him approaching with a package. "Hi, David. How are you this evening?"

"Very good, thank you. This was delivered for you a short time ago." He handed her the package and smiled. "Have a nice evening."

"Thank you, David."

The elevator dinged and the door opened. Brooke stepped back to allow a small group to exit. She went into the elevator and pushed the button for her floor. When the doors closed, she looked down at the package. The only writing on the paper was her name, nothing more. She shook it gently and listened for any clue as to the contents. The sound revealed nothing.

"Guess you'll just have to be patient won't you?" she said to herself.

Once inside her apartment, she took the package to the living room and sat down on the couch. She removed the paper and carefully opened the simple box. She caught her breath. Under the layers of foam was a beautiful ceramic jewelry box. The ebony lacquer sparkled with specks of gold that appeared to be mixed into the lacquer. The top and sides were inlaid with gold; the ancient Greek picture embossed on the lid was of a woman strumming a small harp beside a fountain.

Inside the box, she found a gold pin shaped like a laurel wreath and a note that read simply "Missing you – Paul." She ran her fingers over the lid, tracing the lines of the engraving that penetrated the smooth surface.

She shook her head in frustration. "I love him, Lord. Please help me to work this out. Please don't take him away from me."

A gentle voice in Brooke's head said simply "Trust Me. Just do what you know is right."

———

Paul dragged into the office Friday morning feeling the effects of serious jet lag and being out too late. As he had suspected, Pratt's idea of "early" was 1:00 in the morning. Daybreak arrived far too early, his alarm jarring him from a deep sleep.

"At least it's a long weekend," he thought, making his way from the elevator to his office. He had considered going to Rockport to see his parents for the July Fourth holiday but decided to stay in New York. He wanted time with Brooke and hoped she didn't already have plans. He also had no desire to spend the weekend in an all-too common religious battle with his parents.

"Good morning, Paul," Kelly greeted him when he approached her desk.

"Morning, Kelly. Pratt told me I had a new office. What are you still doing here?" Paul asked, nodding toward her desk.

Kelly shrugged her shoulders. "He didn't say anything about me, Paul. I boxed up everything from your old office and took it down the hall to your new one, but, well, he didn't say anything about MY moving." Kelly had tears in her eyes. "Does this mean I don't have a job anymore, Paul?"

Paul wrinkled his brow and looked toward Pratt's office. "Don't worry, Kelly. Let me talk to Pratt and find out what's going on. I'm sure there's a good explanation." Paul smiled at Kelly reassuringly and went to Pratt's office.

Paul tapped on Pratt's door and turned the knob. "Pratt?"

"Good morning, Paul. Come in! Are you ready to see your new office?" Pratt rose from his desk and crossed the room greet Paul.

"Yes, I am. Actually, that's why I'm here. Why is Kelly still sitting in front of my old office? She won't do me much good there," Paul said with a nervous chuckle.

Pratt clasped Paul's shoulder. "No worries, Paul. If you want to keep Kelly as your secretary, you can. We just wanted to give you the option of someone, shall we say, better, if you'd like." Pratt gave Paul a knowing look. "Kelly's a great girl, but let's face it, she isn't your best first impression."

Paul smiled at Pratt. He understood exactly what Pratt was implying. Kelly was married and though she was far from unattractive, she was conservative and very professional. Pratt was offering him a single, attractive, "playful" secretary – not at all what Paul wanted.

"Thanks, Pratt. I understand what you're offering and I appreciate it. But, Kelly has been my secretary since I started here and I don't think I'd be able to do it without her. She's like my right arm!"

"No big deal, Paul. Whatever you want! Let's get you moved in."

Paul was shown to an office only a little smaller than Pratt's. The walls were wood paneled from the floor up to a chair rail. Above the rail, the walls were painted an egg shell beige that made the wood in the room stand out. The view of the City was breathtaking.

The dark mahogany book cases that lined two of the walls appeared to have been crafted to match the desk that stood in the center of the room. Leather chairs were set in front of the desk as well as around a small table near the window.

Paul stood in awe and took it all in before looking at Pratt. "I hardly know what to say, Pratt. This is fantastic!"

Pratt laughed at Paul's reaction. "You deserve it Paul! Come on. Let's get Kelly moved to her space out here. We'll offer her a raise, too. How does that sound?"

Paul spent most of the day getting settled into his new office. Kelly was relieved to still be working for Paul. Her eyes had filled with tears when Paul stood before her desk and informed her of her "new position" and the pay increase she would receive as the secretary to an almost-partner.

Paul had everything put away – pictures on the walls, private files in the appropriate drawers, his desk in order – by the end of the day. He spent the final hour answering emails and making a list of calls that had to be made when the office opened Tuesday morning. His promotion meant that several of the "smaller clients," as Marshall had labeled them, would be turned over to account managers.

"Your time must be dedicated to our more prestigious clients," Marshall had explained when Paul had objected to turning over some of his accounts. "It's the way the business works, Paul."

Paul completed his list and made a few notes on his calendar before shutting down his computer for the day. It troubled him to be giving up some of the people he'd been working with since he'd started with Appleton, Murphy & Young. He didn't think of any of them as "small clients." Each one had played a role in getting him to his current position. How was he going to explain the need to turn them over to someone else? It just didn't seem right.

"Leaving soon?" Pratt asked from his doorway, startling him from his thoughts.

"Yes, I am. I think I'm still feeling the effects of jet lag. Hopefully, the weekend will help me get back on New York time." Paul rose from his chair and picked up his briefcase.

"Got plans for the weekend?" Pratt asked, crossing his arms and leaning against the doorframe.

"Not too many. I want to help Brooke finish moving her grandfather into his new apartment. And, I'd like to spend a little time with her, but other than that, no real plans."

"Great! I'll call you tomorrow. We should go out to celebrate your promotion!"

Pratt walked with Paul to the elevators. "Enjoy your time with your girl," he said with a wink as Paul stepped onto the elevator.

Paul laughed and waved him off. "Yeah, nothing is quite as exciting as helping a 70-something year old man unpack boxes. I'm sure we'll have a most romantic evening!"

"You never know," Pratt grinned as the elevator doors closed.

"Papa, here's another box for the kitchen," Brooke called out as Shaun unloaded more boxes from the moving truck. "Are you ready for it in there yet?"

Pastor Brian and Shaun had helped her father unload the U-haul with the boxes she'd helped him pack up over the previous evenings. Brooke had gone straight from work that night to the new apartment to help unpack the necessities and get Papa settled in for the night.

"What's listed on the side of the box?" Nick asked from the kitchen.

"Umm…toaster, blender, grinder, coffee pot…"

"Yes! Definitely! That coffee pot is the necessity right now! If we can find the coffee beans, we'll be good to go!"

Brooke laughed as she carried the box into the kitchen. "How do you ever get to sleep at night, Papa? You drink more coffee than I do!"

"Old age will overpower caffeine any day!" he replied with a chuckle.

Brooke cut the tape from the box and unpacked the appliances. Removing the plastic wrapping, she handed each item to Papa to be put where he wanted it. When she finally found the coffee pot and grinder, Papa smiled and said "Break time!"

Brooke laughed and shook her head at him. "I'm surprised you didn't hand-carry that pot and hook it up the minute we got here!"

"Why didn't I think of that?" Papa wrinkled his brow in mock puzzlement.

Brooke laughed again and looked at her watch. "You know, Papa, it's after 6:00. We may want to make this little break a dinner break."

"I know. Your father and Pastor Brian are already on their way to pick up pizza and wings. What time did you say Paul was planning to meet us?"

"He said he'd be here right after work. I'm sure with being out of town for a couple of weeks and the holiday on Monday, he had to get caught up. He might be a little late." Brooke dragged another box into the kitchen. "Hopefully, he won't be too much longer. I was hoping he'd be here to help Shaun with the heavy stuff. Pastor Brian has a meeting tonight and I'd rather not have Daddy lifting any more than he has to."

"Well, you know your father. He'll balk if you try to tell him to avoid the heavy stuff."

"I know! That's exactly why I wish Paul would get here."

"I heard my name in there!" a voice called from the living room.

Brooke stood up and looked at Papa. Papa laughed, "I believe Prince Charming has arrived."

Brooke gave him an exasperated look before going from the kitchen to the living room. She had to resist the urge to run across the room. "Paul," she said, walking to him and putting her arms around him. "I'm so glad you're here."

Paul kissed her tenderly and looked into her eyes. Smiling, he said softly "I missed you too."

"Okay, you two," Papa said from the doorway. "There will be enough time for that later. We have boxes to unpack."

Paul laughed and walked over to him. "It's good to see you again, Nick. I've missed our discussions over these last two weeks."

"I've missed them, too," Nick answered. "Thanks for coming over to help us out tonight. I'm sure you're exhausted and would rather be sleeping tonight."

"I'm beyond exhausted, but if I don't get back on New York time, I'll never recuperate. So, this is the best place for me to be right now. Besides," he added quietly, "it sounds like Brooke really wants to work me to death tonight."

"I heard that!" Brooke said, swatting Paul playfully on the arm.

Paul laughed and pulled Brooke close for another kiss before she returned to unpacking the box in the kitchen. After taking off his tie and jacket, he turned to Nick and asked "Well, where do I start?"

It was nearly 10:00 before Paul and Shaun finished unloading and arranging the furniture. Shaun wished everyone a happy Fourth of July weekend and said his good-byes.

"I should probably be going soon, too," Paul said, trying to stifle a yawn.

"You didn't drive, did you?" Brooke asked. "I'd hate for you to fall asleep driving home."

"No. I took the subway. I'll probably just take a cab. Do you want me to wait so you can ride with me?" Paul asked, hoping Brooke would agree to share his cab.

"I want to stay for a little bit longer. I haven't had much time with Daddy and I want to make sure Papa is settled before I leave."

"Okay. I want to help again tomorrow. What time is everyone getting here?" Paul asked, looking at Nick.

"Brooke is the 'everyone' tomorrow," Nick answered. "You'll have to ask her."

"No one else is coming to help?" Paul asked with surprise.

Brooke shook her head. "Pastor Brian and Lauren have a wedding ceremony tomorrow, and Shaun and Rachel have plans for the day. I want to be here around 9:00 in the morning, but if you want to get some rest, don't feel like you need to be here that early."

"Nine it is," Paul said with a smile. He said good-bye to Nick and Martin and then reached for Brooke's hand.

"I'll walk out with you," she said, smiling at him.

Brooke and Paul walked to the lobby. Paul leaned over, kissed her gently and held her close for several minutes. "I've missed you, Brooke," he finally said quietly, pulling away and looking into her eyes.

"I've missed you too."

"Do you think we'll be done early enough tomorrow for dinner?" Paul asked, running his fingers over her cheek.

"I would think so. There isn't much left to do."

"Good. I'd like to spend some alone time with you. We haven't had much time to talk. I'll see you in the morning, then." He kissed her again and went out into the City night.

"Good morning," Gianna greeted Paul with a bright smile as she handed his cup over the counter to him. "I was worried you had started getting your morning coffee somewhere else," she said accusingly.

Paul laughed. "No, definitely not! I was in Greece for two weeks. Believe me, there isn't another place in New York that serves the coffee you do!"

"Good. I would have been upset with you if you were going somewhere else!" She wagged her finger at him. "Nicholas tells me you are helping him move into his new apartment. That's very kind of you."

"He's become a good friend. I'm on my way over there now and want to take a box of cookies along. What are his favorites?"

Gianna laughed. "Anything with sugar!" She boxed up a tray of cookies and waved away his money. "Tell my stubborn old friend I say 'hello.'"

"I will. Thank you, Gianna!" Paul left the café and started toward the curb.

"Looks like we had the same idea," he heard from behind him. He turned and saw Brooke standing by the café door.

Paul laughed. "Well, good morning. I guess we did!" He reached for her hand and kissed her lightly before waving down a cab.

"Did you enjoy Greece?" Brooke asked once the cab was on its way.

"I did. It was such a beautiful country. I spent the whole time in Athens, but it's a gorgeous city with so much to see. I hope you like the box," Paul said, taking her hand.

"I do, Paul. It's beautiful."

The cab let them out in front of Papa's building. Paul pulled Brooke to him for another kiss. Brooke stepped away and looked down at her feet.

"You're getting shy on me again," Paul said quietly.

Brooke shrugged her shoulders and looked up at him. "This is still new to me, Paul. I'm not used to getting so much attention."

"Come on. Let's go in and finish getting your grandfather settled. I'd like to have plenty of time to pay attention to you tonight."

"I think that does it, Papa," Brooke said, putting the last stack of dishes into the cupboard. "Is there anything else you want us to do?"

"No, I don't think so. Are you staying for dinner or are you leaving us two old men to fend for ourselves?" Papa asked, nodding toward Brooke's father.

"Old?" Martin said in mock surprise. "Who are you calling old? I think you'd better speak for yourself!"

Brooke laughed and shook her head. "Paul and I have dinner plans, so yes, you too are going to have to fend for yourselves!"

"Alright, if you two don't want to spend an exciting evening with your grandfather and your father, fine," Nick looked at Brooke and Paul, pretending to be hurt. "Thanks for all of your help," he said, shaking Paul's hand. "You too, Sweetheart," he said, hugging Brooke.

"Coming to church with me in the morning, Daddy?" Brooke asked her father as she hugged him.

"That's my plan," he said, kissing her on the cheek. "Have a good time tonight," he said, waving to Paul and Brooke as they left the apartment.

"I want to go home and get washed up and changed before we go," Brooke said to Paul as they left the apartment. "Do you want to pick me up or do you want me to meet you somewhere?"

"I'd like to shower, too. So, how about if I pick you up around 6:00? Will that give you enough time?"

"Plenty of time. I'll see you at 6:00."

Paul kissed her good-bye and waved down a cab. Brooke watched him get in and pull away from the curb before making her way to the subway. She felt uneasy as she went down the steps to the subway platform. The feeling stayed with her all the way home and through the afternoon as she readied herself for her date.

"God, what's wrong with me? Why am I feeling this way? Please, Lord, show me what it is and give me Your peace," Brooke prayed as she locked her door and rode the elevator down to the lobby to meet Paul.

Paul was waiting for her by the security desk when Brooke stepped out of the elevator. "You are beautiful," Paul said as she approached him. He took her hand and kissed her softly.

The anxious feeling again assaulted her as she looked into Paul's eyes. "Please, Lord…" Brooke prayed silently as she let Paul lead her out into the night.

"I hope you don't mind, but I got a call from Pratt after I left you this afternoon and he wants to meet for cocktails after dinner," Paul said to Brooke as they pulled up to the restaurant.

"No, I guess that's okay." Brooke tried not to sound disappointed.

"We won't stay long, I promise," Paul said, taking Brooke's hand. "Pratt is hard to say 'no' to and he is my boss."

"I understand. I'll just stay close to you!"

Paul laughed. "I'll protect you. You have nothing to worry about."

The restaurant was crowded with people waiting for a table. Paul took Brooke's hand and led her to the front of the line. "Paul Matthews – table for two," he said to the host.

"Right this way," the host said with a smile, leading them to a corner table near the back of the restaurant.

"Looks like you called ahead," Brooke said with a smile as the host pulled her chair out for her.

Paul sat down and folded his hands under his chin. "Well, I guess I planned ahead a little bit," he said, smiling at Brooke.

Their waiter approached their table, uncorked the wine and poured a glass for Paul to test. Paul nodded his approval and the waiter poured a glass for Brooke. He filled their water glasses and left them to look at the menu.

"Why do I get the feeling you're up to something?" Brooke asked after the waiter had taken their orders.

"Not up to anything. I just wanted to treat you to a nice evening. I haven't spent any real time with you in two weeks." Paul reached for her hand.

The waiter returned with their dinners and topped off their water glasses. Paul sipped his water and looked down at his lap as Brooke blessed their dinner. "I'm still having trouble getting used to that," he said when she looked back up at him.

"Why? Does it make you uncomfortable?" Brooke asked, tilting her head to one side.

Paul shrugged his shoulders. "A little. It just isn't something I've done in a long time." Paul reached over and squeezed her hand. "Don't worry about it. I'll get used to it again in time," he said with a smile.

Paul spent the rest of their dinner telling her about the places he'd visited in Athens. "I wish I had thought to bring my camera tonight so you could see the pictures I took. You would love the pictures of the Acropolis. The Parthenon is lit up at night. I got a great picture of that."

"It sounds lovely, Paul. I'd like to see them." Brooke pushed her plate back and finished her water.

Paul paid the check and stood to pull Brooke's chair out. Brooke took his arm and let him lead her out into the night. She leaned her head against his shoulder while they waited for the valet to bring the car around.

They rode in silence to the lounge where they were to meet Pratt. Brooke took a deep breath before getting out of the car when they arrived. Paul took her hand as they entered the lounge. "I promise we don't have to stay long."

"Paul," Pratt said from across the room. "I've been waiting for you."

"You remember Brooke," Paul said, nodding in Brooke's direction.

"I could never forget such a lovely woman," Pratt said, taking Brooke's hand and pulling her forward to kiss her on the cheek. "I'm glad you were able to join us tonight."

Brooke pulled away from him and slipped her hand into the crook of Paul's arm. She smiled at Pratt. "Thank you for the invitation."

Pratt smiled and nodded toward a table on the other side of the room. "Let's get you two a drink."

The waitress approached the table. "What's everyone drinking?" Pratt asked.

"Just water," Brooke replied.

"Water? Come on Sweetie, surely at least a glass of wine?" Pratt asked with a laugh.

"No, thanks. I had wine with dinner. Water, please," Brooke said to the waitress.

"Coffee for me," Paul said. "I'm driving," he said to Pratt before he could comment.

"This should be quite a party," Pratt responded sarcastically. "Well, Honey, I guess I'll have another vodka & tonic."

The waitress nodded and went to the bar for their drinks.

Pratt stood and smiled as a young woman approached the table. "Paul, Brooke, this is Tiffany."

Tiffany smiled and then excused herself to the ladies room. Brooke watched the woman walk away and looked at Pratt. "Where's Marjorie tonight?" she asked, her voice strained.

Pratt smiled at Brooke. "She and the girls are home, where Marjorie prefers to be."

Brooke nodded and looked at Paul. Paul shook his head as if to say "Don't ask me now."

"Did Paul tell you about his big promotion?" Pratt asked Brooke.

"Yes, he did. It sounds rather exciting," she answered, keeping her eyes on Paul and trying to sound more relaxed than she felt.

Pratt laughed and slapped Paul on the back. "He'll be a rich man soon. He's well on his way."

Pratt looked up with a smile as Tiffany returned and took the seat next to him. She whispered something that made Pratt laugh and shake his head.

Brooke set her jaw and looked at Paul. "I'm sorry Paul. I hate to be the party killer, but I'm so tired. I don't think I can keep my eyes open." She rose from the table and smiled at Pratt. "I apologize. It's been a long week and I'm completely exhausted."

Paul stood and shook Pratt's hand. "Sorry, Pratt. I'll call you tomorrow." He smiled at Tiffany and turned to Brooke. She slipped her hand into his as they left the lounge.

Paul helped Brooke into the car and started the engine. He gripped the wheel and looked over at her. "I'm sorry Brooke, but what just happened in there?"

Brooke was quiet for a moment before looking at Paul. "How can you spend an evening with that man, watching him cheat on his wife? I just don't understand it."

"Brooke, he's my boss. What am I going to say? 'Sorry, I can't meet you for a drink because I think you're a jerk for cheating on your wife?' It doesn't work that way. I'm sorry, Brooke. I had no idea you'd be so uncomfortable. I guess I've gotten used to it."

Brooke shook her head and crossed her arms. "I don't think I could ever get used to that."

"You'd be surprised at what you can adjust to when you're around it all the time," Paul said to her before pulling into traffic.

Brooke stared out the window at the traffic as they drove through the City. "What are we doing here?" she asked when Paul pulled into the parking garage of his building.

He parked and turned off the engine. "Come on. I want to show those pictures of Greece."

Brooke looked up at him as he opened her door and helped her out of the car. "I don't know if this is such a good idea, Paul. Maybe you should take me home and just bring the camera with you the next time we go out."

Paul smiled and took her hand. "Relax. I'm not ready to say good night." He nodded toward the elevator and tugged at Brooke's arm.

Brooke sighed and followed Paul. They rode the elevator up to his condo in silence. The doors opened and Paul stepped out. "Come on," he said to Brooke with a chuckle. "You really need to relax."

Brooke followed Paul into his condo. Paul motioned for her to sit on the couch. "I'll get the camera. Do you want a drink? Wine, soda, water?"

Brooke shook her had and took a seat on the couch. She watched Paul go into the next room and tried to calm the heavy beating of her heart. The disquiet rose up in her again.

Paul returned with the camera. He turned it on and sat down next to Brooke. "Here. Look at these pictures. The first few are of some the streets I explored. The little shop there is where I bought your jewelry box."

Brooke relaxed as she looked through the pictures. He described the areas around the different places he'd visited, pointed out the sites and explained what each one was.

"My favorite had to be the museum. I couldn't take pictures inside, but the artifacts and sculptures were absolutely breathtaking." Paul put the camera on the table after they'd viewed the last picture.

"It sounds wonderful, Paul," Brooke said smiling at him. "I would love to see it someday. I've hardly been anywhere. My family is from Italy and I've never been there. We've been to Canada, of course, and visited a few states here in the US, but I've never been to Europe. Someday, I hope to go."

"You'll love it," Paul said, pulling her close to him. He kissed her hard and pulled away to look into her eyes. "I love you, Brooke. I want to show you all of the places I've been. I want to share everything with you," his voice deep and husky. He pulled her against him again, kissing her more firmly, his fingers clutching her hair.

Brooke's body grew warm as she was filled with desire for him. Her heart beat hard against her ribs, the sound of it echoing in her ears. "I love you too, Paul," she whispered, his lips brushing against hers.

"I want you, Brooke," Paul said, pulling her closer to him.

Brooke's heart beat harder, the rhythm changing from desire to fear. She began to shake as a voice in her head yelled "What are you doing Brooke? Do you know what you're doing?"

Panic filled her as she pushed away from Paul. Shame washed over her as she realized what she had been about to do. She rose quickly from the couch and hugged herself. She shook violently; her teeth started to chatter.

"Brooke? Are you all right?" Paul asked, rising from the couch and reaching for her.

Brooke stepped back and put her hand up to keep him away. Tears welled up as she shook her head at Paul. "Please, Paul. Don't touch me," she choked.

Paul reached for her, but she twisted from his grip. "Paul! Please, I can't!"

He let his hands drop to his sides. "Brooke, I understand being nervous, but you look terrified. What's wrong?"

Brooke shook her head again and choked down a sob. "I can't do this. It isn't right. I love you, Paul, but I can't do what you're expecting me to do." She reached for her purse and moved toward the door.

"Brooke, wait." Paul rushed to the door and pushed it closed. "Please, don't leave like this. Sit back down. If you're not ready, I can wait."

Brooke looked up into Paul's eyes. Tears streamed down her cheeks. "I'm waiting for marriage, Paul."

Paul dropped his hand and took a step back. "Brooke, you're a grown woman. You realize how unrealistic you're being, don't you?"

Brooke smiled weakly and nodded. "I know, Paul. You have to understand, I just can't give you what you want." Brooke opened the door and left.

Paul stared at the door. He couldn't believe he'd just let her leave. He started toward the door and stopped, the voice of his brother running through his head, *"If she has to choose between her faith in Christ and you, you're gonna lose."* Paul closed his eyes at the memory of Jason's words.

Paul turned the deadbolt on his door and went back to the couch, his shoulders slumped in defeat. He sat down and raked his fingers through his hair and looked up at the ceiling. "I guess You won," he said, a sense of loss washing over him. He slumped back on the couch and closed his eyes, the image of Brooke's face streaked with tears etched in his mind.

Brooke walked several blocks before finally waving for a cab. She didn't know what to do. She was overcome with shame and guilt. She hugged herself as the shaking started to take over her body again.

"Miss, are you alright?" the cab driver asked, turning around in his seat. "Do you need to go to the hospital?"

Brooke shook her head and cleared her throat. "No, I'm okay, thank you." She gave him Pastor Brian's address and sat back in the seat. She prayed that he and Lauren would be home.

The lights were off at the house when they pulled up. Brooke paid the driver and declined his offer to wait. Brooke took a deep breath and went up the steps. She rang the bell and prayed again that they would be home.

Lauren answered the door, her bathrobe pulled tight around her. "Brooke? Honey, are you okay?" she asked, taking Brooke by the arm and leading her into the house.

Brooke shook her head and felt the tears start to roll down her cheeks again. "Lauren, please. I really need to talk to Pastor Brian. Is he still up?"

"He is, Honey. Sit down. I'll get him for you."

Lauren returned with Pastor Brian. Brooke looked up and started to sob. Lauren and Brian sat on the couch, one on either side of Brooke, and wrapped their arms around her.

"Child, tell me what's wrong," Brian said after a time. He rose from the couch, gave Brooke a tissue and pulled a chair over so he could sit in front of her. He leaned forward, letting his arms rest on his knees.

Brooke wiped her eyes and told him about the evening with Paul. "I failed, Pastor Brian. I failed horribly," she sobbed.

Brian sat back in the chair and folded his arms. "How did you fail?"

Lauren put her arm around Brooke again and hugged her tightly. "Honey, you didn't fail."

"Yes I did," Brooke said looking first at Lauren and then at Pastor Brian. "Don't you see? I *wanted* to give myself to Paul. If the voice in my head hadn't spoken when it had, I probably would have. I feel like a terrible person. I've failed God."

Brian leaned forward again and took Brooke's hand. "Look at me, Brooke." When her eyes met his, he smiled. "You didn't fail. You didn't give in. You ran when God made a way for you to escape. You *listened* to that voice and left. Honey, that isn't failure."

Brooke nodded and wiped her eyes. "I love him. I know I can't see him anymore, though. Not like we have been. We don't share the same faith and I can't take the chance that next time, I won't be strong enough to run."

Pastor Brian squeezed her hand. "I think that's a wise decision, Brooke. Trust in the Lord. He'll bring you through this and believe me, you'll come out on the other side stronger than you imagined possible. His plans for you are greater than any you could make for yourself. Just surrender to Him."

TWENTY-ONE

THE SUNLIGHT STREAMED BETWEEN THE slats of the blinds and cast ribbons of warmth across Paul's bedroom. Paul rolled over, locked his fingers behind his head, and stared up at the ceiling. He was wide awake at 6:30, despite having slept very little. It had been a late night. Once he did crawl between the sheets, his sleep had been fitful.

The same tear-streaked image of Brooke was in his mind that had been there when he'd gone to bed the night before. He had gone over the events of the evening repeatedly and couldn't understand what had happened. He loved Brooke and he knew that she loved him.

Jason's voice again invaded his thoughts – *"you're gonna lose."*

Paul took a deep breath and threw the covers off in frustration. Sitting on the edge of the bed, he raked his fingers through his hair and shook his head. He had trusted God once. He had planned his life and future around his faith. He had chosen a seemingly godly woman to share his life with. How had that turned out? She had fallen into the arms of another.

"Nope. Not going down that road again," Paul said to himself. "I love Brooke and I'll do whatever I can to prove it to her, but I'm not falling into that pit of legalism and hypocrisy again. If she chooses a list of rules over me, so be it."

Paul stood up and grabbed his robe. He debated meeting Brooke outside her church after the service. He wanted to spend some time with her, to try to come to some compromise. There had to be some way to work it out.

Paul took his coffee and paper out to the balcony. It was a warm morning and the fresh air helped to relieve some of his tension. He read the paper and ate his breakfast before deciding against trying to see her after church. Her church was her territory. Better to meet her on neutral ground.

Paul showered and left the condo. He boarded the subway, uncertain of his destination. He considered going to see Nick and asking his advice, but thought better of it. Brooke probably had told him about what had happened. Nick knew Paul well enough that he may give the benefit of the doubt on his intentions.

Her father was still visiting. He, on the other hand, might not be as understanding. Paul had visions of some Indiana Jones style booby-trap with his name on it waiting for him should he show his face. No, better stay away until her father had returned to Syracuse.

Paul left the subway and walked a few blocks. The sunshine and warm breeze led him to the Park. He stuffed his hands into his pockets and strolled down the path that led to the bench at the pond he and Brooke had shared a few weeks prior. Another couple was sitting on the bench, their hands intertwined, the young man whispering something into the young woman's ear.

Paul turned away, his shoulders slumped. His steps took him to the deli near the zoo. The smell of fresh bread made his stomach grumble. He looked at his watch – 2:30 and he hadn't eaten lunch.

He moved toward the door and paused at the sound of children's laughter ringing through the air. He looked up in time to see a group of children leaving the zoo, papers clutched in their hands. Most were holding the hands of mothers and fathers, a few showing off whatever was on their papers. Families were out sharing their holiday weekend. He was alone, feeling a twinge of regret at not having gone to Rockport.

Paul watched the little group for another moment before going into the deli. He ordered his lunch and went back outside to sit on the patio. He sat at a table near the trees and watched the people come and go. He couldn't shake the loneliness he was feeling. He stared into his glass, wondering again how to get through to Brooke.

"Paul?"

Paul looked up from his glass and saw Shaun walking across the deli patio. He walked over and shook Paul's hand. "I thought that was you. How are you?"

Paul smiled and motioned for Shaun to sit down. "Great. Just out enjoying the summer weather. How about you?"

"I had a class this afternoon and thought I'd grab a quick bite before going to pick up Rachel." Shaun pointed toward the deli entrance. "Mind if I run in and get a sandwich? I'm starving!"

Shaun went into the deli and came back out with his lunch. He sat across from Paul, took a bite of his sandwich and shook his head. "This place has the best roast beef in the city!"

"I can't argue with that!" he said, picking his own sandwich up from his plate and taking a bite. "What kind of class do you have on a Sunday in the summer, Shaun?"

"The school system has a summer program for the elementary school kids. They offer art classes that take the kids to different parts of the City, sort of a summer camp. I usually teach three a week. The woman who does the Sunday classes fell Friday and sprained her hip. I was asked to fill in so that the kids could still have their class. I couldn't say no."

"Sounds like a fun way to spend the summer," Paul said with a laugh. "For the kids anyway!"

"Oh, I love it. Today, we drew our favorite zoo animal. Most of the kids are around seven or eight years old, so you can imagine how interesting some of the drawings were. I had one little boy draw a squid! They don't even have a squid in the zoo! It was hilarious! They are so easy at this age – enthusiastic. And the kids that come to the summer program, most of them anyway, are here because they want to be, unlike the kids during the school year who are there because they have to be."

Paul finished his sandwich and picked up his glass. He took a drink and set the glass back down on the table. Taking a deep breath, he looked back up at Shaun. "Did you go to church this morning?"

Shaun nodded and smiled. "Yes, I did. And, yes, I talked to Brooke. She was telling Rachel what happened. She's pretty upset."

Paul nodded. He toyed with the straw in his drink. "Any suggestions, Shaun? You've known her a lot longer than I have. What can I say to make her understand that I love her and I'm willing to compromise?"

Shaun leaned back in his chair and folded his arms. "Paul, I know without a doubt that she loves you, very much. She won't compromise, though."

Paul leaned forward, crossing his arms on the table. "I'm not asking *her* to compromise. She can keep believing however she wants. I won't pressure her to do anything she doesn't feel ready to do. *I'm* willing to make the compromise."

"True compromise takes two, Paul. What you're asking is for her to give you another chance and you'll be *patient* until she's ready to give you want you want." Shaun paused and considered his words before continuing. "I think I can safely say that Brooke won't refuse to see you. She cares about you. I do believe, however, that your time together will be much different now. I don't think she'll be willing to be alone with you, and I'm certain that your relationship from this point on will be platonic."

"In other words," Paul said, a hint of sarcasm in his voice, "I'm about to get the 'let's just be friends' talk!" Paul shook his head. "I should have known it would end up like this."

Shaun wrinkled his brow and tried to read Paul's expression. "What happened to you, Paul? Why are you so dead set against God and faith? This is what it's really about, isn't it? This isn't about Brooke so much as you and some vendetta against God."

"Let's just say I've been down this road before and didn't like where it took me. You seem to have God all figured out. I doubt you'd understand."

"Try me, Paul. You might be surprised."

Paul looked at Shaun. Shaun sat with his arms crossed, his eyes fixed on Paul. Taking a deep breath, Paul shared with Shaun his religious upbringing, his baptism as a teenager, his failed relationship with Lilly, right through his parents continued push into his adulthood.

"I guess you could say I've had my fill of the hypocrisy and legalism. Don't get me wrong. I still believe in God and Jesus. I just don't believe any more that they spend each minute of the day holding our little hands so that life will be all nice. I learned long ago that sometimes they just don't care," Paul said shaking his head. "So, why live my life pretending that they do?"

"I'm sorry you had to go through that. That had to be hard. But Paul, don't let the actions of a person mold your view of God. Just because everything in our lives doesn't turn out the way we want them to doesn't mean that God doesn't care. Don't reject Him based on the way you've been treated by people."

Paul held up his hand to halt Shaun. "I've heard it all before, Shaun. I know what you're going to say. I'm glad this works for you. I'm glad God has always been there for you. I just can't believe it for myself anymore. I'm going to need some divine proof that He still cares if I'm ever going to jump on that wagon again."

Shaun smiled and nodded at Paul. "I hear you, Paul. Just be careful what you wish for. God just may answer that prayer and it may be in a way that you never expected."

Brooke juggled her sketch book and an over-stuffed picnic basket as she raced down the steps to the subway platform. She was out of breath and wishing she'd taken a cab by the time she was on the train and seated.

She rested her sketch pad against her side and situated the basket between her feet.

"You realize you're breaking one of the cardinal rules in subway safety by carrying so much, don't you?"

Brooke looked up from the basket and laughed. "Hi, Julie. I know. I guess I figured if anyone tried to mug me I could just smack them with the basket. This thing weighs a ton!"

"Where are you headed?" Julie asked, nodding toward the basket.

"I'm meeting Rachel and Shaun in the Park to eat and watch the fireworks. I agreed to bring the food and blanket. They are supposed to be bringing an ice chest with water and soda. I think they got the better end of the deal," Brooke replied with a laugh. "How about you? Are you going to see the fireworks?"

"Yeah, but I'm meeting some friends to take the boat out on the water. We're going to watch them from there. Well, this is my stop. See you at work in the morning." Julie stood up and waved.

Julie stepped off the train and rushed ahead to embrace a young man waiting on the platform. She laughed, kissed him, and waved again at Brooke before wrapping her arm around him walking away.

Brooke felt a moment's regret over Paul as she watched her co-worker. She knew she'd done the right thing, but she still felt like she had lost something wonderful. Why she'd let herself get in so deep, having suspected the differences in their faith early on, she didn't know.

The train slowed and she reached for the basket. Clutching the sketch pad, she stood and waited for the train to stop and the doors to open. She watched as families and couples left the train. She was leaving alone.

She let herself get swept up into the flow of people making their way to the Park. It was a beautiful afternoon. When she reached the path leading to the Great Lawn, she could see blankets spread out like a checkerboard across the expanse. Frisbees flew through the air. The laughter of children and dogs barking filled the air.

She saw Rachel and Shaun waving at her from the middle of the lawn. She waved back and made her way through the crowd. Shaun met her part way and took the basket.

"Good grief! How much food did you pack? There are only three of us Brooke!" Shaun laughed, pretending to struggle with the weight of the basket as they made their way Rachel.

"Hey! You never know if someone else will show up and I like to be prepared," Brooke replied in mock irritation.

"Your dad and grandfather change their mind about joining us? There's plenty of soda and water in the cooler and from the weight of this thing, I think it's safe to say there's enough food."

"No. Daddy and Papa went out to Uncle Vince's yesterday afternoon after church. They planned a big barbecue with most of Rhea's family. I guess there's fireworks somewhere close enough that they can see from the house. I was invited, but decided to just stay in the City," she said with a shrug.

Rachel and Brooke spread the blanket out on the grass. Shaun put the basket down and pulled the ice chest closer to their spot. "Drinks, anyone?" he asked, holding the chest open.

Rachel and Brooke both took a bottle of water. Shaun grabbed a soda. "Am I the only unhealthy one here?" he asked with a laugh.

"Looks like it," Rachel said with a smile.

Shaun took a drink of his soda and looked at Brooke. "I saw Paul yesterday."

Brooke looked up at him and smiled weakly. "Really? Where did you see him?"

"Here in the park. I ran into him at the deli by the zoo. Did you talk to him yesterday? He sounded like he wanted to get in touch with you."

"No. I didn't talk to him. I went to Papa's after church to say good bye before they went out to Uncle Vince's. I spent the rest of the day running errands." Brooke looked around at the other picnicers on the lawn. A group of kids chased a soccer ball. A father and son tossed a baseball back and forth.

Looking back at Shaun, she asked "So, what did he say?"

"He told me about the other night. He wants to come to some sort of compromise with you," Shaun said.

Anger boiled up in her. "Compromise? Did he say what that was supposed to mean? I can't believe he doesn't know me better than that by now!"

Shaun held up his hand. "Hold on, Brooke. He said he didn't expect YOU to compromise what you believe. He believes you two can come to some sort of agreement where he accepts your faith and your desire to wait til marriage so long as you don't try to push what you believe on him." Brooke opened her mouth to speak, but Shaun held his hand up again. "I'm not done, Brooke. Don't get all worked up."

Brooke sat back on her heels and folded her arms. She wanted to ask Shaun why he'd continued to have the conversation with Paul, but decided to be quiet and let him finish.

"I told him it takes two to compromise and that you'd never compromise your faith. I then asked him why he was so set against God. Do you know what he told me Brooke? Has he ever told you anything about his life before coming to New York?"

Brooke shook her head. "Not much. I know he was raised in church. I know he was pretty dedicated for a while, but something happened in college, I guess, that pulled him away. At least, that's what I gathered from what his brother and sister-in-law told me when they were here."

"Brooke, I get the feeling there was some serious legalism in his home. He kept mentioning "hypocrisy" and "rules." He also told me about the Christian girl he was engaged to before he finished high school. She cheated on him and became pregnant by another guy. This was after they had agreed they'd wait until marriage. She refused to name the baby's father and because of that, Paul's parents and the girl's father assumed the baby was Paul's. They never would believe he hadn't touched her," Shaun explained.

Brooke was stunned. She closed her eyes and shook her head. "He never told me any of that. No wonder he's so against the church." She sat quietly, looking down at her empty water bottle. "Shaun, I don't know what to do. I can't do what I know would be wrong. I can't deny my faith because I love someone who has rejected his. Are you trying to convince me to go against everything I believe to be right, to understand what he's been through and go along with this whole compromise thing he's talking about? I don't think I can do that!"

"Brooke, that's not what I'm trying to tell you. No, you definitely can't compromise. You have to follow God's Word on this. I just thought that maybe if you knew what had happened, you'd be able to understand him better." Shaun reached over and squeezed Brooke's arm.

"Well, well, speak of the devil," Rachel said, nodding toward the path.

Shaun and Brooke looked up to see Paul walking through the grass to where they were sitting. Brooke looked at Shaun, an accusing look in her eyes.

"I didn't tell him we'd be here, I promise!" Shaun said defensively.

Brooke rose from the blanket as Paul approached. Paul smiled at her and then nodded toward Rachel and Shaun. "Hi. Great night for this, isn't it? The weather couldn't be any more perfect."

"No, it couldn't," Shaun agreed. He stood and pulled Rachel up with him. He shook Paul's hand and turned to Rachel. "Well, how about if we go for a quick stroll before we eat?"

Brooke looked at Rachel, her eyes pleading with her to stay. Rachel just shrugged her shoulders and let Shaun take her hand and lead her away.

Brooke watched them go and turned back to Paul. "So, how did you know we'd be here?"

"I didn't. It was just a guess. I tried calling your grandfather's and got the answering machine." Paul shrugged his shoulders and put his hands in his pockets. "I thought I'd give it a shot."

Brooke motioned toward the ice chest. "Thirsty? There's water or soda?"

"No, thanks. I just wanted to talk to you for a minute." He took a step toward Brooke. "I'm sorry about the other night. It didn't occur to me that you wouldn't be ready. I thought that we were both ready for the next step."

"Paul, please don't. I've already explained to you why I'm not ready. Things became clear to me the other night. I realize we don't see things the same way."

"Brooke, that doesn't mean we can't be together. I'm willing to try to make it work."

"Shaun told me about your discussion yesterday. Please don't get upset with him for sharing something so personal. He just wanted to help me understand what you've been through."

"I would have been surprised if he hadn't told you, Brooke. Does it help you understand why I feel the way I do, why I pretty much avoid church and the whole religious thing?"

"It does to some degree. I understand that you were hurt by a woman who claimed to embrace Christ." Brooke took a breath and continued, "After meeting Jason and Lydia, however, I don't understand your rejection of your faith. I would think that your brother's faith, even if you feel your parents were a bit legalistic, would convince you of the truth of what real faith is all about."

Paul became defensive. "You can't? With what Shaun told you, with what my parents put me through – how can you say that you don't understand?"

"Paul, please…"

Paul took a step forward. "We love each other Brooke. You can't deny that! How can you feel so strong about your faith when *God* keeps two people from sharing what they feel for each other? How can you say that these *rules* make sense?" Paul set his jaw and glared at Brooke.

"Paul, God didn't make the rules to make our lives difficult. They are meant to protect us…"

"Don't go there," Paul said, cutting Brooke off. "I was raised hearing everything you're about to spew at me. I don't need to hear it again."

"You may have heard it, but it's clear you never took it in. You may have been raised in a Christian home with Christian values, but I believe you never really accepted them as your own."

Paul glared at Brooke before turning to leave. Shaun and Rachel returned as Paul left. Rachel rushed to Brooke's side. Shaun tried to speak to Paul, but Paul pushed him away and stormed off. Shaun looked at Brooke, shrugged his shoulders, and followed Paul.

Brooke sat down and buried her face in her hands.

"It's okay, Honey," Rachel said, sitting down next to Brooke and holding her close.

Brooke looked up and wiped the tears from her face. She could see Paul and Shaun in the distance. Shaun was speaking calmly; Paul was obviously agitated. He finally waved Shaun away and left.

"Well?" Brooke asked when Shaun returned.

Shaun shook his head. "Brooke, I'm sorry, but I think you're going to have to leave him alone for a while. Just pray for him. There's nothing any of us will be able to say to him." Shaun sat down next to Rachel and looked back to Brooke. "If Paul's going to see who God really is, we're going to have to let God show him."

TWENTY-TWO

BROOKE DIDN'T HAVE MUCH TROUBLE keeping her mind off what had happened over the holiday weekend between her and Paul. She still thought about him and prayed for him, but she didn't have time to dwell on it. All of the costumes and props for 'Madame Butterfly' had been approved and with only ten weeks until the opening gala at the Met, they had a lot of work to do.

Heron's team was in the prep room cutting patterns and sorting through notions. Heron was working on the costumes for the main characters while Brooke checked off the bolts of material being delivered. As they were checked off the list, Brooke motioned for Julie to move them to the storage rack.

"Wait, hold on a minute," Brooke said, pulling one of the bolts out of the crate. She unwound a yard of the material and held it up to the light. "This doesn't look right." She went down the list and shook her head, not finding the item she held in her hand.

"Heron, I'm sorry to bother you," Brooke called to her. "Would you mind taking a look at this fabric. I don't think this is what we ordered."

Heron huffed over to where Brooke was standing. "Good God, Brooke. If you can't even check in the material we've ordered…" Heron paused. "This isn't right," she said looking back at Brooke. "This is too light. Let me see the manifest."

Brooke handed the paperwork to Heron. Heron ran her finger down the list and looked again at the bolt end. "No, this isn't even on the list. They sent the wrong stuff." She moved toward the phone then paused. Clearing her throat, she looked at Brooke. "Brooke, how about if you take care of this one. Just ask for Tony. He'll know what to do." She smiled at Brooke and went back to her work.

Brooke watched Heron walk away, stunned by her rare smile and apparent confidence in her ability to handle the problem. "Miracles happen every day," Brooke said to herself, moving toward the phone.

She dialed the number on the manifest and asked for Tony. When Tony was on the other end, Brooke explained the mix-up and requested the correct material be delivered.

"Of course, my dear, of course!" Tony answered with a deep accent Brooke couldn't identify. "Might I ask, where is Heron? She is the one who ALWAYS calls from your team. I heard a rumor she was leaving. Is that true?"

Brooke shook her head. "No, Tony. She's still here. I guess you could say I'm her assistant now. As far as I know, she isn't going anywhere."

"Oh, such good news! Don't worry, Darling. I'll deliver the correct material myself this afternoon."

Brooke hung up from Tony and looked in Heron's direction. She was pinning the sleeve on one of Kimonos for Cio-Cio-San. She looked over at Brooke. "Well? What did Tony say?"

Brooke smiled. "He apologized and promised to personally deliver the correct bolts this afternoon."

Heron nodded. "Good job. Make sure you're here to meet him. I want you to handle it start to finish."

"I will. Thanks, Heron,"

Heron went back to work without answering. Brooke watched her a moment longer, wondering about Tony's question. Brooke shrugged it off as typical industry gossip. She and Heron didn't speak again until lunchtime.

"Brooke," Heron said, pulling her to one side. "I have an appointment this afternoon. Are you sure you can handle Tony on your own? I can have Meryl meet with him if you don't think you can handle him."

"I don't think I'll have a problem. I'll make sure he has the right stuff and then I'll give him what was delivered in its place. If he doesn't have what we ordered, then I'll just hold onto what he sent over."

"Good girl," Heron said, no condescension in her voice. "I won't be back until tomorrow afternoon. Make sure the team stays on schedule. We have too much to do to slack off."

Brooke was again shocked. What was going on? Heron had huge control issues. She had never known Heron to turn any responsibility over to someone else. She wasn't sure if Heron was testing her or if Meryl had instructed her to give Brooke more to handle.

Over the next two weeks, Heron turned more and more over to Brooke. She had even taken two days off, leaving Brooke to oversee the team on her own. When Heron returned, she didn't say a word – positive or negative – about the decisions that were made in her absence. It wasn't until they were at the theatre and a problem arose that Heron's unusual behavior was explained.

"Brooke, do you have a minute?"

Brooke looked up from her pinning.

Sheila, one of the other team members, called from across the room where she was working with one of the extras "I want you to look at this costume."

"Sure. Give me just a second and I'll be right with you," Brooke replied. She finished pinning the costume she was working on and sent the actress to change.

"Okay. What's up?" Brooke asked, walking over to where Sheila was working.

"There's something wrong with this. I think you should see it," Sheila replied, motioning toward the garment.

She stepped away from the woman standing on a stool and allowed Brooke to move closer to examine the costume. The stitches were uneven and the sleeve puckered where it was attached to the bodice.

Brooke closed her eyes and shook here head. "Okay. You can change now. We'll take care of this," she said to the actress. The woman nodded and stepped down from the stool.

"Sheila, who did this costume?" Brooke asked.

"Julie did. I should have noticed before I had the woman try it on, but somehow I missed it. I'm sorry," Sheila responded nervously.

"It isn't your fault. You didn't do the stitching." Brooke looked around the room and found Heron. Looking back at Sheila, she smiled. "Don't worry about it. Get the garment for me once it's available, please, and then just move on to your next assignment."

Once Brooke had the costume in hand, she went to Heron. "Heron, we have a problem. I need to show you some of Julie's work." Brooke spread the kimono out on a nearby table and pointed out the mistakes.

"There is definitely a problem here, Brooke. What are you going to do about it?" She crossed her arms and waited for Brooke to answer.

Brooke looked from Heron to the costume. "Heron, I'm confused. I may have designed this, but I didn't stitch it. Julie did. I thought you should see it so you could talk to her about it."

Heron shook her head. "No, I'm not going to talk to her. YOU are. You designed it. It's your responsibility, not mine." Heron started to walk away.

"Wait, hold on, Heron…"

Heron turned back. "Is there a problem? Are you starting to think you can't handle the tasks associated with your new position? If that's the case, just say so."

"Heron, that's not what I'm saying. I guess I'm just a little bit confused by what's been going on around here lately."

"Confused by what? Meryl promoted you, remember? Part of that promotion involves more responsibility. If he wants you in a better position, fine. I'll do whatever I must to get you ready for that position. If you fall on your face because you can't handle it, well, he'll realize you aren't ready. If you don't fall, then I don't want to be responsible for not giving you everything you need to do the job. So, can you, or can't you, handle this?" Heron asked, again crossing her arms and glaring at Brooke.

Brooke looked down at her feet, said a quiet prayer and then looked back up at Heron. "I apologize, Heron. I didn't realize what you were trying to do for me. Yes, I can handle this. I will show Julie her poor work, give her a chance to do it right and then inform Meryl of the situation."

"Very good. Now, if you will let me get back to work."

Brooke closed her eyes and shook her head. What was she supposed to think? Meryl had told her that she and Heron had to work together. Heron was still the team leader. The only thing he had said was that Brooke answered to him now. It hadn't been clear that she could make decisions about the team without prior approval. If she *had* made a decision on her own, she was sure Heron would have hit the roof.

Brooke picked up the costume and went into the next room. Julie was loading the pinned costumes back into the crates and laughing with one of the other girls.

"Julie, can I talk to you for a minute?" Brooke asked, her heart pounding in her chest.

Julie looked up and smiled, "Of course, Brooke. What's up?"

Brooke motioned for Julie to follow her to the other room. She spread the costume out on the table. "Julie, please look at the stitching on this."

Julie looked at the seams and the puckered sleeve. Her face turned red as she looked back at Brooke. "Am I in trouble?"

"No, Julie, you're not in trouble. I realize we've all been in a hurry lately. I think you were just so focused on getting it done that you didn't take the time to double check your work. The fabric isn't damaged. It will be easy to pull the stitches and redo it. Just slow down, okay?"

Julie nodded. "Do Heron or Meryl know about this, Brooke? Or is it just you and me?"

"Heron knows and I have to tell Meryl. My little promotion, or whatever you want to call it, requires that I fill him in on everything. Don't worry. Heron isn't mad and Meryl won't be either. I'll explain to him the hurry we've been in and that I'm certain this won't happen again."

"Thanks, Brooke. I won't let you down," Julie promised.

Brooke returned to the studio before the end of the work day to talk to Meryl. He smiled when she explained the situation with Julie.

"I hope it's okay that I gave her another chance."

"Yes, Brooke, that's fine. I'm glad you gave her another chance." Meryl paused. "She has made mistakes in the past though, hasn't she?"

"Yes, she has. Rachel and I had to do a lot of extra work on our last show because of her mistakes. But, I didn't think it would be right for me to bring that up since she wasn't working on my costumes then."

"You're right. I'm pleased with your decision. I will be keeping an eye on her, though. If this happens again, I'll have to let her go."

Brooke nodded. "Thanks, Meryl. I understand."

"I'm glad that Heron has taken me seriously about giving you more responsibility. I can see I wasn't wrong in promoting you. What do you think so far?"

"I guess I'm still getting used to it. I'm still trying to figure out what I should be doing on my own and what should still be run by Heron. She is, after all, still the team leader. For right now, I feel better thinking of myself as her assistant."

"Well, don't keep that thinking for too long. Yes, Heron is still the team leader, but I have plans for you. As far as I'm concerned, you and Heron should be working as partners. So far, I think you're off to a good start. Now, get out of here. You should have left half an hour ago!"

"Thanks, Meryl," Brooke said as she left his office.

Brooke stopped by the prep room to make sure the costumes had made it back from the theatre. Once she was sure everything had been returned, she turned off the lights and started for the elevator. Her cell phone rang as she pushed the button.

"Hello?"

"Brooke?" a choked voice asked from the other end.

"Yes, who's this?" Brooke asked.

"Brooke, it's Linda. Honey, you've got to get your grandfather and get to Syracuse now. It's your father."

"Linda, what's happened? Where's Daddy?" Brooke asked, feeling panic rise.

"He's on his way to St. Joe's. He collapsed in the yard. Please Brooke – just hurry!" Linda pleaded and hung up.

———————

Paul rubbed his eyes and stretched his legs out under his desk. He had stared at the computer screen so long that the numbers on the spreadsheet were starting to blur. He looked again at the screen and compared the numbers with the last stock report for the week. He hit the print button and sighed. Two of the stocks that their bigger clients were primarily invested in had been declining.

"Time to make a decision," he said to himself, pulling the paper off the printer. He highlighted the declining numbers and put the pages with the customer files he'd pulled earlier.

"Working late, Paul?" Marcus asked, knocking on Paul's office door while entering.

"Yes. A couple of stocks have me a little worried. Come in. Have a seat," Paul said motioning to the chair next to his desk. "Pratt said you were flying in today. How was your flight?"

"Tedious, as usual. It's after 5:30 on a Friday night. Pratt tells me you were here at seven this morning. Don't tell me you've moved in here?" Marcus asked with a laugh.

"I had no idea it was that late. Hold on a minute, Marcus, please," Paul said before buzzing Kelly. "Kelly, go home. It's late."

"But Mr. Fillman hasn't called back yet. Don't you want me to stay for the phone?" Kelly asked.

"No, he knows our hours and he has my cell number. Go home, enjoy the weekend with husband."

"Thanks, you too. I mean enjoy your weekend, not the husband part," Kelly replied with a chuckle.

Paul laughed and turned back to Marcus. "Sorry about that."

"Not a problem. It's a good thing to take care of your people," Marcus said. "So, when are you leaving for the day? Pratt and Marshall have both mentioned that you've practically moved in to your office over the past couple of weeks. What does your lady have to say about your spending so much time here?"

Paul laced his fingers behind his head. "We're taking a little break. Things were getting too serious too soon."

"Ah, the 'marriage' word came up, did it?"

"It did, but not like you think. I was ready for the next step in our relationship and she swears she's waiting for marriage. I'm not quite ready to take *that* step."

Marcus laughed. "Waiting for marriage? You don't hear that often anymore. Are you sure she isn't trying to bait you?"

"No, I believe she's sincere. And because we don't see eye-to-eye on this one, we thought it best to take a little break, you know, give each other some breathing room."

"Sounds like a good decision to me. You're too young to be tied down anyway. Live a little, Paul, before you get into marriage and family."

Paul nodded. "I think so too."

"So, no lady tonight. That means you don't already have plans, I assume. That's good. We want you to join us for dinner."

"No, I don't have plans. Who all does the 'we' include?"

"Marshall, Pratt, myself, of course, and a friend who flew in this morning whom I'd like you to meet."

"A business associate?"

"Not really an associate, just a friend. He flew in this morning to meet with a friend who's with the U.N. I've invited him to join us for dinner tonight. He'll be here for the weekend and then flies back to France Monday morning."

"Politician?"

"No, he just has a friend who is," Marcus replied. "So, how about dinner?"

"Sounds good, Marcus. I want to run these numbers by Marshall and Pratt before I go," Paul said, rising from his desk.

Marcus and Paul made their way to Marshall's office. Pratt was already seated at the table by Marshall's window, sipping a brandy. "Can I bother you two for a minute?" Paul asked from the doorway.

"Sure, Paul. What is it?" Marshall motioned for him to take a seat.

Paul put the spreadsheet on the table and pointed out the declining stocks. "I'm getting concerned over these. Nothing in the news tells me what's going on with our paper manufacturer, so I can't explain their decline. The other one, though, the plastics manufacturer is going through some kind of reorganization – the owner is aging and ready to step down but doesn't have an heir to pass his 60% ownership to. I guess there's some big disagreement as to what should be done. This one really worries me."

Marshall and Pratt looked at each other and then back at Paul. Marcus smiled a knowing smile, but said nothing. After a moment's silence, Marshall looked back to Paul. "Well, I see your concern. We should encourage our clients to liquidate their stock in our paper people. That one's been pretty short on the gains lately, anyway."

"Okay, that's what I was going to suggest," Paul said. "What about the other one, though? I strongly urge pulling out of that one, too. That to me is the bigger time-bomb. We could find ourselves with completely useless stocks if we hang on to them."

Marshall steepled his fingers under his chin and rocked in his chair. He looked at Pratt. Pratt shrugged his shoulders and folded his arms over his chest.

"Paul, I want to wait on our plastics friends. I think it's a little soon to drop them," Marshall replied.

"They've declined steadily for over a week, Marshall. They've had a rollercoaster ride in the market for some time now. I'm not comfortable with them anymore," Paul countered.

Marcus cleared his throat and nodded to Marshall. Pratt shrugged his shoulders again. Marshall looked back to Paul. "This information doesn't leave this room. I happen to know that there is a buyer for the 60% of that company. It's still in legal, but it's a sure thing. Within a week or two, the stocks should steady and then start to rise again."

"Any idea who the buyer is?" Paul asked.

Marcus raised his hand. "Me. I'm the buyer."

Paul was in the lobby of the Waldorf by 6:45. He wanted to get to Marcus before Pratt and Marshall arrived. Marcus's purchase announcement had troubled him all evening. Something didn't feel right about it. When Paul spotted him, however, he was deep in conversation with a man Paul assumed to be his visiting friend. He would have to either wait for another time to talk to him or find a diplomatic way of bringing it up during dinner. Marcus noticed Paul's arrival and motioned for him.

"Paul, it's so kind of you to join us," Marcus said, extending his hand. "Let me introduce Denis Beck, an old friend of mine."

"Nice to meet you, Mr. Beck," Paul answered.

"No formalities! Denis will do. You are Marcus's friend, therefore you are my friend," Denis replied, shaking Paul's hand with such strength, Paul thought his fingers might snap.

"Come gentleman, Pratt and Marshall will surely find us if we go into the dining room," Marcus said.

Paul followed Marcus and Denis to their table. A waiter hurried to them to fill their water glasses and take their drink orders. "There will be two more," Marcus informed the waiter, who filled two more water glasses.

The waiter was returning with their drinks when Marshall and Pratt arrived. "I apologize for our tardiness, gentleman," Marshall said as he and Pratt took their seats.

Dinner was relaxed, almost casual. Denis asked questions about the business practices common in the United States. Marshall asked Denis about his business and his trip to New York.

"I have a small winery outside of Paris that has been owned by my family for generations. It's modest, but has kept my family comfortable. My trip to New York has been educational and enjoyable, so far," Denis explained with a smile.

Paul was struck by his command of the English language. Despite his accent, he was clear and easily understood.

"Is this your first trip to the U.S., Denis?" Paul asked.

"Oh no. I've been here many times. Today was my first visit to the U.N. That was quite an experience! My friend is new to his post and was most eager to show me around. But, I've been to New York three times now. I've been to Chicago, Miami and San Francisco. I've always enjoyed travel," he said enthusiastically. "My friend Marcus being here was an added bonus!"

Marcus smiled. "Denis and I met at a business expo in Paris several years ago. We've been friends ever since. We try to get together any time we are in the same place at the same time."

When the waiter returned to clear their plates and offered to refill their glasses, Marcus declined. "No, thank you. I believe it's time to take our drinks in the lounge."

"I'm sorry, Sir, but there's a private party in the lounge. Would you care to sit in the lobby? I can arrange for service there," the waiter replied.

Marcus looked around the table. "Well, gentleman. What do you say to strolling down to the little club on the corner? "

"Sounds good to me," Pratt answered, rising from the table.

"I regret, gentleman, that I must return to my room. The time change has completely exhausted me," Denis said.

Marcus reached for the bill.

"No, no, my friend. Please allow me the honor," Denis insisted. "Good night, gentlemen. It has been a pleasure."

The rest of the party walked to the corner lounge. It was busy, but not crowded. They found a table near the back and motioned for the waitress.

"Sherry?" Marcus said looking questioningly at each of the men at the table.

Marshall nodded his agreement.

"Vodka and tonic for me," Pratt answered.

Paul shook his head. "Brandy, please."

Marcus smiled at the waitress, "Two Sherrys, a Vodka and tonic and a Brandy."

She smiled and turned toward the bar. Pratt watched her walk away from the table and shook his head.

"You're looking like a wolf, my friend," Marcus said, folding his arms. "She must be half your age."

Pratt shrugged and laughed. "No harm in looking, right?"

Marcus shook his head and looked at Paul. "I'm sorry you didn't have more time with Denis. You would have found him a most interesting business man."

"I'd have enjoyed talking with him more. I like to find out as much as I can about the different business practices around the world. But, I also understand how exhausting travel can be."

The waitress returned with their drinks and agreed to open a tab in Marshall's name.

"I believe I see an old acquaintance." Pratt said, leaving the table. He was soon laughing with a young woman at the bar.

"Have we ever gone out that he hasn't done this?" Paul asked, irritated.

"No, my friend. I don't believe we have," Marcus replied, shaking his head. "The man just can't help himself."

"I'm sorry. I guess I shouldn't question him," Paul said apologetically. "It isn't my place. I had hoped we'd have a chance to talk business for a while before he was distracted."

"What did you want to discuss, Paul?" Marshall asked. "Is it something Pratt must be included in?"

"No, not really. I'm just curious about the conversation we had before leaving the office today." Paul turned to Marcus. "The company you're buying - they've been an American company for over a hundred years! No one's complaining?"

"No one. Why would they? I can offer financial stability and a promise to keep their workers on. I'm even willing to sign their little Union agreement for the next five years. After that, we'll see. But, this is perfect for everyone involved," Marcus said with a smile.

"How long has this been in the works?"

Marshall and Marcus looked at each other. Marshall shrugged.

"For almost a year now," Marcus answered.

Paul blanched. "A year! We've been encouraging our clients to buy stock in this company when we knew there was going to be a buyout? The owner's retirement didn't even become public knowledge until this week!"

Marcus nodded. "I understand your concern. But Paul, there really isn't anything to be worried about. I have taken care of everything."

Paul looked at Marshall and Marcus. Both seemed to be trying to read Paul's reaction. Marshall cleared his throat. "Are you in any way in disagreement with this? You are, after all, in a decision-making position. Did I make a mistake in thinking we are like-minded?"

"No, Marshall, of course not. If everyone else is happy, I'm happy!" Paul raised his glass. "Let me toast your latest requisition, Marcus!"

Marcus and Marshall raised their glasses in agreement. Paul drained his glass and motioned for the waitress. "I would like to buy the next round of drinks for my friends." Paul turned back to the table and smiled. "I believe we should celebrate."

Marcus smiled back at Paul and clasped him on the shoulder without a word. Paul smiled back, trying to ignore the chill that ran down his spine.

TWENTY-THREE

BROOKE STOOD IN HER FATHER'S backyard, arms crossed, staring down at the dead rose bush. The other three bushes were thick with green leaves and covered with blossoms and new buds. Her father's bush, however, was nothing more than dead twigs pushing up through the ground. She wanted to reach down and yank it out by the roots, but she couldn't bring herself to do it. If there was even a chance it would come back…she just couldn't pull it up.

Brooke wiped the tears from her face. She couldn't get the past three days out of her head. By the time she and Papa had reached the hospital Friday night, her father was in surgery. A nurse had led them to the waiting room on the surgical floor. Linda had been sitting in a corner chair, her face buried in her hands.

Brooke rushed over to her and put her hand on her shoulder. "Linda, we're here. How's Daddy?"

"Brooke, I'm so glad you got here," Linda cried into Brooke's shoulder.

Brooke fought her own tears and pulled away from Linda. "Linda, please, how's Daddy?"

"Not good. He's been in surgery for three hours. They weren't going to tell me anything. I had to lie and tell them I was his girlfriend to get them to tell me that much."

"Why the surgery?" Papa asked, sitting next to Brooke and leaning over to look at Linda.

"Aneurism. I guess there's considerable damage to his heart," Linda replied.

"Linda, tell us what happened," Papa said.

"We were in our yards. He had been working in the rose garden and we decided to pool our food and grill out. He was on his way into the house to see what he had for meat and just collapsed. He was just passed out, not breathing. I ran into the house for the phone, dialed 911, and started CPR. He never woke up," Linda buried her face in her hands again and cried.

"We need to pray," Brooke choked out.

The three of them were huddled together in prayer when Uncle Vince and Rhea had arrived. Within half an hour, Aunt Maria was also there.

It was after 11:00 before a doctor finally walked through the door of the waiting room. Brooke looked up and felt dread wash over her at the doctor's grim expression. She tried to fight the sobs rising up in her as the doctor approached.

"Barsanti family?"

"Yes, I'm Brooke Barsanti, Martin's daughter," Brooke whispered.

She remembered Papa taking her hand as the doctor said, "We're sorry, but your father didn't make it. We were unable to repair the damage from the aneurism. I'm so sorry for your loss." He looked around at Brooke's family standing around her and left the room.

Brooke heard the back door to the house open, the soft music from the living room escaping and interrupting her thoughts. Laughter mixed with the music. The family and friends from her father's funeral were gathered inside, celebrating her father's life. She didn't feel much like celebrating.

The door closed, shutting the music and laughter back inside. The sound of footsteps approaching was all Brooke heard over her own heartbeat.

Pastor Mark stood beside her. Since she'd been a child, Brooke had known him and his wife, Madeline. She had grown up with their boys, attending the same schools and church. Her first crush had been on their oldest boy, Steven, who was now a pastor himself. Mark and Madeline were Brooke's other parents.

Pastor Mark reached over and put his arm around Brooke's shoulder. "Let it out, Honey," he said quietly.

Brooke shook her head and choked down a sob. "I'm trying not to ask God the 'why' questions, but I can't help it. I have a lot of them right now."

"I understand, Brooke. God never told us not to cry when we lose someone. Even Jesus wept when Lazarus died."

She looked up at Pastor Mark. "I know, but Jesus knew He'd raise Lazarus from the dead and bring God glory. I don't understand the 'why' parts of this."

"This *will* give Him glory, too, Honey. We may not know how or why God had to do it this way. But the words I spoke this morning about your father's faith reached hearts. His life was a strong statement of his faith. I also believe that it will in your own life, somehow, bring God glory."

"I know, Pastor Mark. I know in my head that's true. My heart's having some trouble with it." Brooke stared at the rose garden again. "Pastor Mark, did Daddy know he was going to die? He had his will updated. It was on the desk in the living room, opened up and just laying there. It was as if he knew I'd need to see it. The dates on it were from last month."

Mark shook his head. "No, I don't think so. After your friend Ruth's funeral, your father just felt it was time to get his own wishes in order. I really believe this was just as sudden for him as it was for us."

Brooke nodded and wiped the tears again. "I guess I should be thankful for that. At least he didn't have to suffer."

"You know you can come to us anytime. Madeline and I have always thought of you as a daughter. You are more than welcome at our home if you want to get away."

Brooke smiled up at him through her tears. "I know, Pastor. Thank you."

Pastor Mark left Brooke and returned to the house. She watched him go through the door, the music and laughter again escaping as the door opened. *"I suppose I should go back in too,"* Brooke said to herself, moving toward the house. Papa would need her. He was more or less alone. Aunt Maria left for home from the funeral, and Uncle Vince and Aunt Rhea left shortly after. Grandma & Grandpa Merriweather were still there, but she knew they'd have to be leaving soon. The drive to Old Forge was two hours long.

She stopped on the top step and looked around the yard before opening the door. Rain had fallen hard during the funeral, leaving puddles and drops all over the yard. The beads of water that still dangled from the leaves looked like diamonds sparkling in the trees. Brooke smiled to herself. Her father had always loved the yard after rain. She knew God was with her, reminding her of the good things that she would have to hold on to while she walked this difficult path.

———

Brooke and Papa sat in the lawn chairs in the back yard after everyone had left. Linda, Grandma and Grandpa Merriweather and Pastor Mark and Madeline were the only ones who remained to help clean up the mess after the celebration of Martin's life had concluded. Brooke's grandparents kissed her good-bye and left so they could be home before dark. Pastor Mark and Madeline left shortly after. Brooke had to beg Linda to leave, insisting that she and Papa needed time to just mourn.

Once everyone was gone, Papa brewed a fresh pot of coffee and they each poured a cup and went out to sit in the yard and unwind from the stressful day. Brooke pulled the lawn chairs and a small table close to the house where she and Papa could sit to drink their coffee.

Brooke kicked her shoes off and tucked her feet up under her dress. She sipped her coffee and leaned her head back. "Papa, did you look at Daddy's will?"

"Yes, Sweetheart, I did."

She looked at her grandfather. "Why do you think he wanted the house sold? I understand selling the business. I wouldn't know what to do with that. But why the house?"

"I should think to spare you the burden of it. It's a big house, several hours from where you live. It wouldn't be practical for you to have to deal with it."

"I guess I don't understand why I wasn't given the option, though, of keeping it. I grew up in this house. It's my home." Tears welled in her eyes.

Papa leaned forward. "Brooke, do you think you'd want to live here again? Really think about it. Even when you were a little girl, you would have moved to New York in a heartbeat if you'd been allowed. You wouldn't be happy here, Sweetheart, and your father knew it. If he hadn't put the sale of the house in his will, you would have felt obligated to keep it somehow. This way, you aren't in that position."

Brooke knew her grandfather was right. She had always wanted to live in New York. It had been her dream since childhood. "I know you're right, Papa. I just can't imagine anyone else living here."

"Linda mentioned that a couple had actually looked at the house last spring."

Brooke nodded. "She mentioned it to me too. She guessed them to be in their thirties – both are professors at the Environmental Science &

Forestry College. They had a little girl with them who looked to be about four or five and the wife was pregnant. They wanted a place closer to the campus. They'd been driving around, saw the house and asked Daddy if he'd be willing to sell. He told them no."

"She told me the same thing. Sounds like they'd be the perfect people to buy it."

"That would be great if only we knew who they were and how to find them!" Brooke said with a laugh.

"I need a refill," Papa said, rising from his chair. "How about you?"

"Sounds good, thanks," Brooke said, handing him her cup. She leaned her head back again and watched the tree branches sway in the breeze. Birds flitted from branch to branch, singing their evening song.

Papa returned and handed Brooke her cup before sitting back down in his chair. Brooke took a sip of her coffee and watched a squirrel scamper up the tree. She started laughing and sat forward quickly, trying to steady her cup to keep the coffee from spilling.

"What on earth are you laughing about?" Papa asked, watching Brooke juggle her coffee cup.

"A memory." She shook her head and laughed harder.

Papa chuckled. "That must be some memory!"

Brooke cleared her throat and nodded. "Daddy and I were planning a weekend camping trip during the summer Mom was pregnant with Rose. We were going to drive to Old Forge. Mom was going to stay with Grandma and Grandpa while Daddy and I hiked out into the woods and pitched a tent. We hauled the camping equipment out of the shed, checked the tent for holes, you know, stuff like that. Daddy even explained that we would have to hoist the food up into a tree, away from the campsite, to keep the bears away."

Brooke smiled and looked at Papa. "The weekend we were supposed to go, Mom got sick. She couldn't ride in the car and Daddy didn't want to leave her alone."

"I remember that. Your grandmother and I offered to come get you. We thought maybe a visit with us would help you get over not going camping."

"Well, Daddy didn't want me to miss my camping trip, so we pitched the tent right here in the yard, under that tree. Mom packed the picnic basket with s'more stuff and other snack stuff. Dad filled the canteens with water and we pretended to be out in the woods. Mom sat out with us while we roasted marshmallows, then Daddy helped her into the house. He came back out and helped me spread my sleeping bag out in the tent. We were getting ready to climb into our bags when I remembered that the food had to be high up from the bears."

Papa chuckled, "I don't know how many bears there are in Syracuse."

"I wanted it to be as real as possible. So, Daddy got a rope, tied one end to the picnic basket and tossed the other end over that lower tree limb." Brooke pointed to the tree. "He tied the rope off on a tent spike and said 'There, no bear's gonna reach that!' He kissed me good-night and we climbed into our sleeping bags."

Brooke started to laugh. "We woke up the next morning and Daddy lowered the picnic basket. There were holes torn in the top and the granola bars and graham crackers were all chewed up. Daddy looked up at the tree limb and scratched his head. He looked back at me and said 'That must have been one huge bear.'"

Brooke was laughing so hard she could hardly speak. She said between her laughs, "I ran screaming into the house. I could picture this huge, twenty foot bear, roaming around the city, reaching into picnic baskets and eating the food inside."

Papa started to laugh with her. "That sounds just like your father!"

Brooke nodded and cleared her throat. "Mom made him come in and apologize for scaring me. He explained to me that it had to have been a squirrel or a chipmunk, that there aren't bears roaming around Syracuse. I had nothing to be afraid of. For the next three nights, though, I slept with the flashlight and shined it out the window to make sure there weren't any bears in our backyard. It took Daddy setting a live trap and catching a squirrel one night to convince me that's all it was that broke into our picnic basket. He even let me release the little guy. I watched him run up the tree and was finally convinced there hadn't been a bear."

Papa watched Brooke as she finished telling the story, the smile on her lips making her face light up. "You have memories to treasure, Sweetheart."

"I know Papa. I already miss him, though." Brooke rose from her chair and sat next to him. She wrapped her arms around his neck and cried. "I never thought I'd have to say good-bye so soon."

"I know, Sweetheart. I never thought I'd outlive my son. This isn't how it was supposed to be," Papa said, his own tears running down his cheeks. "We'll get through this together, with the help of Almighty God, we'll make it."

Brooke and Papa spent the rest of the week in Syracuse packing the contents of the house. Brooke's grandparents came from Old Forge to help. The boxes Brooke wanted to keep but couldn't take back to her apartment were taken to Old Forge and stored in their attic. The items that had been in her father's family that Brooke didn't want were divided between Uncle Vince and Rhea, and Aunt Maria. Papa made arrangements to have a truck take it all to Vince's in Long Island. "Let the three of them work it out," he said when Brooke asked what should go to Maria's in New Jersey.

An auctioneer was hired to take care of the rest. The auction was scheduled for the same weekend as Rachel and Shaun's wedding. Linda promised Brooke she'd take care of the auction personally. Brooke would be back the weekend after the auction to get the house ready for the realtor. As much as she hated to see someone else living in the house, she knew it was for the best. She hoped it would sell quickly and to a family who would love it as much as she had.

"I think we've got it all pretty much taken care of," Papa said to Brooke Thursday night after the last of boxes going to New York were loaded into her trunk.

"I think so, too. All we'll have tomorrow before we go home is the appointment with Daddy's lawyer about the business. Daddy's employee, Bruce, is going to meet me down there."

"What did you tell him the reason was?"

"I told him I wanted to discuss his completing any of the unfinished work still in Daddy's shop," Brooke said with a smile.

The next morning, Brooke met with her father's lawyer while Bruce and Papa waited in the lobby. "I don't want to make a profit off Daddy's business," she explained to his attorney.

The man shook his head in puzzlement. "I don't understand. Why would you want to take a loss? It's a profitable business. I'm sure you could get a good price for it."

"I don't doubt it. But, the man who works for my father has been there for ten years. I want him to have it. All I want him to do is pay for any fees or costs associated with transferring the business. That's it."

"I can make those arrangements," he replied with a shrug.

Brooke went to the lobby and asked Bruce to return with her. Bruce's eyes grew wide as the lawyer explained what Brooke wanted to do with the business. He turned to Brooke and hugged her. Brooke laughed. She felt the tears start to come again. If felt good to make someone so happy, and she knew her father would have been proud of her decision.

Bruce released her and looked back at the attorney. He asked through excited tears, "Where do I sign?"

TWENTY-FOUR

IT WAS STILL DARK WHEN Paul eased himself from under the covers and crept to the other side of the room. He slipped into sweat pants and a t-shirt and moved quietly to the bedroom door. He turned slightly and looked back before going to the next room. Susan's blonde curls were flowing over the edge of the bed; one hand supported her cheek on the pillow. The sheet covered her body, clinging to every curve. Even the darkness couldn't hide her seductive form.

Paul closed his eyes and shook his head before leaving the room. He went into the living room and opened the doors to the balcony. He stepped out into the darkness. Even at 4:00 am the traffic below was heavy. The City was always moving. He gripped the railing and closed his eyes, feeling the early morning breeze caress his face.

He knew he'd had too much to drink the night before. It was nothing short of a miracle that he made it home alive and without an accident or a ticket. He had never driven drunk before. And what had possessed him to bring Susan home last night? He had spent months trying to get through to her that their relationship was over and now she was asleep in the next room, in his bed. He felt like a fool.

Paul buried his face in his hands. He hadn't even planned to go out. Marcus had flown out early in the day. Marshall was on a business trip to Chicago. Paul had planned to spend a quiet weekend at home. Pratt had called. That had put an end to his plans to stay in.

Pratt was flirting before the second round of drinks. He'd kept trying to convince Paul to go over and talk to one of the women at the bar. Then Susan had walked in. Paul walked over and offered to buy her a drink. His plan had been to use her as a prop, a way to keep Pratt from badgering him about the woman at the bar. He hadn't planned to take her home. The more he drank though, the more he'd been drawn to her enticing smile and irresistible body.

Paul went back into the condo and closed the screen, leaving the doors open to let the breeze and the early morning sounds pass through. He was angry with himself for being foolish. He was angry with Pratt for dragging him out yet again. More than anything, though, he was consumed with guilt. Brooke's image kept flashing before his eyes. Her gentle smile and innocent manner caused his chest to ache.

Paul sat on the couch and raked his fingers through his hair. He loved Brooke. And despite that they were no longer a couple, he felt like he'd betrayed her, that he'd been unfaithful to her.

"Oh God, what am I going to do?" he asked, rising from the couch.

He paced for several minutes before sitting down at the piano. He keyed a few random notes then began the Moonlight Sonata, its quiet melody filling the living room. He could feel the tension starting to ease as the notes flowed.

"Why are you playing so early, and why did you pick something so depressing?" Susan asked from behind him.

Paul stopped playing and turned on the piano bench. Susan was standing a few feet from him, rubbing the sleep from her eyes with one hand and holding his robe tight around her body with the other. Her hair was sticking up and she had black smudges around her eyes from where her mascara had run during the night.

"Sorry," Paul replied. "I guess I wasn't thinking about the time."

Susan walked over to him and put her hand on his shoulder. Paul stiffened at her touch. She let her hand slide from his shoulder and fall to her side. She smiled knowingly at him and simply nodded before turning to the bedroom. She returned a few minutes later. She was dressed in her clothes from the night before, her purse in her hand.

"I'm not going to see you again, am I, Paul?"

Paul shook his head. "No, Susan. I'm sorry about last night. I shouldn't have..."

She interrupted, "Don't, Paul. It was my fault as much as yours. You didn't drag me up here. I was more than willing."

"Let me get my keys. I'll drive you home." Paul rose from the piano bench.

"No, I'd rather take a cab." Susan walked to the door and put her hand on the knob. She turned to Paul and smiled. "Whoever she is Paul, don't let her get away. You love her. Do whatever you have to to make her know that." Susan opened the door and left.

Paul sat back down and stared at the door. The last thing he wanted was for Brooke to get away, but what more could he do? He turned back to the piano and ran his fingers over the black and ivory keys.

Closing the cover, he rose from the bench and went to shower. All he wanted at that moment was to wash away the night before. He stayed under the water until it ran cold. Stepping out and wrapping a towel around his waist, he went to his bedroom and sat on the edge of the bed. He suddenly felt exhausted. Lying down on top of the crumpled covers, he drifted off to sleep.

———————

"How does it look?" Rachel asked as Brooke helped adjust her veil.

"You look beautiful, Rachel. Shaun will fall over when he sees you come down that aisle!" Brooke smiled at her friend.

Brooke and Rachel, along with Rachel's other two bridesmaids, spent the entire morning in the salon. Within minutes of leaving, heavy rain poured down on the City. Umbrellas were useless in the wind and heavy downpour. By the time they'd reached the church, they were all soaked.

Rachel had sobbed. Brooke called Lauren who arrived soon after with a friend. By the time the wedding was scheduled to start, the two ladies had Rachel and her wedding party looking more beautiful than they had when they'd left the salon.

The music started in the sanctuary. Rachel's mother rushed in and gave her daughter a kiss on her cheek and smiled. "It's starting, Pumpkin."

Brooke turned Rachel toward the mirror and squeezed her friend's shoulders. "Just look, Rachel. You're a beautiful bride!"

Rachel smiled at Brooke. "Don't make me cry, Brooke. I don't think Lauren would have time to fix us now!"

Brooke handed Rachel her bouquet and nudged her through the door. "Time to go down the aisle, unless of course you've changed your mind. The emergency door is right there!" Brooke said, pointing to the exit.

Rachel laughed and shook her head. "Not in a million years! There's no way I'm letting Shaun off the hook now!"

They made their way down the hall. Shaun's groomsmen led the bridesmaids through the doors. The music continued to play softly as Brooke walked slowly down the aisle. She could see Shaun standing near the altar, smiling brightly.

Shaun's nephew ran down the aisle. He held the pillow containing the rings under his arm like a football, causing laughter to erupt in the sanctuary. When the laughter tapered off, Shaun's niece reluctantly made her way down the aisle, scattering rose petals as she went.

The music changed and the guests rose. Rachel's father, his head high and tears in his eyes, smiled as he escorted his daughter down the aisle. Shaun beamed as Rachel's father placed her hand in his, giving his daughter to be wed.

Pastor Brian smiled. "Dearly beloved, we are gathered here today to witness the joining of this man and this woman in holy matrimony…"

Brooke waved as the limousine pulled away with Rachel and Shaun waving back through the window. The wedding and reception had been beautiful. Brooke fought tears when Pastor Brian had announced them man and wife. They looked so blissful. Her friends were starting their new life together and she was happy to have been a part of it.

Brooke turned back to the fellowship hall. Most of the guests were leaving. A few people went back inside with Brooke. Lauren was helping Rachel's mother gather up the gifts. "Anything I can do to help?" Brooke asked as she approached the two women.

Rachel's mother glanced around the room. "I don't think so, Honey. I've already boxed up the top of the cake to save for them. The leftover cake has already been handed out. I think we're about done."

Brooke looked around the room. "What about clean up?"

"All set," Lauren answered, nodding toward Rachel's mother. "They've already paid a cleaning crew to take care of it tonight. The church will be ready for services in the morning."

Brooke nodded. "Well, I guess I'll be off then. Papa is sitting outside. I think I'll give him a ride home." She hugged Rachel's mother and Lauren. "I guess I'll see you in worship in the morning."

Brooke found Papa sitting on the edge of the concrete wall that surrounded the church yard. "You ready, Papa? I'll drive you home."

Papa stood and stretched his back. "I'm getting too old for this stuff."

They drove most of the way in silence. Papa glanced at Brooke from time to time, but she appeared to be deep in thought. Brooke pulled into the parking garage of Papa's building and started to pull into a short-term parking space. Papa put his hand on her arm. "I want you to stay for a little while. Just park over there," he said, nodding toward one of the long-term spaces. "I'll let Jamie know it's your car."

Brooke backed out and pulled the car into the space Papa had pointed out. She grabbed her bag from the back seat. Papa looked at her quizzically.

"Change of clothes," she said. "I wore these to the salon before the wedding. There's no way I'm sitting around all night in this gown."

Papa laughed. "You look lovely. You don't think calling for take-out qualifies for a gown and nice shoes?"

"No, I don't. If I were at home ordering take-out, I'd be in pajamas!"

Papa stopped by the parking attendant's station before going into the building. "Good afternoon, Jamie. This is my granddaughter Brooke and that car over there is hers. She may be here for a while. Is it okay if she parks there?"

"Yes, sir. I'll put a ticket on the windshield. It'll be okay," Jamie said with a smile.

Brooke followed her grandfather into his apartment. Papa nodded toward the bathroom. "Go on and change. I'll call for dinner. What are you in the mood for?"

"I'm not really hungry, Papa."

"You will be. Now, what do you want? Chinese, Italian, Thai? If you don't tell me, you'll be stuck with whatever I call in," Papa said impatiently.

Brooke shrugged her shoulders. "Chinese, I guess – Sesame chicken and white rice."

She went into the bathroom and slipped out of the gown. She pulled on shorts and a t-shirt. She took the pins from her hair and brushed out the curls, letting her hair fall in waves over her shoulders.

She looked in the mirror and sighed. She was happy for her friends, but the wedding had made her miss Paul. She wished she could just forget him and be done with it, but she couldn't.

By the time she finished changing and joined Papa in the kitchen, he'd ordered dinner and changed his own clothes. He had a pot of coffee brewing and a plate of biscotti on the table.

"Sit," Papa said, nodding toward the table. He poured two cups of coffee, placed one in front of Brooke and sat down in the chair across from her. "Now talk."

Brooke shrugged her shoulders and looked at him over the rim of her cup. "Not much to say, I guess."

"Nonsense," he said as he set his cup down and crossed his arms. "You've been fighting tears since Shaun and Rachel got into that limo. Is it Paul? Or is it something else? Come on, Sweetheart. I need to talk to you, but I'm not saying a word until you've talked to me."

"Are you okay?" Brooke asked, alarmed by his need to talk.

"I'm fine. I just need to talk. You first, though." He picked up his cup and waited for her to speak.

She took a sip of her coffee and set the cup back on the table. She reached for a biscotti, broke it in two, and dipped a piece in her coffee. "Papa, I have so much to deal with right now, I hardly know where to start. I miss Daddy, I miss Ruth, and yes, Paul is a part of it. I think about him all the time. I woke up this morning with this incredible need to pray for him. The whole time I prayed, I felt this ache in my soul, like something terrible had happened. Then today, watching Rachel and Shaun take their wedding vows, I felt alone."

"I can understand that. It's going to take time. I have to say though, if God tells you to pray for him, there's a reason."

"I know, Papa. It's just so hard. I really want to talk to him, but I don't feel like it's right for me to call him." Brooke's eyes filled with tears.

"I don't think so either. Brooke, I wish I had advice for you. All I can tell you is to stay strong and trust the Lord with this." The buzzer on the door sounded, interrupting him. "That's dinner," Papa said as he rose from the table.

Brooke got up and set the table. Papa had never liked eating out of containers. She poured milk into two glasses and sat back down. Papa brought their dinner to the table, blessed their food, then handed Brooke her containers from the bag.

Brooke scooped the contents onto her plate. "So, what did you want to talk about? Are you sure nothing's wrong?"

"No, nothing's wrong other than I miss your father," he said between bites.

"I'm sorry, Papa. I feel like I'm being selfish, thinking only of myself. Daddy was your son just as much as he was my father," Brooke whispered through her tears.

He cleared his throat, "I guess I'm just feeling a little alone right now myself. Vince and Rhea are always busy. Maria and Tom never have time for me. Tom couldn't even be bothered to attend his own brother-in-law's funeral, for heaven's sake! And Maria was on her way home before we were out of the parking lot of the funeral home. She didn't go to the burial or the life celebration. I just feel, well, alone."

Brooke stood from her chair and went to Papa's side. She leaned over and wrapped her arms around him. "I'm here for you, Papa. You know that."

"I know, Sweetheart. You always have been."

Brooke went back to her side of the table and finished her dinner. "Papa, would you come with me next weekend when I go back to Syracuse?" she asked.

"Of course I will. Do you have any idea what you need to do?"

"Well, I talked to Linda yesterday. The auction was today. I plan to touch base with her on that tomorrow after church. She told me yesterday, though, that the family who had stopped and talked to Daddy in the spring came by earlier in the week. They'd seen the signs for the auction. They still want the house. Linda told me she'd get in touch with a realtor friend who could get things rolling if that's what I want to do." Brooke finished her milk and set her glass back on the table.

"Sounds like a plan to me. What would you have to do?"

"Nothing but sign a bunch of papers, from what Linda said. The buyers have already offered to pay for the survey and the inspection. They'll even pay the closing costs. I just have to come up with a price for the house. Linda suggested having an appraiser come in. I told her that would be a good idea. She's going to have the realtor contact one for me."

Brooke rose from the table and cleared the dishes. "I feel like in a couple of weeks, my home will be gone. I miss Daddy so much. I thought I'd at least have a little time in the house, but it doesn't look that way, does it?"

"This may be God's way of telling you to move on, Sweetheart. He knows what He's doing."

"I know. So much has happened in such a short time. I'm trying to keep my faith. It isn't easy, though, is it?"

"No, sometimes these things don't make sense at all, but I've learned over the years that the things that make the least sense are often the things that give us the greatest rewards later on," Papa said with a smile.

"I hope you're right, Papa. Right now I feel like I'm in the middle of a huge test. One wrong choice and I could fail miserably. I just wish I had a glimpse of the bigger picture."

Papa got up from the table and stood beside Brooke. "We all do, but unfortunately, most of the time we don't get that chance. Right now all we can do is trust and pray.

TWENTY-FIVE

PAUL POURED A CUP OF coffee and sat down to read the paper before leaving for the office. The headline jumped off the page and had him running out the door before he'd had a second sip of coffee. He sprinted to the subway. Out of breath by the time he boarded the train, he dropped into the nearest seat.

He read and re-read the article during the ride. He couldn't believe the headline: "Big-Business Exec Arrested for Solicitation." Pratt's picture was plastered across the page for the whole world to see. Paul shook his head in disbelief.

"This can't be happening," he said to himself over and over as he ran the short distance from the station to the office.

Reporters were packed together like sardines behind the police barrier that had been set up in front of the building. Several yelled to Paul, waving their microphones and notebooks in his direction. He ducked into the building, ignoring their requests for an interview.

The place was in chaos. The lobby was a collection of people huddled in little groups, some whispering amongst themselves, others arguing about what the news meant for the company. Paul looked around, shaking his head at the sight.

"We still have a company to run, ladies and gentlemen. How about we get to work doing it," he shouted boldly, feeling a need to get things in order.

A few looked at him with disdain. Most, however, moved toward the elevators. Paul stopped to speak with the security guard. "Come on, Jerry. I know these people are employees, but please. We don't need the media looking through the glass and seeing this. Try to keep the huddles from forming. If they want to gossip, let them do it on their own floors."

Jerry nodded his agreement.

Paul waited for most of the staff to disperse before making his way to the elevators. He was relieved that no one else stepped through the doors with him, allowing him a few moments to compose himself before reaching his floor. When the car stopped, he took a deep breath and straightened his tie. He tried not to look as panicked as he felt.

The floor had a tomb-like quiet. People were gathered here and there. A few looked up at him as he made his way to his office. Kelly was waiting for him at his door.

"They're in the conference room, Paul. They told me to send you in as soon as you arrived. You're early. You may want to wait. They've been shouting for a while. Marcus even showed up this morning." Kelly's face mirrored the fear Paul was feeling.

"Marcus? Why would this drag him from half the world away?"

She shook her head. "I don't know, Paul, but he didn't look happy when he marched to Pratt's office."

Paul reached over and squeezed Kelly's arm. Trying to look calm, he smiled at her and said "Go back to your desk. I think something has been blown out of proportion. Don't worry. I'll go in and see what's going on."

Kelly nodded. She looked up at Paul once more, her eyes wide with concern, before returning to her desk. Paul felt his own emotions start to roil. How many times had he been out with Pratt and seen him leave with a "date?"

Paul stowed his briefcase under his desk. He checked his phone and email messages and made a note for Kelly to cancel his early morning appointments. She met him outside his office, his coffee cup in her hand. He handed her his appointment cancellations and turned toward the conference room.

The shouting met him before he was halfway down the hallway. Kevin's voice was the loudest, though Paul couldn't make out the words being shrieked until he was right outside the door.

"We're ruined! I tell you, we're ruined!"

Paul downed his coffee. He opened the door enough to peek in. "You wanted to see me?" he looked around the room as he entered.

Marshall was seated at the head of the table, Pratt and Marcus seated on either side of him. The chair nearest Pratt was pulled out. Kevin marched back and forth behind it, wringing his hands. Paul let his eyes settle on Marshall.

"Come in, Paul, and have a seat. I'm sure you've seen the headlines?" Marshall sounded calm, despite the situation.

"Yes, Sir. I came in as soon as I saw the paper." Paul sat down next to Marcus and poured himself a fresh cup of coffee from the carafe in the center of the table.

Kevin resumed his hysteria. He waved his arms like he was caught in a swarm. "We'll never get through this!"

Marcus looked over at Paul, closed his eyes and shook his head. He turned toward Kevin and with an eerie calm said "Kevin, do sit down and stop the dramatics. This isn't the first time a company has faced such a misunderstanding."

"Misunderstanding! This isn't a misunderstanding, Marcus! This is a disaster!" Kevin continued pacing. He muttered under his breath and ran his hand through his hair. "This could ruin us!"

Marcus stood and walked calmly around the table, stopping in front of Kevin. "I advise you to calm down and have a seat, Mr. Murphy."

Kevin set his jaw and glared at Marcus. Pointing a shaky finger at him, he hissed, "You above all should know the danger we face here! What if the Board of Directors demands a full, in depth audit? What if they find out about the money you've made off our stockholders? And what about your little side business, Marcus? What if they find out about that? Do you really think they won't go to the authorities when they find out you supply the people who brought down the towers on 9/11? Do you really think they'll just overlook that little morsel? If I were you, I'd be a little more concerned than you are, MR. REED!"

Marcus took a step closer to Kevin. His voice remained steady, but his eyes grew dark and piercing. "You would be wise to keep your voice down and be mindful of what you are saying." Marcus paused long enough to look around the room and make eye contact with Marshall, Pratt and Paul.

Marcus turned back to Kevin. "You forget, Mr. Murphy, we know you do little to nothing for this company. You're content to draw an income without working for it. We know about the personal charges to the company accounts. We know about your little 'business trips.' We know about the several affairs you've had. It would be most regrettable if those 'minor defects' in your character were to be made known."

Kevin clenched his jaw. He turned to Marshall and opened his mouth to speak. Marshall shook his head as if to say, "Don't say a word." Kevin stormed from the room, slamming the door as he left.

Marcus walked casually back to his chair, and sat down. He took out his Blackberry, sent a rapid text and tucked it back into his pocket. Turning to Paul, he said, "I'm sorry you had to witness that."

Paul shrugged his shoulders and smiled faintly at Marcus, trying to appear unfazed by the situation. "I always thought he was a little unstable."

Marcus sat forward in his chair and folded his hands on the table. "You do realize, my friend," he said, looking at Pratt. "Kevin isn't far from the mark. This could cause panic within the board, and they *could* require an audit if they feel company funds have been used inappropriately."

Pratt nodded his understanding. "I know I should have been more careful. I had no idea the bartender was listening. She was a lovely woman – too tempting to pass up."

Paul cleared his throat. "I'm sorry, but the only thing I know about all of this is what I read in the paper and if it's none of my business I will accept that. But I feel like I've been a part of this inner circle for some time now and the mere fact that I'm sitting here leads me to believe you are making it my business." Paul held out his hands, palms up, and shrugged.

"Paul is correct," Marcus said. Turning to Paul, he proceeded to explain the situation. "Apparently Pratt remained at the Waldorf after a business dinner and was approached by the lovely woman he has referred to. He allowed her to offer her services and state the price at the bar – with the bartender within earshot. The bartender informed the manager, who called the police, and, well, you read the rest in the paper this morning."

Marcus looked at Pratt and continued, "Mr. Young neglected to consider that the establishment is one of high reputation and not some back-alley bar. He failed to recognize the danger of entering into such an agreement without first leaving the lounge." He allowed his gaze to rest on Pratt another minute before turning back to Paul. "Corporate attorneys are absolute magicians in such situations. We need only to keep our wits and we will come through this unscathed."

Marshall finally spoke, focusing on Paul. "Kevin's outburst was regrettable, Paul, as it has given you certain information we weren't sure you were ready to possess..."

Marcus interrupted Marshall. "I think he is aware of the danger involved in disclosing too much information." He looked at Paul. "Paul?"

"I understand," Paul responded. He understood what Marcus was saying, but not the information Kevin had leaked. He wanted to vomit, to free himself from the poison he had allowed to infect him.

They spent the remainder of the meeting discussing damage control and planning a strategy that would save Pratt's image. In the end, it was decided that Pratt would admit to propositioning the woman. He would, however, feign ignorance to the fact that she was a prostitute and deny the mention of money.

Paul felt a wave of nausea come over him again when Marshall stated matter-of-factly that they all knew the truth of Pratt's escapades and would have to deny it if ever questioned, even if it were to go to trial. Paul was certain he'd never be able to lie under oath.

By the time the meeting broke up, everyone was relaxed and almost jovial – everyone except Paul. Marshall and Pratt were discussing lunch. Paul was numb. His mind kept coming back to two questions. Why was Marcus here? Why was Marcus *always* here? He wasn't a board member or a stockholder. And what were they involved in? How much should he believe of what Kevin had disclosed?

Marcus rested his hand on Paul's shoulder. "Marshall, Pratt, I will meet you both in the lobby. I would like to spend a few moments with this young man. He appears to be shaken by this whole situation."

Marcus walked Paul back to his office. He shut the door and motioned for Paul to take a seat. Marcus pulled a chair closer to Paul's desk, sat down and crossed his legs. He set his elbows on the arms of the chair and folded his hands under his chin. He looked at Paul, gauging his disposition. Finally, leaning back in his chair, he said simply "Speak to me."

"Marcus, I know Kevin. I realize for all purposes he knows nothing about this company, except of course when payday is. I also understand that he probably overstated much during our meeting." Paul paused and took a breath. "I have been recently promoted – giving me greater responsibility, as well as privilege, and more sensitive information of late than ever before. I've never heard any of what Kevin disclosed. I guess I would like some clarification."

Marcus stared long and hard at Paul. "I appreciate your honesty, Paul. Kevin, as you so adequately stated, knows very little about the company from which he takes money every week. And, as you also observed, is quite talented in his ability to overstate things. He takes a shred of truth and blows it out of proportion." Marcus smiled at Paul. "My company is, as you know, growing at an exciting rate. And, as you are already aware, stock in my up and coming branches are often 'recommended' to many of your more financially stable clients. It helps me to secure the funds I need to continue to expand my business. I, in turn, will on occasion express my gratitude to your company for their continued support of my growing business."

Paul nodded. He had long ago realized the relationship the company had with Marcus. Though he also realized the legal ramifications of such a relationship, he never really knew the depth of the activity, so chose to ignore it. Paul pretended indifference. "Not all that uncommon, from what I understand."

Marcus smiled again at Paul. "As far as Kevin's other remark, that most unsettling accusation that I have any involvement with terrorists, I am appalled by his implication that I would be associated with such beasts. Another of his dramatizations."

"Where would he come up with such a ridiculous idea?"

Marcus stood and walked to the window behind Paul. "This is a beautiful city – a wealthy city, isn't it Paul?"

Paul knew the question wasn't meant to be answered so he waited for Marcus to continue.

Marcus turned from the window and looked at Paul. "Do you remember what I told you about some of the textiles my companies produce – plexiglass, asbestos, other technical textiles? We have business arrangements with different tribes in Iraq, Pakistan, etc."

Paul gasped. "Which side? The side we support or the enemy?"

"Both." Marcus watched Paul closely for his reaction. "Paul, I don't support either side. Who is to say which side is right and which side is wrong? I do not wish to see harm come to any of our nations, and I certainly don't condone blatant acts of terrorism. But I consider myself to be neutral. Business is business."

Moving from the window and returning to his chair, Marcus continued, "It is also a well-known fact that war in one nation brings prosperity to others. This beautiful city prospers from the 'business' of the war. This company, *your* company, has benefited greatly from the continuing conflict. And you in turn have reaped many of those benefits."

Paul felt the color drain from his face. He couldn't hide the horror he felt over what had just been revealed. Marcus had all but admitted fanning the flames of war in the Middle East to help his business concerns. He had all but admitted supplying the enemies of the United States. He had admitted illegal business practices.

Paul also knew Marcus was not a man to have as an enemy. He could feel the evil emanating from every pore of Marcus's body. He suddenly knew without a doubt that to cross Marcus Reed was an act of suicide – literally.

Marcus stood again and looked down on Paul. "You don't look well, my friend. I believe you need a few days of rest to come to terms with all that you've encountered today. I will talk to Marshall. I'm certain he will agree."

He opened the door and turned back to look at Paul. "I am certain that, given time to consider this situation – as well as your part in it – you will realize the only reasonable decision for you to make is to continue to support this family you've become such a valuable part of." Marcus smiled his venomous smile before turning away and closing the door.

Paul stared at the door. He had no idea what to do. He had to get away. He needed time to figure all of it out, to come up with a way to get out of the entire mess. How, he didn't know. The longer he sat, the more he realized he was in too deep to just walk away.

Paul printed his appointment schedule for the remainder of the week and shut down his computer. He grabbed his briefcase, shut off the light in his office, and closed the door. He stopped at Kelly's desk and handed her the printout.

"Kelly, please do me a favor and cancel my appointments for the rest of the week. In light of our problem, I would like a few days to consider what to say to people if they ask what's going on."

"What is going on, Paul? Frankly, I'm a little nervous," Kelly replied, her voice quivering.

Paul smiled. "Don't get worked up. We do have a problem. There's no denying that. But, we'll get through it."

"Okay, Paul. What do you want me to tell everyone?"

"Just that I'll get back to them at the beginning of next week. Make those calls for me and get some lunch. I'm going out for a while."

Paul left the building and had to dodge reporters again. He opted against the subway, concerned that someone from the press would find him and badger him all the way to his stop. He flagged down a cab and gave the driver Nick's address. He needed to talk and if anyone could shed some sensible light on the situation, it was Nick.

———————

Paul picked up sandwiches and pasta salad from a nearby deli before going to Nick's apartment. He knocked on the door and hoped he was home.

Nick answered the door, wiping his hands on a towel. "Paul, what a surprise! I haven't seen you in weeks! Please, come in."

Paul entered the apartment and set his briefcase on the floor near the door. "I hope you haven't eaten yet, Nick. I thought it might be nice to share lunch."

"No, I haven't eaten yet. Go into the kitchen and make yourself comfortable. I'll be right out," Nick nodded toward the kitchen before going into the bathroom.

Paul went into the kitchen and put the bag on the table. He slipped out of his suit jacket and draped it over the back of one of the chairs. Opening the lunch bag, he removed the contents and placed them on the table. He noticed a paper clipping on the table as he folded the paper bag and put it to one side.

"Martin Nicholas Barsanti, devoted father and beloved son, died at St. Joseph's Hospital in Syracuse, NY..." Paul read.

Nick entered the kitchen and Paul looked up from the clipping. "I'm so sorry Nick, I didn't know about Martin."

Nick shook his head. "How would you have known if you didn't see it in the paper? It was quite sudden."

"Still, I'm so sorry. How's Brooke?"

Nick smiled. "She's a strong woman. She mourns, of course, just like I do. But she's given it to God and He's getting her through." Nick turned away from Paul and got plates, utensils and glasses from the cabinets and set the table.

"What are you drinking?" Nick asked, taking milk out of the refrigerator.

"Just water, please."

Nick filled a glass with ice and water and handed it to Paul.

"Have a seat, Paul," Nick said, motioning toward a chair.

Paul sat down and opened the containers. They each took a sandwich and spooned pasta salad onto their plates. Paul pushed the containers aside and stared down at his lunch.

Nick cleared his throat. "What's troubling you, Paul? I know you didn't show up here just to share lunch with an old man, especially after not coming by for so long."

Paul looked up and chuckled. "I *have* thought about you, Nick, believe me. I just didn't know how to do it after Brooke's and my breakup."

"You knew me before you knew my granddaughter, and while I don't completely understand all that happened between you two, I still consider you to be my friend. So come by any time. Now, what's the matter?"

Paul took a deep breath and plunged ahead into the situation he found himself in. He started with his early successes in the company, included his promotions and the information he possessed. He finished with the events of the day.

"I guess more than anything, I need advice. Nick, I respect you and believe you will be honest with me about your opinion on all of this."

Nick sat back in his chair and crossed his arms. "How deep are you involved with all of this Paul? I mean *really* how deep? Are you just scratching the surface, or have you had knowledge of these business practices all along?"

"I've know about Pratt all along. He's never been overly discreet in his extra-marital activities. As far as the business itself, I recently learned of some unethical transactions. The information that was dumped on me today was all new." Paul shook his head. "Nick, Marcus didn't even try to deny it. It was like he had this smug, no one can touch me, air about him."

"Unethical transactions – you mean illegal, but you rationalized it."

Paul nodded. "Yes, I guess that's right. I kept telling myself that it was all in how you looked at it."

"And this friend of your employer, 'Marcus,' you say he's from overseas, he isn't an American?"

"He's part Canadian and part Turkish. His home base is in Turkey, but he has business concerns and homes in Italy, Greece, Canada, as well as homes in Spain and Ireland. The man seems to be everywhere." Paul buried his face in his hands. "What should I do, Nick? I want to do what's right. I don't want to have anything to do with these people, but I'm scared. Marcus knows a lot of people and he strikes me as the kind of man who takes care of anyone who gets in his way, if you know what I mean."

"I've known people like that," Nick answered. "The question, Paul, isn't what *should* you do, but what are you *willing* to do – what are you willing to give up to do what's right?"

"I know you're right. I have a lot to think about. Marcus suggested I take a few days to 'come to terms' and 'realize my need to support the family I've become a part of.' Maybe I should take him up on it."

"I think that's a wise decision. I'll pray for you Paul, and I'll have Brooke do the same. Don't worry, I won't give her all of the details if you'd prefer. In the mean time, what's this Marcus's last name? I can do some digging for you while I pray."

Paul looked at Nick, puzzled. "His name is Reed, Marcus Reed. What do you mean by 'doing some digging?' How exactly will you do that?"

Nick smiled. "I still have connections, despite my old age. I'll see what I can find out. You, young man, find a place to get away and get your thoughts together."

Paul left Nick's apartment, his jacket draped over his arm and briefcase in hand. He walked several blocks to Central Park. It was a warm afternoon. By the time he reached the Great Lawn, sweat trickled down his spine and soaked his shirt. He was surprised by the number of people in the park in the middle of a Tuesday afternoon.

He took the path to the pond and sat on the bench he'd shared with Brooke many weeks before. He dropped his jacket and briefcase on the bench and loosened his tie.

Sunlight danced over the ripples in the water. Ducks paddled around the pond, quacking to each other as they went. A dog sniffed at the tasty remains of a hot dog in a trash basket. Children laughed and shouted in the distance.

Paul leaned forward and buried his face in his hands. How did he get here? What had driven him into this madness? He sat up and leaned his head back. He had to get away. Nick was right; he needed time to sort things out. He couldn't stay in the City. He knew, even if he called Marshall and Pratt and explained his need for time, he'd be hounded non-stop to have dinner or a "few" drinks. He needed to leave the City.

Paul closed his eyes. He had a sudden desire to go home. For the first time in months – no, in years – he wanted to see his father. Paul sat up straight on the bench. He knew his father would have a few things to say to him that he'd rather not hear, but he also knew his father would have sound advice.

Paul rose from the bench and grabbed his jacket and briefcase. He hit the speed dial for Marshall on his cell phone and put the phone to his ear. He debated lying to Marshall about his plans but decided to be honest about going to Rockport. If they happened to check up on him and discovered he wasn't where he said he was, he could find himself in bigger trouble.

"Marshall Appleton."

"Marshall, it's Paul."

"Paul, how are you holding up?"

"Okay, I think. Listen, I would appreciate a few days to get my thoughts together on all of this. Marcus suggested taking some time off, and, frankly, I think he's right. I think I need to get out of town and away from the press. If I'm not here, they can't badger me. I want some time to consider what I need to say to them, as well as our clients, when I return." Paul held his breath and waved down a cab as he awaited Marshall's response.

"Marcus told me you may want to do that, and I agree. Take off until Monday, Paul. Do what you need to do to figure out your position in all of this."

"Thanks Marshall. I appreciate it. I'm going to my parents'. Maybe a few days on my father's boat will give me a much needed respite. I'll have my cell if you need to get in touch with me."

Paul took the cab to his condo and packed his suitcase for a full week. He left a note for the cleaning lady and was on his way out of the City by 3:00. He drove all the way to Rockport, praying that he'd find some answers before he had to return New York.

TWENTY-SIX

PAUL PULLED INTO HIS PARENTS' driveway shortly after 10:00. Lamplight shone through living room windows. He was relieved to see that someone was still awake. He knew they would suspect something was wrong. He rarely visited unannounced and never in the middle of the week unless it was a holiday. The last thing he wanted to do was startle them if they were asleep.

Paul cut the motor and pulled the key from the ignition. He opened the door and took a deep breath before stepping out of the car. He opened the trunk and pulled out his suitcase, briefcase and laptop. He slammed the trunk closed and took another breath before heading toward the house.

He heard the back door open and met his father coming out of the house. "Paul? What are you doing here?" His father reached to take Paul's suitcase.

Paul shifted his laptop case on his shoulder and switching his briefcase to his other hand. "I had to get away for few days, Dad. I hope it's okay that I just showed up like this," Paul replied, following his father into the house.

"Of course it is, Son." His father led him through the kitchen and into the living room. He put Paul's suitcase next to the stairs and motioned toward the couch. "Have a seat and tell me what's going on."

Paul put his briefcase and laptop on the floor next to his suitcase. He walked over to the couch and sat down.

His father sat down at the opposite end of the couch and leaned forward, his hands folded on his knees. He watched Paul and waited for him to speak.

Paul leaned his head against the back of the couch and closed his eyes. He rubbed his forehead and raked his fingers through his hair before sitting up straight and looking at his father.

"Where's Mom?" he asked, looking around the room.

"She's at your brother's. Lydia had one of those tote bag parties and your Mom went over for it. You know, one of those women only things. I think it's just an excuse to get away from us men for awhile," Steve said with a chuckle. "She should be home soon."

Paul nodded and looked around the room again. He leaned forward and rested his elbows on his knees and folded his hands under his chin. He looked over at his father. "Dad, I have a serious problem, and I don't know what I'm going to do."

Steve sat back on the couch and nodded. "I thought something must be wrong. You don't usually come home like this. Is it job-related or woman-related?"

"Job-related."

"Son, what have you gotten involved in? We're talking something illegal here, aren't we?"

Paul nodded. "Dad, my involvement is minimal, but I'm a senior manager now. I'm part of the core group in the company. If I can't come up with some solution, I could end up in as much trouble as the rest, despite my limited involvement."

"How limited Paul? Are you actively involved in it or just aware of it? What kind of activity are we talking about here – drugs, smuggling, what is it?"

"Dad, I've never made a decision that was in itself illegal. I have knowledge, though, of illegal activity. Illegal stock purchases, that sort of thing, I've known about part of it for some time now and because it was more or less superficial, I've ignored it. I like my job and comfortable life."

Paul looked up at the ceiling and shook his head. "Dad, there's more, though. I found out this morning that the people I work for aren't who I thought they were." Paul looked at his father. "They are involved with a man – a foreigner – whose businesses supply enemies of our country. They've known about it and continue to support this man."

Paul rose from the couch and stuffed his hands into his pockets. He looked down at his father and shook his head. "Dad, I don't know what to do. This man is dangerous. I know, without a doubt, that my career is over if I don't go along with this. I'm afraid though, that my life could be in danger, too." Paul turned away and walked to the other side of the room.

241

Steve stared long and hard at Paul. He opened his mouth to speak but changed his mind. He folded his hands on his knees and looked away from his son. "What do you think you're going to do?" he asked, still looking away.

Paul walked back to stand in front of his father. "Dad, I can't support them. I can't. The people this man supplies are the same people who attacked our country and continue to plot against us. He admitted to me that he supplies both sides, just so he can prosper." Paul sat on the couch near his father. "I need your help, Dad. I need your advice. How do I do this?"

"You need to go to the authorities, Son. That's the only right answer."

Paul nodded. "I know that Dad." He reached out and put his hand on his father's arm. "Dad, I'm scared. I've never been more afraid in my life."

Steve put his hand over Paul's. "I understand that. We'll figure this out."

Paul spent the next hour giving Steve the details of what had happened over the course of the day. They moved into the kitchen where Steve put the tea kettle on the stove and piled cookies on a plate. He put the plate in the middle of the table and took mugs out of the cupboard. He emptied cocoa into each of the cups.

"How sure are you that this guy is capable of doing you physical harm?" Steve asked, pouring boiling water into the cups. He put spoons into each cup and set one in front of Paul before sitting down to the table.

Paul stirred his cocoa, took a sip, and reached for a cookie. "Dad, you'd have to see this guy to believe him. He has a bodyguard who follows him everywhere. He has more money than anyone I've ever met. There's just something about him. It's like evil just oozes from every pore of his body. He warned the Vice President of our company to keep quiet this morning during our meeting. Kevin looked terrified of the man. I just can't explain it."

The door opened. Marian entered, interrupting their conversation.

Paul rose from the table as she closed the door. "Hi, Mom."

"Paul! I saw your car when I pulled in. Are you okay? Why are you home?" She dropped her keys on the counter before walking over and reaching out to him.

Paul put his arms around her. Exhaustion and grief washed over him. He felt sobs start to rise up and despite his attempts to fight the tears, he broke down in her arms.

Marian held him and let him cry. Paul was not a crier. She looked at Steve in puzzlement.

Steve shook his head as if to say *"I'll tell you later."*

Paul finally pulled away and reached for a napkin. He wiped his eyes and sat back down at the table. "Sorry, Mom. I'm really tired. I think I'll go up to bed if you don't mind. Dad can fill you in if he wants." Paul emptied his cup, got up from the table and put the cup in the sink. "I'll see you in the morning," he said before leaving the kitchen.

He picked up his luggage and went to his room. He closed the door and sat on the edge of his bed. Exhaustion overtook him. He undressed to his boxers and climbed under the covers. He reached over and turned off the light, the darkness enveloping him. He drifted off to sleep, feelings of hopelessness pulling him into an abyss of despair.

It was late morning before Paul awoke. He pulled on his jeans from the day before. He opened his suitcase and pulled out a clean t-shirt. He left his bedroom and walked down the hall, pulling the t-shirt over his head and slipping his arms into the sleeves. He followed the smell of coffee down the stairs and into the kitchen. His mother was at the sink washing strawberries.

She looked up and smiled at him as he poured a cup of coffee. "Did you sleep?"

"A little," he said, rubbing his hand over his face. He took a sip of his coffee and sat down at the table. He looked over at his mother. "Did Dad tell you what's going on?"

Marian nodded and put the strawberries into a bowl. She put the bowl on the table and sat down in the chair nearest to Paul's. "He told me," she said, reaching to touch his arm. "Have you come to any decisions?"

Paul shook his head. "No." He took another sip of his coffee and set the cup down. "Mom, I feel like there's no right answer. It feels so impossible." He put his head in his hand and looked down at the table. "I want to stop them, Mom. I *want* to go to the authorities. I don't want to be a part of this anymore, but I'm worried about what's going to happen to me. Will I go to jail – or worse?"

Marian took her hand away and sat straighter in her chair. "I wish I could tell you what to do. I don't have the answers, Honey. You know what the right answer is. I know you, Paul. In the end, you'll figure it out. I'm praying for you. I've never stopped."

Paul looked over at his mother and smiled weakly. "I know Mom. Thanks for that. I don't feel like God hears my prayers anymore. Maybe He'll listen to yours."

"Honey, God hears your prayers. Don't ever think He doesn't."

Paul rose from his chair. "I think I'll take a shower and go out for a while." He kissed her cheek and left the kitchen.

Paul showered and put on clean jeans. He put the t-shirt he'd worn earlier back on and unpacked his suitcase. He opened the window shades and let the sun stream into the room before plugging the wireless modem into his laptop. He had dozens of emails. He sent personal messages to the larger accounts, offering cryptic answers and promising to contact them early the following week. The rest he forwarded to Kelly.

He spent a few minutes scanning the news pages, checked the opening stock numbers and then shut down his computer. He grabbed his cell phone and went downstairs. His mother was still in the kitchen. "I'm going for a walk, Mom."

Paul went out into the yard. He considered walking the few blocks to his grandmother's house, but decided instead to go to the marina. The sun dominated the sky, promising a hot day. Paul went to his car for a hat and his sunglasses.

He checked his phone messages as he walked toward his father's shop. He had a few from clients – most he had already responded to by email. The other messages were from Marshall and Marcus. He wanted to ignore them, allow himself time to think clearly without having their constant input. He knew, however, that would be impossible.

He stopped before the walkway that led to the shop. He dialed Marcus and sat on a bollard under a tree. He got voice mail. "Marcus, it's Paul. I received your message. I appreciate your concern. I plan to spend the day on the water. I'll be in touch."

He ended his call to Marcus and dialed Marshall, hoping to get Marshall's voice mail as well. He didn't.

"Hi, Marshall. I got your message. I didn't get in until late last night and I slept late this morning. I just checked my phone a few minutes ago."

"That's okay, Paul. I wanted to make sure you made it safely. You were under a lot of pressure yesterday. It could've made for a difficult drive."

"Well, thanks. I appreciate that. How's the situation?"

"No real change. Pratt gave a statement to the press this morning. Kevin has more or less disappeared. We haven't heard from him since he stormed out of the meeting yesterday. His wife even called. He never went home last night."

"Hmmm, that doesn't sound good, does it?"

"Oh, you know Kevin. He's probably just hiding out somewhere – a 'friend's' house, or he may have gone upstate. His in-laws have a place in the mountains. He'll be in for his paycheck Friday, you can be sure of that," Marshall said with a chuckle.

Paul offered a forced laugh. "You're right about that! I'm going out on my father's boat for a while. The phone reception's terrible on the water. I'll be in touch."

"Okay, Paul. We'll be waiting to hear from you."

Paul ended his call and stuffed the phone deep in his pocket. He wiped the perspiration from the back of his neck and went down the walkway to the shop. He went inside and stopped at the sound of Herbie's off-key singing coming from the stock room. Paul had to laugh. It was a welcome sound.

"Hi Herbie," Paul said from the doorway.

"Paul! Oh boy, this is cool! I had a funny dream about you last night and now you's here! That's so neat!" Herbie smiled at Paul and gave him a childlike hug. "You wanna help, Paul? There in that box is tons of stuff to put away,"

"Maybe after I talk to Dad. Do you know where he is?"

"He's down at the dock where that guy has his boat. You know, the guy from the T.V," Herbie said, pointing toward the window.

"The senator?" Paul asked, looking in the direction Herbie had pointed.

"Yeah. He wants us to do somethin' different with his boat."

Paul nodded and put his hands in his pockets. "Well, maybe I'll help for a few minutes. Then I'll go talk to him."

"Oh, that's great, Paul!" Herbie clapped his hands and took Paul's arm. He led him to the box and showed him how to put the supplies in their proper places. Paul smiled and shook his head. He knew where everything went, but let Herbie show him anyway.

He spent half an hour with Herbie, putting screws, bolts, washers, and other small parts into supply drawers. The man's enthusiasm and innocent chatter helped Paul forget the problems he was facing for a while.

Paul said good-bye to Herbie and left the shop. He strolled down the walkway to find his father. Steve was standing on one of the docks talking to a local fisherman. Paul approached and extended his hand to the fisherman.

"Hi, Paul," he said, shaking Paul's hand. "Your father told me you were visiting for a few days. How's New York?"

Paul smiled. "Busy, but I love it. I had the chance to take a few days off, though, and thought it would be nice to see Mom and Dad during the summer for a change. That doesn't happen very often."

"I know Marian must be happy. Well, enjoy your visit, Paul. It's good to see you again," the man waved and stepped onto his boat. "I'll drop those traps off later, Steve," he said before having one of his deckhands untie the boat.

"If I'm not there, just give them to Herbie. He'll leave them in the shop for me," Steve said, waving back at him.

Paul and Steve walked together from the dock back to the walkway. "I know it's early, but let's get some lunch," Steve said to Paul.

Paul nodded and stuffed his hands into his pockets. They walked in silence to the diner that overlooked the water. It was busy, but they didn't have to wait long for a table.

The waitress smiled and hugged Paul. "So good to see you, Paul. How's life in New York?"

Paul smiled and lied, "Great, Connie. Life's good! How's your family?"

"They're good, Paul. Thanks for asking. What can I get you?" she asked, her pen poised over her order pad.

"Iced tea and the fish sandwich," Paul answered. He closed the menu and put it back in the slot on the wall by the table.

"How about you, Steve?" she asked, turning to Paul's father.

"Same for me, Connie. Make mine coffee, though, instead of tea."

Connie left them and returned quickly with their drinks. Paul squeezed lemon into his tea, and Steve emptied sugar packets into his coffee. They each took a sip of their drinks.

Steve put his cup down and leaned forward, his forearms resting on the table. "Come to any decisions?"

"Not really," Paul replied. "I feel like I need to be alone for a while, Dad. Do you mind if I take the boat out?"

"No, Son, of course not. It's all yours. But are you sure you don't want some company? I have extra help at the shop for the summer, as always. I can take the afternoon off."

Paul shook his head. "Thanks, Dad, but no. I really want to be alone. I need to think."

"Okay, Son. I can respect that." Steve pulled his keys out of his pocket and removed the boat keys from the ring. He handed them across the table to Paul. "There's bottled water and staples in my refrigerator at the shop. Don't go out without them. There's nothing on the boat."

"I won't, Dad. Thanks." Paul put the keys into his pocket.

Connie returned with their lunch plates and topped off their drinks. "Let me know if you need anything else," she said with a smile before walking away.

"Herbie was telling me the senator has asked for more work on his boat," Paul said, squeezing ketchup on to his fries.

"That man is definitely keeping things profitable this season. You know, he's not a bad guy. He's intelligent and easy going. We've become friends since he's been here. You'd probably like him," Steve said before biting into his sandwich.

"I probably would. You've always been a good judge of character, Dad. Do you think he's guilty of what he was accused of?"

Steve wiped his mouth with his napkin and shook his head. "I don't think so. But, really, who knows for sure – except for him and the woman who accused him."

They spent the rest of their lunch talking about how good the season had been for Steve. They finished their lunch and Paul insisted on paying the bill. They left the diner and walked back to the marina. Steve went into the shop and packed up water and snacks for his son.

"Sure you don't want some company?" Steve asked when Paul turned toward the dock where Steve's boat was tied off.

"Yeah, I'm sure." Paul stepped into the boat and took the supplies from Steve. "Thanks Dad. I appreciate it."

Steve untied the boat. "God, protect him," he prayed as he waved to Paul.

Paul guided the boat out of the slip and steered it slowly out of the marina. Once he was clear of the small space, he increased his speed and rushed out into the open water. The water sprayed against his skin as he turned quickly, the cool mist a relief from the beating sun.

He slowed the engine and moved closer to the shore. He found an out-of-the-way spot under a cluster of trees whose branches stretched out over the water. He dropped the anchor and sat on the edge of the boat.

He closed his eyes. The breeze rippled the water, causing it to lap against the sides of the boat. The only other sounds were from motors in the distance and seagulls screeching overhead.

Paul wished he could just motor off and not look back. He didn't know how to face the problems that had developed in his life. He felt like there were no right answers. Whatever decision he made held serious consequences. He knew he couldn't continue to support the practices in his company. He also knew, though, that going to the authorities meant he would have to forfeit his position and change the lifestyle he enjoyed – maybe even face prison time. He didn't even want to consider what Marcus might do to him.

Paul opened his eyes and slipped down onto the floor of the boat. He pulled a pillow off the bench and shoved it under his head. "I don't want to think about anything," he said to himself, closing his eyes again and stretching out in the boat. He folded his hands over his chest and tried to concentrate on the sound of the water.

The sun was starting its descent by the time Paul steered the boat back into its slip. He cut the engine and tossed the rope onto the dock. His father came out of the shop and fastened the rope to the bollard.

"So? Did you enjoy the water?" Steve asked as Paul stepped up from the boat.

"Yeah, I did. I spent the whole afternoon anchored under a cluster of trees. It was a nice break," Paul replied, shifting the pack with the remaining water to his shoulder. "I'm starving, though! Do you think Mom cooked, or would you guys like to go out?"

"I'm sure she cooked. Pete dropped lobster and shrimp off when his boat pulled back in. They had a very good catch. You should see the lobster he came back with! We won't go to bed hungry tonight!"

Steve went back into the shop long enough to turn off the lights and lock up. They went up the walkway toward town. The house was in sight before either spoke.

"Did you get any thinking done while you were out there?" Steve asked.

"Yeah, I did a lot of thinking, but still don't have a concrete solution. I'm definitely not going back and acting like I'm in agreement with it all. I just don't know exactly what to do yet."

Steve stopped before they reached the backdoor of the house. Paul walked ahead.

"Son, hold on a minute," Steve said.

Paul turned back toward Steve. "Yeah, Dad?" He walked back to stand beside him.

"I hope I haven't overstepped my bounds here, but I presented your situation to Burt Maxwell…"

"The senator! Dad! What were you thinking?" Paul interrupted.

"Just calm down. I presented it hypothetically. I didn't mention names, company, or even city for that matter. I asked one of those 'If-I-had-a-friend-in-this-situation' questions. Don't get all excited." Steve reached over and grasped Paul's arm.

"You've got to be careful, Dad. You're going to hang me." Paul shook his head and looked off into the distance. "So," he said, looking back at Steve. "What did he say?"

"He had some suggestions that may keep you out of trouble. Well, big trouble anyway. You'd have to go to the authorities and cut some kind of deal with the District Attorney in New York, but he thinks you'd be able to work something out. I don't understand it all and I'd rather he explained it to you, if you decide you're willing to tell him everything."

"I don't know, Dad. I need to think about this one. Could he guarantee me some kind of protection against Marcus?"

"Paul, how sure are you about this guy? You sound like one of those overly-dramatic movies we see on cable. Are you sure you aren't just being paranoid?"

Paul shook his head and sighed. "Dad, trust me. I'm sure. That's the one thing I AM sure of in all of this."

Paul sat up in bed, his heart racing. His sheets and shorts were soaked with sweat, his hair plastered to the sides of his head. Pushing the sheets back, he swung his feet around to the floor and raked his hands through his hair. It was the dream again. He put his face in his hands and shook his head. Why did he keep having the same dream?

"Well, almost the same dream," he thought. It had started out the same. The same gentle rocking of the boat, the easy lapping of the water against the hull. The sun shined bright on his face; the sails filled with the light breeze. The buoy could be heard in the distance, and he could see himself resting in the boat, his hands folded on his chest, a slight smile on his suntanned face. Herbie had even appeared, offering him the loaf of bread before vanishing into thin air.

In an instant, though, the sun had vanished and darkness filled the sky. Thunder rolled, the wind became strong. The rain started to hammer the cabin and the waves surged. Water was filling the boat faster than he could pump it out. The wind and waves raged against the boat, tearing the sails and pounding the hull. Paul was too far from shore to make it back before the boat sank.

He fell to the deck and wrapped his arms around the mast, squeezing his eyes shut. He clung to the boat with all of his might. He heard wood snapping and felt the mast tremble as the top broke away and plunged into the sea. He could hear the hull breaking apart as the waves ripped away at the boat. The water had filled the boat and was pulling it into the depths of the sea.

Paul heard a voice call to him just as the thunder rolled again. He was able to wrestle himself awake. He didn't know who had called to him or what they had said. He only knew that, in his dream, he was about die.

He shuddered at the memory of it. He pulled his robe on and went to the kitchen. It was only 5:30, but he knew he'd never be able to go back to sleep. He started the coffee pot and opened the kitchen curtains. Birds hopped around under the feeders, pecking at the seed that had fallen to the ground. His mother loved to watch the birds in the morning.

The coffee maker gurgled as the last drops of coffee dripped into the pot. Paul took three cups from the cabinet and set them by the coffee maker. He filled one and took it to the table.

"I thought I was smelling coffee," Steve said, his slippers scuffing along the floor as he walked across the kitchen. He poured himself a cup and sat across from Paul. "Did you sleep?" he asked.

"A little," Paul answered. He took a drink of his coffee. "I've had the same dream – or should I say variations of the same dream – for a couple of months now. The version I had this morning scared me half to death."

"You're under a lot of stress. I don't doubt that could stir up some nightmares. Do you have plans today?" he asked before sipping his coffee.

"I thought about seeing Grandmother. Then I might come down to the shop. I don't know. I haven't really decided yet."

"Feel like working? Herbie's the only person I've got today. The kid I have helping me from the school has some college visitation planned today. I could sure use your help."

"Maybe I will," Paul answered, surprising Steve. "Don't look so shocked Dad! Maybe a little manual labor will help me think straight!"

Steve laughed and rose from the table. "Well then! Let's get going before you change your mind!"

Steve cooked breakfast while Paul showered and dressed.

"I showered last night," he said when Paul offered to take over the cooking after his shower. "It won't take me long to throw some clothes on."

They were seated at the table, finishing their breakfast, when Marian padded into the kitchen. She poured herself a cup of coffee and sat down with them. She smiled when Steve told her of their plans for the day.

"You two get going," she said, shooing them out of the kitchen when Paul offered to wash the dishes. "I'll take care of these."

They walked together to the marina, discussing the work Steve had to do on the Senator's boat. Herbie was waiting at the shop, leaning against the side of the building.

"You's late, Mr. Matthews!" Herbie said when Steve unlocked the door and disarmed the alarm.

"I know, Herbie. Sorry about that. Paul's going to help out today. Will that make up for my being late?" Steve asked, turning back to Herbie.

"Oh yeah, sure! This is great!" Herbie exclaimed, beaming at Paul. "You can help me with my stuff!"

Steve laughed. "We'll see, Herbie. I had hoped Paul would help me get started on the new cabin paneling in the senator's boat."

"Oh, okay." Herbie shrugged his shoulders and went to the stock room to finish unpacking some boxes.

Steve handed Paul a tool belt. The two men gathered up the tools they'd need and left Herbie to watch the shop. They spent the morning ripping the old paneling from the walls of the boat cabin. By lunchtime, Paul was drained.

"I haven't worked like that in years, Dad. I have sore muscles I forgot existed!"

Steve laughed. "It's good for you! You giving up for the day or are you sticking around?"

"I'll stick around. I need to check in with Marshall, though. I don't want him getting nervous. Want me to meet you at the diner?"

"Sure. See you in a few minutes."

Paul walked to the end of the pier as Steve headed down the walkway toward the diner. Paul hit the speed dial for Marshall and held the phone to his ear. Marshall answered and Paul could hear laughter in the background.

"Marshall, it's Paul."

"Paul. Good to hear from you. I had hoped to hear from you earlier," Marshall replied, a hint of irritation in his voice.

"Sorry Marshall. I guess I wasn't thinking. I've spent the morning working with my father. Any news?"

"Pratt's meeting with our attorneys this afternoon. We still haven't heard from Kevin. Nothing for you to worry about though, Paul. Everything's under control."

"Good, that's a relief."

"Keep in touch with us, Paul," Marshall said before ending the call.

Paul stared down at his phone and shook his head. "I really wish I knew what to do," he said to himself. He put his phone into his pocket and turned toward the walkway.

Herbie was standing a few feet away; his hands were pushed deep into his pockets.

Paul walked over to him. "Herbie, are you going to get some lunch?"

Herbie nodded and looked out over the bay. He turned back to Paul. "Paul, can I tell you about something?"

Paul sighed. He really wasn't in the mood for Herbie. He had too much to think about. The last thing he wanted at the moment was one of Herbie's stories.

"Sure Herbie. I have to meet Dad soon, so tell me quick."

Herbie pointed to the bench near the shop. Paul walked over and sat down. Herbie shuffled over and sat down next to him. He shifted his weight and folded his hands over his knees before looking at Paul.

"Paul, I think you need to hear a few things that my Daddy told me before he went to be with Jesus," Herbie said with surprising authority in his voice.

Paul was startled by the change in Herbie's character. He didn't have the same child-like sound to his voice. His speech sounded older - normal. Paul wasn't sure what to think of it. "Okay, Herbie. I'm listening."

Herbie looked out over the water. "My Dad told me when I was a kid that God has all the answers to our problems. I know you're having some bad problems right now, Paul. I heard you talking. I know, too, that you know about God." Herbie glanced at Paul before looking back out over the water. "Knowing about God isn't enough, Paul. My Dad said that God and Jesus and the Bible are like having bread. You can have bread in your house but if you don't eat it, you'll still be hungry."

Herbie took a breath and looked into Paul's eyes. "You can slice the bread up, put butter or jelly on it, but if you don't eat it, it won't do you no good."

Paul's heart beat harder in his chest. His dream invaded his thoughts, Herbie's smile and the loaf of bread in his hand coming clearly into his mind. Paul wanted to speak, but Herbie kept talking.

"Paul, God and the Bible are like that. You can have a Bible, but if you don't read it, you'll never know what it says. And if you do read it, but don't let God talk to you through it, you'll never know what God wants to do for you."

Herbie rose from the bench and looked down at Paul. "You're the one who has to pick it up and read it, Paul. You're the one who has to open your heart and let God talk to you. He can fix your problems, but you have to let Him." Herbie stuffed his hands into his pockets and smiled at Paul before turning away and shuffling up the pier toward the walkway.

Paul watched him go. Every part of him was numb. Herbie had seemed to grow into a man. He couldn't believe this overgrown child had such faith. He also couldn't deny that God was trying to get his attention.

TWENTY-SEVEN

BROOKE WAS RELIEVED WHEN LUNCHTIME arrived. She had been restless all morning. She'd said quick, silent prayers, but the overwhelming feeling that something was wrong refused to leave her.

"Julie, I'm going to lunch. I'll be back in an hour or so," Brooke said, walking over to where Julie was working. "You should probably go eat, too."

"Okay, Brooke. Maybe I will. My hands are killing me! I think I'll be doing beadwork in my sleep!" Julie laughed.

"I know what you mean," Brooke replied with a laugh, before leaving the prep room.

A warm breezed greeted her as she left the building and walked down the block to a café. Most of the patrons were sitting at tables on the sidewalk, enjoying the pleasant weather. Brooke ordered her lunch and took it to the courtyard next to the studio.

"Lord, bless this food and please, whatever it is that has me feeling like something's wrong, you know what it is. Take care of it," Brooke prayed before biting into her sandwich.

She leaned her head back and felt the breeze on her face. The sun shone bright and hot. She wished she could work outside and feel the summer warmth all day. She dropped her lunch wrappers into the trash and took a quick walk around the block.

"God, why can't I shake this feeling? I really wish I knew what was going on," she prayed as she again was burdened with restlessness.

She stopped outside the studio and looked up at the blue sky. Paul's face invaded her thoughts and dread washed over her. "God, is it Paul? Is he the one I need to be praying for?" The anxiety became stronger.

Brooke returned to the courtyard and sat on a bench under a shade tree. She closed her eyes in prayer, her burden for Paul growing heavier.

"Lord Jesus, he needs You. Please, reveal Yourself to him." Tears streamed down her cheeks as her words turned into sobs.

She spent the remainder of her lunch in prayer. Peace washed over her as she rose from the bench and walked to the studio. Her cell phone rang as she pushed through the doors into the lobby.

"Hi, Papa," Brooke answered. "Is everything okay?"

"Yes, I'm fine," Nick said. "Don't always assume there's something wrong with me when I call you."

Brooke laughed. "Okay, Papa, I'm sorry. So, what's up? Are you still going to Syracuse with me tonight?"

"Oh, yes, I'm still planning to go along with you." Nick paused and cleared his throat. "Sweetheart, have you seen the newspaper today?"

"No, I haven't. Why?"

"Paul's employer was in the news again. Their Vice President, Kevin Murphy, was found dead this morning – apparent suicide."

"Suicide! Oh, no, Papa!"

"I just thought you should know. I don't know if Paul knows yet. I haven't heard from him since I talked to him Tuesday."

"No wonder I've had such a burden for him today. If you hear from him, please let me know, Papa."

"I will, Sweetheart. I'll see you tonight," Nick replied before hanging up the phone.

Brooke stepped into the elevator. "God, please," she prayed as the doors closed. "Please be with Paul."

———

Paul walked to his grandmother's house late in the morning. His muscles were sore from the work he'd done with his father the day before on Mr. Maxwell's boat. He hadn't done such hard work in years and despite his efforts to stay in shape, his body was hurting all over.

He had tried calling Marshall and Pratt all morning with no success. He thought it odd that no one was reachable and that his own cell messages were few. He'd left messages on their voice mails before checking in with Kelly for his own messages.

"Grandmother, it's me," Paul shouted into the house as he turned the knob and walked into the entryway.

"Paul, I'm in the kitchen," she called back to him.

Paul walked through to the kitchen where he found her drying dishes. He leaned over and kissed his grandmother on the cheek. "No piano students?" he asked, looking into the living room.

"No, they're all away on vacations with their parents. It's a welcome break."

"I'll help," he said, putting the dishes into the cupboards as she finished drying them.

"Your father tells me you are facing a serious problem at work," she said, handing him a glass. "Care to tell me about it?"

Paul shrugged his shoulders and put the glass into the cupboard. "It could take a while."

"Well, have lunch with me. That should be enough time."

Paul made sandwiches while his grandmother filled two glasses with iced tea. They took their lunch out to the patio where they sat in the shade of an umbrella. Paul summarized his situation while they ate their lunch.

Paul finished his lunch and pushed the dishes aside. He looked over at his grandmother. "Well? Any suggestions?"

She dabbed her lips with her napkin. She sat back in her chair and folded her hands in her lap. "Do you have any ideas of your own yet?"

"I've been over this so many times..." he shook his head and folded his arms. He looked out at his grandmother's well manicured lawn and sighed.

"And?" she asked, waving a hand toward him to continue.

"I think I need to go to the authorities and hope for the best. Dad talked to Burt Maxwell, presenting it to him as a hypothetical. I guess he had some thoughts that could keep me from facing any serious charges. But honestly, Grandmother, as worried as I am about going to prison, I'd be more worried if I felt like I could just let this go. What kind of a man have I become that I've allowed myself to even get involved in this? I don't even know who I am anymore!" Paul shook his head and looked away again.

"Paul, if this man can help you, I believe it's time you sat down and talked to him. I don't often agree with your father, despite the fact that he's my son. We've always had different views on things. But, in this case, I believe he's right. Perhaps our former senator can offer you some advice worth considering." She rose from the table and went into the house.

Paul gathered up the dirty dishes and followed her inside. He helped clean up the kitchen before kissing her good-bye and walking back to his parents' house. His phone chirped.

"Hello?"

"Paul, it's Nick Barsanti."

"Nick, how are you?"

"I'm good, Paul. I just wanted to check on you, see how you're doing," Nick paused. "Have you seen the news or spoken with your employer today?"

Paul stopped at the end of his parents' driveway. "No, I haven't. What's going on, Nick?"

"Paul, it was in the paper this morning that the body of Kevin Murphy was found in a cabin in the Adirondacks. They believe it was a suicide."

Dread washed over Paul. He pulled the phone away from his ear, closed his eyes and clenched his jaw. "It just keeps getting worse and worse, doesn't it?" he said to himself.

"Paul? Are you still there?"

Paul put the phone back to his ear. "I'm here, Nick. I'm just so shocked. Kevin has never been my favorite person, but this really surprises me. He doesn't strike me as the suicidal type."

"Well, I've got a call in to my in-laws in Old Forge. Brooke's grandparents live up there. I'd like to hear what the locals have to say. If I find anything out, I'll let you know," Nick said. "In fact, Brooke and I are going to Syracuse this weekend to take care of a few things. Maybe I'll see if they can meet us there. Either way, I'll let you know what they have to say."

"Thanks, Nick, I appreciate it."

Paul stuffed the phone back into his pocket and went into the house. His father was at the marina and his mother had gone out. He went up to his room and pulled out his laptop. He got online and found the article about Kevin. The time on the article was from late morning. Why hadn't

Marshall or Pratt called him? Even if they hadn't received his messages, they should have called with this news.

Paul pulled out his cell phone and considered calling Marshall. Changing his mind, he put the phone back into his pocket and hurried down the stairs. "I want to talk to Dad first," he said to himself.

Paul raced to the marina. He found his father at work on the senator's boat. "Dad," he called into the cabin. "I need to talk to you, if you can spare a minute."

Steve came out of the cabin, pulling off safety goggles and work gloves. "I need a break anyway." He grabbed a bottle of water and stepped out onto the dock. He wrinkled his brow. "What's the matter, son? You look worse than you did Tuesday when you pulled in here."

Paul told him about the phone call from Nick and the article about Kevin. "Dad, according to the article, no one had heard from Kevin since Tuesday morning. They estimate his time of death to be sometime Tuesday night." Paul shook his head and rubbed the back of his neck. "Kevin didn't act like he was suicidal when he left that meeting. He was mad – I mean *really* mad."

Steve walked to a bench under a tree. Paul followed and sat down next to him. "Dad, I've left messages all morning, and no one has called back. Kelly didn't even say anything when I talked to her this morning."

"Maybe she didn't know, Son. As far as your employers, maybe they're tied up with details from this whole thing."

"You're grasping, Dad. I know these men. They should have called me by now."

Steve nodded and looked out over the bay. He crossed his arms and looked back at Paul. "What do you want to do, son?"

Paul took a deep breath. "I think I need to talk to Burt Maxwell before I come to any real decisions. I'm at a total loss right now."

Steve took out his cell phone and dialed. He held the phone to his ear. "Burt? Hi. It's Steve Matthews. Remember that scenario I shared with you the other night? I'd like to discuss that with you further, if you don't mind." He was quiet for a few moments. "One hour, on your boat? Sure, sounds good." Steve ended the call and looked back at Paul. "Done. He'll meet us in an hour on his boat."

Steve went back to the boat to clean up his mess before going home to shower. Paul went home long enough to retrieve his laptop and briefcase. He sat on the bench by the senator's boat and waited for his father. He closed his eyes and tried to remain calm.

He opened his eyes and saw his father walking toward him, Burt Maxwell by his side. He rose from the bench as the men approached.

His father nodded toward Paul, "Mr. Burt Maxwell, this is my son, Paul."

The senator reached for Paul's hand and smiled his huge, toothy smile. "Pleased to meet you, Paul." He motioned toward the boat.

The three of them made their way into the cabin of the boat. They avoided the room being remodeled and sat in the kitchenette. Mr. Maxwell took water and soda from the refrigerator and set it on the table before sitting down.

"Okay, Steve. Tell me what I can do," Burt Maxwell said, looking at Paul's father.

Steve nodded toward Paul. "I think I'll let my son give you the details."

Burt folded his hands on the table and looked expectantly at Paul. When Paul didn't speak, he shrugged his shoulders. "I'm here, Paul. I'm gathering from the story your father shared with me the other night, you're in some kind of trouble. I can't help you if you don't spill it."

Paul sat back in his chair and folded his hands on his knee. "Sir, I don't want to be rude, but may I ask you something before I tell you about this?"

Burt Maxwell laughed. "Of course you can, Son. I bet I can already guess what it is, though." He smiled and stared into Paul's eyes. "You're going to ask me whether I was guilty of those sexual harassment charges."

Paul nodded.

"I'm gettin' used to it," the senator replied. "And, I understand. How can you trust me to help you with something this sensitive if I'm guilty of harassing that woman?" He reached for a bottle of water and took a drink before continuing. "The answer, Son, is no, I'm not guilty. If I'd been guilty, I would have paid her off and moved on. Instead, I let it go to trial and I was found innocent of all charges. The only reason I resigned when I did was to open my spot for another candidate. There was no way

I would get voted in to another term, and why let the other side win? It just made sense."

"Thanks for that, Sir. I hope I didn't offend you. I just had to know," Paul said.

"No problem. Now, let's get down to business. What exactly is your story?" he asked, leaning forward and resting his elbows on the table.

Paul took a deep breath and told Burt Maxwell the whole story. From Marcus' purchase of the troubled plastics manufacturer to his interests in the Middle East, Paul took him through every detail of the information he had. He shared with him the trip to Greece that resulted in a new client for the company and Marcus' visitor from France who had a friend at the U.N. He ended with the apparent suicide of Kevin Murphy.

The former senator sat back in his chair. He crossed his arms and cupped his chin in his hand. He stared long and hard at Paul. He looked over at Steve and back at Paul. "Paul, I have to know — exactly how involved are you? What, precisely, have you done for this employer of yours?"

"I knew about the business purchase in its final stages, not before. I knew about Pratt's extra-marital activities. I have always had an uneasiness about Marcus. But, that's the extent of my involvement."

"You encouraged your clients to purchase stocks in the company Mr. Reed was purchasing?"

"Yes, but I wasn't aware of Marcus' purchase offer at that time."

"You encouraged your clients to purchase stock in Mr. Reed's other business interests?"

Paul nodded. "I did, but I was not aware of his involvement in the Middle East."

Burt Maxwell rose from the table and pulled a notebook out of a drawer. He scribbled furiously, asking Paul to clarify names, dates, and the most commonly recommended stocks within his company. He pushed the pad away and looked at Paul.

"I'm going to make some phone calls. I will be in New York in two weeks. I want you to go home and pretend you are 100% behind your little corporate family. Take notes, keep your eyes and ears open, and, when I call, have information for me," Burt instructed.

"Okay," Paul replied. "I just make believe none of this bothers me?"

"Yes, that's exactly what you do. In addition to all of this, I want you to plan an intimate little dinner party in honor of your friend Marcus Reed and put me on your invitation list. I will call you early in the week and give you a couple of other names, depending on what I can find out. You have to make this man believe you are in his camp. I want the guest list when it's complete so I can do some checking on these people."

Paul's cell phone chirped. He pulled the phone out of his pocket and looked at the display. "It's Marshall," he said, looking up at Burt.

Burt shrugged, "So answer it. Remember, you are just another happy employee."

"Hi, Marshall, thanks for calling me back. I heard a rumor that something happened to Kevin. Is it true?" Paul asked, running his sentences together to keep Marshall from interrupting.

"Yes, Paul. Unfortunately it is true. An autopsy is being done, but they are certain it was suicide. The calling hours and funeral won't be until Tuesday. Don't feel you need to cut your weekend short."

"Marshall, I think I may head back early."

Burt scribbled a note on the notepad and handed it to Paul.

Paul read it quickly and nodded to Burt. "I think I'll start back tonight. That way, I can be in town if I'm needed."

"Paul, you do what you feel you must. I admit it would be good to have you here right now. This has all been so difficult," Marshall said.

"I understand Marshall. I'll get back as soon as I can."

Burt nodded his approval. "Start for New York tonight. You'll be too tired to complete the drive. Spend the night somewhere - get a receipt so you can prove your attempt to get home. Take some time to relax before you jump back into the furnace, so to speak. Go to the office as soon as you get in tomorrow and do whatever you can to convince them you're still on their side."

"I'll do my best. Anything else I can do?" he asked, handing the notepad back to Burt.

"Pray this works," Burt replied, taking the notepad back. "I'll do whatever I can Paul, but only God knows how far this will go."

Paul drove to the bed & breakfast in Biddeford he'd stayed in the last time he'd visited his parents. He settled into his room and then went out to find someplace to get a late dinner. He walked the streets and found a little café that was still open. He ate a light meal and went back to the bed & breakfast.

He strolled out into the garden and sat on the bench near the fountain. He watched the water flow in the fountain before going back to his room. He made a call to Marshall, informing him of his decision to spend the night in Biddeford.

When Paul woke the next morning, rain was pelting the windows. Lightning flashed through the sky; the thunder rumbled loudly overhead. Paul showered and dressed quickly. He packed his bag and took it to his car before enjoying the breakfast provided with his stay.

He was on the road by 9:00, but took his time driving back to New York. He was in the City before 3:00, the afternoon traffic forcing him to a crawl. The rain had followed him from Maine, drenching the streets of New York. He slowly made his way to the office, parked his car and walked purposefully through the lobby to the elevators.

Paul stopped by his office, leafed through the pile of messages on his desk. He booted up his computer and checked his email before going down the hall.

Pratt's office was empty, but the computer was on and his jacket was draped over a chair. Paul found him in Marshall's office, a brandy in his hand, laughing at something Marcus was saying.

Paul tapped on the open door and entered. "I got here as soon as I could."

Marcus crossed the room and gripped both of Paul's shoulders. "I must tell you, Paul. We are most relived to have you here. This has been a difficult week."

Paul offered a grim expression. "I couldn't stay away after what happened to Kevin. I belong here."

Pratt jumped up from his chair and poured a drink for Paul. "Have a seat Paul."

"Did your time away help you?" Marshall asked.

"I think it did, Marshall. I'm rested now and feel like I can get back to work," Paul said before sipping his drink.

"That's good news. As you already know, the calling hours and funeral for Kevin will be Tuesday. While it's a blow to our company, we must admit that Kevin wasn't really a big contributor. We won't replace him immediately. That would be inappropriate, but I think it's safe to say that it will be business as usual."

"Is there anything I need to know, anything I've missed this week?" Paul asked.

"Not too much. Mostly legal matters from Pratt's arrest. It doesn't appear it will do any real damage. We will, of course, have to stroke our clients a little, put their minds at ease, but that's to be expected. It also doesn't appear that the Board of Directors is too upset," Marshall explained. He took a sip of his drink and continued, "Marcus' new business purchase will be finalized Wednesday. I think that brings you up to speed."

Paul took another sip of his drink. "This may not be the best time," he began, "and please, if I'm out of line, let me know. But, I would like to give Marcus a dinner party, at my condo, to celebrate his newest acquisition."

Marcus cocked his head to one side and looked at Paul with a warm expression. "Paul, I am most honored."

Marshall looked at Pratt and shook his head. "I don't believe it would be the least bit out of line. I think it's a wonderful idea, Paul."

Paul smiled. "Good, I'm glad to hear that. I'd like to keep it small, intimate – only our closest friends. I'd appreciate any suggestions you might have for the guest list."

Marshall folded his hands and rested them on the edge of his desk. "I think we can manage that," he said, looking at Pratt and Marcus with a nod.

Marcus rose from his seat. He walked over and clasped Paul's shoulder. "Welcome back, Paul," he said with a smile.

TWENTY-EIGHT

PAPA'S LAUGHTER AND THE SMELL of coffee roused Brooke from sleep Saturday morning and led her into Linda's kitchen. She found Papa and Linda seated at the table, sipping coffee.

Linda looked up at Brooke. "How'd you sleep, Honey?" she asked as she stood and poured coffee into another cup and motioned for Brooke to sit.

Brooke shrugged and accepted the cup. "Okay, I guess. I had trouble not thinking about Daddy."

Brooke and Papa had arrived the night before and settled into Linda's spare rooms. It was strange to Brooke to be sleeping next door to her childhood home rather than in it. Every time she closed her eyes, she could see herself curled up in her own bed in her old room, her father asleep down the hall.

"Those rooms are empty now," she had thought, trying to put out of her mind the fact that nothing of hers remained in that house and another family would be moving in and sleeping in those rooms soon. She had cried herself to sleep, missing her father and wishing she could have seen him one last time.

Linda reached over and patted Brooke's hand, startling her from her thoughts. "It's okay, Honey. It'll hurt for awhile."

Papa insisted on cooking what he called an Italian-American breakfast – crisp bacon, spicy sausage, scrambled eggs with his own secret seasoning, and toast. He brewed another pot of strong coffee, put a plate of fresh fruit and biscotti in the center of the table and told Linda and Brooke to help themselves while he did the cooking.

"When did you get this, Papa?" Brooke asked, taking a biscotti from the plate.

Papa turned to Brooke and smiled sheepishly. "I borrowed your car keys early this morning and drove to the bakery near the University."

265

"Borrowed, huh?" Brooke laughed.

"Of course! I put them back didn't I?" Papa chuckled as he put the toast and a platter with the sausage and bacon on the table. "Besides, I didn't think you'd mind since it was for something as important as breakfast!"

Papa scooped the eggs onto three plates and handed one to Brooke and another to Linda. He sat down with his own plate as Linda refilled coffee cups and poured juice.

She sat down and smiled. "I can't remember the last time I had someone cook me breakfast. Thanks, Nick!"

"Don't mention it. Don't get used to it, though. Tomorrow, it's your turn," he said, giving Linda a wink.

Linda laughed. "I think I can handle that!"

Brooke helped clean up after breakfast and spent the rest of the morning with the realtor, her father's lawyer, and the family who'd put the purchase offer on the house.

Mike and Janet Phillips were pleasant, warm people. Their five year-old daughter, Brittany was quiet and shy. Brooke finally got the little girl to talk to her by asking about the baby.

Little Brittany pointed to the four month-old baby in her mother's arms and said "That's Sarah and she's *my* baby!" She smiled at Brooke and moved closer to the infant.

The morning went well. The realtor had hired a cleaning company to clean the house and polish the hardwood the week before. The Phillips' were pleased with the condition of the house and agreed to sign the papers that morning. Brooke, to the dismay of the attorney, gave them permission to start painting and wallpapering the house.

"But, Ms. Barsanti! What if the sale falls through? Do you really want to let them make changes before it's final?" the attorney asked.

In the end, Brooke agreed to put in writing that should the sale fall through, no compensation would be made to the Phillips' for any of the work. No major structural changes could be made and the appliances currently in the house would be kept until the closing.

All of the preliminary paperwork was signed and notarized. The final paperwork would be sent by courier to New York for Brooke's signature when the time came, and then the Phillips would be able to move into the house.

Once the formalities were complete and the realtor and attorney left, Brooke spent some time with the family. Mike and Janet were both professors. Mike taught landscape architecture. Janet was a Biology professor. Both were in their thirties and loved the university area.

By the time they buckled their fussy infant into her carseat and drove off, Brooke felt better about selling the house. She knew they'd love it as much as her father had, and would take good care of it.

Grandma and Grandpa Merriweather had arrived sometime during the morning while Brooke was occupied with the house. Grandma and Linda made salads and desserts while Grandpa and Papa went to the market for steaks and shrimp for the grill. Brooke was greeted by the aroma of her grandmother's peach cobbler when she walked into Linda's kitchen.

Brooke helped Linda carry salads and trays to the patio where Grandma was busy filling glasses with ice. Papa and Grandpa were standing over the grill, laughing. Brooke smiled. It was nice to have part of her family together again.

"How much longer will that take?" Grandma asked, looking toward the grill.

Grandpa opened the grill and poked at the steaks. "They still have a little while."

"Don't forget to put those vegetables on," she said, nodding toward the foil package on the grill's shelf.

"I think we've got it under control, Nellie," he replied, motioning toward Papa.

Grandma shook her head. "The last time you let yourself get distracted at the grill, Richard, we had charcoal instead of steaks!"

Grandpa handed the fork to Papa. "Maybe you'll be able to do a better job. I'll just watch!" He folded his arms and looked over at Brooke's grandmother with a smile.

The three women laughed.

"Let's leave those two alone for a while and walk over to Martin's yard," Linda said, motioning for Brooke and Nellie to follow.

"What are you planning to do about your father's car?" Linda asked, nodding toward the garage.

Brooke shook her head. "I hadn't really thought about the car. I guess I need to figure that out too, don't I?"

"Honey, your father's car is in much better shape than yours," Grandma said. "Why don't you keep it and sell yours?"

Brooke looked over at her grandmother and laughed. "Grandma, I'm not really a Cadillac person. I like smaller cars."

"So, sell the Caddy and get yourself something a little safer, more reliable. That old Pontiac of yours is what, twenty years old? It looks like it's going to fall apart!"

"I probably will. Like I said, I just hadn't thought of it."

They walked through the yard and stopped at the rose garden. Brooke's smile faded as she looked down at the dead rose bush that had once been her father's. "I guess I'll have to dig that up, won't I? I'm not sure I can do it. I know it's dead, but it's always been here."

"I know, Honey. That's why I wanted you to walk over here with me," Linda said, putting her arm around Brooke's shoulders. "I'll dig it up, if you want me to. I'll even give it a couple of more weeks if you want, though I doubt it will revive at this point."

Brooke nodded. "I appreciate that, Linda. I know Daddy wouldn't want it left for the new owners."

"Steaks are done!" Papa shouted.

The women made their way back to Linda's yard and finished setting the table while the men took the meat off the grill. They sat down, joined hands and bowed their heads.

"Thank you, Lord, for this precious time you've blessed us with," Grandpa prayed. "Bless this food, this fellowship and this dear family. In Your precious Name we pray, Lord Jesus, Amen."

Trays and bowls were passed around the table until each person had a full plate. They ate in silence for a few minutes, enjoying the quiet presence of family. Plates were empty before Papa looked over at Grandpa Merriweather and broke the silence.

"So, Richard, were you able to find anything out about Kevin Murphy?"

Richard wiped his mouth with his napkin and rested his elbows on the table. "Not much," he replied. "He apparently got into an argument at the convenience store on Tuesday night with someone no one recognized. It got pretty heated before Mr. Murphy stormed out. He got into his car and drove toward his camp. The other guy got into a black Lincoln and drove back down the mountain. Neither of them was seen again until Murphy's body was found."

Papa leaned back and crossed his arms. "So, he was followed to Old Forge. At least, that's the way it sounds to me."

Richard nodded. "That's the way I see it too. But following someone doesn't necessarily mean they intend murder."

"Murder!" Brooke exclaimed. She looked between her two grandfathers. "The newspaper said it was a suicide!"

Papa looked at Brooke. "I know, and with the pressure from the current situation in their company, it's likely that's exactly what happened. But Paul isn't so sure. I told him I'd ask around, so I am."

Brooke shook her head. "Paul's in serious trouble, isn't he? You told me he needed prayer, but you never gave me any details, other than what I've already read in the papers. What's going on, Papa?"

"Sweetheart, I promised him I wouldn't tell you anything. I think that should be up to him, should he choose to. Yes, he is in serious trouble. Right now, all we can do for him is pray."

———

After church let out Sunday morning, Brooke took her Grandmother's advice and drove her father's Cadillac to the Honda dealership. Papa followed in her old Pontiac. She test drove the Civic Hybrid that had caught her eye and at once decided to buy it. The dealership offered top-dollar for the Caddy. The old Pontiac wasn't worth anything, but they agreed to take it off her hands.

Brooke had enough in the bank to pay the rest in cash, but with the banks closed on Sundays, she paid the balance with her credit card, knowing she'd be able to pay the bill in full when it came in. She drove off the lot with a brand new car.

"Why do you young people always want foreign cars?" Papa asked as Brooke merged into traffic on the Thruway, headed toward New York. "This doesn't help our economy, you know?"

Brooke laughed as she set the cruise control and turned off the navigational system. She'd driven this route so many times, she didn't need it. "You sound like Daddy. I know, but I really liked this car. Besides, look at it this way, I'm helping with foreign relations."

Papa chuckled. "Rationalize it any way you want. It's too late now, anyway."

"You're right, it is!" Brooke said with a smile. Her cell phone chirped in her purse. Brooke nodded toward the backseat. "Papa, can you reach that and answer it for me?"

Papa turned and reached behind Brooke's seat. He dragged her purse into his lap and pulled out her phone. "Hello?"

"Who is it?" Brooke whispered, glancing at Papa.

Papa shook his head and held up his hand. "Hi, Paul. Yes, we're on our way back now. It'll be after dinner time before we get back in."

Brooke kept glancing over at Papa, wanting to get his attention. "Why is he calling, Papa? What's going on?" she whispered.

Papa waved at her and shook his head again. "Sure, Paul. I'll see what Brooke has planned and I'll give you a call when we get closer to home." Papa paused. "Not a problem Paul. I'll see you later."

Papa ended the call and dropped the phone back into Brooke's purse before putting it behind her seat again.

"Well?" Brooke asked impatiently, glancing over at Papa.

"He knew we were together, that's why he called your phone."

"And? That doesn't tell me much, Papa. Is he okay?"

Papa nodded. "I think so. He wants to see me tonight, if we get in early enough. He wants to update me on what's happening and he has a favor to ask." He turned to look directly at Brooke, "Of both of us."

TWENTY-NINE

BROOKE STEPPED OUT OF THE cab in front of Paul's building and waited for Papa to pay the driver. Papa slid out and offered Brooke his arm. "You look lovely, my sweet granddaughter."

"You don't look bad yourself," she said, smiling nervously at him. "I can't believe I let you talk me into this."

"Paul needs our help, Sweetheart. He needed a hostess for his dinner party. He couldn't ask just anyone. Most of the women he knows would be flitting aimlessly around the room, trying to be the center of attention. He needed someone objective, someone he could count on to be sociable but not complicate things. You're level-headed and intelligent. You can do this. And don't worry, Paul understands that your being here in no way means that you are dating again."

Brooke sighed and let Papa lead her into the building. Papa stopped at the security desk and gave the security guard their names before they continued to the elevator.

They rode in silence up to Paul's condo. Brooke took a deep breath as the doors opened, trying to calm her nerves.

"Relax," Papa said, as they stepped out.

Brooke tucked her purse under her arm. "Here, let me fix your tie. The bow looks a little lop-sided. I guess it's a good thing I *did* come along," she said with a smile.

"What would I do without you?" he laughed before ringing Paul's doorbell.

Paul opened the door and motioned for them to enter. "I've hired someone to answer the door for the party, but they aren't here yet." Paul shook Papa's hand and then leaned over to kiss Brooke's cheek. "I really appreciate all of your help. The caterer was here right on time. The tables were delivered this morning and the wait-staff arrived shortly after the caterer. The smells coming from the kitchen have had my stomach growling all afternoon!"

"It's my pleasure to help a friend," Papa said. He looked around the room. The living room had been rearranged. A small band was setting up near the piano. Around the room were tables covered with white tablecloths and set with fine white china. A bud vase with a red rose and baby's breath decorated the each of the tables with simple elegance. A small, portable bar was standing in the corner opposite the band.

"Do you have enough tables?" Papa asked, turning back to Paul.

"I think so. I had more apologies than acceptances for tonight. I wasn't thinking clearly. Labor Day weekend isn't the best time to plan a dinner party, I guess. Marshall will be here and Marcus, of course. Pratt and Marjorie, Burt Maxwell, and a few of his friends from the Senate with their wives. Marcus' friend from France, Denis Beck is in town."

"Denis Beck?" Papa asked, surprised by the mention of the name. "Owns a winery outside of Paris?"

Paul wrinkled his brow. "Yes. Do you know him?"

Papa nodded, a distant look in his eyes. "I knew him when I was still living in Italy. He's an old business acquaintance."

The bell rang before Paul could ask any more questions. The rest of the staff Paul had hired for the evening arrived. The doorman stationed himself by the door. The bartender tied his apron around his waist and started emptying bags of ice into the ice buckets. Two waitresses went quickly around the room, checking the tables.

The bell rang again. Paul looked at Brooke and smiled, "You ready to help me turn on the charm?"

Brooke looked over at the door as the door man announced "Marcus Reed and Marshall Appleton, Sir."

"I guess I'll have to be." She smiled as Paul took her hand and led her to the door.

Paul looked around the room as the band played a slow jazz piece. Dinner was finished and the guests were clustered in small groups around the room. Marshall was deep in conversation with Gregory Fillman and a senator. Burt Maxwell stood with his arms crossed, listening intently as Pratt talked and gestured with his nearly-empty glass. Nick and Denis Beck were talking on the balcony.

Most of the wives were huddled near the band. Only one couple took advantage of the music. Senator Jim Poole and his wife, Tara, swayed to the music, her cheek resting on his shoulder. His eyes were closed, a smile on his face, oblivious to everything in the room, save his wife.

Brooke was standing near the balcony doors talking with Marjorie Young. The moonlight was streaming through the doors and cast a soft glow around Brooke. Her chiffon evening gown flowed gracefully over her body, giving her an angelic look. Her dark hair spilled over her shoulders and down her back. Paul wanted desperately to march across the room and take her in his arms, to hold her close and surrender to the music.

"She is a most beautiful woman, isn't she?" Marcus asked, coming to stand beside Paul.

"Yes, she is," Paul agreed.

"How did you win her back, Paul?" Marcus sipped his champagne and looked at Paul over the rim of the glass.

"I haven't exactly won her back yet, but I did manage to make her realize how much I need her."

Marcus nodded knowingly, smirking as he looked across the room at Brooke. "In other words, you agreed to behave yourself if she would agree to come back into your life." He looked back at Paul. "You gave in to her demands. Did you agree to marry her?"

"No way! Nothing like that. I'm not ready for marriage, and I'm sure she isn't either. We're just giving ourselves a little more time to figure things out. In reality, her grandfather was more instrumental in her being here tonight than I was."

"I'm sure he realizes your situation. He knows you'd be able to take care of his granddaughter most generously. Be careful, my boy. If you don't watch yourself, you'll find yourself trapped!" He smiled again and turned away from Paul.

Paul watched Marcus cross the room and join Marshall in conversation. Nick and Denis passed through the balcony doors and stopped to talk with them before joining Paul.

"I believe your evening has been quite a success, Paul. I have also enjoyed catching up with my old friend here." Denis raised his glass to Nick.

"I was surprised when Nick told me he knew you," Paul said with a smile. "He said you knew each other through business, but he never explained how a carpenter and winery owner would become associates."

Denis smiled at Paul. "Europe is smaller than it looks. Our countries are connected in many ways. It's easy for businessmen from different nations to become friends."

"Must be," Paul said. "Nick was in Italy. Marcus is based in Turkey. It seems like you guys know everyone!"

Denis Shook Paul's hand. "I thank you for your generous invitation. I must be leaving, but I was most honored to be here."

"The honor's mine, Sir."

"Give me a call before you leave, old friend," Nick said, embracing Denis. "We have a lot to catch up on."

Denis smiled at Paul and Nick and crossed the room to say good-bye to Marcus.

The guests seemed to take Denis' departure as a cue that the party was over. Marjorie helped a stumbling Pratt through the door and to the elevator.

Burt Maxwell shook Paul's hand and whispered "I'll call you Monday" before slipping out the door.

Within half an hour, Brooke, Nick and Marcus were the only remaining guests, Marcus' ever-present body guard continuing his vigil near the door.

"What a lovely evening, Paul. I appreciate your honoring me like this," Marcus said, ordering a brandy from the bar. "How about if we sit on your balcony while I finish my drink?"

"Sounds good. It *is* a little warm in here." Paul turned to Brooke and Nick. "Would either of you like another drink?"

Nick shook his head.

"No thank you, I've had my limit," was Brookes reply.

Paul gestured for them to go out onto the balcony. Marcus and Nick sat down near the railing. Paul reached for Brooke's hand and led her to a chair before seating himself.

Marcus sipped his brandy and looked at Paul. "How do you know Burt Maxwell?"

"He's friends with my father. His boat is docked at Dad's marina in Maine."

"Really? The way you described your father, I wouldn't think he'd want to be anywhere near Burt Maxwell. After all, sexually assaulting a woman would have to be against his religion," Marcus said sarcastically. He looked over at Brooke and smiled. "What do you think, my dear?"

Brooke tilted her head and smiled back at him. "No, I don't think God would condone such a terrible act, Sir. But, from what I read, Mr. Maxwell was found innocent."

Marcus laughed. "Darling, you shouldn't believe everything you read. I have no doubt his money bought his innocence."

"Why, then, didn't he just pay the girl off and be done with it?" Brooke asked, trying to mask her irritation at Marcus.

Marcus leaned forward. "Because, my dear, it looks better in the news if a court finds him innocent. That doesn't mean money wasn't tossed around to bring it about." Brooke felt her face turn red as he smiled condescendingly and let his eyes move over her body. "You'd be surprised at how easy it is to sway even the most righteous when enough money is dangled before them."

Nick cleared his throat. "I'm sorry to bring this to an end, but I am exhausted. I think the champagne has started to get to me." He rose from his chair. "Thank you for having me, Paul. It was a great party. I haven't enjoyed myself like this in ages."

Paul stood and shook Nick's hand. "Thanks for coming. I appreciate your help with everything."

Brooke started to rise, but Nick motioned for her to sit. "I don't want to break you two love birds up already. I can get myself home." He waved back at them and walked into the living room. He stumbled and grabbed the door leading from the balcony. "Maybe I do need a little help." He looked at Marcus. "Would you mind helping me out and getting me to a cab?"

Marcus chuckled. "Of course. I need to be going anyway." He stood up and walked over to Paul. "Thank you, Paul. I will see you Monday."

Paul and Brooke walked Marcus and Nick to the door.

Marcus nodded to his bodyguard. "You can have the car brought around." The man nodded and left the condo.

"Be safe, Papa," Brooke said, pulling him close for a hug. "What are you doing?" she whispered.

Nick squeezed her tightly and whispered back, "Just trust me." He pulled away from her and winked. "Okay, Mr. Reed. I'm ready to go!"

Paul and Brooke waved to them as they made their way to the elevator. Paul closed the door and looked at Brooke. "What is your grandfather up to?" he asked.

"I have no idea. He acted like he was intoxicated, but in truth, he didn't have two drinks all night. I'll bet he's hoping to get some information out of Marcus. What, I don't know."

"I don't know how much Marcus would say anyway. The man doesn't volunteer much."

"You should know my grandfather by now, Paul. If he wants the man to talk, he'll talk." She looked around the room. "I'll help you clean up a little before I go. It'll take you half the night to clean this up."

"That's okay. The caterer has already started cleaning up the kitchen. I have a cleaning crew coming in tomorrow to take care of the rest. Don't worry about it." He reached for Brooke's hand. "Please don't leave yet, though. I promise I'll behave myself. I just want to talk for a while."

Brooke nodded. "Okay, but only for a few minutes."

Paul led her back out onto the balcony and motioned for her to sit. "Brooke, I don't know how to thank you for your help tonight. Having you here helped me to relax a little. I've been a nervous wreck for over a week."

"No need to thank me, Paul. Papa explained everything. I'll do whatever I can to help you, though I have to admit I don't know what else I can do. Being the smiling hostess is about all I *can* do," Brooke said, then added with a laugh "unless you want theatre tickets."

"You believe that I'm not directly involved, don't you Brooke? Please tell me you trust me?" Paul leaned forward and clasped his hands between his knees. "I have to know you believe me."

"I do believe you, Paul." She looked away before continuing. "Please don't be hurt by this, but I believe you put a high value on status and money. I think that you'd be able to overlook a small indiscretion on the part of your employer if it meant you'd keep your position and allow you the luxury you enjoy." Brooke looked again at Paul. "What they're involved in, however, far exceeds what I believe you'd be willing to go along with."

Paul stood up and looked out over the City. He rubbed the back of his neck and sighed. "I'm living in the middle of millions of people and I feel very much alone right now. I know what I have to do, but I'm completely terrified of facing these people by myself."

Brooke rose from her chair and stood beside Paul. She rested her hand on his arm. "Paul, you aren't alone. Papa and I will be here for you. We're praying for you. We've asked people we trust to pray for you. God won't abandon you – and neither will we."

Paul looked into Brooke's eyes. He let himself swim in her beauty before reaching up and running his thumb over her cheek. "I still love you, Brooke. I hope you realize that."

Brooke reached up and took his hand from her face. "I know, Paul. And I still love you." She released his hand and walked across the balcony to the door. She stopped in the doorway and turned back to him, resting her hand on the door frame. "We just can't be what you want us to be. God has to come first in my life." Hugging herself, she shook her head and went inside.

Paul rose from the chair and followed her. "Brooke, please don't leave yet."

"I have to, Paul. Good-night." She picked up her purse and left Paul standing in the doorway.

———

Paul directed the rental company to the freight elevator as they removed the tables and chairs from the condo. The cleaners were finished with their work and the caterers had already left with the dishes that had remained from the night before.

Paul looked at the clock. *"Not bad,"* he thought. *"Noon and everything's finished for the day."*

He paid the cleaning company and thanked them for their work. He picked up the phone and dialed Nick's number. Nick's machine answered as Paul's doorbell rang.

"Hi Nick. I figure you're probably in church. If you get a chance, please give me a call when you get home," Paul said into the phone while answering the door.

Paul laughed when he opened the door and saw Nick standing there. He looked at the phone and then back at Nick. "I was just calling you. I guess you can disregard the message when you get home. Come in. I thought you might be in church."

"Usually I would be, but I overslept this morning for the first time in years. Last night exhausted me. Your friend Marcus talked me into having coffee with him. We ended up at the café until after midnight. I didn't get home until after 1:00 this morning. I'm too old for these late nights."

"Your leaving with Marcus is why I was calling. I'm curious to know how it went."

"Not much to tell, I'm afraid," Nick said, taking a seat on the couch. "He asked about my friendship with Denis and my former business in Italy. He asked a lot of questions about you. I think he was trying to determine the depth of your loyalty."

"Do you think he's convinced?" Paul asked, shifting in his chair.

"I think he believes you're completely dedicated to him and your company. I'd still be careful, but I believe he's convinced."

"I tried to get some more personal information out of him – asking him questions similar to what he'd asked me," Nick continued. "He and Denis met a few years ago at some business convention and soon became friends. He did tell me about some of his business interests. He made a point of mentioning that he never lets anyone or anything get in his way, but that's about it. I was hoping for more, but he's very superficial in his conversations. He doesn't mind telling how much wealth he has. He doesn't like to say much about how that wealth came about, however."

Paul nodded. "I'm not surprised. Brooke was confident you'd be able to get him to talk, but I've known the man long enough to know he's not too open."

"Not to worry." Nick smiled. "The truth always comes out. You'll see."

Paul shook his head and sighed. "I wish I had your confidence. Nick, you and Brooke seem so at ease, so relaxed about everything. How in the world are you both able to always see the good, the positive in everything?

How do you stay so calm, despite everything you've been through? I just don't know how you do it."

"Has Brooke ever told you about her grandmother, my late wife, Sophia?"

"No, not really," Paul replied, disappointed that Nick was changing the subject.

"My wife Sophia was always a strong, determined, sometimes angry woman. She wasn't pleased with our coming to America, but she understood the necessity. We were already thirty and childless, but settled in our life in Italy. She didn't like change."

"Her Italian blood always ran a little hotter than most, but it seemed to boil when we stepped off the boat here." Nick chuckled at the memory. "She hardly spoke to me for about a month after we arrived. It wasn't long, though, and we settled into our life. We both already spoke English, which helped a lot. We had a little money, so we were able to buy in the Village and avoid the tenements, and I was able to quickly set up my business. We found a church and started going to mass every Sunday, which helped us to develop friendships."

Nick rose from the couch and pointed toward the kitchen. "Would it be rude of me to suggest that I make us some coffee?"

Paul leaped from his chair. "I'm sorry, Nick. No, I should have offered."

The two went into the kitchen. Nick insisted on making the coffee. "Just tell me where everything is, you sit." Once the coffee was brewing, they pulled stools up to the island and Nick continued. "Within six months, Sophia was pregnant and we started our family. Rather than joy, she seemed to feel more anger. She resented having to raise her family here and not in Italy."

Nick stood from the stool and poured coffee for them both. He took a sip and nodded. "I don't mean to ramble. I am making a point. My Sophia stayed angry for years. She'd yell and scream when she wasn't happy, usually in Italian. She'd throw things and storm around the house. She was always extreme in her discipline of the children. Broom handles often found the backside of whichever child needed it."

"The summer after Martin graduated high school, she went too far. He always worked the mornings with me and then had an afternoon job with a family friend. He worked for me that day, as usual, but he was given the afternoon off from the other job. He never told us and chose instead to spend the afternoon with friends. Sophia found out when she tried to reach him at work. We had a shrine to the Mother Mary in the corner of the dining room. Sophia was standing by it when Martin entered the kitchen. Sophia took up the porcelain statuette of the Holy Virgin and threw it across the room at Martin. It shattered against the wall beside him, the pieces showering down and cutting his cheek. Martin packed up and left home that afternoon." Nick shook his head at the memory. "He didn't come back again until his sophomore year of college, not even for Christmas."

Paul leaned forward, his elbows resting on the island. "Brooke never told me any of this."

"She may not know herself. I'd be surprised if Martin ever told her. Anyway, once Martin and Elizabeth were married, we saw a little more of him but it was still seldom. His new bride had converted him from Catholicism. They went to the Assembly of God church that Elizabeth had grown up in." Nick paused, "Did you know Brooke's other grandfather was once a pastor?"

"Yes, she did tell me that."

Nick nodded, "That conversion really upset Sophia. She admitted that Martin was a better man because of his wife, but she had a hard time with the religious change. Once Brooke was born, though, Sophia relaxed a little. We spent more time visiting in Syracuse. Brooke would come spend time with us. Then, when Elizabeth became pregnant again and had terrible problems, she needed help. So, Sophia moved in with them for a while to help with Brooke and the household, cooked meals, helped Martin. She became very close to Elizabeth during that time and it broke Sophia's heart when she died. The newborn baby's death shortly after made it worse."

Paul shook his head, "I can't even imagine. That must have been terrible for your family."

"It was, but Sophia came home a changed woman. She spent another month in Syracuse, helping Martin and Brooke cope with what had happened. She watched Martin, though mourning the loss of his wife and baby daughter, cling to God and trust in His divine mercy. That sent her to Martin's church asking questions. She wanted whatever it was that allowed him to be so serene through such tragedy. She gave her life to Christ and was a peaceful, joyful woman from that time on." Nick stared into his coffee cup.

He cleared his throat and looked up at Paul through tears. "Sophia found out two months after she returned home that she had cancer in both breasts and her lymph nodes. We sold the house in the Village and moved into the apartment above my shop, so she could be closer to the hospital for her treatments. Not once did she complain. Not once did she rail against God. The cancer was advanced. She was in a hospital bed in the living room within months. The night she died, she took my hand and told me with a smile that she knew she was going to be with Christ that night, but that she couldn't go peacefully until she knew that I was right with God. Sophia's change was what convinced me that Christ truly is the answer. There was no other explanation for her transformation. I gave my life to the Lord that night. She died before sunrise."

Nick rose and poured another cup of coffee. He wiped his eyes and cleared his throat before sitting back down. He sipped his coffee and shook his head as if trying to clear his thoughts.

"I shared that with you for one reason – to help you understand that God alone gets us through these things. You wonder how Brooke and I have been able to cope and remain calm through it all? We can't, Paul – it's Christ in us, holding us up through the pain and suffering. Without Him, we'd surely fail."

THIRTY

THE PREP ROOM HUMMED WITH activity as the team worked to complete the last minute costume adjustments. Only two weeks remained until the Opening Gala at the Met and there was still work to be done.

Brooke and Julie were putting the finished costumes on the rolling racks, grouped by actor and scene, and checking them against their lists. Others on the team were finishing hems and sorting through accessories. Heron moved around the room, double-checking the racks against her master list.

"Julie, we're missing the costume for the number three extra in the wedding scene. It should be finished," Brooke said, checking each of the costumes on the rack against her list.

"It is. I finished that one last week," Julie said, looking through the closets.

"We need to find it. This rack is going over to the theatre this afternoon," Brooke put the list down and helped Julie with her search.

Heron walked over to the closet and crossed her arms. "Well, ladies, what's the problem?"

Julie looked first at Heron and then at Brooke. "Um, I," she stammered. "I can't find one of my costumes!"

Heron looked at Brooke, "Well?"

Brooke shook her head, "I don't see it, Heron. I'm sure Julie completed it." Brooke looked back into the closet. "Julie, would you have put it somewhere else? This is your work closet, it should be here."

"I don't know! I don't know what happened!" She shouted and started to storm out of the room.

Brooke reached out and clasped her wrist. "Calm down! This won't accomplish anything. Now, stop and think. Did you check the other racks? Maybe you put it with the wrong scene. Just look."

Julie threw her arms up and marched to the other side of the room. Brooke shook her head and looked at Heron.

"I'll look, Heron. I know you have a lot to do." Brooke went to where several racks stood full, waiting to be checked off the list.

Heron followed her. "I'll help, Brooke. We need that costume."

Brooke nodded. They each took a rack and started looking. Julie soon joined them, apologizing for getting upset.

Neither Brooke nor Heron said anything. Brooke handed Julie one of the lists and pointed to the corresponding rack. After a few minutes, Julie shouted "I found it!"

Heron walked over and took the costume. She shook her head and held the costume up. "This isn't labeled, Julie! How many times have you been told to label these!" Heron shook her head again and marched across the room. She grabbed a label, filled it out and attached it to the garment before putting it on the appropriate rack.

"I'm glad the crisis is over," Meryl said from the doorway, startling the women. "Heron, Julie, I want to talk to you both before you leave today. Brooke, I'd like to see you now, please."

Brooke followed Meryl down the hall to the conference room. Meryl stopped in front of the door and turned to Brooke. "There's someone here that I'd like you to talk to. This meeting is confidential, Brooke. This isn't to be mentioned to anyone else in this company, including Heron. Do you understand?"

Brooke looked at the closed door and back at Meryl. "I understand."

Meryl smiled at Brooke and opened the door. A tall, slender man stood by the window, his hands clasped behind his back. He wore a cinnamon-colored, tailored suit. He turned toward them as Meryl closed the door.

Brooke gasped and looked back at Meryl. "Adam Nichols."

"I'm glad to see you know who this is," he said, motioning toward the man. "Mr. Nichols, this is Brooke Barsanti, the young woman I told you about."

Adam crossed the room and took Brooke's hand. "I'm pleased to meet you, Ms. Barsanti. I appreciate your taking some time to talk to me today."

"Mr. Nichols is here to follow up on a reference for Heron. She has applied for a position with his company, and he has asked to speak with one of her co-workers. I believed you to be the best person for him to speak with. I know you will be honest and fair," Meryl added before leaving Brooke alone with their visitor.

Brooke watched Meryl leave and then turned back to Adam Nichols. She sat down and folded her hands in her lap. "Mr. Nichols, I am honored to speak with you."

"As Mr. Rivers has indicated, Heron has applied for a position with my company. We travel all over the country, taking the best shows on Broadway to cities throughout the United States and Canada. I need someone I can rely on to assist my costume director. I need to know that the individual who receives this position will not only do excellent work, but will also be fair and impartial as the second in command of the costume team," Mr. Nichols explained.

Leaning back in his seat and folding his arms, he continued, "Mr. Rivers has already assured me of Heron's dependability and unparalleled talent. What I need to know from you – someone who works directly with her on a daily basis – what is she like to work with?"

Brooke looked down at her hands and said a quick, silent prayer before speaking. She and Heron had experienced more than their share of differences over the few years they'd worked together, but Brooke wanted to be truthful.

"Mr. Nichols, Heron is, without a doubt, the most talented and capable woman I have ever worked with. She has taught me a great deal during the time I've worked with her. She is strict and she *is* a perfectionist. She can be difficult to work with at times, but I believe it's because she expects the best each one of us has to offer. It has been a pleasure for me to work with her." Brooke smiled, feeling for the first time the truth in those words.

Mr. Nichols rose from his chair and reached for Brooke's hand. "Thank you, Ms. Barsanti. Mr. Rivers told me you would be honest with me. I appreciate your time." He gathered his papers and nodded to Brooke before leaving the room.

Brooke stared after him for a long moment, stunned to think Heron could be leaving. Despite the differences they'd had, Brooke couldn't imagine the studio without her. No one in the industry could replace Heron.

"Who in the world is Meryl going to bring in to fill her shoes?" Brooke asked herself as she rose from her seat and left the room.

Meryl was waiting for her. "So, how did it go?"

"Good, I guess. He didn't ask me too many questions. He seemed satisfied with what I told him, though." She looked at Meryl. "Is Heron really leaving?"

"It looks that way, though I can't say for certain. I don't know if she has the job, but Adam seemed pretty happy with what he heard about her. I'd be surprised if he didn't offer her the job." He reached for Brooke's hand and patted it paternally. "I appreciate your willingness to put your differences aside and be honest about Heron. I knew you were the right person to speak with Adam." He squeezed her hand before releasing it and turning toward the elevators.

Brooke returned to the prep room and found the team still bustling around to complete their work. Only Heron glanced up at Brooke, an expectant look in her eyes. Brooke simply smiled and nodded before she returned to her work, hoping the small gesture would encourage Heron.

———

"Kelly, could you run stockholding reports on this list of clients, please," Paul asked, handing her a long list.

Kelly took the paper from Paul's hand and glanced over the list. "Paul, fewer than half of these are your accounts," she said, looking perplexed.

"I know. I have a couple of appointments at the end of the week and want to get a feel for what's working and what isn't before I go. How long do you think it'll take for you to get this back to me?"

Kelly shrugged. "Not long – a few keystrokes and whatever time it takes the printer to spit them out. I'll bring them to you when they're finished."

"Thanks," Paul said and returned to his office, closing his door.

He took a deep breath and sat back down to his computer. Burt Maxwell had called before 9:00 AM, asked a few questions, then gave him instructions. Paul was to get as much information as possible on the clients invested in Marcus Reed's and his daughter's businesses. He wanted the value of the stocks and when they were purchased. Paul was to put the information together and meet him the next day for lunch.

"Monday morning's not the best time to rush," Paul thought as he dashed through his work, trying not to forget anything. By lunch, he'd completed the absolute necessities. He had rescheduled his Tuesday meetings and compiled the client list for Kelly, making sure to include clients he knew had no interest in Marcus' businesses, just in case someone else got a look at the list.

Paul put together a spreadsheet of the clients and was saving it to his flash drive when Marcus knocked and entered Paul's office. "You look busy," Marcus said, pulling a chair closer to the desk.

Paul closed the spreadsheet and pulled up the stock report. He looked at Marcus and nodded. "You know Mondays," he said with a smile. "What can I do for you, Marcus?"

Marcus folded his arms across his chest and looked at Paul. He cocked his head and smiled. "Why so formal, my boy? You look like you've been caught cheating by your teacher. Something the matter?"

"No, nothing's wrong. It's just a busy morning. I have two meetings with potential clients the end of the week and I want to make sure I'm ready. And, honestly, I think I'm still feeling the effects of the party Saturday night," Paul replied, rubbing his forehead. "I feel like I could take a nap."

Kelly tapped on the door and slipped in quietly with the reports Paul had asked for. "Thanks, Kelly. Why don't you take lunch before you start anything else?" Kelly nodded and left the room.

Paul flipped through the pages and tucked them into a folder. He looked up at Marcus. "Want to join me for lunch?"

Marcus shook his head and stood to leave. "Thanks, but I have another commitment. I just wanted to stop in and thank you again for the party Saturday night."

"My pleasure, Marcus." Paul logged off of his computer and rose from his chair.

"By the way," Marcus said, turning to Paul after they were outside his office. "How well do you know Ms. Barsanti's grandfather?"

"Fairly well, I think. I met him before I met Brooke, and I've spent considerable time with him. Why?"

"No reason, really. I just found it amusing that he and Denis knew each other – you know, small world and all of that. Just my curiosity. Enjoy your lunch," he said, turning toward Marshall's office.

Paul went back into his office and grabbed his briefcase and the folder containing the reports Kelly had run for him. He exited his office, tucking the papers into his briefcase as he made his way to the elevator, unaware that Marcus was watching him from Marshall's doorway.

———————

Brooke stepped onto the sidewalk from the dark subway tunnel and squinted at the late-day sun. It had been a long day. She wanted to go home and relax, but she had accepted Papa's invitation to dinner and didn't want to disappoint him.

She joined the mass of people waiting at the crosswalk and rushed across the street when the light changed. She waved to the security guard as she entered the building and made her way down the hall to Papa's apartment. Brooke inhaled deeply and smiled. She could smell dinner cooking before entering the apartment. Her stomach grumbled as she knocked on the door and turned the knob.

"Hi Papa," she called.

"I'm in the kitchen, Sweetheart. Come in here and slice some bread for me."

Brooke went in and kissed him on the cheek. She washed her hands and slid the bread knife from its place in the storage block. "I'm starving, Papa! I could smell your manicotti in the hallway!"

"That's good because I think I made enough for an army. You'll have to take some with you." He nodded toward the vegetables in the colander. "Could you cut those up for me? I need them for the salad."

Brooke got a clean knife and spread the vegetables out on the cutting board. Papa wiped his hands on his apron and looked over Brooke's shoulder as she chopped.

"Looks good. Now, while you're taking your frustrations out on those mushrooms, why don't you tell me what's got you in a mood tonight."

Brooke halted her chopping and looked up at Papa. "I'm not in a mood. I'm just tired."

"Honey, I know you. You have a look when you have something on your mind. So, talk. Tell me what happened today." Papa reached for the olive oil and a dressing shaker.

Brooke finished the vegetables and wiped her hands on a towel. "I don't know. I guess it was just one of those days." She took plates and glasses out of the cupboard and started to set the table. "It was really busy, for one thing. The Opening Gala is in two weekends. We're more or less ready, but there's always something. Julie goofed up again and nearly lost one of the costumes that had to go to the theatre today. Meryl witnessed the entire process. Julie not only didn't follow procedure, but she also lost her temper and flew off at Heron. Her little temper tantrum got her fired this afternoon."

Papa looked over at Brooke. "Meryl fired her – this close to a big show?"

Brooke nodded. "This isn't the first time she's messed up, though. Her work isn't great and she is a little absentminded. I think Meryl realized enough is enough. It's just bad timing. In addition to losing Julie today, Meryl informed Ruby and me that we are going to Ithaca for a week! We'll be back in time for the Gala."

"Ithaca!" Papa exclaimed. "Okay, what in the world is there for you two to do in Ithaca? I thought it was more or less a college town?"

"Apparently, Ithaca's drama department is doing some kind of weekend arts thing for local high school students and the college has asked Meryl to send a couple of people to demonstrate the costuming process. We have to leave Thursday night, meet with the college on Friday and then spend the weekend working with the high schoolers. Monday through Wednesday, we're doing a hands-on with the college drama department. We won't get back until late Wednesday night. And…" she began, turning to look at Papa again.

"Oh, no, there's more?"

"Yes and I've saved the best for last!" she said sarcastically. "Heron will most likely be leaving the studio."

"Leaving for what?" Papa asked, setting the salad and the bread on the table. He motioned for Brooke to move aside. "Let me get dinner out of the oven. You pour the wine and fill the water glasses. You can finish telling me what's going on once we're seated."

Brooke filled the glasses and sat down. She put salad into two bowls and waited for Papa to sit. Papa blessed the food and looked at Brooke. "Now, where were we? Oh, Heron is leaving - to where? How do you know she's leaving?"

Between bites, Brooke told him about the interview with Adam Nichols. "I wouldn't be surprised if she has the job. Meryl seemed pretty confident that she would have it," Brooke concluded, dabbing her lips with her napkin.

"Did Meryl say anything about her replacement?" Papa asked, scooping another helping of manicotti onto his plate.

"I don't know what Meryl plans to do. There are a couple of women on the other teams who may be qualified to take over Heron's position, but I'm not really sure. I don't know them very well. I guess I'll just have to wait and see."

"Sounds like you've had quite a day," Papa said, reaching to take her plate. "I know you're full, but you can't say no to dessert. I had Gianna make her chocolate cake you like so much!"

Brooke helped Papa clear the table and loaded the dishwasher while he fixed the coffee and sliced the cake. "Come on, sit back down. That can wait," Papa said, motioning for Brooke to leave the rest of the dishes.

"We haven't talked since Saturday night, Papa. How do you think the party went?"

Papa nodded. "I think it went well. I talked a little to Marcus Reed. I think he believes Paul is loyal. I also don't think Paul is going to have to wait long for something to happen."

"What do you mean?" Brooke asked pushing her empty plate away and raising her cup to her lips. "Is Paul in more trouble?"

"No, nothing like that. This is between us, Brooke. You can't tell anyone, even Paul," Papa said sternly.

"This is the second time today I've been told to keep a secret," Brooke said with a chuckle. "You know I won't say a word, Papa."

Papa sat with his elbows resting on the table, his coffee cup held in both hands. He took a sip and put the cup down. He looked at Brooke, his eyes becoming serious and unwavering. "Brooke, I still have friends who, shall we say, know things. After Paul confided in me his predicament, I started making some phone calls."

He crossed his arms on the table and leaned toward her. "Paul's friend Marcus Reed is being watched rather closely in Italy, France, and here in the United States. I don't know if the Canadians are looking at him or not, but at this point, I wouldn't be surprised. Italy and France are getting close to picking him up. The U.S., well, they are in need of a little more before than can go after him. Paul is in the perfect spot to get the few morsels they still need – against Reed and against Paul's employer."

"Is Paul in danger, Papa? Is he paranoid, or is there a real threat against him?"

"I think if he's careful, he should be fine. Burt Maxwell was going to give him an "assignment," so to speak. If Paul produces what Burt thinks he's going to produce, it should give the Federal Trade Commission and the District Attorney's office enough to at least question Reed and instigate a full blown investigation into Paul's employer."

"What if Paul isn't careful? How bad could it be?" Brooke asked, the coffee cup in her hand suspended between her mouth and the table.

"I would hope Marcus Reed wouldn't be stupid enough to threaten Paul physically, but let's just say that my friends in Italy believe he was behind three different 'suicides' there. After Kevin Murphy's suspicious suicide, I think anything is possible."

Papa leaned forward again, his eyes drilling into hers. "Brooke, right now, Paul needs all the prayer we can offer up for him. If he isn't careful, he could be in real trouble."

THIRTY-ONE

PAUL LEFT THE OFFICE AT 8:00 Friday morning to meet with a potential client in Stamford, CT. The meeting was a success, with an immediate signed contract. He grabbed a deli sandwich at a local café and ate in the car, rushing to make an early afternoon appointment in White Plains, NY. He left that meeting feeling confident that with a few minor contract modifications, it too would result in a new client.

Paul got into his car and looked at his watch. *"Perfect – only 3:00,"* he thought. *"I'll have time to get back to the office and tie up a few loose ends before I start my weekend."*

Paul followed the Friday traffic out of town and merged into the stream of cars on Route 287. Travel was slow, but within a half hour, he was turning onto Route 87. *"An hour, and I should be back in the City,"* he thought. He adjusted his mirror and was settling into the steady flow of traffic when his cell phone rang.

"Paul, I need you to go by Andrew Wallace's office in Greenwich before you head back. I have reason to believe he's planning to move his accounts to another company. I know you're the one who can convince him otherwise. I'll email you his account info to review, since he's not one of your accounts. Just be casual, take him to dinner. You know what to do, Paul," Marshall instructed in a breathless stream, not allowing Paul an opportunity to say a word.

"Okay, Marshall. I'll do what I can." *"Great,"* Paul thought. *"Greenwich is twenty minutes in the opposite direction."* He shook his head and did a u-turn toward Route 287.

Paul pulled into the parking lot and took out his laptop. He spent a few minutes reviewing his account before going into the building. It was a small account, but an old one. Mr. Wallace was a valued client.

Andrew Wallace was a large, imposing man with an even larger ego. He was eager to allow Paul to take him to dinner, insinuating that Marshall should have shown his appreciation for his business personally. It didn't take Paul long, however, to convince the man that he was a valued client.

It was after 9:00 before Paul left the restaurant and called Marshall. "I think he just needed his inflated ego stroked a little," Paul laughed when Marshall congratulated him on saving the account. "Marshall, he was surprised when I mentioned our concern that he was going to pull his account. What made you think that's what he planned?"

"Oh, you know how it is, Paul. It may have just been industry gossip, but I couldn't take that chance. Have a good weekend, Paul."

Paul pulled out of the restaurant parking lot. He was exhausted. It had been a long day and an even longer week. Between the steady pace at the office and the usual lunch and dinner outings as well as having several meetings with Burt Maxwell, Paul felt he couldn't handle another minute of the week. The most stressful part of it was trying to continue to look like the loyal employee while gathering the information the retired senator was asking for. He felt like a Judas.

Paul also had the added stress of a confrontation with Marshall over some stock decisions he'd made for two new clients. Since learning the truth about Marcus' business practices, Paul refused to encourage anyone to invest in those stocks.

Paul had been called into Marshall's office Wednesday evening. "Paul, please explain your decision to ignore our request to invest the bulk of the Dayton and Vigis accounts into these stocks," Marshall had said, waving the pages in the air as Paul entered the room.

Marcus sat near the window, his arms crossed, staring at Paul. There hadn't been any of the usual pleasantries - no "hello, have a drink, please sit down" – nothing.

Paul had stopped in the middle of the room and looked at the two men. He knew why he'd been summoned, so he made sure he was prepared when he entered the office. He'd cleared his throat and turned his attention to Marshall.

"I spent the early part of the week reviewing the stock holdings of some of our more profitable clients." Paul handed him the spreadsheet he'd carried into the room.

Marshall had glanced at the paper and handed it to Marcus before motioning to a chair. "Please sit down, Paul and continue."

Paul had set down and looked back at Marshall. "I believe you can see from the spreadsheet that the stocks I've selected on their behalf will generate far greater returns than the ones you recommended. I apologize if that was a mistake. I thought it would be the best way to develop the proper relationship with our newest clients. Once we've gained their trust, then we can encourage them to move their interests to these other stocks."

Marshall had glanced at Marcus before speaking. "I guess we can't argue with your logic, Paul. I think you have an excellent point."

"Thank you. I appreciate that you continue to trust my judgment."

Paul had risen from his chair and was turning to leave the office when he was gripped by an unexplainable anxiety. He turned around to look at Marcus. For a brief moment, he had been assaulted by an icy glare that caused the hair on Paul's arm to stand up. Just as quickly, Marcus' expression had become casual.

"Are we still having our dinner meeting?" Paul had asked, trying to appear unfazed.

"Yes, we are," Marshall replied. "We'll see you at the Waldorf at 7:00."

"I'll see you there," Paul had said before leaving the room.

The evening had gone well. Dinner was relaxed and light-hearted. They had walked to the corner tavern after dinner, Pratt having been banned from the lounge at the Waldorf after his solicitation arrest. The rest of the night had been spent laughing and joking just as they had for months. Paul had gone home feeling more at ease, thinking that Marcus again trusted his devotion.

Paul's thoughts were yanked back to the present as heavy rain began to pelt the car. He turned on the wipers and slowed down as the water quickly pooled on the road. The wiper blades couldn't keep up with the rain hitting his windshield.

Paul sighed. "Where in the world did this come from?" He leaned closer to the windshield and reduced his speed more as he approached the exit to Route 287.

Bright lights flashed in his rearview mirror. He took his eyes from the road and stared at the black car speeding into his lane, the distinct Lincoln emblem on the grill catching his attention. His eyes widened as the luxury car came speeding toward him.

Paul gasped and clutched his steering wheel tighter as the Lincoln slammed deliberately into the rear panel of the Mercedes. His heart beat wildly in his chest as his car hydroplaned. He spun the wheel, fighting the pull of the water on the road. The Lincoln again sped toward him, crashing again into the rear of the sports car. He lost control, the vehicle's front end shooting over the guardrail.

Paul held his breath, his equilibrium lost as the car flipped wildly. Time seemed to slow as it continued its descent. It landed upside down in the treetops. There was a moments silence before a loud snap and the car shifted rapidly downward.

"Oh, dear Jesus!" Paul exclaimed as the airbag deployed, landing a solid punch into his face and sending him into darkness.

———————

Nick sat up in bed, sweat covering his body as he jerked awake from the strange dream. He swung his legs around and reached shakily for the water glass on the night stand. He took a gulp and put the glass back.

"Dear God, what was that all about?" He looked at the clock. "Hmmm… only 11:30. Well, after that little thriller, I don't think I'll be going back to sleep any time soon." He grabbed his robe and went to the living room.

He switched on the television and turned up the volume before going into the kitchen. He filled the kettle with water and dropped a tea bag into a cup.

"Breaking news tonight on I-87 outside the town of Elmsford," Nick heard from the television. *"A late model Mercedes was discovered less than an hour ago, flipped over and hanging in the trees. A passing motorist saw what looked like steam rising from the drop off. The motorist reports that he saw tire tracks leading to a damaged guard rail. He found the Mercedes dangling in the branches of the trees where it landed after flipping over the guard rail and down the embankment. A large section of guard rail was embedded in the car's frame, keeping it suspended, preventing it from plunging further down the embankment."*

"Driver was probably drunk," Nick muttered to himself as he poured the boiling water over the tea bag. He took the cup into the living room and sat down on the couch.

He sipped his tea as the newscaster continued, *"Special equipment and the jaws of life had to be brought to the scene to extract the driver without causing the car to shift and plunge further down the embankment. The driver of the vehicle, 26 year-old Paul Matthews of Central Park West, was airlifted to St. Luke's Hospital."*

Nick sputtered in his tea and rattled the cup abruptly into its saucer, spilling tea onto the coffee table. "Oh my God!"

"No additional information is available at this time and the cause of the accident is unknown. If anyone has any information related to this incident, please contact the New York State Police at the following number..."

Nick turned off the television and rushed into his bedroom. He dressed quickly and raced out into the night and hailed a cab. "St. Luke's Hospital, the emergency room."

"Oh Jesus! Please, sweet Jesus, be with Paul right now," Nick prayed as the cab sped down the city streets, weaving through traffic.

The cab bumped the curb in front of the hospital. Nick sprinted through the doors of the ER. "I'm here about Paul Matthews," he said breathlessly to the receptionist.

"Are you family?" she asked.

"No," Nick said. "But, I'm a good..."

The receptionist shook her head and interrupted. "Family only."

Nick gave her an exasperated look. "His family is in Maine! He and my granddaughter..."

"I don't care if *you're* his lover, if you ain't family, you ain't getting any information."

Nick walked from the reception desk to the nearby waiting room, raking his hands through his hair. "What can I do, Lord?" he prayed, pacing back and forth in front of the door. He sat down in a chair and put his face in his hands. "Please, God, tell me what to do." He rubbed his face and looked up in time to see Pastor Brian racing toward the reception desk. He jumped up and jogged toward him. "Brian!"

Brian turned to Nick and clasped his hand. "I saw the news. How is he? Is Brooke with him?"

Nick shook his head. "Brooke's out of town for work. She isn't here. I have no idea how he's doing. I came over when I saw the news, but they won't tell me anything because I'm not family."

"Well, let me see what we can do." Brian motioned for Nick to follow him to the reception desk.

"Excuse me. I'm Reverend Brian Jefferson. Paul Matthews was brought here this evening."

The receptionist smiled up at him. "Yes Reverend, he is in the ICU right now. Let me call a nurse for you. I'll have her meet you in the waiting room."

Brian smiled at Nick "One of the perks of being a clergyman – I'm related to everyone."

The nurse entered the waiting room. "Reverend."

"Can you tell me anything about our friend?" Pastor Brian asked when she stood before him.

"He has broken ribs and a broken nose, probably from the airbag. His left shoulder was dislocated, likely from the seatbelt, and he's covered with cuts and bruises. Otherwise, he's doing fine. As a precaution, patients are kept in ICU for twenty-four hours after a serious accident." The nurse shook her head in disbelief. "Most accidents of this sort result in head injury or internal bleeding. Mr. Matthews is a very lucky man."

"Not luck," Pastor Brian said with a shake of his head. "He's very blessed!"

———

The sun streamed through the window and warmed Paul's face. He squinted against the brightness. He tried to sit up and pain shot through his ribs, causing him to gasp and clutch his ribcage.

"You'd better take it easy, Paul," Nick said, coming to stand by Paul's bed.

"Nick. What are you doing here?" Paul asked, looking around the hospital room.

Nick took the control for the bed and pushed the button to adjust the head. "Let me know when you're comfortable, Paul. You have broken ribs and a dislocated shoulder. You need to be careful. To answer your question, I saw your accident on the news Friday night."

Paul nodded when the bed was where he wanted it. "That's good, thanks." He looked around the room at the vases of flowers, the stuffed animals, and bunches of balloons. "How long have I been here?"

"You were brought in Friday night. It's a little after noon, Sunday." Nick pulled his chair closer to the bed.

"I've been out that long?" Paul reached up and felt the bandages on his nose. He winced and pulled his hand away from his face. "Do I have a head injury, too?"

"No, nothing more than what was caused by the airbag, but that was minor. You've been more or less out of it since you were brought in, though." Nick cleared his throat, leaned forward and folded his hands on his knees. "Paul, the State Troopers are going to talk to you. There doesn't appear to be any witnesses to your accident. Do you remember what happened?"

"I was on my way back from a late appointment and was run off the road by a black Lincoln. I have no doubt Marcus was behind it and I'm certain Marshall was involved. He's the one who added my last minute meeting that kept me until after 9:00, a meeting that surprised the client I met with."

"You're sure it was a Lincoln? It was raining pretty good Friday night."

"I saw the emblem in my mirror. It may have been raining and dark, but the headlights from that car glared in my rearview mirror so fast that it startled me. That shield on the car's grill was unmistakable," Paul replied grimly.

Nick patted Paul's arm and rose from his chair. "You rest. I'll let the nurses know you're awake."

"Tell them I'm starving and ask if they can get some of these tubes out of me! One in particular has got to go!" Paul said with a laugh.

"I'll see what I can do," Nick said, smiling at Paul before closing the door.

Paul looked around the room at the gifts. He noticed the flowers and teddy bear on the nightstand and reached painfully to pull the card from the bouquet. "I wish I could be there to help you, Paul. You are in my thoughts and prayers – Brooke," Paul read aloud. Tears filled his eyes. "I still love you, Brooke," he whispered before putting the card back in the holder.

He looked up and wiped the tears from his face as the door opened. A nurse entered, pulling a monitor. She was followed by Nick, Pastor Brian and Shaun. "You're awake," she said with a smile. "You have visitors, but let me get your vitals before you get too comfortable." His blood pressure, temperature and pulse were checked. "Very good. Strong and healthy," she said, keying the information into a laptop. She checked the bag hanging on the side of his bed, noted its contents and whispered, "We'll get you off this in just a minute." She winked at him and left the room.

Paul turned to his visitors. "Pastor Brian, Shaun – thanks for stopping by."

"Brian was here with me Friday night and most of the day yesterday. We've been taking turns, so to speak," Nick explained. "I had the morning shift today so he could preach. I'm going to say good-bye now and let him take the afternoon shift." He reached for Paul and clutched his hand. "Brooke sends her love. She's working in Ithaca and can't get away. I promised to look after you for her. You rest and get better."

Pastor Brian sat in the chair Nick had pulled up to the bed. Shaun found another one on the other side of the room, carried it over and sat next to Pastor Brian.

"What happened, Paul?" Brian asked, leaning toward Paul.

Paul repeated the ordeal, just as he'd explained it to Nick. "I thought I was going to die," he said after giving them the details of the accident. "I know where I was. I don't know how I survived that drop off."

"When you were found, the car was cradled in tree branches, a mangled section of guardrail holding your car up. If the car had hit anywhere else, you would be dead." Brian described the accident scene, based on the news report. "I believe God was watching out for you, Paul." He fixed his eyes on Paul. "My question to you Paul – what are you going to do about it? God doesn't send that kind of protection without a purpose."

Paul looked at Brian and Shaun before looking toward the door, hoping they'd be interrupted. He wasn't ready for the conversation that was coming. He knew Brian was going to ask him to make a decision. *"God, please, not today,"* Paul thought, furrowing his brow. *"I'm not ready."*

A soft voice invaded his thoughts. *"When will you be ready? When will you stop running?"*

Paul's expression softened, and he looked back at Pastor Brian. "Let me tell you what's been going on in my life lately – work, family, Brooke – I need to share it all."

Brian nodded. "I'm listening, Paul."

Shaun rose from his chair. "I'll get coffee for us, Brian," he said, leaving the room.

Paul told Brian about his Christian upbringing, Lilly's betrayal and what it did to his family and the resulting rejection of Christ. He described the years he poured into college, his pursuit of wealth, and his many empty relationships.

"I was doing what I wanted. I was happy - until I met Brooke. I love her, Pastor Brian, but I was unwilling to let go of my success for her. Now, I've lost her." Paul covered his face and sobbed.

Brian leaned back in his chair. "It isn't your success that you're unwilling to let go of, Paul. It's your pride. You have spent your entire adult life trying to convince your family and yourself that *you* are all you need."

"Over the past few months, I've struggled with the knowledge that my life isn't what I thought it was. What I've discovered about my employer has turned my stomach to acid. I believe they are behind my accident."

"Nick shared some of that with me. We've been praying for you for some time now, Paul."

"Through all of it, for several months now, I've had this crazy dream," Paul said, shaking his head.

He and Brian looked up as Shaun returned to the room. Shaun walked quietly to where Brian sat, offered him a cup of coffee and sat back down in the chair he'd occupied before. He looked at Paul expectantly.

"Tell me about this dream," Brian encouraged.

Paul took a breath and shared the details of his dream. Brian and Shaun exchanged glances several times during Paul's account. When he finished sharing the dream, he told them of the conversation he and Herbie had the last time Paul was in Rockport. "The man is mentally handicapped. He's forty going on twelve – seriously. He's a sweet, hard-working man, but when he wants to tell you something, it's usually a story a child would share."

Paul paused and rubbed his forehead. "The afternoon he told me the story about his father, his voice changed, his demeanor changed. It was like talking to a forty year old, like he had somehow suddenly grown up. It threw me! I had never had a conversation like that with him before.

When the conversation ended, he was again mentally twelve. I just couldn't figure it out."

"I've heard stories like that before. I can't explain it, but it seems like when God chooses to use the child or child-like individual, he gives them a kind of authority. I don't know how else to describe it. It sounds to me that God gave Herbie a word you needed to hear," Brian said.

Shaun leaned forward in his seat. He looked down at the coffee cup he clutched in his hands. "Jesus and His disciples got into a boat so that they could cross to the other side of a lake. While they were in the boat, Jesus – who was exhausted from tending to the multitudes of people – fell asleep in the boat. A storm came up and tossed the boat around. Waves crashed against the boat, water poured in faster than the disciples could bail it out. Finally, when they reached the point of desperation, they cried out to Jesus to save them from certain death. Jesus awoke, calmed the waves and then chided his followers for their lack of faith."

"I know this story. I grew up in church. I know them all. What does that have to do with my dream? The fact that there was a boat and a storm are the only parallels. There wasn't a simple-minded man sitting in the boat with Jesus talking about eating bread!" Paul exclaimed, exasperated.

"I think that's part of the problem, Paul," Pastor Brian said. "You *know* it all in your head, but you don't let it *take root* in your heart. You may know the story of Jesus calming the sea, but you don't see that you have a storm in your own life that only Jesus can calm. There may not have been a simple-minded man sitting in the boat with Jesus, but *Jesus* was there. *He* was able to explain things to the disciples."

Pastor Brian paused and searched Paul's face before continuing. "Jesus isn't sitting in your boat. You kicked Him out a long time ago. God is using Herbie to explain things to you – this simple-minded man who comprehends the seemingly complicated things of God. God is trying to show you that you need to cry out to Him. Knowing *about* Him isn't enough any more than, like your friend explained, having a loaf of bread in the house will keep you from feeling hungry. You have to cry out to God just as you have to pick up the bread and eat it. God's calling to you, Paul. Your dream, your situation at work, your accident – they're all proof. Don't wait too long to answer. Next time your car flips over a guard rail, you might not be so blessed."

Brian and Shaun rose from their chairs as the door opened. A Trooper entered and looked at Paul. "Mr. Matthews, I need to get your account of the accident. Could you please excuse us, gentlemen?" he asked Brian and Shaun.

"We're praying for you," Brian said, clasping Paul's hand between his own. Shaun smiled and nodded. The two men departed, leaving Paul alone to again recount his horrific ordeal.

THIRTY-TWO

PAUL'S HOSPITAL DOOR SWUNG OPEN early Monday morning. A smiling Burt Maxwell entered with a basket of various fruits and delicacies in one hand, a briefcase in the other, and a trail of officials on his heels.

"How's our patient?" Burt asked, setting the basket on the bedside table.

"I've been better," Paul replied. He nodded toward the men accompanying Burt. "Who are your friends?"

Burt checked the door. His expression became serious as he looked back at Paul. "Paul, I'd like you to meet Tom Stewart from the FTC; Joel Wright with the Attorney General's office; Blake Mills, District Attorney's office; and Claude Blanchard, a temporary representative from France at the UN." Each of the men stepped forward and shook Paul's hand as Burt Maxwell introduced them.

"I believe you are acquainted with a friend of Mr. Blanchard's, a certain Denis Beck," Burt said.

"Okay, gentlemen, I think we need to get started." Burt motioned for them all to pull chairs closer to Paul's hospital bed. "I've already asked the nurses to keep everyone out unless it's Denis Beck, Nick Barsanti or a member of law enforcement. Anyone else will be told you can't be disturbed."

Paul adjusted his pillows and looked at the men seated around his bed. "Okay. What are we doing?"

"We're getting ready to go after Appleton, Murphy and Young as well as Marcus Reed and his bodyguard. We have enough evidence now to move forward with an investigation. We need to get statements from you to help us convict them. We also need statements from you to keep you from ending up in the same hole they're going to end up in," Burt explained. "Now, if you want a lawyer here before we get going, I understand, but the sooner we get moving, the sooner we can get this done."

"I'll help however I can. I'll worry about the lawyer later," Paul replied.

"Good man!" Burt exclaimed. "Mr. Mills, why don't you begin."

Paul spent the next three hours answering questions about the accident, Kevin Murphy's frame of mind the day Pratt's arrest made the news, what Paul knew about Marcus Reed. Paul felt like he'd been tried and convicted by the time they were done.

"How much trouble am I in?" he asked when the men started closing their laptops and tucking extensively scribbled-on legal pads into their totes.

Tom Stewart cocked his head. "You will likely be facing minor charges – since you were aware of some questionable practices and never reported them. But the fact that you are cooperating with us now should keep you out of any real trouble. I still strongly recommend contacting an attorney as soon as possible." He shook Paul's hand and followed Joel Wright and Claude Blanchard from the room.

Burt Maxwell and Blake Mills stayed behind. Burt put the three vacant chairs back in their original places and sat back down next to Blake. He nodded to Blake. "Go ahead. Tell him what you've got."

Blake Mills took several photos from his briefcase and handed them to Paul. "These are stills taken from the security footage at the convenience store in Old Forge where Kevin Murphy was seen the day he went to his cabin."

Paul flipped through the pictures. He pointed to one of the photographs. "This is Marcus Reed's bodyguard! Marcus is seldom without him."

Blake crossed his legs and nodded. "Burt called us with a tip that this guy could somehow be connected to Kevin Murphy's suicide. Burt said he'd been given information by someone about the two being seen together there. Your account of your accident led us to look further. The license plate on the Lincoln in those stills was traced to a luxury car rental company. Guess who was listed as the renter in their system?"

"Marcus Reed."

"Exactly. We went over this morning and asked questions. The car was exchanged Saturday morning. The driver claimed that he had hit an obstruction in the road. They gave him a new car and he left. We demanded access to the GPS and found that it had travelled your route and was in your exact location at the time of your accident Friday night. The damage to the Lincoln was consistent with the kind of impact you described in your statement to the State Police. We also learned that the car was at Mr. Murphy's cabin around the time the coroner believes he shot himself. Mr. Reed's bodyguard was brought in for questioning."

"So, do I need a body guard of my own?" Paul rubbed the back of his neck and shook his head. "If this guy knows that I know he's the one who rammed into me Friday night, I'm dead!"

"We still have him. He denied it all until we waved certain documents containing the charges he'll be facing in Italy and France should we choose to turn him over to either country. I think he realized he'd be better off facing our legal system because the big, strong man broke down and admitted everything. Mr. Reed has already been taken into custody," Blake said with a smile.

"That's a relief," Paul sighed. "Maybe now I can stop looking over my shoulder!"

"Don't be surprised if you lose your job before the end of the week, Paul. As soon as your employers find out you're cooperating with us, they'll have you out the door. I've seen it too many times," Burt warned.

"At this point, I don't care," Paul responded. "I don't feel right about being there anymore anyway."

"You rest," Burt ordered as he and Blake left Paul's hospital room.

Rest was not possible. Nick visited daily and the nursing staff was prodding him every half hour around the clock. Burt Maxwell was back early Tuesday morning with more questions.

Paul's lawyer met with him Tuesday afternoon, leaving Paul confident that there was nothing to worry about. "Minor stuff, really," he assured him. "I wish you'd called me before you talked, but I don't think you've done any real damage to yourself. You're cooperating and that gives us something to work with."

Paul was relieved when his doctor finally released him from the hospital Wednesday afternoon. He was tired and ready to go home. He was given strict instructions to rest. His doctor had already notified Marshall that Paul would not be returning to work for a minimum of two weeks.

Nick offered to drive him home. He helped Paul into the car and loaded the many gifts into the trunk. The only flowers Paul kept were the ones from Brooke.

"Where are the rest of them?" Nick asked, settling the vase on the floorboard between Paul's feet.

"I gave them to the nurses and asked them to distribute them to the patients who didn't have any. I kept all of the cards, but how would we have possibly gotten all of those arrangements back to my place?"

"I have no idea! I was starting to wonder if you were going to become a florist!" Nick started the engine and buckled his seatbelt. "Are you ready to go home?"

"More than you could possibly know. Maybe now I can really get some rest," Paul said as Nick pulled out of the hospital parking lot and into traffic. "I can't wait to sleep in my own bed and not have people coming and going constantly."

Paul winced throughout the ride home, the potholes and bumps jostling him and sending bolts of pain through his ribcage. "I know you can't help it, Nick," he said, noticing Nick's attempts to avoid them. "You miss one and there's always another waiting."

Nick helped Paul to his condo. The security guard followed with Paul's bag and the gifts. Paul settled onto the couch with a sigh of contentment. Nick went into the kitchen and brewed a pot of coffee.

"Do you want me to stay?" he offered, handing Paul a steaming cup.

"No, thanks. I talked to my mother this morning. She and Dad should be here sometime this evening. I'll be fine until they get here."

"Well, don't hesitate to pick up the phone if you need me. Do what your doctor ordered, Paul!"

Paul sipped his coffee and leaned his head against the back of the couch. He wanted to sleep. He rose stiffly from the couch and went to his bedroom. He slipped out of his clothes and slid between the sheets. *"Home, peace and quiet,"* he thought. Closing his eyes, he drifted into sleep.

The sound of the doorbell woke Paul from his sleep. The shadows had changed position in his room. He looked at the clock as he carefully inched his way to the edge of the bed and sat up. 7:00 – he'd slept for three hours.

Paul pulled his pants on and moved slowly to the door. "Coming!" he shouted when the bell rang again. He opened the door, expecting to see his parents. It was the security guard escorting a courier with several cardboard storage boxes.

"Mr. Paul Matthews," the courier said. "Please sign here." He handed Paul a clipboard and an envelope.

"Appleton, Murphy & Young," Paul read. "Well that didn't take long," he said with a sigh. He signed the clipboard and handed it back to the courier.

Paul closed the door and opened the envelope. "Well, Burt warned me," he said to himself after reading the termination letter. Included was a list of the contents of the boxes – the items taken from his office and a legal notice that he was banned from returning to the office building. He was instructed in the notice to contact personnel if he believed any of his personal items were missing.

Paul's emotions roiled as he flipped through the pages. All of the hours, the dinners, lunches, weekends given up to move up the ladder in the company – all for nothing. He looked around his condo, realization setting in that he wouldn't be able to afford his luxurious life for long. He had a sizeable savings account and a good 401K, but that wouldn't last long if he continued his current lifestyle.

Paul dropped the papers on the sideboard and went to the kitchen. The coffee Nick had brewed had cooked to a syrupy glob in the bottom of the pot. He turned off the coffee maker, put the pot in the sink, and returned to the living room. He didn't want to sit around. He wanted to go out.

"Car's totaled," he reminded himself. "Not that I could drive with these pain killers in my system, anyway. I'm not sure the subway is a good idea right now, either." Paul shook his head. "I've got to get out of here for a while." He grabbed his keys and left the condo.

He stopped by the security desk. "I'm going out for a little while. My parents will be here soon. Could you let them in for me when they get here?"

"Of course, Mr. Matthews."

Paul stepped outside and hailed a cab.

"Central Park," he instructed, ignoring the cabbie's reaction to his swollen face and bandaged nose.

The cab stopped near the path to the Great Lawn. Paul paid him and strolled down the path. People went out of their way to avoid him, detouring from the path and into the grass to stay away.

"I must look terrible," Paul thought after a small group of walkers stared at him as they passed him by.

He left the path and settled onto his and Brooke's favorite bench. The sounds of the City lingered in the air. Club music spilled out into the night. The chatter, laughter and shouts of the nocturnal could be heard in the distance.

A chill on the breeze reached out and prickled its way into his skin. Paul shivered and rose from the bench, moving closer to the pond. He stared into the water. Moonbeams slivered faintly around the edge, snaking toward him on the ripples in the water. He looked up at the castle, its battlements rising against the darkening sky.

He turned from the water and sat back down on the bench. "I've lost it all," he said to himself. Sobs rose up and wracked his body, his ribs protesting the pain.

"I don't know what to do," he cried into the night. "God, please, I don't know what to do."

"Stop running," the quiet voice whispered.

Paul wiped the tears from his face with the back of his hand. He cleared his throat and looked up at the sky, its light fading to gray. Stars were starting to twinkle as the darkness took over.

"God," he began. "I haven't really talked to You in a long time. I turned away from You a long time ago. I feel like a coward coming to You now when I don't know what else to do. But, well, I don't know what else to do. I know you've been trying to get my attention – the dream, the car accident, Brooke. I'm here God. I'm ready to stop running. Please, Jesus, help me. Give me the strength I need to go forward – whether I lose everything, go to jail, whatever consequences I have to face, give me strength."

A slight wind rustled the leaves. Paul closed his eyes and let the gentle breeze caress his face. He was still worried about what would happen to him, but the fear was gone. An incredible peace filled him, a peace he hadn't felt since he was a kid.

He rose from the bench and looked again at the pond. He took a deep breath, catching it quickly as the pain shot through his ribs. *"Pain is good,"* he thought. *"It means I'm still alive."*

He turned toward the path and walked back to the edge of the park. He waved down a cab and went home, knowing that whether his parents had arrived yet or not, he wouldn't be going back alone, the peace still wrapped around him like a blanket.

———————

Brooke tried calling Paul as soon as she returned home and learned he'd been released from the hospital. She got his voice mail on both his cell and his phone in the condo.

"Hi, Paul, it's Brooke. I'm home from Ithaca and wanted to see how you're doing. Please call me back and let me know how you're feeling." She ended the call and sighed.

She put the phone back in its cradle and went to her bedroom to unpack her suitcase. The trip had turned out to be a lot of fun. The high school kids who'd participated in the program were enthusiastic and remarkably talented. The college group was even more encouraging. They were all either drama or art majors and soaked up everything she and Ruby shared with them.

It had also been a nice change of pace. Brooke enjoyed the time away from the studio and the hours of free time available. She and Ruby had spent their leisure time hiking some of the paths to the many waterfalls in the area, visiting bookstores and antique shops, or just sitting at one of the cafés enjoying a cappuccino and people-watching. It had been a long time since Brooke had been able to just relax.

Still, she was glad to be home. She relished the thought of climbing into her own bed and sleeping on her own pillows. Getaways were nice, but home would always be better.

She finished her unpacking and went to the kitchen. She brewed coffee and searched the refrigerator for a light supper. "Hmmm, looks like I need to go to the market," she said, taking the jam from its place on the shelf.

She pulled out two slices of bread and covered them with peanut butter and jam. She took her sandwich and coffee to the living room. She opened the doors to let in the cool air.

She sat down on the couch and took a bite of the sandwich. "Not gourmet, but it will have to do." She sipped her coffee and looked out at the stars starting to twinkle in the night sky. She thought of Paul.

"God, please be with him, wherever he is. I want him to be okay." A slight wind drifted through the windows, rustling the curtains. Brooke closed her eyes as the breeze brushed her cheek. "Thank you, Lord," she said with a smile. She leaned her head against the back of the couch, reassured that God was with Paul.

———————

Brooke groaned when she took her cell phone from her purse Thursday afternoon and saw that she'd missed a call from Paul.

"What's the matter?" Sheila asked as Brooke dialed Paul's number and got his voice mail again.

She left another message and dropped the phone back into her purse. "Nothing. Just playing phone tag with someone I'd really like to talk to right now."

Sheila cocked her head and gave Brooke a sly smile. "A guy?"

"Ex-boyfriend."

"Oh, sorry."

"It's no big deal," Brooke said with a shrug. She motioned to the rack of costumes. "Come on, let's finish this. The Gala's tomorrow night."

Brooke and Sheila finished loading the costumes onto the rack and rolled it to the waiting delivery truck. They followed the truck to the theatre and double-checked the costumes before returning to the studio. Sheila said "Good-bye" and left for the day. Brooke stayed late to clean up the prep room and make sure nothing had been left behind.

"You're working late," Meryl said from the doorway.

Brooke looked up at him. His wife stood beside him, dressed in an elegant evening gown. Meryl was wearing his tuxedo.

"What's the occasion?" Brooke asked with a smile.

"Our twentieth anniversary," Meryl replied, drawing his wife close. "We're having dinner at the Waldorf and then attending an exclusive movie premier."

"Congratulations," Brooke said. "I hope you have a lovely evening."

Meryl's wife smiled, "Thank you, Brooke. I know we will."

"I wanted to catch you before we leave," Meryl said. "Adam Nichols gave Heron the job. She'll be here to get us through the two opening weeks at the Met, but then she'll be gone."

"I'm not surprised," Brooke replied. "I'm a little disappointed, though, if you can believe that. Have you decided on her replacement yet? I guess I'm curious to know who my new supervisor is."

Meryl crossed the threshold into the room. "As a matter of fact, I have decided on Heron's replacement. I will be your supervisor, Brooke. I want you to take over Heron's job."

Brooke looked at Meryl with shock. "Me? Meryl, most of the team is twice my age. What will they say?"

"No more than they said when Heron was promoted at a young age. Brooke, I know you're more than capable of this. You are a talented, dedicated young woman." He extended his hand. "So, what do you say? Will you take the job?"

Brooke smiled and shook Meryl's hand. "I accept."

Meryl announced Heron's resignation and Brooke's promotion the following morning. Everyone congratulated Heron on her new job and most seemed genuinely excited about having Brooke as their team leader. A few people grumbled, but Brooke figured they'd get over it with time.

"Gala's tonight, people. Get busy and remember, everyone who's attending the Gala must be there at 5:00 tonight – formal attire, people! That means a tux, Stuart," Meryl said, pointing to one of the prop designers.

The meeting broke up, the teams rushing to finish any last-minute issues. Brooke and Heron went to the theatre to be on hand for the dress rehearsal in case repairs were needed for any of the costumes.

Brooke watched the people rushing around on the sidewalk as the cab crept from the studio to the theatre. *"Everyone's in such a hurry,"* she thought.

"Brooke," Heron said, interrupting her thoughts.

Brooke turned to her. Heron smiled weakly, a troubled expression on her face.

Brooke furrowed her brow. "What's wrong, Heron?"

"Nothing's wrong, Brooke. I just have to tell you something and, well, I'm not very good at this." Heron looked down at her hands. Taking a deep breath, she looked again at Brooke. "I owe you an apology for the way I've treated you these past few years."

Brooke shook her head. "You don't owe me anything, Heron."

"Yes, I do. I don't understand your faith, but that's no excuse for mistreating you. Honestly, I think it's more that I'm jealous of your ability to believe. I've never been able to get my mind around the whole God-thing. You seem to have it figured out," Heron shrugged and looked out the window before continuing. "I also want to thank you. Adam shared with me the remarks you made during his interview with you. Your words struck deeper than Meryl's recommendation. I appreciate your willingness to set aside our differences to help me in this. Anyone else would have seen it as an opportunity to tear me down."

Brooke smiled. "I meant every word, Heron. It has been a pleasure working with you. I will treasure all that you've taught me and I will truly miss working with you."

The cab dropped them in front of the theatre. Heron paid the driver and moved toward the entrance.

"Heron," Brooke said, reaching for her to wait. "One thing before we go in – if you really want to find faith, if you really want to believe – stop trying to figure it out. Just surrender and let God reveal Himself to you." She smiled at Heron and went into the theatre.

For several minutes, Heron stayed outside and stared at the door, pondering Brooke's words.

THIRTY-THREE

BROOKE STOOD WITH THE REST of the team and applauded the cast returning to the stage to take their bow. The theatre erupted in thunderous ovation when the actress who filled the role of Cio-Cio-San, the female lead, glided fluidly across the stage. Her beautiful smile and graceful bow sent the audience into a near frenzy. Her performance had been flawless. Her voice was filled with such emotion that the audience felt what the character was feeling – joy as the parasols danced in the actors' hands during the wedding scene, serenity as she brushed her fingers over the orchids in the garden, pain when her American husband revealed his betrayal, anguish when the lovely young woman had thrust the blade into her abdomen, ending her life. The audience eagerly celebrated her indescribable talent.

Brooke wiped the tears from her eyes and crept quietly from her seat, following Meryl and the rest of the team away from their section. Brooke's hands had touched every costume in the show, but seeing everything come together on stage was like seeing an artist's canvas after the final strokes of paint had been applied. The scenes were truly beautiful. Brooke was filled with pride and a sense of accomplishment as they left the theatre and made their way to the private dinner party that awaited the cast and crew.

She always enjoyed the dinner parties after the opening and closing nights of shows. Hollywood stars mingled with politicians. Stage royalty laughed with newscasters. Brooke stifled a laugh when Stuart from the props department – usually in holey jeans and speckled in paint – moved stealthily in his tuxedo and well-polished shoes to the bar and sidled up next to an elegant diva. The young women looked Stuart up and down, sniffed and strutted away. Stuart merely shrugged and edged toward his next target.

"Enjoying the party?" Meryl asked as he approached Brooke.

"I always do," she replied with a smile. "I love watching the people, seeing the way everyone just blends after a show. Kind of feels like a family gathering."

"It does, doesn't it! Well, enjoy the rest of the party." Meryl smiled and walked over to where his wife was speaking with one of the actors.

Brooke looked at her watch. "After midnight. Time to go." She stopped to say "good night" to a few people before leaving then made her way out of the building and into the night. The Gala had been a success. She slipped into a cab and gave the driver her address.

She pulled her wrap around her shoulders and looked out the window. Couples strolled down the sidewalks, holding hands and laughing. The only way the night could have been better was if Paul had been there to share it with her.

"God, I know it wasn't Your will for me to stay with him," Brooke prayed quietly. "Why can't I get him out of my mind and heart? Please, Lord, why can't you take these confusing feelings away?"

She closed her eyes and sighed as the gentle voice in her mind whispered "Just trust Me."

———————

Heavy showers drenched the City Saturday morning. Thunder rumbled and lightning flashed as sheets of rain passed down the streets. Brief power outages rerouted subway trains and closed the smaller businesses.

Brooke sipped her coffee and watched from her living room window the rain pounding car hoods and rooftops. She'd planned to go to the market early and then meet Papa for lunch. She hadn't spent time with him since before her trip to Ithaca and she missed him.

The sound of the rain pounding on the windows took her ambition and replaced it with laziness. She wanted nothing more than to stay in and lounge around in her pajamas all day. Maybe she'd just read a good book. She took another sip of her coffee and walked over to the couch. The phone rang before she could sit down.

"Ms. Barsanti, this is Office Marks with the NYPD."

"Yes, good morning, Sir."

"I'm calling to let you know you can claim your property from the station at any time. The trial is moving forward – both parties have admitted to the crime," Officer Marks said.

"Even Melissa? I don't understand." Brooke sank onto the couch in disbelief.

"Melissa originally claimed that the boyfriend forced her to help him break into Miss Howell's home. She claimed he was completely on his own in the act. The details of her story changed several times, however. When we presented her statement to the boyfriend, he became furious and gave us every detail, including her help getting into the house and her attempt to keep Miss Howell from reaching the door. He pulled the trigger, but Melissa didn't make any attempt to stop him."

"Why? Why did they choose Ruth? Sir, she never hurt anyone. She always went out of her way to help people – even Melissa," Brooke's voice choked.

"They both had serious drug problems, Ms. Barsanti. They saw it as a quick fix to their drug debts. I don't think either of them believed Miss Howell would come home, and when she did, they panicked."

Officer Marks paused, allowing Brooke a moment to calm her emotions. He cleared his throat. "I just wanted to call you with the update. You can come to the station any time to pick up your belongings. Your statement will be sufficient for the trial. We won't need to bother you again unless more of your stolen items are recovered, though at this point, it's doubtful. Thank you, Ma'am."

Brooke hung up the phone and looked out the window at the falling rain. Tears ran down her cheeks. Her part was over, Officer Marks had told her. Ruth was still gone, but at least now she could put the ugliness behind her and remember the wonderful woman Ruth had been.

She didn't want to stay in anymore. She wanted to go to the police station and then to Papa's. She wanted that closure right away. And she needed to see Papa desperately. The market could wait.

———

Papa smiled gently as Brooke tearfully recounted the phone conversation with Officer Marks. He ran his finger over the delicate brooch and put it back on the table next to the bangle, relieved to have those items back in the family.

He reached across the table and clasped her hand with his, comforting his granddaughter. She had been through so much in her life and it hurt him to see her having to endure more heartache.

Brooke released his hand wiped her eyes. "I'm sorry to cry about her again, Papa. I guess today kind of reopened the wound. I'm a little bit relieved, though, too. I feel like it's, well, over." Brooke shrugged and smiled weakly. "I miss her, and missing her made me miss Daddy. Does that sound silly?"

"No, it doesn't sound silly."

Brooke cleared her throat. "I'm doing my best to not ask God the 'why' questions. I know He has a purpose."

"He does. But it's natural to want to know why. You're human, with human emotions and human limitations. God knows that. I believe he's preparing you for the rest of your life. He has plans for you, Brooke. You can't move to a new season until the old ones have passed."

"Thanks Papa. You always know what I need to hear."

"How's the new promotion going for you?" Papa asked, changing the subject.

"Good. The Gala was a complete success last night. Meryl is putting in a proposal and portfolio for 'Les Miserables.' So, in addition to the nights I have to be at the theatre for 'Madame Butterfly,' I have to be sketching costumes for the portfolio. I don't mind, though. I'd rather be busy."

"I don't blame you. I've never liked to sit around either – unless I'm eating," Papa said with a laugh.

"Does this mean you're ready for lunch?"

"Sweetheart, I thought you'd never ask!"

The week kept Brooke busy. She had the Monday and Tuesday night shows, as well as the upcoming weekend shows. Meryl called her early Wednesday morning, apologizing for calling so early after a late work night.

"I need you here ASAP, Brooke. Our deadline for the Les Mis proposal was moved up – I have to have it all in by the end of the day Thursday."

Brooke readied herself quickly, grabbed breakfast on the run and was in the studio before 8 AM. She worked on sketches until after 7:00 that night, missing her Bible study. She was back in the studio early Thursday morning, racing to get everything to Meryl in time.

"I'll take your weekend theatre work, Brooke," Heron offered when she arrived Thursday morning. "I don't have any real work anymore. I'm more or less just sitting around right now. And you'll be dead on your feet."

Brooke looked at Heron with disbelief. She'd never offered to take anyone else's theatre work. "Thank you, Heron. I appreciate that. Are you sure you want to give up your weekend?"

Heron smiled at Brooke. "I don't mind. I'd kind of like to do it one last time. You'd be doing me a favor."

Brooke smiled back at Heron. She leaned forward and offered her a hug. Heron at first tensed up then relaxed as Brooke pulled her into a sisterly embrace. "I'm going to miss working with you, Heron." Brooke's voice was thick with emotion.

Heron pulled away and wiped a tear from her cheek. "I'm going to miss you too, Brooke." She reached out and squeezed Brooke's elbow before walking away.

Brooke rushed around the rest of the afternoon. She and the rest of the designers finished the sketches with a little time to spare. She dropped them at Meryl's office.

"Wish me luck," Meryl said as he grabbed his briefcase, portfolio and jacket and rushed down the hall to the elevators.

Brooke returned to her work space to clean up before leaving for the day. She put her supplies away and wiped down the table. She rinsed out her coffee cup and sent the rest of the team home. She was locking up her supply drawers when Meryl's secretary approached with a young man. He was carrying a large envelope and clipboard.

"Are you Brooke Barsanti?" he asked.

"Yes," she replied.

"Please sign here."

She signed the board and accepted the envelope. "Thank you."

He nodded to her and let Meryl's secretary lead him back out of the room. Brooke watched him leave before sitting down and opening the envelope. It contained the final paperwork on her father's house. The financing had gone through. All that remained was for Brooke to sign the papers before a notary and send them back to the realtor.

Brooke put the papers down on her table and covered her face with her hands. "I knew it was coming Lord. Please, I beg You, help me to get through all of this – Ruth, Daddy, losing Paul. Please Lord." She put the papers back into the envelope and left for the night. She'd have to stop by the bank in the morning to have the papers notarized. Her childhood home now belonged to someone else.

"Good to see you again, Mr. Matthews," the pastor said, shaking Paul's hand as he and his parents exited the church Sunday morning.

Paul smiled and turned toward his parents, "Pastor, I'd like you to meet my parents." Paul's eager expression changed to disappointment when he realized the man had already started speaking to the couple behind him – wealthy, famous, hotel royalty.

"Don't worry about it, Son," Steve said quietly, reaching out to touch Paul's shoulder. "There's a long line behind us. I'm sure he wants to get people on their way."

They went down the steps from the church to the sidewalk and waved down a cab. Paul gave the address for the condo and turned to his parents. "I had thought about taking you to Brooke's church. That's where I took Jason and Lydia when they were visiting, but it's a little more, well, upbeat I guess you could say, than what you're used to. I thought this would be more comfortable for you. Honestly, this is the first time I've been to church since they were here and it had been even longer before then. I guess I can't blame the man for not being more interested in my family."

"It's okay, Paul," his mother said with a smile. "I'm just happy you're going back again. The news of your renewed faith…" Marian choked up. Paul reached over and took her hand.

The cab pulled up to Paul's building. Paul paid the driver and led his parents inside. They went through the lobby, entered the elevator and remained quiet until the doors closed. Paul pushed the button for his floor and looked at his father. "What time do you plan to leave?

"Right after lunch. We have a long drive. Unless you want us to stay longer. I can make arrangements, Son."

"No, that's okay. I appreciate it, but I think I'm okay to take care of myself again. I have a busy week ahead. As soon as I can, I want to come home for a while, though," Paul said as the elevator doors opened. They went down the hall and Paul put the key in the lock. He laughed as he pushed the door open. "That is, if I don't find myself on the other side of a jail cell door by this time next week."

Steve reached for Paul's arm as they entered the condo. "Son, a lot of people are praying for you. God knows what He's doing. Just have faith."

Paul looked at his father and nodded. "I know, Dad. I appreciate it."

Steve pulled Paul into his arms and embraced him. "I'm proud of you, Son. You're doing the right thing – not only in your faith, but also in your life." He pulled away and held Paul at arms length. "God will honor that, Son."

THIRTY-FOUR

PAUL SAT IN THE COURTROOM with his attorney, Todd Lawrence. He gripped the arms of the chair and silently begged God to help him control his temper as Gerald Bauer, the assistant DA, whined to the judge about the need for adequate punishment for Paul's "heinous" crime.

In an attempt to avoid the case going to trial, sentencing in a closed hearing had been mutually agreed upon by Paul and his attorney, the DA's office, and the judge. The only other people in the courtroom were the bailiff, court reporter, and two security guards. Two State Troopers waited outside the court room to escort Paul to jail, should that be the outcome of the hearing.

Only an hour into the hearing and Paul was starting to question the wisdom in agreeing to it. The picture Mr. Bauer was painting of Paul was more that of an ax murderer than of a businessman with poor judgment.

"Your Honor," Mr. Bauer moaned, "Mr. Matthews must be held accountable for his involvement in these illegal business practices. Anything less than a $500,000 fine and five years in prison would be a monstrous breach of ethics."

Todd Lawrence shook his head and spoke up. "My client is cooperating in every way, on every detail of the continued investigation into his employer as well as Marcus Reed and his terrorist-supporting businesses..."

"How do we truly know the depth of Mr. Matthew's involvement in that activity?" Gerald Bauer shouted his interruption.

"Gentlemen, please," the judge said. "Gerald," he said, turning to the Assistant DA. "Has anything surfaced that would lead you to believe that Mr. Matthews has been involved in anything more than what he's already turned himself in for?"

"Well, no, but..." Gerald began.

"Then stop the dramatics. I'm not a jury that you need to sway. The man is obviously cooperating in every way. He went to the authorities, remember? They didn't have to go to him first." The judge shook his head and motioned toward Paul's attorney. "Mr. Lawrence, please continue."

Todd cleared his throat. "It is our request, Your Honor, that consideration be given to my client's cooperation. The attempt on his life and termination of employment by his employer offer proof of his lack of previous knowledge of his former employer's illegal activity. We request that a fine be imposed and jail time be avoided."

"Oh, please!" Gerald exclaimed, rolling his eyes. "Your Honor…"

The judge rose abruptly from his seat. Everyone scrambled to their feet. The judge sighed and shook his head. "Counsel," he said, pointing to Todd and Gerald, "in my chambers, NOW!" He adjusted his robe, nodded to the bailiff, and left the courtroom.

Paul watched as Gerald Bauer marched out of the room, his nose stuck up in the air. Todd looked at Paul and shrugged. Leaning toward Paul, he whispered, "If you believe in prayer, I suggest you try it now. It's never a good thing to be called into chambers."

"Thanks for the reassurance," Paul said as Todd strode out of the room. Paul sat down and put his face in his hands.

"Would you like a cup of coffee, Sir?" the bailiff asked, his deep voice echoing through the room as he approached Paul's table.

"That would be great, thanks."

The bailiff left the room and Paul bowed his head. "Lord, I know I've messed up and have to pay for my wrong choices, but please, God, I'd really, *really* like to not go to jail."

Paul opened his eyes and looked up as the bailiff handed him a Styrofoam cup. He dropped a handful of sugar and powdered creamer packets along with a napkin and stir stick onto the table.

"Thank you," Paul said.

"Welcome," the bailiff said with a smile and returned to his post.

Paul added one packet each of the sugar and creamer and grimaced as he sipped the burnt concoction in the cup. Three sugar packets later, Paul was able to choke down the tar-like substance.

Paul looked around the room as he waited for the judge and the attorneys' to return. Everything was old, but polished and in clean, perfect order. The American flag stood at attention in one corner. The New York State flag stood in the corner opposite, leaning slightly on its ancient pole, bowing toward the Stars and Stripes in apparent humility. On the judge's bench were the scales of justice, a reminder to Paul that there must always be balance – penalty for wrong-doing that fits the deed.

Paul sighed. "Is this a sign, Lord, that I'm headed to jail?"

The quiet voice in his mind said softly, *"There's also reward for right."*

Peace flooded over him and he was able to sit back in his chair, close his eyes and relax.

Paul opened his eyes as the doors opened into the courtroom. The bailiff stood straighter. "All rise," his voice boomed as the judge reentered the courtroom.

Todd Lawrence gave Paul a broad smile before turning back toward the bench. Gerald Bauer looked haggard as he mumbled in monotone to the judge, "We the people of the State of New York agree to withdraw the request for the imprisonment of Paul Matthews and hereby accept as penalty a fine of $250,000.00"

The judge nodded his agreement and turned to Paul and Todd. "This court agrees. Mr. Matthews, I expect full payment within three months, or a jail sentence will be imposed."

"I understand, Your Honor," Paul answered.

The judge banged his gavel and announced "Court is adjourned."

The men rose as the judge exited the courtroom. Gerald Bauer stuffed papers into his satchel, hastily snapped it closed and stormed from the room, glaring at Todd and Paul as he marched by.

Paul reached to shake Todd's hand. "Thanks for whatever you did in there. I'm really thankful to not be headed to jail."

"Don't thank me. The judge is the one who more or less attacked Bauer." Todd shrugged his shoulders. "Bauer has never liked me. He has this tendency to seek the maximum possible sentence whenever I'm representing someone – regardless of the situation. I think the judge realized that and pushed Bauer to be a little more flexible."

"Well, however it happened, I'm truly grateful."

"We'll pursue the suit against your employer and Marcus Reed as planned, but Paul, don't count on anything big coming from that. The suit the State and Feds are filing will take priority over whatever we decide to do. This thing could take years – literally. And our part of the damages may not amount to much. Don't wait to get that fine paid."

"Don't worry, I won't," Paul assured. "I'll get rid of everything if I have to – savings, 401K, possessions – whatever it takes."

"Your 401K will probably be frozen for awhile, at least until after the FTC does a full audit. No one in your company is going to be drawing out of it for a while," Todd said, leading Paul from the courtroom. "You'd better not count on that as a way of paying this either."

"I'll figure it out, don't worry."

"Well, let me know when you've got the funds together. We'll get you cleared up so that we can move on to the next step in all of this." Todd shook Paul's hand again and left the building.

Paul stuffed his hands in his pockets and looked up toward the ceiling. "Well, God, any suggestions?"

"Estate buyer," a deep voice said from behind him. Paul jumped and turned around. The bailiff was standing near the door leading into the courtroom.

"Pardon?" Paul asked.

"Estate buyer," the bailiff repeated. "The phone book is full of people who'll come and buy up your stuff. You'll take a loss, of course, but if you have anything worth anything, you could get what you need to pay your fine." He held up Paul's briefcase and smiled. "You left this at the defendant's table."

———

Paul watched as his condo was emptied of its contents. He hadn't wanted to give up everything he'd worked so hard for. He realized, however, that he didn't have a choice – sell everything to pay the massive fine or face prison time. Staying out of jail, Paul decided, was worth giving it all up. So, he'd taken the advice of the bailiff and called an estate buyer.

The buyer, Vic Warner, had entered Paul's condo with wide eyes. Paul's passion for antiques showed in every corner of the condo. Mr. Warner had strolled casually through the rooms, running his hands over the valuable furniture. He stopped and smiled broadly at the breakfront in the dining room, opened drawers and examined the notched corners, scribbling furiously on his note pad after each perusal. He nodded his approval at the sideboard. The secretary in the living room held his attention the longest, his hands running over the edges and knobs like a lover caressing his bride.

The only things in the apartment he hadn't been interested in were the leather sofa, the kitchen stools, appliances, electronics, and a few odds and ends. Paul had to keep him away from the family items that he would never consider selling. He had begged for the artwork, but Paul had already made arrangements with a local gallery for an auction that would net far more than the estate sale could even hope for. Two of the paintings had been purchased at a local starving artists' event when the painter was still an unknown. His work had since been discovered and was now in great demand.

"Thousands," the gallery owner had said to Paul after examining the pieces. "No doubt in my mind – and that's just for these two," he'd said, nodding toward the companion paintings.

The afternoon was a steady procession of numbering and cataloging each item, wrapping it securely and then moving it from the condo. Paul sat back on a kitchen stool and watched each step of his life being dismantled.

He shook his head and sighed. "It's just stuff."

He rose from the stool and went into the kitchen. He ground coffee, poured water into the coffee maker, and leaned against the counter. He crossed his arms and closed his eyes, listening to the sound of the pot gurgling.

"Mr. Matthews," Vic Warner said from the kitchen doorway, "we're finished with the cataloging and wrapping. The piano movers have arrived. Do you have the key for the cover?"

Paul nodded and pushed away from the counter. He went into the living room and opened the seat on the piano bench. The key was resting alone inside the bench, the books and sheets of music already removed and tucked safely away.

As Mr. Warner reached into the bench to remove the key, Paul felt as if his heart was being removed as well. His hands had spent many hours stroking the keys of that piano, the sound harmonizing with his thoughts. Of all the things being torn away from him, the piano was causing the most pain.

He stuffed his hands into his pockets and nodded to Mr. Warner, who motioned for the movers to begin dismantling the instrument. They quickly had it apart, secured and wrapped for moving.

"I'll see them down to the truck," he said to Paul as they carefully lifted the pieces and took them through the door.

It wasn't long before the remaining items were removed from the condo. Paul shook his head as the foreman handed him the clipboard containing the list of items being removed. Paul reviewed the list, signed the form and accepted his copy.

"All gone," he said quietly, staring down at the paper in his hand.

"It's a lot to lose. I guess that's one good thing about not having much – there's nothing for anyone to take away from you," the foreman said to Paul before stepping into the hallway.

The door closing echoed through the room, the emptiness amplifying the sound. Paul looked around at the nakedness. All that remained were the leather sofa, the flat-screen, entertainment center, a couple of lamps and the marble-top table that had been in his grandfather's office. Stacked in his bedroom and the spare room were the boxes he'd packed with the items he intended to keep.

Shaking his head, he went back into the kitchen. He poured himself a cup of coffee and settled down on one of the stools. He leaned forward on the counter, the feeling of loss overtaking him. He tried to choke back the tears, his body trembling as the sobs rose up in him. "Oh, God," he tried to pray.

"Just let it go," the quiet voice inside said.

Paul dropped his head onto the counter and gave in to the tears that had risen up, their flow a cleansing torrent.

———————

"One Hundred Eighty-five thousand Dollars," the gallery owner said.

Paul looked down at the check in his hand. "I don't believe it," he said, reviewing the breakdown that accompanied the check and noting the bulk of the proceeds had come from the companion paintings. He looked back up in disbelief. "I only paid a hundred dollars for BOTH of those paintings!"

"I told you they were worth something. The buyer has been trying to get his hands on every piece that guy painted for some time now and jumped at the chance to add them to his collection."

Paul thanked the gallery owner and left the shop, a sense of relief washing over him. "Only sixty-five thousand to go," he said to himself as he folded the check and stashed it in his pocket. He pulled out his cell phone and dialed his attorney.

"Wow!" Todd exclaimed when Paul told him how much the art auction had brought in. "Get to the bank, get a cashiers check made out to the State of New York and get it to me right away. We'll run it down to the cashier at the courthouse this afternoon. Wow!" he said again before ending the call.

Paul took the cashiers check to Todd's office. Todd pulled a form up on his computer, typed in the check information and made copies of both the check and the form before grabbing his jacket and briefcase and racing from his office with Paul. They climbed into a waiting cab, and Todd instructed the driver to hurry to the State Office Building.

Todd looked at Paul and took a deep breath. "This is our good news for the day," he said waving the envelope containing the check and the paperwork for the court. "Ready for the bad news?"

Paul looked at Todd and wrinkled his brow. "Please don't tell me they've decided to hit me with a bigger fine."

"No, they couldn't do that," Todd said with a chuckle. "I got a call today from Joel Wright with the Attorney General's office. Marcus Reed has been escorted from the United States and turned over to French Authorities."

Paul's jaw dropped. "What do you mean? What does that mean for us? He had Kevin Murphy killed and tried to have me killed! I don't believe this!"

"He's facing some pretty serious charges in both France and Italy. Believe me when I tell you that the legal systems in both of those countries make our system look like a walk in the park. Remember we still have his bodyguard, driver – whatever you want to call him. He will be facing the murder and attempted murder charges."

"Marcus was the one who sent him to do it, though," Paul said in disgust as the driver pulled up to the State Office building. They slipped out of the cab. Paul paid the driver and turned back to Todd. "I can't help feeling like I'm being cheated somehow, and Marcus is literally getting away with murder."

"I know, Paul. I understand where you're coming from. There's nothing we can do about Marcus now." He put a hand on Paul's shoulder, halting him in front of the building's entrance. "Your former employers are a different story, however. The FTC and SEC have already started their action against them. Appleton, Murphy, & Young won't get off so easy."

———

The news broke the following Monday afternoon. A reporter stood on the busy New York sidewalk and pointed to the building of Paul's former employer. *"Sources tell us that the Federal Trade Commission and the Securities and Exchange Commission have conducted audits into the business practices of Appleton, Murphy, & Young. In addition to the discovery of serious inconsistencies in their financial statements and manipulation of their balance sheets, the company has been actively investing its clients' funds in foreign companies alleged to be supplying known terrorist cells."*

The camera left the reporter and zoomed to the doors of the office building. The image of Marshall Appleton and Pratt Young being escorted from the building by authorities filled the screen. Marshall marched along, his head held high in defiance. Pratt, however, pulled his jacket lapels over his face, in an attempt to hide himself from the cameras. Both men ignored the questions being shouted to them by the media.

Paul clicked off the power and put the remote control on the arm of the couch. Taking a deep breath, he leaned his head back. It wasn't over yet, not by any means. He would be called in to take the stand during Marshall's and Pratt's trials. Todd had already warned him that the defense lawyers were known to be brutal.

He rose from the couch to finish packing. Vic had called early that morning to tell him that the estate auction was complete, netting fifty-five thousand dollars. Paul had picked up the check, liquidated his savings, and gone with Todd to pay off the fine.

They'd run into the judge outside the courtroom. "I think that's a record," the judge had said with a smile. "Most people wait until the last possible minute to pay these things. Good luck to you, Mr. Matthews."

Paul had left the building feeling free.

Paul taped up the last of the boxes in the kitchen. The movers were coming within the hour to take everything to Rockport. Paul was spending the night in a hotel and planned to drive home in a rental car the next morning.

He dropped the packing tape on the floor next to the box. The doorbell rang, announcing the arrival of the movers. There was little to load up. They were finished in less than two hours. He signed the form, thanked the driver and closed the door.

He put his hands on his hips as he surveyed the empty shell that had been his home for two years. Soon, it would belong to someone else. His realtor had already shown it to two prospective buyers, the latter offering more than the $1.4 million being asked for it. The sale of the condo would pay off the mortgage and give Paul some survival money until his 401K was released or he found another job – whichever came first.

"Think of it as a fresh start," Nick had said when Paul stopped by to see him over the weekend. "God never lets you lose it all without offering you the chance to receive even greater things."

"I'll take whatever you have to offer, Lord," Paul prayed as he put his luggage in the hallway outside the door. He turned off the lights and closed the door. He turned the key in the lock for the last time.

THIRTY-FIVE

BROOKE RUSHED DOWN THE SIDEWALK from the subway entrance. The original plan had been for her to meet Papa for dinner at 6:00 pm. It was after 6:30. She pulled the restaurant door open and breathlessly gave Papa's name to the hostess.

"Right this way," the woman said with a smile.

Brooke followed her to the corner table where Papa sat sipping ice water. When he saw her approach, he rose from the table with a smile and leaned forward to kiss her on the cheek.

"I was starting to worry," he said with a chuckle.

"Sorry. The studio has been a madhouse these past few weeks," she said. She glanced quickly over the menu. "Have you ordered yet?"

"No, Sweetheart. I waited for you, but I'm ready if you know what you want."

"I'm starving," she said with a laugh.

They gave the waitress their orders. She returned with Brooke's iced tea as well as a basket of warm bread and their salads. Papa offered the blessing for their dinner.

Papa mixed the dressing into his salad and looked at Brooke. "So, are you going to tell me about your madhouse? I haven't seen you in two weeks and we've hardly spoken on the phone!"

"I know, Papa. I've missed you so much! I've come to rely on our conversations. I feel, well, lost without them," Brooke said with a slight laugh. Brooke took a bite of her salad and a sip of her tea before continuing. "Heron's leaving has left a real void. No one was hired to replace Julie or Rachel. We've been really short-handed and it's taken its toll."

"Is Meryl going to do anything about it?" Papa asked, taking warm bread from the basket and spreading butter over the steaming surface.

"He did this week, thank God! He promoted one of Ruby's team members and hired three designers to work with him. They've been assigned the 'Madame Butterfly' costume maintenance. Ruby's team is working on the 'Christmas Carol' contract and my team has the 'Les Miserable' contract."

"Good heavens! Are there any shows in the City that Meryl doesn't have?" Papa asked with a chuckle.

"I know! It does seem like we've taken them over, doesn't it?" Brooke laughed. "It's a huge relief. My team was trying to keep up with the 'Butterfly' maintenance as well as the designing for 'Les Mis' and quite frankly, I was starting to wonder if the whole promotion thing was a mistake."

"I'm sure Meryl realizes you're capable, but Honey, you're also human. That's more than anyone can be expected to keep up with."

The waitress returned with their entrées. She topped off their glasses, removed the empty salad plates, and added fresh bread to the basket. "Anything else you'd like?" she asked.

"No, thank you. This is good for now," Papa answered with a smile.

They were silent for a few moments as they began their meals. Brooke sipped her tea and twirled pasta on her fork. Papa wiped his mouth with his napkin. "Did you see Paul's former employers were in the news again last night?"

Brooke nodded. "I did see that. Is there no end to what these guys have done?"

"It's bad enough they played around with their books and supported that Reed lunatic, but to hear they've dipped into the employees 401K accounts," Papa paused, shaking his head. "It's not even their money – it's the employees' money!"

"I wonder what this will do to Paul," Brooke said, more to herself than to Papa. She looked down at her hands and then back up to Papa. "Have you talked to him since he left?"

"Earlier in the week."

Brooke nodded and reached for her water glass. She took a sip and put the glass back on the table. She looked back down at her hands.

"I think you still love him."

"I still pray for him every day. I also pray every day that God will take the feelings away. Must I still love him if we can't be together?"

"Why can't you? Faith is no longer an issue, remember? He turned his life back over to Christ after he left the hospital. Every conversation I've had with him indicates his sincerity and desire to be what God wants him to be." Papa crossed his arms and leaned back.

"He's in Maine, Papa." Shaking her head, she picked her fork up and twirled more pasta. "He has a lot to deal with right now. Besides, if he were still interested, don't you think he would have called me – or something?"

She dropped the fork on her plate and pushed her half-eaten meal away. "It's all so confusing."

"It can be." Papa slid his empty plate back and rested his elbows on the table. "Have you considered, though, that the reason he's holding back is because he knows he hurt you? Or perhaps he's afraid you wouldn't want to be dragged through this whole mess he's tied up with right now?"

The waitress returned to the table with coffee and their check and cleared the dirty dishes away.

Brooke stirred sugar and cream into her coffee. "According to the news, Marcus Reed was extradited to France. Did Paul explain why that happened?"

"Paul's 'friend' Mr. Reed is facing some serious charges in both France and Italy," Papa said with a shake of his head. "Apparently, he's had some in depth involvement in the Italian Mafia – including some suspected financial support during the time they struck Italian law enforcement in the early nineties."

"He's been involved that long and they didn't catch him until now?" Brooke asked in disbelief.

Papa nodded. "He's quite clever. He's hidden much of his activity in his business finances. He's being accused of supporting terrorist cells, the forced takeover of several weak businesses in Italy and France – the list is rather long."

"So, why is he in France if there are so many charges in Italy? I would think the mob-thing would be pretty big."

"He's facing murder charges in France in addition to his tainted business practices. My friend Denis shared with me that the men Mr. Reed had killed were somehow related to one of the ministers as well as a member of the Constitutional Council. Those are extremely serious charges." Papa sipped his coffee.

Brooke watched Papa as he set his cup on the table and dabbed his lips with his napkin. She folded her arms and cocked her head to one side. "Papa, exactly how do you know Mr. Beck and why is he so comfortable sharing all of this information with you?"

Papa removed his napkin from his lap. He folded it carefully and put it on the table. He leaned forward and smiled at Brooke. "Because, Sweetheart, he is with French Intelligence."

He picked up the check. Taking his wallet from his pocket, he pulled out several bills and tucked them into the slot. He looked back up at Brooke. He smiled at her again and said quietly, "And I was once with Italian Intelligence."

Brooke's shoulders slumped and mouth dropped open in astonishment. "You're serious!"

Papa smiled sheepishly. He rose from the table and motioned toward the door. "Let's go for a short walk."

The two of them left the restaurant and walked together down the sidewalk. Papa paused in front of a small café. "Feel like another coffee?" He didn't wait for her answer before opening the door.

Once inside, Papa ordered two cups of coffee and directed Brooke to a table near the window. He sat across from her and sipped his coffee.

"Well?" Brooke asked impatiently. "When are you going to fill in all of the missing details of this information you just dropped on me? You were really part of Intelligence – like the FBI, CIA, or…" Brooke paused and shook her head as if trying to find the right description. She laughed and said "Or MI6."

Papa laughed and shook his head. "Honey, you've watched *way* too many movies! No, it wasn't anything like that. There are different kinds of intelligence."

"So, what did you do?" Brooke crossed her arms on the table, her coffee forgotten.

"My last project was to gather information on the Italian Mafia. The people I had been dealing with somehow found out who I was. Your grandmother and I were in real danger, so we were moved to the United States where we'd be safe." Papa shrugged his shoulders as if to say "no big deal" and put his coffee cup to his lips.

Brooke wrinkled her brow and shook her head. "So you weren't really a carpenter in Italy?"

"Of course I was. That's what my father and grandfather did, so that's what I knew. The other thing was just, shall we say, a side job."

Brooke laughed and shook her head again. "I just can't believe it! Here I thought I was part of an ordinary, every day, boring family!"

Papa remained silent, sipping his coffee.

Brooke grew serious. "That's why it was so hard for Grandma to come here. I always thought you wanted to be a part of the American dream, just like everyone else, and maybe she was just coming along. That must have difficult for you." She reached over to take Papa's hand.

"It wasn't easy. But God knew what He was doing all along. If we hadn't come to the U.S, your father never would have met your mother and we wouldn't have you. He had a plan and we were a part of it." He smiled at Brooke and squeezed her hand. "Don't get in the way of what He has for you, Honey. Ask Him what He wants for you and then let Him have His way."

Brooke and Rachel left the church together Wednesday night after Bible Study. Brooke hugged Rachel. "I'm so happy for you and Shaun!" She pulled away and smiled. "Congratulate Shaun for me, and remember - I want to do the baby shower!"

"Don't worry. I wouldn't want anyone else to do it! We aren't due until April, so we have plenty of time," Rachel said with a smile, her hands embracing her still flat belly protectively. "I'm just so excited, I can hardly stand it!" She waved to Brooke and turned to flag down a cab.

"I'll call you, Rache."

Brooke walked to the subway tunnel and waited for her train. She was happy for Rachel and Shaun. She knew they would be wonderful parents.

She boarded the train and sat down. She stared out the window at the people standing on the platform - so many were couples or families. Brooke felt alone. Thoughts of Paul flooded her mind, intensifying her feelings of loneliness.

"I miss him, God," she prayed quietly as the train moved through the tunnel. *"I wish I knew what I was supposed to do. I know we shouldn't ask for signs..."* Brooke let the thought trail off.

When the train stopped, Brooke disembarked with the mass of humanity flooding the platform. She trudged up the steps to the sidewalk and walked to her building.

"On duty again tonight, David?" she asked as she entered the building and passed the security desk.

"Yeah, other guys are sick. It's okay, I can use the overtime."

"Well, have a good night." Brooke went to the elevator and pushed the button.

"Oh, hold on," David said, rising from his seat. "This was delivered for you today." He handed Brooke a small package.

"Thanks David."

She stepped into the elevator and pushed the button for her floor. When the doors closed, she looked at the return address on the box. "What's Linda sending me?"

She went into her apartment and put her Bible and purse on the counter. Taking the scissors from the drawer, she slit the brown paper on the package.

On top of the layers of wrapping was a single page with Linda's handwriting:

Brooke, I hope this finds you well. The new family in your former home is bringing me great joy. They are happy, friendly people who truly love the house the way it's meant to be loved. I know what that means to you.

A couple of weeks ago, I set out to dig up your father's rose bush like you asked me to and was met with a surprise. A single rose had blossomed on the dead vine. I took a picture of it so you could see it for yourself. I also snipped the rose from the bush and took it to the florist near the university. She preserved it for you.

Honey, I hope you receive a little joy from this small token that I believe God sent to you. I have no doubt He is showing you His love in this small wonder.

Much love, Linda

Brooke set the letter on the table and pulled apart the wrapping. Under the first layer was an envelope with the picture Linda had taken of the rose bush. The bush's branches were twisted and brown, completely devoid of leaves or life except for a single, defiant red rose that forced its delicate petals through death's grip.

Brooke choked back tears as she stared at the photograph. She shook her head and set the picture down so she could empty the rest of the packing from the box. Nestled in the bottom, wrapped gently in tissue paper and bubble wrap was the fragile rose that Linda had snipped from the lifeless bush. The florist had preserved it with a delicate glaze that froze the blossom in perpetual beauty.

Brooke cupped the rose in her hand and looked up to the ceiling. She laughed through her tears, realizing the miracle she held in her hands. God had answered her. She knew what He wanted her to do.

The chill of autumn gripped the marina in Rockport. Summer was over. The leaves were surrendering their green to the bright oranges and reds that nature used to paint the horizon. The sun was setting earlier and rising later. The earth was preparing for the slumber of winter. The boats that remained at the marina were shrink-wrapped and in storage barns for protection from the coming freeze. The absence of the boats gave the docks a look of abandonment.

Paul stood at the end of the pier and watched as the sun started its descent. A burst of wind raised goose bumps on his arms. He shoved his hands into the pockets of his khakis, closed his eyes, and lifted his face into the wind.

He thought about the weeks he'd spent with his father in the shop. Paul treasured those hours he'd shared with his father – hours of getting to know each other again, of laughing and of forgiveness. The sailboat was complete and waited in the storage bay for its maiden voyage in the spring.

Paul opened his eyes as Herbie shuffled up next to him. "Steve says you might be going away again?" he asked in his childlike voice.

Paul looked over at Herbie. "I might be. I have to go back to New York to take care of some things, but I might go back to stay. That's been my home for a long time, Herbie."

Herbie looked over the water and nodded. He stuffed his hands into his pockets and turned back to Paul. "Are you still eating the bread?" His voice carried the authoritative tone Paul had heard months earlier.

Paul smiled at him and replied "Every single day. I realize now how hungry I was, and I don't ever want to be that hungry again."

"Okay, good. That's real good. Bye, Paul." Herbie's voice was again childlike.

"Bye, Herbie." Paul watched as the man shuffled toward the sidewalk. When Herbie was out of sight, Paul returned his gaze to the water.

The harbor was quiet except for the sound of the waves crashing in the distance against the breakwall and the gentle lapping of water against the pier supports. Paul thought about his future, the choices that lay ahead. His father had offered him half of the business at the marina. Paul knew it wasn't an offer made lightly.

He wanted to return to New York, however. He loved the City and couldn't imagine living anywhere else. He loved the challenges associated with financial management. Numbers were his life.

He realized, though, that it would be a difficult journey. He still had the trial against his former employers to face. He would soon have to find a job. Three had been offered to him. Two were with management firms in New York. The other was offered by a former Appleton, Murphy & Young client, Gregory Fillman. He wanted to make Paul his CFO.

Paul knew that whatever his decision, if it involved remaining a part of the financial world, the FTC and SEC would be watching him like hawks for a long time.

He also knew that he could never again make a decision without first seeking God's will. To do so would mean certain failure and heartache.

Paul closed his eyes and again turned his face into the wind. "God, I need to know what to do. Never again do I want to make a decision without Your guiding hand. Please, Lord, help me to know exactly what Your will is for my life."

Paul opened his eyes as the purple and red of the sunset splashed over the sky. The beauty of it reminded him of Brooke. Thoughts of her beautiful smile and sparkling eyes made his heart ache. "I still love her, Lord," he said quietly into the dusk.

Paul gave the sunset one last glance before turning back toward the walkway leading away from the marina. He scrunched his shoulders up to his ears and shoved his hands into his pockets against the chill that forced its way through his clothes. He kept his eyes on the ground as he walked up the sidewalk and through the grass leading to his parents' house.

He looked up and halted as he reached the end of the driveway. Standing in the side yard, her dark hair spilling over her shoulders, her eyes sparkling, was Brooke.

Paul's heart beat wildly in his chest, its heavy rhythm filling his ears and numbing his senses. He walked over to stand close to her.

She smiled at Paul as she looked up into his eyes and shrugged her shoulders. "I've missed you," she whispered, her body trembling as she fought to control the tears welling up.

Paul reached out to cup her face in his hands. He smiled down at her as he drank up her scent and absorbed her beauty. "I've missed you too, Brooke. And I love you – more than you could ever know." He pressed his lips against hers and felt her arms encircle his waist.

Paul held her tighter and nestled his cheek in her hair. His future had never been so clear. He thanked God that this precious woman was part of His plan and an undeserved answer to prayer.